15/03/09

MW01101760

# RESTORATION

# RESTORATION

## A Novel

### Murder, the Mob, and a 1964 1/2 Mustang

# TED GRIFFITH

James Lorimer & Company Ltd., Publishers
Toronto

James Lorimer & Company Ltd. acknowledges the support of the Ontario Arts Council. We acknowledge the support of the Government of Canada through the Book Publishing Industry Development Program (BPIDP) for our publishing activities. We acknowledge the support of the Canada Council for the Arts for our publishing program. We acknowledge the support of the Government of Ontario through the Ontario Media Development Corporation's Ontario Book Initiative.

The Canada Council | Le Conseil des Art
for the Arts | du Canada

ONTARIO ARTS COUNCIL
CONSEIL DES ARTS DE L'ONTARIO

Cover design: Cathy MacLean

**Library and Archives Canada Cataloguing in Publication**

Griffith, Ted
Restoration / Ted Griffith.

ISBN10: 1-55028-886-5
ISBN13: 978-1-55028-886-5
I. Title
PS8613.R55R43 2005      C813'.6      C2005-903275-8

James Lorimer & Company Ltd., Publishers
35 Britain Street
Toronto, Ontario
M5A 1R7
www.lorimer.ca

Printed and bound in Canada

*For my sons, Jamie and Mike.*
*Never give up.*

The author gratefully acknowledges the support of his instructors and fellow students at the McMaster University Certificate of Writing Program. The contributions of Bob Neilson, Cathy Vasas-Brown, and Greta Paso to the manuscript are immeasurable.

Special thanks to Salvatore for sharing his keen insight, observations, and love for the communities in the novel. Continuing mentorship from the seminar leaders at the Surrey International Writers' Conference has guided me for many years, and their input is reflected. Any acknowledgement would be incomplete without stating my sincerest gratitude to two people: Elsa Franklin, for her guidance; and my business partner, Jeff Martin, whose enthusiastic support of this other career has been unyielding.

Carol already knows her special role in my life and in my writing career, as, of course, does Dayle.

# Prologue

## Thursday, May 14, 1964

Roberto Constantine turned the wheel of his new convertible, a skeleton-white Mustang with its red roof open to the sky, towards the towering backlit Texaco sign. Beaming over the iron-hardened horizon, the red neon insignia burned bright like the star of Bethlehem, drawing him like a Magi to the oil stained station at the corner of Kenilworth and Barton. It was an odd sight, buried beneath the evening pall of the blast furnaces.

He found the station empty of any vehicles save a few tired cars, their scarred hoods raised, each awaiting the mechanic's ultimate decision as to their death or rebirth. All of them, rusted or bruised, lame or awaiting a part from a far-off land, lay beneath a twilight sky punctuated with Hamilton's orange-grey afterglow. It had been decades since he had last noticed the flaming backdrop of the fiery roman candles that framed the city's twin steel plants and the storms of cooling steam that rose from their rolling mills like ghosts fleeing the site of their deaths. It was urban wallpaper, familiar, stained, and somehow comforting.

"Goddamn car dealers," he muttered to his wife.

Teresa had joined her husband on the Mustang's inaugural joyride. Her left arm was outstretched along the seat back's fresh poppy-red upholstery; her fingers played absently with the short black curls at the back of her husband's neck. A chill had settled into the spring night. But the loin-warming rush of success heated the evening's ride, fueling the intoxicating allure of the Ford Motor Company's newest creation.

"I pay eight grand for a car that's worth four," Constantine complained, "and that Shyster McAllister doesn't even give me the courtesy of a full tank of gas. Eight-grand for a car worth four," Constantine continued to mutter, "and that shyster McAllister doesn't even give me the courtesy of a full tank of gas."

"Stopping to stretch is not so bad an idea," Teresa said, fondling the string of Mikimoto pearls around her neck. "Besides, I want to see how well these pearls match the car's finish."

It's two hundred miles from Dearborn, Michigan to Hamilton, Ontario. Two hundred and nine from the Ford Plant on Cherry Street, where the new Mustangs are assembled, bolt-by-bolt, day-by-day, to Bay City Motors on Cannon Street. In between, there are thirty-two Ford dealers, each as anxious as Benjamin J. McAllister Jr., to be the first in Canada to deliver the new 1964 ½ Mustang. Until yesterday, he'd only seen pictures. Since word of the new model first hit the news in December, barely an hour would go by without a phone call from a prospective buyer or a query from one of his salesmen asking *when* and *how much*. In a week, the most eagerly demanded new Ford ever built would be playing rabbit for sixty-four race cars at the Indianapolis 500. Then the whole god-damn city would be beating down his door. But if his shipment of stock Mustangs didn't arrive soon, all he would have had to show would be row after row of Falcons, Fairlanes, and Galaxie 500s.

He did have one edge. Roberto Constantine. Jeweller. Man about town. And for Hamilton, a commodity almost as rare as a 1964 ½ Mustang: a wallet as big as his ego. No one in this town bought a car without seeing it first. No one put in an order for a new model without at least kicking the tires of one of its sisters on the lot. And no one except Roberto Josepi Constantine, God bless his soul, paid one hundred percent *over* the sticker price. Today, McAllister would deliver the first of the new Mustangs in Canada. Media from as far afield as Toronto and Montreal were in the unusual position of jostling with their Hamilton juniors for access to the moment. For Benjamin J. McAllister Jr. the world didn't get any better than this.

Roberto Constantine arrived at the dealership in a 1963 Cadillac driven by his wife, Teresa. Even he was surprised by the phalanx of hangers-on peering through the floor-to-ceiling windows.

"Pull over," Constantine told his wife, pointing towards a row of new Galaxie 500s framing a pair of blue-on-blue Fairlanes. Before she could stop, he reached across the dash and angled the rear-view mirror towards him.

He had turned thirty the week before; the new Mustang was to be a birthday gift. To himself. As soon as he heard of the car's introduction — his older brother Sal had seen a few pictures in the paper last fall — he'd called McAllister, written the cheque, and counted the days until its delivery. That was one hundred and eighty-two afternoons ago.

Constantine combed his hair, watching every follicle fall into place. He'd piled a handful of Vitalis onto his head in an attempt to control the waves of thick black hair. Teresa tried to run her fingers through the back of it, but he pushed her hand away.

"Leave it alone, doll. The press is gonna be all over the place, taking pictures. McAllister told me he's gonna want one framed to hang up in his office, permanent. The little shit. It's him that should be paying *me* for all the publicity I'm getting him."

Teresa lit a cigarette, waving the smoke away from her face. "I just don't understand it. You men and your cars."

Constantine grabbed the crotch of his pants. "It's the *cogliones*." He pretended to squeeze. "The balls, baby. Getting this car, before anyone else, it's about balls. And that little shit in there, he thinks

11

he's ripping me off." His smile broadened. "But no more than the shit I've been selling him for years." The jeweller straightened the hairs in his pencil-thin mustache with his finger. He smiled at himself. "I guess if McAllister don't notice a few pieces of glass here and there in his wife's rings, I can overlook the highway robbery he's pulling off with this car." Constantine looked at Teresa. "But I will remember, and the next strings of stones he buys to wrap around his wife's little wrist, every damn one of them's gonna be paste."

"I thought there was honour among thieves."

"Not a chance." He closed his fingers into a fist. "Fucking car dealers. They didn't invent thieving. They just got the government to make it legal." Constantine shifted his eyes back to the mirror and started to dab his eyebrows.

"Stop your fussing," Teresa whispered conspiratorially. She brushed some lint off the shoulders of his suit jacket. Constantine turned his chin away to avoid being scratched by her cocktail ring, a ruby-diamond cluster the size of a ping-pong ball that danced by his neck with each brush of her hand.

"You're gorgeous," she told him. He turned to face her. She pretended to straighten his tie, but he didn't need it. His ensemble was perfect — Italian silk, well cut, pressed, and brilliant in the sheen of the late afternoon sun. "Now go in there and get your car. It's the last virgin you're ever gonna score, so enjoy it." She kissed him on the cheek.

"Don't worry, doll. I got something for you too." He tapped the breast pocket of his jacket. "Get a sitter for the kids. I'll pick you up in about an hour and we'll spend the night showing off Hamilton's two most beautiful possessions." Constantine looked at his wife's chest. "Okay, three."

Red velvet ropes and brass stanchions, borrowed from the lobby of Pantages Theatre, stood guard around the Mustang convertible, the visiting celebrity in town for its own premiere, resplendent in its white tux with red trim. McAllister had let the crowd in early;

his salesmen worked the room passing out business cards and souvenir brochures. Kids grasped balloons and a select few were even given a model Mustang complete with working wheels, doors, trunk, and hood. A six-year-old boy barely taller than a wheel well crouched at the side of the showroom clutching his model car so tightly it seemed as if he was dreaming of somehow fitting himself behind the miniature steering wheel.

McAllister had closed the service bays and sent the mechanics home early, after cleaning the floors and bringing the hoists and air guns up to showroom condition. Webber, the service manager, guided the overflow of gawkers through a tool-by-tool description of the service area, right down to the wattage in the fluorescent lamps used to illuminate every nook of the injured engines and overworked transmissions.

The dealer spotted Constantine approaching the open bay doors. He strolled towards him, his arms outstretched, pulling at the fabric of his plaid jacket. He extended his right hand towards his new favourite customer.

Constantine scowled. "Why was I told to come here? To the service entrance?" He adjusted his shoulders. "My money not good enough for the showroom?"

McAllister shook his hand. "Just a little showmanship, my friend. You, of all people, should know these things. I want a grand entrance, as well as an exit. I got a couple hundred people in there," he motioned towards the showroom. "A dozen press, even a TV camera crew."

"All I want is the car," Constantine lied.

"Then let's go." McAllister put his arm around him. "I do need a favour, though."

The pair strolled leisurely up the ramp towards the showroom, the air still full of the scent of fresh rubber and grease. "I've already done you one," Constantine answered. "You're gonna be bathing in my money for months."

"Don't I wish it were so." McAllister stopped for a moment, bringing Constantine to halt mere feet from the closed door to the showroom. "Your money paid for the car, at full retail, plus a premium for early delivery, express freight, and most of all, cash for greasing the palms of a half dozen Ford execs on both sides of the border. The goddamn Ford of Canada president was supposed to get this car, you know. To get it away from him, I had to agree to buy all last year's remaining Falcons from both US plants. That's two hundred and seventy-eight cars, all with the personality of your brother. Cold, grey, but functional. I'm gonna have to sell them cheap … as cabs."

Constantine chuckled under his breath. He slipped his hand underneath the lapel of the car dealer's jacket. "Why is that my problem? You took my money quick enough. What do you expect?"

"I expect that the mayor is gonna be here and I want you to take him for a ride in that Mustang. Let the press ride alongside and take pictures."

Constantine rolled the Mustang over the rubber hoses, ringing the bell inside the service station.

"Lucky we made it this far," Constantine said. "Fucking McAllister. He had me drive the mayor halfway around the harbour before he'd let *me* take *my* car out on my own."

"It'll be in all the papers tomorrow," Teresa said. A bejewelled crucifix hung between her rope of pearls, catching the light of the pumps.

"It goddamn well better be." Constantine honked the horn in an attempt to coax an attendant out of the station. A slight boy with a limp hobbled towards them. His grey overalls identified him as Neil.

"Just my luck," Constantine said. "Must be hire-the-goddamn-handicapped week."

Teresa gave him a playful push on the shoulder. "Really, Robbie. There's a place in hell with your name on it."

The attendant continued his awkward gait towards the Mustang, slowing down to gaze at the new car's silhouette. Before the kid had a chance to open his mouth, Constantine barked, "Fill it up with premium."

Neil nodded, continuing his slow walk around the vehicle, his hand inches away from the well-polished steel, as if he was using Braille to find the gas cap. Stopping at the trunk, he found the rounded cap and removed it with the care he might have give to opening a rare bottle of wine, had he ever had the opportunity. He heard the sound of a well-throttled muffler approaching, followed by a double ding of the bell, and turned to see a pair of large motor-cycles enter the lot. One stopped behind him, the other pulled over to the driver's side of the Mustang.

The lead biker gave the heavy cycle a couple of revs, then killed the engine. He dismounted like a cowboy stepping down from his stallion. He removed a pair of sunglasses, tucking them into the pocket of his leather vest.

"Nice wheels," he said to Constantine, his smile revealing a pair of gold caps.

Constantine said only, "Thanks," and turned his head to look at the gas jockey. "Hurry up."

"What's your hurry, pony boy?" the lead biker said. He looked as if he weighed more than his bike. His legs were massive, a pair of tree-trunk suspension bars that pushed his height to six-foot-six or more.

His wing man had taken up root behind Neil, shooing him away. The second biker was blond with a dirty brown beard, his eyes hidden behind a set of mirrored lenses. He took the abandoned pump in his hand and resumed filling the Mustang's tank. "You want I should check your oil?"

Teresa grabbed her husband's arm. Constantine reached over to grasp her hand.

"Relax, pony boy," the lead biker said. He put his foot up on the driver's side door, his scuffed black boot resting inches from Constantine's face. "We saw you drive by and just wanted to get a closer look at the car." He took his foot down and began to walk slowly around the car as his partner continued to fill the tank.

Out of the corner of his eye, Constantine saw the hobbled gas jockey pedalling a bicycle off the lot and into the darkness of the city street.

"I suggest you visit a dealer," Constantine said. "They'll let you take a test drive." His voice was slow and steady, as if he was trying to calm a rabid dog.

"I was hoping that you'd let us take this pony for a ride," the biker said. He walked over to the passenger's side, leaned over the open roof, and stared down at Teresa, his eyes on her pearls, then on her cleavage, then on the car. Instinctively Teresa shied away from him, but the car was small and she found herself longing for the Cadillac's size, speed, and power windows.

Constantine got out of the car and moved towards the biker in an attempt to get between him, his car, and his wife.

"Robbie," Teresa said. "No. Please."

Constantine continued moving towards the biker. The wing man had finished his work and also began moving toward his partner.

"You should leave us alone," the jeweller said. "This won't work out well for you."

The biker's large smile revealed a set of dental work that had been forged by a cross between a dentist and a machinist. He lifted the heel of his boot and came down hard on the quarter-panel above the passenger side wheel well. The steel was crushed underfoot.

"You goddamn son of a bitch!" Constantine yelled. He resisted the urge to grab the biker by the throat. "You don't know who you're fucking with. I know people! One call! One fucking call," he held up his index finger, "and you're dead." He stared down the second biker. "Both of you. Fucking dead."

Teresa started sobbing. The second biker crossed his arms. His partner came around to the front of the car, then kicked in the headlamp on the front passenger side, rocking the car as the glass shattered and the chrome ring twisted into the shape of a boot.

Constantine returned to the driver's seat. He started the engine. "One call, asshole, and you're wife's a widow."

The biker stood in front of the bar, his boot now pressing heavily onto the hood. He ground his toe between the "O" and the "R" in the word Ford. "You know, I'd give you a dime to make the phone call." He pointed over to the pay phone attached to the wall by the station's office. "But I don't have to. Those people you know? They're right over there." He gestured towards the street where a long black Lincoln Continental had appeared. It was idling by the curb, its exhaust adding to the acrid texture of the smoke from the steel plant.

Another pair of bikers pulled up, blocking one of the entrances to the gas station. Moments later another pair set themselves up at the only other exit. Teresa gripped her pearls and prayed.

"You should follow me," the gold-toothed biker told Constantine as he remounted his motorcycle. "Stay close. Like your life depends on it."

# 1

## Thursday, January 17, 1991

A couple of cars, a couple of times, a couple of weeks — it wasn't like *he* was stealing the cars. Still, Dominic couldn't help feeling like a mortician who moonlighted in bootleg body parts. And he could never get past the thought that the quarter-panel he'd be chopping off a Chevrolet for the Romanian one night might end up on the driver's side of a Pontiac he'd be repainting for his brother the next day. At Tony's shop, Dominic's job was to hide the damage of the road. Here, he inflicted it.

That morning, he'd called the Romanian, who told him the time and place. This was routine. After Dominic had worked the day at his brother's City-Wide Collision, off he'd go to another abandoned building for another all-nighter and take apart a perfectly good car, piece by piece. Each night, he'd close his mind to the consequences. There he'd be — Dominic DiPietro, the mortician cutting up cadavers, when all he really wanted to do was bring them back to life.

He was grateful that the Romanian was in charge of the muscle. Dominic was strong enough, but underworld auto-parts dealers needed a team of brutes for the really heavy work, like transmissions, differentials, and engine blocks. Dominic was built for speed, so the Romanian had recruited bikers from local affiliated gangs. They were easy to spot, with their club leathers, insignias, and affinity for bandanas and tattoos. Nastasi filled out the balance of his chop shop roster with a changing number of transients whose command of the English language, like his, had yet to fully emerge.

Dominic's impact on the operation was immediate. The first night he worked with the Romanian's crew, he'd immediately jumped in and stopped everything before they reduced the car's value to scrap metal. Nastasi had sent them all to a derelict truck factory on Burlington Street. There, Dominic found the Romanian's bruisers pulling the parts off a Corvette as if the event was an Olympic speed trial. Dominic slowed them down. He showed them where to find the seams, the weak points, the carriage bolts, and coached them in the gentle tugs that kept the wiring schematics in place and — most of all — saleable. That was the first time he ever saw the Romanian smile, his teeth black and ragged, like a wolverine after a meal of fresh meat. On that first night, Dominic showed the Romanian and his crew how to pull seventy thousand dollars worth of parts from a thirty thousand dollar car, all because Dominic's real love was not hacking automobiles to pieces, but putting them back together.

For this, the Romanian gave him five hundred dollars a car, in cash. The same amount for a night that his brother Tony paid him a week, less deductions for taxes, insurance, and City-Wide Collision's social fund. The Romanian's money was good, and tax free, but by Dominic's own calculations he'd have to chop three cars a week for fifteen years to put the money together for his own business. At that rate, he'd be dead before he ever saw his name on a shop. He'd bet on it.

He left each night's chop shop before the sun rose over the harbour, a little richer in his jeans, a little lower in his self-regard, and knowing he'd never see the place again. During the three months he'd been chopping for the Romanian, he'd never gone to the same place twice. Still, the Romanian was incessant in prodding Dominic to take on more jobs.

"You are genius," the Romanian would tell him, usually as he was admiring the skill at which Dominic had just stripped off a fuel injector or disassembled a transmission. The Romanian spoke in deep nasal tones that he mumbled into his chest, forcing his listeners to pay close attention to every word he said. Often, there were gaps in his speech, as if he was on a constant search for the right word in his adopted language. "I make you rich," he'd tell Dominic. "People pay money, good money, for parts you make me." But a couple of cars, a couple of times a week, was as close to Hamilton's underground as Dominic wanted to slither. Gambling and women excepted, of course.

After each night with the Romanian, he'd shower and change at City-Wide and tell himself quiet lies of penance as he stroked yet another car back to life for his brother. *It's about freedom,* he'd tell himself. *It's about making cars so beautiful that people will stop and stare and want to mortgage their children's future.* When he was chopping, he'd say the same prayer, only in consolation. *Sorry,* he'd whisper to each stolen car as he fired up the acetylene torch. Then he'd let his fingers caress its curves. It if it was old enough, he'd admire its classic lines, its chrome, and the firmness of its body. Then, he'd slice it into a hundred pieces.

It was nine a.m. by the time Dominic returned to his day job. By nine-thirty, the paint gun was hot, its air-fired engine dripping green from his recent assault on a Malibu. The gun was attached to Dominic's gloved hand as if he'd been welded to it. A paint-suit covered his body completely, and his mask engulfed him, a pair of face-hugging goggles and two air filters that extended around his mouth like oversized insect's eyes attached to his head. He looked like a spotted, bug-eyed monster dredged from the marshes of Cootes Paradise or the Amazon jungle.

The last car through the paint booth had been green, and now so was he. Dominic lifted the goggles from his eyes and inspected the finish coat of General Motors Green Number 8 he had just lain down. The colour chip identified it as Forest Green. Heaven on a hood was Dominic's goal. He moved his eyes along the hood from the newspapers that covered the windshield to the masking tape that kept speckles of over-spray from dancing on the headlights. He slid the respirator from his face and let it rest on the top of his head, his eyes following the gentle horizon of the Malibu's emerald hood. Unprotected, he laid his cheek a bare millimeter from the hood and gazed across its flatness, scanning for any imperfections. To Dominic, the slightest flaws looked like pits and scars across a green full moon. He took off his gloves and stuffed them into his coveralls.

The pump of the air pistol pounded in his ears. He pointed the paint gun at a groove in the hood too faint for any eyes but his to see. He gave it a millisecond burst, and it vanished. He caught another, then another. Thirty minutes later he'd inspected the entire Chevy and retouched a dozen flaws, yet he couldn't stop shaking his head.

Dominic put the gun down and exited the paint booth. The protective whoosh of positive air pressure pushed him into the main shop. From the doorway, he could see his brother Tony talking to Nunzio, the shop's principal body man. Both men were perched underneath a hoist inspecting the frame of a twisted Mazda RX-7.

Tony turned to look at Dominic when he heard the opening *shhh* of the air-controlled door. "What's been taking you so long in there? You'd think you were working on a Rolls Royce or something." He was a full head and shoulders taller than Nunzio, who'd cranked the RX-7 high enough on the hoist for his hands to reach inside its wheel wells. He moved out from under the car and away from the work area.

"I go now to catalogue for parts," Nunzio said. If not articulate, in either English or Italian, he remained a man of a certain expertise.

Plus, he was smart enough to realize that when you worked in a family business and were not of the proper bloodline, the best place to be when an argument was about to break out was on the other side of the building.

"The sanding job was crap," Dominic said. "Herman must be using the sandpaper to scratch his ass, 'cause he sure as hell ain't using it on the cars. How am I supposed to paint on top of that crap?"

"You paint what gets sent to you." Tony came out from under the Mazda and walked towards Dominic. Built like a professional wrestler, Tony's chest and stomach were iceberg large and solid. He looked like he could carry the weight of every bruised car on his shoulders.

"It needs another sanding and another coat. Maybe two." Dominic was stripping out of his coveralls. Underneath he had on a black Led Zeppelin T-shirt and a pair of black, well-worn jeans. His dirty blond hair looked glued to his head in patches that spiked and splayed at will.

"Don't get out of those yet. I got another three cars in the paint line." Tony looked at his watch. "And by the time you're finished those, I'll have the Cadillac and that Mercury ready to go in."

"That Chev's gotta sit in there for a least twenty minutes. Then I'm giving it a second coat."

"That *is* its second coat. The insurance company's not paying for a third. No extra sanding, no nothing. You're done with it."

"It's gonna look like shit." Dominic squared his shoulders, but he already knew what the result would be. Tony's business. Tony's rules. Dominic gets fucked, again.

"It'll be fine," Tony waved his hand dismissively. "Just get this paint line moving. We got cars to get through. There are twenty more where these came from and I got insurance adjusters crawling up my ass waiting to get these pieces of tin back on the road."

Dominic started to zip up his coveralls. "This is shit and you know it. That car's gonna blister in a year unless we fix it."

"There's no profit in overwork. Somebody's got to pay for it and it ain't gonna be me. If the customer's paying with his own money, then you can give it your show-and-shine best. But not a minute more labour or another ounce of paint unless somebody's paying for it."

"My talents are wasted on this kind of crap," Dominic said. He slipped his paint gloves back on.

"Talent paints pictures," Tony said. "You paint cars, for *me*. Now get your ass back to work."

The echoing voice of Lisa Fortunato, the office administrator, carried over the speakers of the shop. "Dominic, line three. Dominic, line three."

Tony raised an eyebrow. "Make it quick." He returned his attention to the Mazda.

Dominic ignored him and picked up the phone on wall. He pushed the third line. "Yeah."

It was Walter Janowitz, the shop's paint supplier, as rich a resource of information as he was with clear coats, primers, and body-filling plasters. He insisted that Dominic meet him after work at Hanrahan's, a strip club. Dominic knew that it was a favourite hangout of the paint salesmen. It was where Walter took a lot of his clients. But Dominic wasn't his client. His brother was.

Walter baited him. "I got some really good news for you." He needn't have bothered. The canteen truck had yet to make its morning delivery, but Dominic could already taste the desperate need for a drink. By six, he'd need several.

He hung up and returned to the paint booth, the pressure-sealed doors closing behind him. Beside the door was his toolbox. It contained a series of nozzles for his paint gun that could lay a patch of paint three feet wide or a millimetre. It also held a six pack of paper air filters — he went through one every hour — three sets of contact lenses, five handkerchiefs — two clean and three in various stages of colour spew and sputum — fourteen screwdrivers of all

24

sizes and configurations, two lengths of heavy gauge extension cords, a portable lamp — one hundred watt halogen for accurate colour control — another halogen lamp, a flashlight small enough to be held between his teeth, and a peanut butter sandwich, of indeterminate age, preserved by the spice cabinet of chemicals that called his toolbox home. He lifted the top tray and set it aside. From the bottom of the toolbox, stuck deep in a corner and surrounded by three rolls of masking tape, each a different width and weight, Dominic pulled out a paint-speckled bottle of Smirnoff Vodka. From his pocket he took out a bottle of Advil, unscrewed the top, and spilled five of the muddy brown painkillers into his hand. Using the vodka as a chaser, he swallowed the handful whole. He wasn't going to wait for Walter.

He stood up and gave his head a shake to mix the liquor and the pills. He put the mask back on his head and snapped on the respirator, then flipped the switch for the air hoses. They began to purr. He picked up the spray gun and grimaced, grabbing his shoulder for support. A sharp pain sliced down the length of his arm and shot out of his shoulder. He switched hands and rolled the offending shoulder while breathing deeply and praying for the painkillers to kick in. They did, chasing the pain enough away for him to return the weight of the spray gun to his right hand.

Dominic looked over at the Malibu and pointed the spray gun at the floor. He gave it a couple of test shots.

"Sorry, honey." He was still rolling his shoulder in an attempt to loosen the grip of the pain. "But walking wounded is as good as either of us is going to get today." He pushed the button that powered up the chain-driven conveyor. The Chevrolet rolled away and into the drying area. A Toyota Corolla was pulled into its place. Dominic ran his bare hand across the sanded hood. *You could be so beautiful.* He hoped Janowitz really had some good news. He could not remember the last time he'd had any that hadn't come out of a bottle or a bet.

# 2

Walter's news was good. Too good. Dominic put back four shots of tequila while trying to digest what the paint salesman told him.

"My boss is calling in the equipment loan at Nick's," Walter said. They were sitting at the back of the club, as far as possible from the pounding of the dancers' music. Still, Dominic had to lean forward and strain his ears to hear over the din.

"Nicky just didn't know how to run a shop properly," Walter said. He was keeping up with Dominic shot for shot. He waved over a large-breasted waitress. She looked a few years past her days as a dancer, but was fit enough to keep the regulars happy. Walter ordered a double round of shooters and two bottles of Molson Canadian. "We were always having to go in and do extra work for him on warranty claims. He had a great set-up too, he just wouldn't put out any money for a decent paint man. If he'd had a guy like you there, he'd have given your brother a run for his money."

"I know the place. It's over on Cannon Street, by the stadium."

"Hard to believe that a guy who has twenty-five thousand people walk by his front door every time there's a football game can't make a go of it."

"It always comes down to quality," Dominic said. The waitress had returned with their drinks. Dominic threw back the first tequila before the second one hit the table.

"Slow down, honey." She leaned into Dominic's face. "There's more to this place than beer, you know."

"Thanks." Dominic poured the second tequila down his throat. "We'll have two more."

The music blared, but now it was slow and easy. This dancer was going to take her time.

"So Nicky's gone, eh?"

"As of Friday. Monday we start hauling out the equipment."

"Damn, that's a shame." Dominic nursed his Molson.

"It doesn't have to be. My boss told me that if I can get another guy in there, he'd leave the equipment and help set him up."

"No shit."

"We got no place else to put the stuff, anyway. The equipment is good and everything, but it's not as good as what your brother's got. It's worth about a hundred grand, on paper. But without an operator, it's worthless."

"So what are you asking me?"

"You wanna take over Nicky's shop? Say the word, Dominic, it's all yours."

Dominic drained his beer. "Whatever word you want, I'll say it."

"The word is twenty grand. The rest we'll finance."

Dominic found himself wishing he hadn't finished that beer. He needed another long one, the kind that comes directly from the end of a keg. "That's a lot of money."

"Dominic, I'll give you the straight deal. I don't know all the particulars, but Nicky's into us for the entire value of his business. Like I said, that's a hundred large. At least. My boss co-signed his lease, so now we're stuck paying rent on a place we can't use, and we got all this equipment gathering dust. It's a shame, Dominic. A real fucking shame. The worst part of it is that I didn't even put Nicky into the place. That was my boss's doing. He's got a soft spot for the little Greek. But now I'm stuck cleaning up the mess." Walter leaned over the table. Dominic could see the paint salesman's nostrils opening and closing like a thoroughbred warming up for a race. "You come up with the twenty grand, and I *know* I can convince the boss to carry the rest. He'll be jumping for joy that head office doesn't find out what kind of screw-up he's been. All you gotta do is buy your paint and supplies from me exclusively. That'll be enough for now."

"That, and twenty-five grand."

Walter opened his throat and drained another shot. He pushed the remaining one towards Dominic. "My boss is gonna want to see some commitment, in cash. But you must have access to that kind of dough. Don't you?"

Dominic took the tequila. He thought of the coffee can hidden in his mother's basement, filled with the money he'd earned from the Romanian. Ten thousand dollars. *Twenty nights, twenty cars, three months.* "I could get you half. For the rest, I'd need some time."

"How long?"

Dominic did Romanian car math in his head. "Probably six more months."

Walter shook his head. "Dominic, I've been watching you. I know that a man with your talent can really make a go of it. But I can only keep my boss off this place for five or six days. Even a month is out of the question. He wants this deal done or I swear he's gonna blow the place up himself to get rid of any evidence of his fuck up. If you want this, if you *really* want this, you're gonna have to move fast. Maybe you could borrow the money from your brother?"

Dominic let out a sad chuckle. "How long have you been selling us paint? I'd have a better chance buying a lottery ticket."

"What about a bank? I know a guy who could write you up a business plan, cheap. That, plus your experience, I know it'll satisfy the most uptight loans officer."

"Sorry. This tequila has a better credit rating than I do. There isn't a banker in this town who'd loan me so much as a pen."

"Listen to me, Dominic. I've known you long enough to know

that working for your brother is a dead end. He's one of my best customers, but you, my friend, he has some kind of hate-on for. What'd you do, steal his girlfriend or something when you were kids?"

Dominic shook his head. "No. Just being born. I think that was enough for Tony. His lifelong ambition was to be an only child."

"Whatever, you gotta get past it. It's a ... what you call it?" Walter snapped his fingers a couple of times. "An albatross. This thing you got going with your brother, it's some kind of albatross hanging around your neck. You're going nowhere until you get rid of it. If I were you, I'd fight like a demon to get this place. Opportunities like this don't come along very often, if ever."

A demon, Dominic thought. He had plenty of those to choose from.

# 3

Dominic sucked in his breath and sat down beside Magilla. The tight squeak of the compressed stool interrupted the silence in the donut shop. The hour was early — too early for drunks and far too late for the street trade on Barton. The few hangers-on, the ones with no homes worth returning to, littered the shop, nursing their morning-after versions of self-medication — coffee and nicotine. Dominic had left his buddy Sammy, a welder who was as lean as one of his torches, to act as lookout outside the donut shop beside the yellow and red newspaper boxes from the *Hamilton Spectator*, the *Toronto Star* and the *Buffalo Daily News*

Before Dominic was strong enough to hold a paint gun in one hand, he'd known that Magilla, or someone like him, made this place his office. These were the things you came to know if you were an Italian boy living in Hamilton's north end — like who was beating his wife, when one of the neighbours came up for parole, on what street corner the best weed could be bought, and where, if you wanted to, you could place a wager on anything that moved: cars, horses, hockey pucks, or footballs.

The bookie with hair as greasy as yesterday's french fries took up the better part of two stools. The counter was his regular spot to meet bettors face to face. Dominic played along with the bookie's ritual by ordering a honey dip donut and a double-double coffee, then sliding the order over to him. It was the signal that Dominic had a bet to lay down, something Magilla already knew, but the bookie had a routine and Dominic knew he wasn't about to change it. The ritual made him feel important, like you had to know some kind of secret code before he would lay book for you. For the moment, Dominic played along. He had no choice. Every other bookie he'd called had already turned him down. Magilla was Jewish, and Dominic knew that from the local mob's perspective on street management Magilla's circumcision made him reliable, but expendable.

"You look like you lost some weight," Dominic said. He could fit himself inside one leg of the bookie's pants. "I hope this doesn't mean business is bad."

"Fuck off." Magilla took a sip of the coffee and rubbed his perpetually runny nose. "God, I hate this fucking weather. One more cold and I'm moving the business to Florida."

"Criminisi will let you do that?"

"That little Mussolini may own the book to this slag heap of a city, but he's not everywhere. I could set up shop down south. In a heartbeat. They race dogs down there, like they was horses. Give 'em racing names and everything. I'll take Florida over this fucking place, anytime." Magilla sniffed and rubbed and slurped.

"Well, stay away from the beach. You in a bathing suit has got to be bad for the tourist business."

"Fuck you." Magilla wiped his face with a handkerchief that was already stained with sweat. "What'd you want?"

"Bills over Giants, ten grand."

Magilla turned to Dominic. The slits that passed for eyes were so puffed and dark he looked as if he'd just been on the losing end of heavyweight fight.

"The Super Bowl is the biggest sucker bet of the year, DiPietro, and your credit's not that good."

He opened a small ring-bound notebook that sat by his coffee.

31

Magilla looked down at a page devoted exclusively to Dominic's wagering history. There was a lot of red ink on it.

"I know what I'm doing," Dominic said.

"Okay, but ten, with points? No way. You're already into me for five."

"No points. I'm not making that mistake again. Bills to win. Straight up." Dominic looked over the bookie's ample shoulder. Outside, Sammy was finishing off the last drags of a butt and looking ready to bolt.

Magilla took a long sniff that caught the air like a waking snore. "Still, this ain't the kind of action I can take, not with the situation you're in. I got people, and they're already pissed at me for letting your ledger get this far in the red."

"These people, they're the same people who'll let you pack up and move to Florida?"

"Yeah, the same. You see, they don't care if I fuck off to Florida or fuck your sister. They don't even give a fuck if you don't pay your debts, only that I cover them. You see, DiPietro, it's my neck on the line here, not yours."

Dominic could see that was a lot of neck, but the sight of it did not make what he was about to do seem any less risky. He pulled two large rolls of bills from his jacket pocket. They were wound tight, and held together by a rubber band. "This should loosen your collar. There's five grand to cover my losses, and another five as a down payment against my action this Sunday."

Magilla took the two rolls in his hand. He seemed to be weighing them rather than giving each bill the once-over and a count.

"That's a lot of fresh for a little shit like you. You must be doing pretty well with the Romanian."

"That's none of your business."

"My only business is that you make good on your bet."

"So I've done it." Dominic looked at the pile of his savings. There were a lot of bumpers, quarter-panels, and transmissions wound up in those rubber bands. "We're even. And now I want back in the action."

Magilla took one of the rolls and put it his pocket. "Then let me do you a favour." He picked up the other roll and placed it in Dominic's hand. "Keep the change."

Dominic pushed the money back towards Magilla. "Take it. I won't lose."

"Yeah, you and a hundred other dumb fucks. You think I do this for fun?"

"Magilla, it's the Super Bowl. I can make as much in one bet as I can working nights all year for the Romanian. And I don't have that much time."

"You can bet the Pro Bowl next week. Or the Leafs, any time. You got like a hundred hockey games left to do some real damage."

"No, it's gotta be this Sunday." Dominic moved closer and whispered in the fat man's ear. The odour of the bookie's shirt travelled up his nose, but he ignored it.

"Listen," he said. "I need this win, bad. I got plans."

Magilla laid his hand on the cash. "So what the fuck are you giving this to me for?"

"I need twenty-five grand to close a deal."

"Then what you need is a banker, DiPietro. Not a bookie."

"Magilla, you're the best banker I got. So take the bet. You've got five grand against my action right there in front of you."

"Still, you lose …"

"I won't lose."

Magilla took the other five thousand and put it into his jacket pocket.

"But if you do, I will be seeing that skinny little ass of yours perched right here on Monday morning with the other five. Right?" He looked at his notebook. "Or certain parts of your face are going to be rearranged, like you was a Picasso."

The bookie wrote down Dominic's bet. It was done. Dominic rubbed his own nose, as if to make sure it was in its rightful place.

Sammy greeted Dominic outside the donut shop, the cold turning his lips a dangerous shade of blue. "You leave me out here any longer and you'd be calling the paramedics. They'd be chipping my frozen body off the sidewalk. I should have stayed in the car, with the engine running."

"You did good, Sammy. I needed you outside to cover my back, and you did great."

Sammy blew into his hands, then buried them in the pockets of his leather jacket. He held them close to his belly. "All this money and mob stuff, it twists my stomach into knots. That's where I carry my stress, you know. And its not like it's even my money. Next time, get Leo to stand on guard for thee. One look at him would scare anyone. And he knows how to use a knife."

They started walking toward the car, a City-Wide Collision courtesy car.

Sammy stopped and looked back at the bookie through the floor-to-ceiling windows of the donut shop. "How old is that Magilla, you figure?"

"How should I know?" Dominic kept walking.

"The guy looks pretty fucking old. At least sixty."

"Forty, sixty, twelve, who gives a shit?"

"You don't think I'm gonna look like that when I'm sixty, do ya?" Sammy was skinny enough to floss with. Dominic often wondered where he found the strength to use his welding gear.

"What do I look like, a doctor?" Dominic opened the passenger door and got in. Sammy slid into the driver's seat and started the engine. He turned the heater on high as well as the fan, but all that came out of the vents was air chilled by Hamilton's January winds. The car was a faded blue Nissan Sentra with a full set of balding tires and a couple of front quarter-panels borrowed from a sister Sentra and covered in the brick-red patina of a primer coat. A City-Wide Collision logo on the door might have been the sole reason the door stayed in place.

# 4

"Still, I could end up that way. Eating donuts and becoming fat like that. I think I'll stick to tea." He touched his stomach, as if to examine it. "You know anything about that green tea stuff? Supposed to be real good for you. Do they sell green tea in there? They should, you know, and whole-grain donuts, baked, not those fried hunks of cholesterol. They'll kill ya."

"Something always does." Dominic pulled a pack of du Mauriers from his jacket and lit one. "There's only one sure bet in this life. None of us is getting out of here alive." He rolled his window down an inch or so and blew a puff of smoke through the crack.

"Maybe so. But that's no reason for doing business with goons like him."

"Magilla falls into the category of a necessary evil. There's no one else in town who'd cover that kind of bet. I know. I checked."

"I don't know how you sleep." Sammy rubbed his stomach. "I'm about to put my breakfast all over this dashboard, and all I did was drive you there."

"I try not to think about it."

"Maybe you should start. Magilla's been known to go to pretty obscene lengths to get paid."

"Sammy, you know shit about this kind of stuff."

"Shit, Dominic, is what you've gotten yourself into." Sammy was driving with one hand on the steering wheel and the other buried in his pocket, holding onto his stomach. He only took it out to shift gears. "Just a couple of months ago, a guy working at the Rolling Mill, he got into Magilla for about thirty thousand. Had a thing about betting on hockey games — NHL, AHL, International League. Hell, he'd lay his life savings down on figure skating if they starting using sticks."

"So?"

"Well, *so* is about what happened to him when he couldn't cover his bets. You see, Orville — that's his name, Orville — he liked to hang at this sports bar on Barton Street. Fast Willy's. You know it. They have like a hundred TV sets spread over the bar so he could watch all the NHL games at once every Saturday night."

"I've been there."

"Been there? Man, you never left." Sammy pulled his hand from his pocket, but miscalculated the timing of the gear shift and clutch, so that jostling both men to the windshield and back. "One Saturday night, Orville's watching the late west game, Canucks versus the Kings, in LA. It's about one o'clock in the morning and Orville's at the bar, thinking he's lucky that Magilla wouldn't take his action because the Canucks are getting their asses kicked. Orville would bet the Canucks even if they had your mother playing goal." Sammy got the car up to speed and the ride smoothed itself out. "So he's sitting there, counting the money he didn't lose, when two of Magilla's collectors show up, big goddamn biker guys, looking like they didn't just ride their Harleys, they bench-pressed them. They escort Orville downstairs to the basement, where they tell him to strip to his underwear."

Dominic let out an uneasy laugh.

"This is no joke, man. You and Orville are about to meet in hell."

You see, cause when Orville's down there in Fast Willy's basement, after taking off his socks and shoes, his shirt and his pants, Magilla's guys shove him into this humongous walk-in freezer and

36

lock the door behind him. It's Saturday night, more like real early Sunday morning, and the bar won't open up again until Monday afternoon. So they leave him there, sitting in his underwear, inside this man-sized ice cube maker for thirty-six hours."

"At least he would have arrived at the morgue well-chilled."

"No, he didn't die. Magilla can't collect from dead people. More than that, he's done his homework. He knows that Orville, like all of us at the steel company, has insurance benefits. We got life insurance, dental insurance, eye glasses insurance, and *especially* disability insurance."

"Disability insurance?" Dominic repeated.

"Yeah, D and D, as in disability and dismemberment. You know, the kind of insurance like if you lose a finger, the insurance company pays you ten thousand dollars. Lose a toe, another ten. Lose a leg, twenty-five grand, stuff like that."

"Oh."

"Oh, is fucking right. Because when they let old Orville out of that freezer he's frostbit all over his hands and feet. The only thing that kept Orville's dick from becoming a Popsicle was that he kept it cupped in his frozen hands for the whole night."

"Jesus."

"Damn right. Magilla's collectors, they drop him off at a hospital where the docs lop off four toes, a pinky finger, and both his earlobes."

Dominic was doing the math in his head. "About thirty grand worth."

"More like fifty. An aggravation tax, I think Magilla called it. Orville had to tell the insurance company he'd gone ice fishing for the weekend and fallen through some frozen fucking hole. Which was one hell of a story 'cause I think all this happened last October."

"So, Magilla's not as stupid as he looks." Dominic tossed the cigarette out the window.

"But you, my friend, are. It must have something to do with those paint fumes you keep sucking in. Because if I recall, you're working for your brother and the only benefits you get are lungs full of cancer-causing chemicals and the weight of Tony's thumb pressing down on you every moment of your life."

"That's the whole point, Sammy. This gets me out from under him. The Bills win, I'm out of there."

"And if you lose?"

"That's not an option," Dominic said to the windshield.

"Then I'll be praying for you, Dominic. Because as I see it, your fingers and toes aren't worth the body they're attached to."

# 5

Hamilton is bordered by a long-dead sea that hovers over the city and its people as if those living below it reside on the bottom of some vast kitchen sink. At its center lies a bay, a once pristine natural harbour that has evolved into the city's open sewer and into which drains the detritus of a half a million people.

It is a city built on the promises of industrial prosperity, layered thick like the toxic sediment at the bottom of its harbour. Yet, like a drunk who keeps spilling martinis at a black-tie dinner, Hamilton can't help but embarrass itself. So it hides away, a leper ashamed not of its blisters and its foul-smelling body, but of the long-forgotten spiritual misdeed that must have given birth to it. The nooks are its streets. The crannies are its alleyways and lanes cast full of garbage and ruin. Its buildings, the closer they get to the great drain at its centre, wallow like rotted mould and discarded bits of food that its caretakers have yet to wash away. When the wind blows off the lake in January, the rain falls sideways and the air ices it into slivers of glass that pierce frozen cheeks and dance like iron filings on windshields.

Sammy slid the balding tires of the City-Wide courtesy car around an iced-up corner, bumping the sidewalls into a curb as if he was taking Dominic on a bumper-car ride through the city rather than to a large Italian-owned grocery store. Dominic wanted to talk to Leo Deluca, a friend since the two had shared a choir book and cigarettes when they had attended Saint Emmanuelle's Church together. Today Leo was a butcher, which meant that Dominic could talk to him by simply stepping up to the meat counter.

Inside the store Dominic wove through the crowded aisles and headed towards the back. Sammy followed, stopping occasionally to look at a label or avoid a woman more focused on her shopping list than the direction of her cart. He slipped his slender hips around parked carts and aisle-end displays of imported pastas, canned whole tomatoes, and multinational fortresses of pickles, antipasto, and cans of Australian pears and apricots.

Leo was trimming veal behind a glass counter full of fresh cuts of beef and pork. Dominic's old choir buddy looked like a man who took his profession home with him. His chest and belly appeared ready to burst under the weight of a chain-mail apron. He was a modern knight, welded together by ancient armor and wielding a knife that could cut through bone. His arms hung easily from shoulders broadened by two-hundred-pound hindquarters carried from the meat locker to the butchering block.

"Don't leave any fingers in there," Dominic said. Without looking up, Leo raised a gloved hand and unfurled a single bloody finger wrapped in steel.

Dominic walked around the glass counter. He stopped to smell the fresh-cut steaks. Sammy inspected packets of cheese a few aisles away.

"Nose out of there," Leo said. He waved his butcher knife at Dominic. "You shouldn't even be back here." He looked at Sammy, who waved back with both hands. He had a block of cheddar in one hand and a wedge of Brie in the other. "Put that down, now."

An elderly woman was inspecting the beef section. She shot Leo a glance of maternal disapproval.

"Who's gonna stop us? Not him." Dominic gestured at a pig's head lying pink and puckered at one end of the table. "Listen, I just came by to see if you were coming with me to Hanrahan's tomorrow afternoon, for the Super Bowl."

"No. Christina and I are going over to Gino's house." Leo said. "You not coming?"

Dominic had picked up a small trimming knife and was trying to spin it like a top on Leo's chopping board. Leo sneered, then grabbed the knife. "You are dangerous."

"Only to myself." Dominic forced a smile. "But no, I'm not going to Gino's. His wife is always trying to set me up with one of her friends. This game is too important to be bothered by some over-eager husband-shopper. All I really want to do is watch football and drink too much."

"Yeah," Sammy said. "Dominic's laid a bundle down."

Leo closed his eyes. "Then you really are dangerous." He exhaled and slid the trimming knife into a slot along one edge of the chopping board, then picked up his butcher knife.

"It's only a bet. It's not like I'm robbing a bank or anything."

Sammy said, "Good bet too, Leo. Dominic's got the Bills straight up."

"Keep out of this, Sammy."

"No, well, I was just trying to help …"

"I'm not looking for any favours here."

Leo pointed his butcher knife square at Dominic's heart. "No … I suppose you're looking for money. Again."

"No, no, I'm fine."

"Dominic, I've worked with meat long enough to know the difference between grain-fed steer and triple-A bullshit."

"No, really." Dominic picked up a piece of Genoa salami and took a bite. "I just wanted Sammy to drive me here to see if I could convince you to quit hanging out with the *wives* and spend an afternoon with your best friend watching the biggest sporting event of the year."

"Friends like you, I don't think I need so much, not anymore. And the wives are right about one thing. A good woman might help settle you down."

"Now you're making me loose my appetite." Dominic put the

uneaten portion of salami on the butcher table. Leo brushed it into a garbage bin with his knife.

"Well, since you're so flush that you're flashing your money around with the bookies, then maybe you can pay me back the fifteen hundred you owe me."

Dominic gritted his teeth. "Ah … no. Not today. My cash is all tied up right now. But tomorrow. On Monday. For sure."

Sammy was fondling soft-ripened cheeses. "Dominic had to pay off Magilla and lay a deposit down on his Super Bowl bet."

Leo stabbed his knife into the top of the table. "You are such a fool, man."

"Leo, it's none of your business." Dominic turned to Sammy. "Why don't you go check out the organic produce or something?"

Leo wiped the blood from his hands onto his apron. He looked like he'd just fought a war, and won. "They're shits, you know, these mob types you're dealing with. They give every Italian in Hamilton a bad name."

"He's a Jew, actually."

"So was Judas." Leo pulled the knife out of the table. "And I seem to remember that he worked for the Italians too … the worst kind of Italians, the kind of Italians that make me wanna puke." Leo spoke with his hands, a troublesome trait for a two hundred and fifty pound man wielding a knife the size of his forearm and sharp enough to cleave a tree trunk.

"It's because of shits like them that people think that every Italian is connected." Leo punctuated each word shit with a thrust of the knife. "Doing business with them is like paying for sex, Dominic. It's not right." Dominic took a step back.

The elderly woman turned in a slow-motion huff and walked away from the meat counter and out of earshot. Leo sawed off a half dozen veal chops on the band saw then trimmed the fat away with his knife.

"Everyone's got a right to make a living," Dominic said.

Leo lowered his voice to a whisper. "I got no time for anyone who doesn't put in a day's work for his paycheque." He slid the butcher knife into the sheath hanging from his belt and walked the veal chops over to the meat counter, fanning them in the display case beside skinned rabbits and thin slices of scallopini. "They're killers, you know."

"You make it sound like I'm running drugs for them or something."

Leo shook his head. "That wouldn't surprise me. Not anymore. You're a long way from the choirboy I grew up with."

"Hey, Leo," Sammy said. He had returned to the cheese display. "Is this stuff made from soy milk or something? I mean, I won't get sick or nothing if I eat it?"

"You eat it, you pay for it."

"Sammy," Dominic said, "It's cheese. It's dairy. Eat it and you'll be breaking out in hives before the second bite hits your stomach."

Sammy dropped the cheese on the floor like it was a plate of smallpox. Leo's voice returned to its booming volume. "Pick that up. And put it back where you found it." Sammy obeyed Leo's order but used the tips of his fingers to grab the cheese. Leo picked up three legs of veal and carried them over to the band saw. He sawed off veal shanks as if he was lopping off the end pieces of fire logs.

"Look, Christina is starting to ask questions about that term deposit. You know that I borrowed that fifteen hundred for you against it and now it's due. I can't put her off much longer." He placed a shoulder of veal on a Styrofoam tray and covered it in clear plastic wrap.

"I'll get it to you. Monday. I promise."

"You're pushing me, man. If I don't pay the bank back the money I borrowed for you by the end of the month, they're gonna call in that term deposit — and then my marriage is for shit." Leo leaned on the enormous butcher block and shook his head. "Man, I don't know why I let you talk me into going behind Christina's back.

That's your style, not mine." He lined up another leg of veal along the band saw and took a couple of quick passes to test the blade and the bone. "Now you're fucking around with this Italian trash."

"I know, Leo, I know. You've got me starting to see the light. The Pope's gonna make you a saint one day."

"Sure, after I'm dead. About the same time I see that fifteen hundred bucks." Four shanks ready for osso bucco fell from the veal leg.

"Monday. I promise."

Sammy had wandered off to safer territory, the bulk islands. He was lifting the plastic covers, picking out a nut, or a cracker, sniffing it, then putting it back. "You know, you really should put a list of ingredients on these things. You could be selling people anything out of these bins."

Leo ran out from behind the meat counter and hurried to put himself between Sammy and the food.

"Just get out of here, would ya? Christ, you're both gonna get me fired."

"Alright," Dominic said. He began to walk out from behind the meat counter.

"Not that way," Leo said. "Christ, I don't want anybody to see that you were even here. Go out the back."

Leo directed Dominic to leave by way of the open-window meat locker. Sammy following him, conspicuously averting his gaze from the sides of beef hung from hooks and ready for their buddy the butcher's magic with a knife and saw.

"Why are we going this way?" Sammy asked. "Now we gotta walk all the way around the building to where I parked. I'm already as cold as those cows."

Dominic ignored the question. "You see a pay phone on the way in?" In order to cover Leo's loan, he'd have to risk another bet on the Bills. It was either that, or cut up three cars by Monday morning for the Romanian, and he hadn't heard a word from him in days.

# 6

The Romanian shuffled his feet and tried to turn away from the wind, his long black hair blowing back around his head. It wrapped his face in a fence line drawn with thousands of strands of blackened barbed wires. His eyes were too dark to see into, more like black holes that allowed light to enter but not leave. His teeth were etched imperfections capable of ripping into a man's throat or breaking bones like pencils. But while Bela Nastasi thrived on a diet of human misery, he couldn't evade the harbour air and the chill that threatened to shatter the blackened enamel off his Eastern Bloc dental work.

The coldest place in the universe is a Sunday night in January on the docks at Hamilton Harbour. Tonight was that night, cold like you'd never endured unless your job was to move stolen cars and run laps between a ship loading up for the Ukraine and a warehouse hidden a quarter mile down the pier. The wind off the water and sub-zero air could freeze your hand to a car's bumper faster than the most permanent glue.

The moon's light hinted at warmth with the sincerity of a dockside whore. Tonight, Nastasi supervised a half dozen fellow Romanians and a hastily assembled posse of refugees from Eastern Europe, most of whom had immigration papers as authentic as a bootleg Michael Jackson cassette. Six recruits from a local motorcycle gang stood vigil at positions well-suited to a clear view of the comings and goings of the lone port police officer and the shift workers departing from a neighbouring chemical-processing plant.

Through the rows of oncoming headlights Nastasi could see the wet snow flying almost horizontally across the docks. He could just make out his brother Octavio a hundred yards away. He thought he could see Octavio talking to Spagnoli, though it was hard to tell. The snow stung his eyes and the light from the overhead lamps on the pier reflected off the ice, making it difficult to see much of anything. The light played tricks with his eyes. Nastasi worried that someone would skid out and hit a pole or, worse, another car. That would be two losses he could not afford.

"Slow down," he shouted, as a nearly new Honda Accord skidded by him. "Idiots," he said to himself. "I brought idiots with me from Bucharest." He walked towards his brother.

"Tell the Transylvanians to be more careful." His brother didn't react. Nastasi got closer and shouted again, this time in Romanian. Still no reaction. He jogged over where his brother stood, almost slipping onto the dock when his foot hit an icy patch.

"Octo! What are you doing?" Still his brother seemed to ignore him. He was directing traffic as if he was a police officer standing beneath a malfunctioning traffic light. As Nastasi approached, he could see the problem. Octavio was wearing earphones attached to the Sony Walkman that Nastasi had given him for his birthday. When he was close enough to pistol whip him, Nastasi ripped the earphones from his brother's half-frozen head.

Octavio yelped and turned into the wind to face Nastasi.

"I need you to concentrate here," Nastasi said, pointing at his brother. "It took me months to convince the Italians to hire us. I won't have you, little brother, screw it up. Get these cars out, but tell the Transylvanians to slow it down. The pier is freezing up. I don't want any accidents."

"Is okay. I do it." Octavio began to replace the earphones.

46

"Stop this!" This time Nastasi swung the back of his open hand across his brother's head. Octavio shook off the blow and rubbed his sore ears.

"Is Super Bowl," he said. "Bills are tied going into halftime."

"Our mother must have adopted you. My father would not have given me such a stupid brother as you." Nastasi pulled the Walkman out of Octavio's coat pocket and tossed it into the harbour.

"You want to listen to your American football? Go swimming."

Octavio looked ready for a fight, but only shrugged and returned to his duties. The younger Nastasi stopped each car as it came out of the building and told the driver, in Romanian, to be careful and keep it slow. A lone Transylvanian, returning on foot from the ship's cargo hold, ran into the relative safety of the warehouse to fetch another car. The warehouse, painted on the outside with the Hamilton Harbour Commission logo and its designation as warehouse 14, Pier 2. Just four vehicles remained: a Cadillac, two Jeep Cherokees, and a three-year-old Mercedes-Benz.

Spagnoli had paid off the ship's captain to keep his crew off the pier while the cars were loaded aboard. That gave Nastasi and his men less than thirty minutes to load twenty-eight cars into the grain hold of the tanker. The captain, Nastasi knew, was reliable. He was Irish, with enough years spent at sea and in the jails of various international jurisdictions to warrant the trust of his bosses. But he wasn't so sure about the Hamilton stevedores, who were scheduled to start work in an hour. The last thing Nastasi needed was forty men with union cards and attitude showing up and demanding to know what the hell a half-dozen illegal immigrants were doing working the docks.

What they were doing, of course, was loading stolen cars onto a ship headed to the Ukraine. While that in itself was illegal in every country in the world, it wouldn't be the crime that would rouse the ire of the Hamilton stevedores. Loading and unloading was their job, by contract. Nastasi just hoped that the pay-off to their union chief was enough to keep the grunts off the pier for now. He half expected Spagnoli to show up seconds before the stevedores and insist that some catastrophe had prevented him from stalling them.

The noise of tire squeals and the crunch and grind of steel against steel caught his attention. He ran through the sleet towards the sound. A few metres in front of the ship, a Mercedes had broadsided a garbage dumpster. The driver was getting out of the car when Nastasi grabbed him by the collar. It was Petrov, the pie-faced Bulgarian. Nastasi dragged the rest of him out of the car and threw him onto the icy concrete pier.

"You fucking fool! Look at what you've done!" He walked around the car and inspected the damage. A scar ran along the length of the passenger side. The door was badly dented and the tempered glass window had cracked and was ready to collapse.

"This will cost thousands. They will not pay now. They will not pay! Not for junk! Not for this!"

"I will fix," Petrov had the sad, dull eyes of a cow, and looked permanently drugged. He rose to his feet.

Another driver came out off the ship and ran over to the site of the accident. He slipped on some ice, landing on his right wrist. He got himself up and limped forward holding his wrist. "What is going on?" he asked.

Nastasi pulled Petrov, bumped and bruised, towards him. "You cannot fix it. What are you going to do, take it into a body shop? Is stolen, you fool!" He pushed him against the Mercedes so hard the driver slid up the hood and cracked the windshield.

"This car is fucked. Fucked, fucked, fucked! You understand, you Bulgarian piece of shit?" He yanked Petrov off the car and threw him back down to the pier. The other driver stepped into the shadows to save himself from Nastasi's wrath. Octavio ran over from his position by the warehouse.

"Bela!" he shouted. "Stop. Please."

Nastasi kicked Petrov in the stomach. "He is worthless shit. He cannot drive. He cannot steal. He cannot shit without instructions on how to wipe his ass."

Petrov moaned as air escaped his lungs, but the force of Nastasi's steel-toed boots was softened by layers of winter clothes and Nastasi's inability to get much leverage on the ice-covered concrete. Nastasi kicked him again this time in the head. Petrov lay silent. A small pool of blood congealed by his nose.

"Get up, you lazy son-of-whore! Get up and be good for something."

Petrov rolled over, dazed but coherent enough to sit up. Nastasi stood straight, catching his breath. With one hand he pulled Petrov to his feet and dragged him over to the damaged side of the Mercedes.

"This! This is what you are to me. A piece of junk that was once a Mercedes. Now is worthless. You, car, all of this worthless!"

"Is … is still good car," Petrov spat out. Blood followed his words, painting a small red line on the car's silver finish.

Nastasi pulled a handgun from his pocket, a Glock, and pointed it at the driver's head. "You are not worth the bullet," he said.

He raised the gun over his head and brought the butt end down against Petrov's skull. Blood splattered over the scarred passenger door as Petrov slumped to the pier and was buried in the shadow of the car. Nastasi wasn't done. He drove the heel of his boot down onto Petrov's head.

"I … have … no … time … for … this!" Once, twice, three times he pounded his boot into Petrov's lifeless body before his brother pulled him away.

Nastasi spotted the other driver standing in the shadows.

"You," he pointed to him. "Get behind the wheel of this car."

"Open the trunk," Nastasi told the new driver. The trunk of the Mercedes popped open.

Octavio said, "What you do?"

Nastasi grabbed one of Petrov's dead arms. "Make yourself useful,"

49

he told his brother. Octavio took the other arm and helped his brother drag Petrov's body to the rear of the Mercedes. They rolled him over the back bumper and into the trunk. Nastasi slammed it closed.

"Get it into the ship," Nastasi pointed towards the freighter. "Better we deliver damaged goods than nothing. These cars must leave, now!"

The new driver had to lean past the steering wheel to get his left hand in a position to start the car. He put the car in gear and directed it toward the ramp, moving much slower this time.

"Last fucking car," Nastasi swore to himself. He removed a walkie-talkie from his jacket and cracked open the signal.

"Boris, are you ready?" He was still breathing hard.

"Ready boss. Ready and loaded."

"I will give you signal in a minute. Bring the boom over the grain hold."

"Yes, boss."

Nastasi climbed up the icy stairs to the ship's deck and walked the twenty feet to the opening that announced the entrance to the grain hold. His men had been arranging the cars at the bottom of the empty hold, leaving only a few feet between each vehicle. He saw the damaged Mercedes with its extra cargo being parked, the last vehicle in the last row of twenty-eight cars fresh from suburban driveways and mall parking lots. The driver got out, looked up at Nastasi standing three stories above him, then back at the Mercedes. Nastasi waved him away from the car and barked into the walkie-talkie. This time his brother was on the other end.

"Pull tarps over vehicles," he said. He watched as Octavio and the four other men pulled orange tarpaulins over the cars. In a few moments the cars were completed covered in thick orange vinyl.

"Everyone outside," he said into the walkie-talkie. He checked his watch. Spagnoli was supposed to keep the ship's crew off the pier until eight. They had ten minutes. Nastasi walked over to the guardrail on the ship's port side and waited until all four men were safely outside.

"Alright, Boris," he shouted into walkie-talkie, "load up."

Boris had swung the large boom crane over the opening to the grain hold. He lowered a long wide aluminum tube into the hold, then released a hundred thousand bushels of prime Canadian prairie wheat. Nastasi covered his mouth and nose so as not to breathe in the chaff. Within two minutes, the cargo hold was full, the cars completely covered in wheat destined for the Ukraine. Nastasi walked down the ramp to his men. He looked again at his watch.

"Get out of here before the stevedores arrive." He grabbed the injured driver by his broken wrist. "Not you." The driver let out a painful sigh.

"You make a mistake like your friend there and you go home in a container, on one of these things." Nastasi jerked his thumb in the direction of the ship's cargo hold.

"Is how I got here," the driver said, forcing a smile.

"I do not want to see your face for a while," Nastasi said. The errant driver appeared relieved at the dismissal.

Nastasi heard a shout over the din on the pier.

"Are you done?" a voice said. It was Spagnoli, his bowlegged frame outlined beneath the street lamps.

"Get lost," Nastasi told the driver.

"You got to get everyone out of here," Spagnoli said, his voice tense from the run to the pier.

"We are done," Nastasi said. "Everything inside, including your friend Petrov."

Spagnoli looked up at the freighter towering above his head. "He was no friend of mine." He struggled to catch his breath in the cold. "You brought him over here."

"So now I send him back."

"Just as well. I told you that we're never gonna pull off the domestic side of this business without local talent."

"I not trust the locals. They are lazy. This country, it makes every-one weak."

"We don't have no choice. I'm going to talk to Criminisi. Either we get more local talent or I'm out."

Nastasi dug his hands into his jacket to keep them warm. "I know a guy. A local kid. He could work out very well."

# 7

Dominic sipped a bottle of Molson Canadian, occasionally sucking back a larger dose to wash down an ounce-by-ounce parade of tequila shots. He passed on the ritual of licking salt off his hand and sucking a lemon wedge, choosing instead to concentrate on the two naked women on stage. They rolled on top of each other in a pool of oil large enough to lubricate the chassis of a Mack truck. Their awkward grappling and simulated moans were more persuasive than those of the Buffalo Bills' defensive line, which struggled to keep pace with its opponents. Between the television behind the bar and the vigorous floor show up on stage, Dominic's line of sight was dominated by arms and legs — some naked, some padded, some lithe, most muscular, and all heaving in a steady torrent. It was hard to tell which was more natural: the steroid-enhanced physiques on the big-screen televisions or the silicone-enhanced breasts that the nubile oil-wrestlers on stage pretended to take pleasure in.

Sammy found him perched awkwardly on a stool with a row of glasses laid out in front of him like so many spent shotgun shells. One was ready to fire. There were two minutes to go in the Super Bowl.

"How's it look?" Sammy asked. The bar was dark, save for the stage lights and the reflected glow of the four large-screen televisions, all of which were tuned to the dying minutes of the game.

Dominic looked away from the girls. The light distorted Sammy's face; his cheekbones appeared sharp despite the darkness.

"Nobody's doing anything. Both teams are too scared too win. It's tied. I'm just happy I bet the game straight up. If I'd taken the points, I'd be dead already." He butted out his cigarette, squinting as the rising smoke stung his eyes. "What are you doing here, anyway? I thought you were going to Gino's."

Sammy pulled up the empty stool beside him. "I was there for the first half. But by halftime, Gino got called away to a job and his cousin Vinnie had to go to work out on the harbour. I figured the best place to be was with you. Just in case you needed a getaway driver."

Dominic lit another cigarette, blowing the remnants of the first drag towards the stage. "Thanks. Let's hope this all ends up with me buying you a round, instead."

He pointed to one of the large screens. "Over fifty-nine minutes of football and all they can come up with is ten lousy points?" He looked back at Sammy. "There's only one thing you can count on. Cars. They'll never let you down." He waved at the bartender, ordering another pair of shots.

"I can think of a couple of cars that have let me down, usually on the highway, with smoke spewing out from under the hood."

"Nah, Sammy. That's about you." Dominic lined up three empty shot glasses in front of him, like he was setting up to play a shell game. "If you took proper care of your wheels, they'd last you forever. Hell, Sammy, in a hundred years you and I will be dust but I guarantee you that somewhere there's a car, today, that will still be rolling down the road. A new engine, bodywork, everything. You take care of a car, it takes care of you."

The song came to a finish and the girls rolled off the stage. Their ability to garner the crowd's attention had plummeted as the game clock clicked towards zero. The Buffalo Bills had gathered enough strength to reach the Giants' thirty-five yard line. The hump-thump beat of the dancers' music became a distant memory as the noise of the crowd in New Orleans rose from the tinny television speakers.

The jerseys of the Buffalo Bills' field-goal team filled the television screens. The bartenders stopped pouring. A few dozen steeltown men held their breaths. Even the dancers stopped gyrating. All eyes were fixed on the field-goal kicker, Scott Norwood. His job, kick a tiny piece of inflated pigskin over the heads of the oncoming New York Giants and through twin uprights of steel spaced thirty feet apart. Three points and a Super Bowl Championship for the Bills. Nicky's shop for the younger DiPietro and a life away from his older brother.

The New York Giants called a time out to stop play just before the ball was snapped. Norwood halted his approach.

"Why did he stop?" Sammy said.

"They're chilling him out," Dominic said. "The Giants are making him think about it a little longer. They're trying to rattle him."

"Well, it's working on me and it's not even my money."

"They can take all the time they want," Dominic said. "This is right in Norwood's range. It's as good as over." He put back another tequila, but didn't take his eyes off the screen.

The teams settled into their opposing positions again. The Giants had one more time out to call as the camera closed in on Scott Norwood's bowed helmet. Dominic could almost see Norwood's eyes flicking from the goal posts to the opposing lineman to the spotter who would hold the ball for him and across all the opposing players to see if someone was going to call his bluff again.

No one did. Norwood kicked the ball through and over the approaching tidal wave of three hundred-pound behemoths bearing down on him. It left his foot right. It flew right. It stayed right. All the way to the end zone. Wide right. By at least the length a parking space. Game over. Giants win.

Dominic stared into one of the giant screens, then another, then another, his empty eyes searching anywhere for a different result.

The screens all glared back at him with the same grim message of defeat.

Each showed the same swarm of New York Giants fans running onto the field. The goal posts, the ones that failed to capture the ball from Scott Norwood's foot, were being bent to the ground as if they were bowing to the championship team or perhaps giving a thin one-finger salute to Dominic's dreams. The cameras cut to a shot of the field-goal kicker, his head down and his teammates turning away from him. There was no *we'll get them next time*, no *good try* uttered into his ear. The only guy more alone than Scott Norwood at that moment was Dominic DiPietro.

He stood up, stumbled sideways to the side door of the bar, and let himself out into the alleyway. After fumbling with some cash to pay the bartender, Sammy followed. By the time he reached the alley, Dominic was face down in a cooling puddle of his own vomit and crying into the cobblestones.

"Sammy," Dominic looked up. "What does a Picasso look like?"

# 8

Dominic awoke on Sammy's couch, his shoulders buried in the deep pile of the upholstery and his eyes looking at the paint peeling from the ceiling. Sammy was sitting in a chair beside the sofa. He had on a pair of headphones. The only light in the room came from a muted black-and-white television that was tuned to the evening news from a Buffalo station. Dominic could see the reporter interviewing people on the street, and though the sound was off, he could tell by the angry faces and finger pointing that football fans in Buffalo were ready to lynch Scott Norwood. He was ready to join them, but was unsure about what end of the rope he should attach to himself.

"How are you feeling?" Sammy took off his headphones. He was framed by a poster of Marlon Brando from *The Wild One* and another of James Dean behind the wheel of the Porsche he would later die in.

It was midnight and as the clock ticked over to the new day, Dominic realized he had less than twelve hours to come up with Magilla's money, or his own mother wouldn't be able to recognize his face in a police line up. Scott Norwood had kicked Dominic's future past those uprights. All that landed in the end zone was a dead football and a life Dominic wasn't convinced was worth living. He'd feel better if he knew Magilla was going to have him killed.

But surrendering his body to the Jew for surgery — or worse — then having to return and face Tony were two evils he could not face.

"I feel like I just woke up from a suicide attempt, and I need to try again." He sat up on the couch, his head bowed to the ground. "Where'd you put my jacket?"

Sammy got up and pulled Dominic's leather jacket from a hook by the front door. He tossed in on the couch. Dominic fished around the pockets for his bottle of Advil, then poured a handful down his mouth.

"You got any beer?"

Sammy got him a glass of water from the kitchen. "This is all you need, for now."

"Thanks." Dominic finished the glass and rested his head against the back of the couch. "But I'd have preferred a Budweiser."

"What are you going to do now?" Sammy sat back down.

"I don't know. Call ahead to the emergency room and get myself an appointment for later today. Or maybe just run away. Lose myself in Toronto. Or better yet, slip across the border to Buffalo. Then I'd have a whole country between me and this city."

"He will find you. There's a reason they call it organized crime."

After lighting a cigarette, Dominic stretched out on the sofa. He blew smoke at the ceiling, talking as much to himself as to Sammy. "You remember when we were kids, playing in my dad's Plymouth? I do. I remember the toughness of the cloth bench seat, and the hard steel wheel. It had a chrome ring inside it that worked the horn. You and I, we must have spent entire days in that car, hidden in the garage. It was another world."

"Yeah, I remember. We pretended it was a spaceship, and we'd fly it to Neptune, fighting aliens along the way."

"Or bank robbers. We'd pretend we were bank robbers on the lam, firing our guns out the windows at the cops."

"Yeah, we were a regular Bonnie and Clyde."

Dominic sat up and butted out the cigarette. "Well, Bonnie, that car was magic. I've been in love with them ever since. I'd go down to my dad's shop and sweep up, just to be around the cars and watch the guys fix 'em. Tony never did that. He worked in the office from day one. Never wanted to get his hands dirty. To him, cars were cash. But I loved them."

"Listen, Dominic, I'll do what I can. I got a few thousand dollars put away. It's yours."

Dominic smiled at Sammy. "Thanks. But I don't think Magilla will have any ears for an installment plan, not unless the interest is so high that any money you give me would postpone my appointment with his muscle." He let out a deep sign. "Keep your money. I'm not a good investment."

He wanted to return to a state of unconsciousness where the real world couldn't get him. He wanted to go back to the front seat of his dad's Plymouth and fly it to Neptune. But he knew that he had only once place to go.

As he walked towards the donut shop, Dominic could see them both through the window — a pair of slobbering dogs guarding the gate to his own personal hell. Magilla was putting back a honey dip. Beside him was the Romanian, blowing smoke in the bookie's face. Dominic had never seen Nastasi in the light of day. He looked battered in the morning sun — the night hid so much of the damage to his face. In the clear light of day, the Romanian looked like he'd been freshly dug from a grave. The sight made Dominic halt in his tracks. *What the hell is he here for?*

He thought briefly about coming back later. But he couldn't return to City-Wide and risk a personal visit from Magilla's collectors. So he gathered his composure, swallowed hard, and pulled open the door. He was greeted by the stale smell of cigarette smoke. It was only the second time he'd ever seen the Romanian smile.

Magilla struggled to turn towards the door. He waved Dominic over to an empty stool beside him. "Here, Dominic. I've even got coffee waiting for you."

Dominic took the seat. He didn't say hello to either man. He looked at Nastasi, then quickly averted his face, hoping that if he ignored the Romanian the whole process could be over with before he was required to engage him in any way.

"I'm sorry it didn't go the other way for you," Magilla said. "I could call someone, you know. We could have it arranged for you."

Dominic swallowed. "You could have what arranged?"

"You'd be doing a lot of people a favour," Magilla told him. "Breaking Norwood's legs. I think we could start a collection." He laughed and the rolls of fat on his neck rippled.

Dominic took a deep breath. "I'm here," he spat out. "But I'm busted."

Nastasi rubbed the pockmarks on his cheek. "I figure as much. That's why I ask to join Magilla this morning." He reached over and placed his scarred hand over Dominic's. It felt like a bear claw closing over him.

"Magilla wasn't so sure you'd show," Nastasi said. "But you and I, we work together. I told him I know you better than that."

Magilla slurped his coffee. "It's good you're here, Dominic. I didn't want to have to chase you. Exertion, of any kind, is a waste of calories. Makes me grumpy."

The Romanian lit another cigarette. He offered one to Dominic, who accepted it. "Our boss, Alfonso Criminisi, has asked us to speak with you."

Dominic tried to swallow, but his mouth was as dry as steel wool. "How does Mr. Criminisi know me?"

Magilla stuffed the remainder of a donut into his mouth. "When I call in a ten thousand dollar bet, you should know that I'm always gonna get asked who the high roller is."

"I answer him," Nastasi said. "That was fortunate. I vouch for you with Mr. Criminisi, or Magilla would not have been able to take your sizable bet."

"I guess I should thank you, but somehow words fail me."

"I'm sure. But we Romanians have a saying. There is no reward without risk. And Mr. Criminisi was very impressed with your ability to take on such risk. But, now we have a problem. Not only did Magilla take your bet, I had to vouch for it. Do you know what this means, Dominic?"

The steel wool in Dominic's throat was starting to choke him.

"It means since you cannot meet your obligations, I have to do it for you."

Dominic rubbed his shoulder. "I'm good for this. Just not today."

The Romanian sat back, crossing his arms and cocking his head a little. "This, I know. You are a good man."

"But I gotta close my book on this," Magilla said. "If not, Mr. Criminisi is gonna take this loss out on me, not you."

"Then I really should be getting to work." Dominic began to stand.

The Romanian stared at him until he sat back down. "You don't owe Magilla anything. As of now, you owe me."

Dominic didn't know whether to breathe a sigh of relief that Magilla wasn't going to have his face carved up like a salami or cry because the Romanian had picked up his marker.

"Think of it this way," Nastasi told him, as though he could see the fear in Dominic's eyes. "I paid you for forty cars, in advance."

Dominic did the math. "That's a lot of interest."

"No interest. Take all the time you want. But now, I pay you two hundred and fifty a car, not five."

Dominic put his hands around the coffee cup in front of him. It was cold.

"There is another way, DiPietro," Nastasi said. Dominic looked at him but said nothing. His body was trying to escape but his brain wouldn't let him leave. "I know what you want. You talk to my men when you're working. About how much you love cars. And how much you hate your brother."

They were long nights, Dominic remembered. Long nights with

hard work and too many beers, all of which had loosened his tongue.

"I don't hate Tony. I don't hate anyone. I just want my own business."

The Romanian used the nail of his thumb to pick at his ragged teeth. "So let me help you. This debt you owe me. You could make me partner."

"Or," Dominic said, "I chop more cars for you, for free, for the next year."

"Yes. It is for you to decide. But the other would be a much better investment, for both of us."

"Give me a few days to think about it."

Nastasi stood up. "Good. This is very good. My wife, she reads my cards everyday. This morning she told me I would make a good investment today. I must go home and tell her she was right."

The Romanian handed him a piece of paper. There was a phone number on it. "When you are ready, we will talk about our restoration business. Meanwhile, let me get you some more cars to chop."

# 9

Dominic walked into the body shop with the attitude of a man who'd just dodged a bullet yet remained scarred by the sound of the shot and the shrill scream of air rushing past his ear. He was unable to purge himself of the smell of the Romanian's sweat or the sight of his drool-laden smile. Dominic had avoided Magilla's knife, but in the process he had relinquished any pretence he might have had of remaining on the edges of Nastasi's vicious underworld.

He popped a handful of Advils and walked through the shop. He passed the paint booth, the mixing area, the plastic plaster workers, and the fender-bender pullers and entered the locker room to change. The bench between the rows of lockers was empty save for a Russian immigrant named Dimitri, who sat smoking a cigarette.

"Good morning, Dommie." Dimitri stood up. "I so glad you here. Could you do something for me?" His voice was thick with vowels found only on the streets of a Europe that Dominic had no knowledge of.

Dimitri walked across the locker room towards a row of vending machines. There was one that dispensed canned soft drinks, another that dropped hot coffee or chocolate into paper cups decorated with various poker hands, and a snack machine that tossed chocolate bars, potato chips, and chewing gum into a drawer at the bottom.

"I need cup of coffee," Dimitri said, "but change for it is in my right pant pocket." Dimitri's right wrist was wrapped in a tensor bandage. "I cannot get my hand into pocket. Is too thick with bandage."

Dominic looked at Dimitri's wrist. "You want me to buy you a cup of coffee?"

"No. I have money. I need you to get it from my pocket."

"Jeez … I'd, ah, rather just buy you a cup myself." Dominic fished in his own pockets for change. They were empty.

"Is okay, you just reach in and get money. Fifty cents. It's there. Wife put it there last night. But she forget I can't get into pocket with right hand."

"Alright. But don't be telling anybody about this." Dominic stood in front of Dimitri and reached into the body man's right pocket with his left hand. Unfortunately, Pockets aren't made for frontal assaults. Dominic had trouble reaching deep enough into the pocket, and Dimitri kept shifting his hips as if this might help in some way.

"Stay still," Dominic said.

"I try, is just funny. Feels funny your hand in my pocket."

"Well, stop enjoying it. Here." Dominic removed his hand from Dimitri's pocket. He'd successfully extracted three quarters and a dime. He handed them to the body man.

"There," Dominic said. "Now don't be asking me to drop the money in the machine."

"Thank you, Dommie. You're a good boy."

Dominic hated it when anyone at City-Wide called him boy. It reminded him of his stature in the place. The *junior* DiPietro. He left Dimitri and approached his locker. He tried to slip his key inside the lock, but it wouldn't fit. He tried again and inspected his key ring to make sure he was using the right key. Then he checked the locker. Right locker. Right key. Wrong lock. He flipped the lock up with one hand, bouncing it off the locker's tin frame like the hammer in a rusted bell.

Dimitri leaned back on the bench and sipped his coffee from a cup marked with three kings, a queen, and a two of diamonds. "You got to see Tony," he said. "He change your lock this morning."

"What?"

"I don't know nothing," Dimitri wove his cigarette in defence. "It was this way when I got here."

Dominic punched his closed fist hard into the locker. Through clenched teeth he said, "It's not Scott Norwood who needs his legs broken, it's Tony."

Tony DiPietro's office was built on a specially constructed mezzanine over the shop's main floor. Floor-to-ceiling windows looked down upon the entire work area of City-Wide Collision. The office wall was full of community awards and photos of Tony with politicians and visiting dignitaries.

A credenza sat behind Tony's mahogany desk, both one-of-a-kind pieces imported from Italy. The top of the credenza was like an altar to Tony's family, adorned with framed pictures of his wife, and their new son, Aldo. On the far left corner, behind the picture of Tony giving away his sister at her wedding, was a picture of the entire DiPietro family taken just after their father's death. Aunts, uncles, cousins and children all gathered in shades of black and grey on sunny spring morning. To their right sat Tony and Dominic's mother, Sophia, and their sister, Angelina. Dominic was on the far left. Dominic looked like a street hood trying to avoid initiation into a rival gang.

Dominic climbed the steel staircase to Tony's office and saw his brother holding court with two men. They were seated at the large table in the middle of the room, looking over an artist's rendering of a new operation. He considered returning later, after Tony's visitors had departed, then discarded the notion. He rapped once on the door and walked in without waiting for a response.

Tony was on the phone when Dominic entered. "Tell that piece of shit I'm done with him." Tony barked into the phone but his eyes

65

were flaring at Dominic. "Yeah, I'll see him. But he better be giving me the deal of the goddamn century. Tell him to come by at the end of the day." He hung up the phone and turned his attention to his visitors.

"My apologies, gentlemen." Tony came out from behind his desk and put one arm around his younger brother's shoulders. "Dominic, I'm glad you're here. You know Councillor Constantine, don't you?"

"It sounds like I should."

Tony turned to one of the men, a dapper gentleman with a full head of white hair, eyes that beamed wisdom, and a smile that was practised and perfect. He wore a charcoal suit that was well tailored to his elder statesman frame. His tie was red, and, like all of Tony's, probably Italian.

"My brother, you've got to forgive him. He doesn't read the city pages. Unless your name is attached to a car or a football team, he wouldn't know who you were."

"That's alright," Constantine said. He rose to greet Dominic, the drape of his suit falling perfectly. "I'd rather read about football than about me, especially the way the papers in this town cover politics." He put his left hand in his pocket. "That Super Bowl was a heartbreaker, eh? I wouldn't want to be in Scott Norwood's shoes. He better hope nobody knows where he lives."

"Yeah," Dominic said. "A real heartbreaker, Councillor."

Constantine walked over to Dominic with his right arm extended. He shook Dominic's hand. "Please, call me Sal."

Tony said, "That's soon-to-be-mayor Sal."

"Tony, I haven't announced anything. Not yet, at least. I remain a humble member of city council."

"Then I'll put my chequebook away," Tony said. "No, Sal, you're gonna do it. This city is ready for its first Italian mayor."

The younger of the two visitors got up from his seat. His voice was clipped. "I'll believe it when I see it," he said.

Constantine said, "Dominic, this is my nephew, Jackie. He's going to be helping me with my campaign when the time comes."

Dominic shook the younger Constantine's hand. His figure was athletic and wound tight like a boxer. He wore his jacket unbuttoned, allowing the large panels of silk and wool to fall open below his torso. Dominic could feel the air fill with competitive heat.

"Nice to meet you, Dominic," Jackie said. He took a business card from his pocket and handed it to Dominic. It read Jack Constantine, Attorney, Constantine, Gravelle, and Zaffiro.

"Jackie's taken over the firm now," said Sal, his pride rising pink against the starched whiteness of his collar. "He's giving me a hand on the fundraising side, too."

Tony said, "Dominic works in one of our paint booths."

"I can tell you right now, Dominic," the elder Constantine said, "you do one hell of a job. My wife's car got dinged last summer. It came out of here better than I bought it."

"That would have been an '88 Chevy Blazer, silver, with leather interior," Dominic said.

"That's amazing," Jackie said. "How many cars you paint in a year, and you can remember every one?"

"Not all of them," Dominic said. "But I could never forget a car that Tony tells me to babysit like our own mother wrapped it around a pole."

"Dominic," Tony said, his arm still tightly wrapped around his brother's shoulder, "I was just showing the councillor the designs for the new twenty-four hour shop."

Dominic knew nothing about a twenty-four hour shop. Tony never told him anything about the business.

"I'm sorry, Sal, but could you and Jackie give me a few minutes to talk with my brother, alone? Collision business. Please, take a tour of the shop. Say hello to the staff. Do a little pre-electioneering. But don't worry. Every one of them will be voting for you come November. Some even twice."

Constantine laughed. He and his nephew shook hands with Tony, nodding as if they'd agreed to something important, then backed out of the office. Tony shut the door behind them. He paused for a moment. Dominic could see his brother's massive back expand through his shirt as he took a deep breath.

"You little fuck," Tony said, and turned around to face Dominic. "I should throw you through one of these windows. Treat you like the piece of human garbage you are."

Dominic sat down at the board table covered with drawings and building plans. He pretended to look at them. He could smell the anger coming off of Tony. "Now what's your problem, Tony? Am I using too much paint for you? Or are the cars coming out looking too good?"

"It's not the cars I'm worried about. It's your gambling. Ten thousand is a lot to lose, especially when you don't have it."

Dominic looked at his brother. "How ..."

"I just know. I know about everything, Dominic. Your gambling, your drinking. If it's a piece of shit and it's attached to you, I know about it."

Dominic felt naked in his defeat.

"There's only one thing I don't know." Tony said. "How are you going to pay these goombahs?"

"I made an arrangement."

"An arrangement. What kind of arrangement?"

"That's none of your business."

"Damn right it's my business. In case you haven't noticed, you not only carry my name around with your debts, but the City-Wide Collision name as well. Tell me, Dominic, what's going happen when word gets out that you're dealing with local mob guys? I've been breaking my back for years trying to build a decent reputation for this company and you're *this close* to bringing it all down with you."

Dominic stood up to leave. "You're making too much of this. I made a bet. I lost. I got a guy holding a marker. Once I make good, this all goes away. That's it, Tony. Your precious little City-Wide Collision has nothing to do with this." He started walking towards the office door.

"I'm not done with you. Not yet."

Dominic wanted to keep walking, but something in his brother's voice made him stop.

"This is a family business," Tony said. "You fuck up like this, it makes us all look bad."

Dominic turned to face him. "Cut the crap, Tony. It's me you're talking to, not some Rotary Club. This is your business. Not mine. Not our sister's. Not our mother's. Your only part of my life is as my boss. If you got a problem with me, then fire me."

Tony opened the humidor on his desk. It was ebony and shone like the hood of a hearse. He pulled out a Montecristo and fondled its length before cutting off the tip.

"I'm not going to fire you. But I do need to keep a closer eye on you."

Dominic remained silent, one hand fumbling in a pocket of his pants.

"Starting today, I'm moving you out of the paint shop. From now on, you're in the office." Tony fired up the cigar and took a draw. The smoke lingered in the air between the brothers. "Lisa needs help coordinating with our insurance companies. You'll assist her with claims management."

Dominic felt the bottom fall out of his stomach. "I'll be pushing fucking paper around a desk."

"Maybe you'll start to see the value of money and hard work. That's what Papa and I built this business on."

"But I'm a body man! I'm the best damn paint and body man in this place."

"I've got a stack of résumés from guys who can replace you before your paint gun gets cold, and couple of new guys pushing brooms who are just itching for a chance to lay some shine on these cars."

"Please don't do this to me."

"Listen. In a couple of years, we'll be painting cars with robots. Paint guys like you, you'll be dinosaurs. I'm doing you a favour. Learn the business side, Dominic. It's where the future is."

"Fuck the future. I'm not working in the office."

"It's your choice. The office, or the street. I mean, you could always try your hand at selling insurance, or maybe you could start a decorating business with that faggoty little friend of yours."

"All I know is the car business," Dominic said. "Fuck, it's all I want to know."

"Then take this as an opportunity to get to know the business better. You can't spend the rest of your life on the labour side of the equation, not if you want to make something of yourself, and not with that shoulder of yours. I'm doing you a favour."

"I could work for somebody else."

"Not on your fucking life." Tony pointed the cigar at him. "Not in this town. With the buying power I got, whoever hire's you won't be able to buy so much as bucket paint. They'd be out of business in a week, and they'll know it."

Tony got up from his desk to formalize his victory. He opened a closet, took out a polo shirt from among a pile of similar shirts and tossed it at Dominic. "Here. It's our new customer service uniform."

Dominic held the garment in his hand like a funeral shroud. "It's purple."

"More like fuscia, I think. That's what the designers called it. They told me it's supposed to make us look more professional and trustworthy."

"The only things that should be purple are hot rods and Popsicles."

"Well, it's fuscia, and it's what I expect to see you wearing to work every day. I'm hoping the trustworthy part wears off on you."

"Man, I wouldn't paint the ugliest car in the world this colour."

70

"Your days with a spray gun are over." Tony spoke through the lit Montecristo in his mouth. "Here." He pulled out a ring with two keys attached and tossed it across the desk. "The new key to your locker, as well as the office."

Dominic stared at the keys, then picked them up and shoved them deep into the pocket of his jacket.

Tony stood up and started walking toward the door. Dominic followed, the corporate shirt thrown over his shoulder.

"Now get down there and talk to Lisa. She'll show you the ropes. Snowstorm's coming tonight. All the business we could ever want will be pulling into our bays tomorrow morning. The insurance companies are gonna be writing cheques with a goddamn printing press."

Dominic made his way down the steel staircase; the weight of the keys seemed to pull him bodily down the steps. Tony stood at the top and waved at his guests to make their way back. The sweet smell of Cuban tobacco smoke mixed with the acrid air of epoxy and paint. Ignoring it all, Dominic made his way back to his locker.

# 10

By the end of the day the foul weather Tony had predicted had fallen on Hamilton like wet cement. As Dominic filled out forms, faxed out paperwork, and made follow-up phone calls to a dozen insurance companies, the roads, along with every telephone pole and tree, became coated with ice, freezing Hamilton into a Hallmark card of winter wonder. Only, this card could kill. From the shop floor, Dominic could see Tony standing beside Walter, staring out the window, arms crossed, a sixty-dollar Cuban between his lips. He was sure Tony could hear every tire-sliding crunch and crash between here and Toronto. It was apparent in the set of his shoulders, which were arched in satisfaction. Tony, Dominic knew, was having a very good day. Dominic was working in the claims office, and was wearing purple.

One of the six garage bay doors opened and an ice-slicked tow truck backed in, pushing a Lincoln Continental twisted to the edge of recognition. The white and yellow flash of the truck's emergency lights bounced around the shop. Nunzio hurried over to close the door as soon as the truck reached the shop's interior. Dominic recognized the Ace of Spades logo on the front of truck. It matched the one on the baseball cap that the driver, Dominic's friend Gino Busseri, wore.

"It's a wild ride out there, Dominic." Gino jumped out of the truck and walked around to the rear to unhook the Lincoln. "There are cars sliding everywhere. I gotta get back out, right away. I figure another hour of this weather and I'll pull a dozen cars off the Skyway Bridge before dinner."

Dominic walked over to the tow truck's hoist controls and helped Gino drop the load. The controls were iced over. Dominic put on a pair of work gloves to handle them.

Gino leered at Dominic's new uniform. "What's with the duds?" He rolled a pair of towing wheels out from under the car. "Little cool out there for a game of golf."

"Don't ask." Dominic eased the tow truck's controls so that the Lincoln dropped gently to the shop floor. He took off the gloves and put them back in the truck.

Gino was about to step into the truck when he motioned Dominic to come closer.

"Dominic." Gino looked cast a conspiratorial look around the shop. "You want to get together at Hanrahan's later? With this weather, it'll be a tomb. Nothing but you, me, and beautiful women, each one of them naked and bored."

Dominic looked out the shop window. This kind of weather wouldn't normally motivate him to go anywhere. He'd prefer to spend the evening doing some extra sanding on a couple of cars, maybe even sneak a few more coats of paint or clear coat onto the long line of cheap fix-its that Tony was pushing through the shop. But now he was wearing a purple shirt. He was corporate. Before, the cars kept him going. Now, all he had was an in-basket of insurance claims and worries about what lay ahead with the Romanian.

"I'm gonna pass. You're not the only guy with a tow truck who's living off Tony's spiffs." Dominic looked through the windows. "There's gonna be a conga line of dented fenders lined up here in another hour. I better stay."

Dominic reopened the garage bay doors and let Gino drive out. As he closed them, he heard Tony and Walter walking down the

73

steel staircase to the shop floor. Dominic looked at Walter, but the paint salesman wouldn't meet his eyes.

Tony was showing Walter to the door. He shook Walter's hand. "Get those papers over to me as soon as you can." He was grinning, yet another smile of triumph. Dominic was sure it was for his benefit, not Walter's. As soon as the paint salesman left the building, Tony turned to Dominic and said, "You remember Nicky, that crumb of a Greek who tried to set up a shop in the east end? Well, I just bought his shop from Walter's guys." Tony headed back up the stairs with an energetic bounce to his large frame.

Dominic lit a cigarette and let the smoke settle around him.

Halfway up the stairs, Tony stopped and turned around. "It's gonna take a couple of months to get Nicky's place up to the calibre of City-Wide, so in the meantime I got him working here."

"Nicky?" Dominic's mouth was open, his eyes wide.

"Yeah. He's a lousy businessman, but pretty good with a paint gun. So I'm having him take over your paint booth." Tony smiled at Dominic, a dare.

Their eyes stayed on each other, but Dominic knew his brother had all the ammunition. So he just dropped his cigarette on the shop floor. He ground out the butt with the heel of his shoe. "Yeah, I hear he's pretty good." Tony was still staring at him, waiting for the argument, the tantrum, the fight that would not only put Dominic in his place, but also prove to his workers that the elder DiPietro was in charge. Always in charge.

"I gotta get back in the office," Dominic said. "Lisa needs me." He heard the stomp of Tony's feet going up the staircase as he walked in the opposite direction, towards the locker room. He wasn't sticking around. He would go to Hanrahan's, get drunk, and if there was enough cash left in his jeans, get laid. If Gino showed up, all the better. But, for sure, he was getting out of here.

Dimitri was in the locker room, reading the *Hamilton Spectator*. He was having trouble turning the pages with his injured hand.

74

"I cannot believe what you North Americans will pay for an automobile," he said. "The steel company makes the steel, ships it down the road to Ford or General Motors, who make it into some fragile kind of automobile that cracks at the softest bump. Then, they sell it back to you for tens of thousands of dollars. What could you want this for? You insure it, put gasoline in it, then it breaks down, and you fix it. You get it banged up and you bring to a place like this and an insurance company charges you ten times the cost of the repairs in more insurance for twenty years. What is this? For what, getting around, going places? It makes more sense to take a bus."

Dominic slipped the new key into his new lock. It fit like it had been lying in wait for him.

"It's not about the steel," Dominic said. "It's about the feel. It's about the shape of the steel and the colour of the paint and the way the car makes you feel powerful, special, like no one in the world can hurt you. Cars are like clothes. You don't drive them, you wear them."

"I wear these overalls that Tony gives me," Dimitri said. "I take a bus to work and send half my paycheque back home to my mother. I no waste my money on cars." He said "cars" like he was trying to cough up a piece of food stuck in his throat.

Dominic opened his locker. No more overalls. In their place were three more City-Wide Collision fuscia polo shirts and a pair of khaki slacks. He slammed the door closed.

"Purple," he said. "Goddamn fucking purple!"

"Stand up," he told Dimitri. He walked over to the body man and reached into his right pocket. He pulled out a quarter. "Thanks." He walked across the lounge towards the pay phone and dropped in the coin. He looked at the telephone number the Romanian had scrawled. He dialed and waited.

# 11

Dominic stood on the sidewalk outside the entrance to Switzer's, a deli on the west side of the city. His eyes were alert against the pewter sky for signs of Magilla's pending arrival. He was still wearing his purple polo shirt, but hid it beneath a blue blazer that hadn't felt his shoulders in years. The bookie's Lincoln Continental drove past him. He watched as Magilla squeezed the three tons of steel into a parking space ten percent too small for its length. Magilla appeared to be parking by feel, coming to a stop each time he hit another car or the curb. With his rear taillight jutting three feet into the street, Magilla killed the engine, thus conceding the loss but still walking away with the trophy. He got out of the car and lumbered towards Dominic. The bookie was breathing so heavily he was expelling a wall of fog in front of him with each step.

"Nice parking job," Dominic said.

"It's in. What do I care, anyway? Like someone's gonna give me a ticket."

"Listen," Dominic said, "before we go in, put me down for a C-note on the Oilers tonight."

"Now? We're going in for lunch with Criminisi."

Dominic blinked twice. "Criminisi? What do you mean, Criminisi? I called the Romanian. He told me that you, me, and another one of his guys were going to get together and talk. Just talk. He didn't say a word about Criminisi."

Magilla held up his massive hand. "What did you expect, anyway? You wanna to work with us? This is like any other job. It ain't just us making the decisions. The boss has got to get a look at you." He grabbed Dominic by the collar. "And this blazer. You're wearing a blue blazer for a meeting with me and the Romanian? No. You knew the boss would be here. A good little Italian boy like you doesn't put on a fancy jacket like this unless he's going to church or a job interview."

Dominic straightened the blazer's collar. "Yeah. I guess so. But I was hoping otherwise."

"A word of advice. When we get in there, watch that mouth of yours. The boss has got class. He'll have nothing to do with you if you start mouthing off and swearing. Mr. Criminisi is a very Godly man. Goes to Mass every week."

Despite the February chill, Dominic felt a rivulet of sweat roll down his spine. He took a step back towards the curb. "I should think about this some more."

"You got no time for thinking. Nastasi offered you his help. You're a lucky man. For some reason, that Romanian piece of shit likes you. Now Criminisi's waiting to talk to you." Dominic tried to pull away a little farther. Magilla put his hand around his upper arm, holding him firm. "Nastasi's not a guy you say no to. Not if you like walking around town without looking over your shoulder, and especially not after he's done you a favour."

"Okay." Dominic shook off Magilla's hand. "Let's go."

Magilla put his hand on Dominic's chest. "One more thing. I should warn you about something."

Dominic knew there was a lot Magilla could warn him about. The list could last through lunch and well into after-dinner drinks. He'd been trying to ignore the laundry list of ill thoughts that had been wrestling for his attention.

Magilla wiped his dripping nose. "The boss is very sensitive about his upper lip. Don't stare at it. He's had a dozen plastic surgeries, but no one's ever gotten it right. He left it too long. See, in the sixties the old man was known for his skill with a knife. Hell, I think he still keeps one strapped to his ankle. Years ago, some punk kid out of Rochester challenged him to a blade duel — a regular ego fight with steel. The kid caught Criminisi in the mouth with an eight-inch slicer. Damn near cut out his entire upper palate. Kid didn't live long enough to see the damage, though. Criminisi stuck him deep in the gullet and drew his knife clear across his torso as easy as he was gutting a salmon. But the boss is one stubborn son of a bitch. He wouldn't let anyone take a look at his mouth for weeks. He said the little punk had just nicked him." Magilla put his hand down and led Dominic to the restaurant's door. "He still can't chew very well. So don't be looking at him odd or nothing."

Magilla pushed open the door and led Dominic to a booth with three men crammed into it. There was Bela Nastasi, a younger man whom Dominic did not recognize, and an older man whom Dominic had never met, but whose reputation preceded him like the knowledge of a pending hangover from a night of bad whiskey.

Criminisi stood up but the change in stature was minimal. He was a tiny man who looked older than his years. His thinning hair, red but fading to a pale orange, was combed across the top of his head. Criminisi carried himself like an old movie star, but his face was tired. His mouth was curled; his upper lip split a hair off centre.

"Mr. Criminisi," Magilla said. "I'd like to introduce you to Dominic DiPietro, Tony's brother. Bela and I, we've been doing some business with him."

"Yes, so I hear." Criminisi shook Dominic's hand. Dominic couldn't help but notice his large gold ring. Dominic could see the pride with which the mob boss wore it, as if it were a trophy. Square and flat, like a Scrabble tile, the ring was embedded with more diamonds than Dominic had even seen in one place. On Criminisi's wrist there was more gold. He wore a bracelet of linked gold chain, each link the size and weight of a wedding ring, as if he'd taken a link as a souvenir from every person he'd ever killed.

"I have heard many good things about you." The mob boss directed Dominic to a place in the booth beside Nastasi. He took it, still feeling the hardened etch of Criminisi's hand on his palm. Magilla pulled over a chair from a nearby table and situated it at the end of the booth. His body formed a barrier between Criminisi's lieutenants and any ears in the deli that may have had a tendency towards eavesdropping.

Nastasi motioned to the gentleman sitting across from him. "This is Theo Spagnoli. He works the import side of our business."

"You can call me Teddy."

"Import?" Dominic shook Spagnoli's hand.

"Yes," Criminisi said. "There are many items of interest that our organization brings into the city; mostly soft drinks, candy, and olive oil. Diversity has become one of the keys to our success. Bela is in charge of our local acquisitions. Magilla, as you know, our bookmaking operations. And Teddy, well Teddy has big plans for us in the automotive sector. Don't you?"

Spagnoli turned towards Dominic. "I am hoping. If we can find the right people."

Criminisi patted Spagnoli on the back. "So you can see, Dominic, we are not, as my American associates would call it, a one trick pony." He reached across the table to pour Dominic a glass of beer from a pitcher.

Dominic waved him off. "Thanks, but no. I have to go back to work, and Tony would have my head if I showed up with beer on my breath."

"He is a serious man, your brother," Spagnoli said.

"You know him?" A waitress came by with a tray of glasses and a pitcher of water. She poured, and Dominic wrapped his hand around his glass.

"No. But you can't build a business like his without being serious. From what I hear, he keeps a tight rein on his people."

"That he does." Dominic looked at his watch. "Which means I don't have a lot of time, or he's liable to send out the police looking for me."

Lunch had been pre-ordered. The waitress came over and covered the table with platters of pastrami, corned beef, freshly sliced dark rye bread, potato latkes, coleslaw, and knishes. Any remaining space was quickly filled with bowls of sour cream and pickled dills larger than Magilla's thumbs. Most of the order seemed specially prepared for the bookie. He loaded his plate like the table was his personal buffet.

Criminisi put a latke on his plate. "I don't have a lot of time left in our business." He placed a dollop of sour cream on the fried potato pancake. "The time comes when a man wants to retire and enjoys the spoils of his work, and his family." He motioned for Dominic to help himself to the food.

"Maybe you want to retire to Florida, with Magilla." The bookie made a choking sound.

"Magilla's not going anywhere," Criminisi said. "Not for a long time."

The bookie managed to clear his throat. "Why would I?" He coughed again. "There's plenty of opportunity for me right here. In Florida, gambling's legal. I'd have to find another line of work." He took a drink of water and peered a warning of silence at Dominic.

"You would be very expensive to keep," Criminisi said. "And, I have a lot of work to do before I can put myself out to rest on the porch." He looked at Dominic. "That's why, when Bela told me that you were looking to do more work from us, I was interested in meeting you in person. Our operation needs good people to grow. Only then, can an old dog like me spend his days lying in the sun."

Nastasi had built himself a pastrami sandwich. He was spreading mustard on the bread. "I see Dominic's work close up. He is best I've ever worked with."

"So you've told me. But I need to know more than what he's

done. I need to know what he can do." Criminisi slid a morsel of latke in his mouth.

"Dominic, there is sort of a retirement hierarchy in our business, which is why I came to Hamilton. I started out in Jersey, when I was about your age, then I moved up to Niagara Falls and Buffalo. Good towns with good people and businesses. But Hamilton is the right size for someone my age. I can know everyone. I can see everything. When you get older, your eyes can sometimes fail you." He waved two skinny fingers at his eye. "It's an important lesson, you know, taking on only what you can manage. You succeed that way. Take on too much, well, even if it works out, someone is very likely to take it away from you."

Dominic busied himself assembling a corned beef sandwich, nodding as frequently as he dared, unsure of what to say, if anything. Even his water tasted foreign and was difficult to get down. He was aware of every sip, swallow, breath, and twitch. His awareness was acute. He felt like prey.

"You like Hamilton?" Criminisi asked Dominic.

"Like it? Yeah, I guess so. It's home. It's familiar. Comfortable, I guess."

"And you, Theo?" Criminisi said.

"Yeah, I like it enough. It's a good place to do business."

"I like Hamilton," Criminisi said. "It reminds me of Jersey. This is a working man's town. People work hard here and they do not have the airs of big city people, like in New York."

"Or Toronto," Nastasi said.

Criminisi laughed a little. He spoke to Dominic. "We always kid Theo. He's a Toronto boy. But now that he's here with us, I think he's come to see the light."

"Yeah," said Spagnoli. "I seen the light. It was shining on one of those automated banking machines. I drove a backhoe through the wall and carried it away." The chuckle that emerged from Spagnoli's throat was like a dare.

81

Criminisi said, "I've always thought that Theo was really here to spy on us, as a *porta pachet* for one of the Toronto families."

Spagnoli said, "Don't believe it, Dominic." He waved a fork in front of his face. "I'm just a guy like you trying to make his way in the world. It's tough for us. You gotta take. Nobody's gonna give you anything. But I spy for nobody."

"It doesn't bother me anyway, Theo," Criminisi said. You can tell your big city friends anything you want. We only let you know so much."

Spagnoli turned the conversation to business. "Dominic, so you know a lot about cars?"

"I do, but mostly about the body." Dominic was trying to get comfortable being squeezed in beside Nastasi. It wasn't working. The Romanian stank of stale sweat and cigarettes. Dominic was becoming desperate for a smoke himself. There were ashtrays fighting for space on the table, but so far nobody had lit up. He said to Nastasi, "You don't happen to have a cigarette, do you?"

"No." Dominic took a deep breath in the hope that the smoky stench of Nastasi's clothes would pacify his lungs for the moment.

"This shop you want to own," Criminisi said, "it would be a body shop?" He used a toothpick to clear away pieces of food that had become stuck in places which his tongue couldn't reach.

"Yes, Mr. Criminisi … Well, no, not really. It wouldn't be like a traditional body shop. That's my brother's business. It wouldn't be good to be in competition with him."

"Yes, this is what I had thought," Criminisi said. "So when I heard you were thinking about going into business for yourself, it worried me. It's not good for family members to compete. Makes Sunday dinners very uncomfortable. Not good for the digestion, and that, my boy, can do you much harm over the years."

"I don't want to make anyone in my family uncomfortable. I want to do a different kind of work than my brother, on my own."

"This is good to hear. I've known your family for a long time. I remember your father well. Over the years, he and I would do each other favours."

Dominic drained his glass of water. "You knew my father?" Dominic felt the need for some Advil. A good handful, and a shot of tequila. He refilled his water glass instead.

"When he was first starting out, like you. Cash flow, you'll find out, can get a little slow sometimes. These Canadian bankers, they don't like Italian businessmen very much. They think we are all Mafioso, the Black Hand." Criminisi held his liver-spotted hand in front of his face. "Such nonsense. These banks, they are very hard to borrow money from. That's why I have this business: to help out people, like your father, like you." He reached out to Dominic, placing his hand over the young DiPietro's. "Not to worry. Your father was a very honest man. He didn't do anything that you wouldn't be proud of. Though he wouldn't have boasted about it."

Spagnoli seemed anxious to get on with business. "Alfonso," he said, "Dominic should be getting back to work. It would be best if you and Dominic spoke soon."

Criminisi stood up from the table, wiping his mouth with a napkin. "Yes. We should not keep this young man too long, and we have much to discuss."

# 12

Spagnoli began to stand up, but Criminisi waved him off. Dominic squeezed by Magilla, who was finishing off a piece of cheesecake. He followed Criminisi to the coat rack by the front door. His desperation for a cigarette had been replaced by the urgent need to use the washroom. He tried to ignore the urge and waited beside Criminisi, who slipped on a beige cashmere overcoat.

"You did not bring a coat?"

"No." The only jacket Dominic had that was suitable for the weather was a greasy City-Wide Collision ski jacket, one that he wore outside in the lot during the winter months.

"You young people. You think you'll never get sick. Such a limited view of your own mortality." Dominic followed Criminisi outside. The older man extracted a cigarette and offered the pack to Dominic, who accepted. As they walked away from the restaurant, Dominic noticed that Nastasi was following, about ten steps behind them.

Criminisi turned down an alley that ran alongside the deli. "So, tell me your plans."

"I want to restore classic cars — old Mercedes, Lincolns, and Cadillacs."

"That's nice. Me, I like the old Maseratis and Ferraris."

"A Ferrari is a fine car, Mr. Criminisi," Dominic said. "But as for the Maserati, a smart man owns two."

"They are that good?"

"No, you need the second one for parts."

Criminisi laughed, a small laugh, a gesture that Dominic could tell was rare by the way it had to be forced through the rickets of the old man's body.

"You can make me laugh. That's a rare thing for a man my age. I've seen too much. This shop you want, there's no one around here doing this kind of work?"

"In Hamilton? No. And there's a real need for it. Rich people — people who love their cars — will go anywhere to have them restored. They'll even come up from the States. And they will spend money on their cars as if they were their own children."

"This won't compete with your brother's business?"

"No, Mr. Criminisi. If we were in the clothing business, my brother would be mending suits and hemming trousers. And he would do it well. But me, I want to be a tailor, a fine one, creating made-to-measure cars for my customers."

"This restoration business: I assume it will cost a lot of money to set up. Money that you, at the moment, do not have."

"Yes. The capital equipment is very expensive." Dominic felt his nerve rising. His back straightened and he attempted to look Criminisi in the eye. "It's not the kind of money that a bank would lend me."

"Nor would I."

Dominic felt the cold of the winter afternoon slap him in the face.

"No. It would be an unwise investment. You could not pay me back."

"But I could, sir. In time. I would just need enough time to get the business on its feet."

"My young friend, I have not even lent you any money and already you are asking for more time." Criminisi slipped his arm in Dominic's and continued down the alley.

"Let me tell you how this business works. Everyone at that table is a good earner for me. The car parts you create for Bela, he sells.

85

Half the money he sells them for comes to me. The same goes for the bookmaking business and Theo's exploits with a backhoe."

"I see."

"As you know, not everyone who works for me is Italian. The business has grown past that. People like Bela and Magilla allow me to keep a certain distance from day-to-day affairs. I don't like to meet very often. That is the job of my people."

Dominic kept silent, walking deeper into the laneway with Hamilton's mob boss on his arm.

"In you," Criminisi continued, "I can see the potential to be a very good earner, and this is how you can finance your restoration business." They stopped walking and faced each other. "You are a smart boy, but naive. Betting money you did not have, then letting yourself be hoodwinked by Bela — this tells me that you take risks, but let your emotions write cheques that your life can't cover."

"I was like you many years ago. I wanted the whole world, and I wanted it right away." Criminisi clenched his fist. "So much so, that I would do anything — absolutely anything — to get it. And I, too, got in trouble."

He took Dominic's hand. If not for the diamond ring, it could have been Angelo's. Dominic hadn't felt his father's hand in sixteen years.

"I'll let you in on a secret," Criminisi said. "In this life, you don't get a chance to truly say thank you to those that help you along the way. What you have to do is give the same sort of help, when you can, to someone else.

"I was not much younger than you when I was in upstate New York. I had my eye on some merchandise that regularly travelled, by truck, along the back roads to Lake Placid. There was a truck, every Wednesday night, delivering luxury merchandise to the tourist shops by the lake. Week in, week out, it travelled into the village, returning in the morning. I got a crew together, and we hijacked it.

"We pulled the truck over and opened the trailer." Criminisi shook his head. "There was no merchandise. It was a rolling whore-house. The trailer was divided into small rooms, complete with lights, toilet, and shower. Inside were six girls and three guys from New York City who ran them from the Poconos to Lake Placid to Stowe, Vermont, and most every tourist town in the northeast. They busted my face and dragged my smart little ass back to New York. I was five minutes from a permanent swim in the East River when the boss there decided to give me another chance."

"Why would he do that?" Dominic asked.

"He told me that he liked my attitude. He liked the way I seized an opportunity, if not the opportunity I seized. It's time I repayed that favour. What you need, my son, is for someone to give you the chance to earn the money to start your own business. I want to do that.

"My business interests in Hamilton have recently expanded. I need access to a body shop such as the one you are proposing. Cars come into my hands that sometimes need to be … reconfigured, made to look different from when I first took possession of them. Would this be something that you could help me with?"

Dominic's right hand started to shake, sending a rising tide of fear up his arm. The ache in his shoulder flared as surely as if Criminisi had laid a strip of hot steel next to it. "It would be difficult. What I was thinking about was a very small shop. I'm not sure that I could handle any more than a few cars a week, to start."

Dominic had to pee so badly he thought his bladder would burst. He wanted to run. Nastasi stood guard at the alley's entrance.

"Most of my business these days is in real estate and other small ventures. I own a few strip malls, plazas, that sort of thing. In one of them, in the east end of the city, there is a ten thousand-square-foot shop that the previous tenant had to vacate. Unexpectedly."

"What business was he in?"

Criminisi shook his head. "It is no matter. Let us just say that he wasn't very good at it. Not like you're going to be. Not like me.

Unfortunately, he could not see the value in certain relationships that you or I would consider assets."

Dominic looked at the ground. The cracks in the pavement looked deep, deep enough to crawl inside.

"I suppose it could work …" Dominic swallowed. "Are there garage bay doors?" He hoped the answer would be no.

"Oh, yes," Criminisi nodded. "Front and back, triple doors on each side. When I built the place, I thought about putting a used car lot there, or maybe a service station. The land and the building are zoned for automotive service, which includes body shops. It is all quite above board." Dominic felt the shaking stop. The fire in his shoulder burned softer, but the ache remained.

"It could be your place, Dominic. I'll help you equip it with everything you need. In exchange for this, I need you to help me on the import side of my business."

Dominic wanted to sit down. His head was a storm of questions and emotions. Fear and flight were fighting with greed and anticipation. "You're going to start importing cars?"

"Yes. Used ones, and soon. But for the time being, you will continue to work for Bela, only out of my shop. Rather than going where he tells you, he will bring the cars to you. Every night."

"So all this talk is about getting me to chop more cars?" Dominic looked at Nastasi standing point at the entrance to the alleyway. He was smiling, for the third time ever. The Romanian had been pushing for this all along. "I don't want to do this anymore. I told Nastasi, and with all due respect to you, Mr. Criminisi, and Magilla, I want to restore cars, not destroy them." He looked at the entrance to the alleyway, where Spagnoli had joined the Romanian.

Criminisi placed his hands in the pockets of his cashmere coat. "I cannot force you to do this. But I can promise you that you will be restoring cars. Cars that I bring you at first, then, in time, for customers of your own. But we need to expand our business first, as a means of funding your restoration project." He pointed a finger at

Dominic. "More cars, more parts, more earnings. Together, we both get what we want."

"How long would you need me to do this?"

"Not long. I have arranged for a large shipment of cars to arrive in a few months. Your restoration shop has to be ready by then, and I want you to lead a team of your own choosing."

"You want *me* to staff it?"

"Oh, yes. I know you've trained Bela's people. You've done well with them. They're brutes, yet you convinced them to take their time. Bela has told me how patient you were with them, how you taught them to be careful and work as a team. This is a sign of leadership, the kind of leadership I am going to need if I ever want to be that old dog in the sun."

Dominic looked in Criminisi's eyes. He saw no warmth, no anger, no emotion at all. All he saw was business, a business without Tony attached to it. He stood silent for a moment as if waiting to find the courage to agree.

"I guess I could do that," Dominic said.

"Good," Criminisi said. He slapped Dominic on the back. "You see? This is not so hard. Here is the agreement I propose."

Criminisi talked for several minutes. Dominic didn't hear a lot of the details. His mind was distracted by the danger inherent in the relationship he was about to enter. He was also dancing with the increasing pressure of a full bladder. Then, in shock, he almost let the pressure explode down his pant leg.

"For now," Criminisi said, "I'd like you to keep working with your brother."

Dominic stepped back. "That, I can't do. It'll kill me."

"I do not understand this," Criminisi said. "This damnable hurry you are in. It makes no sense."

"I can't work for Tony, not anymore."

"You have much to learn. My wish for you is that you take the time to do so. After that, you will find life much easier, and more enjoyable."

"I find nothing about working for my brother enjoyable or easy."

"But it is nonetheless important that you do so. He has you working during the day, yes? Nine to five?"

"Yes. All I do all day is fill out insurance forms."

Criminisi lifted one eye brow and buried his hands deep in his overcoat. "All the more energy for your nights, then. But you be respectful of your brother. He can cause you problems which you cannot imagine."

Dominic resigned himself to the fact that the mob boss was not going to give him everything he wanted, not on the first day. But there was more promise for the future in what Criminisi was offering than there was in any life he could imagine with this brother.

"I know your brother. I remember him when he worked with your father. He is ambitious and competitive. He is a man who has to win, whatever the costs."

Dominic nodded.

"He won't understand you starting your own business. He would see it as competition and, worse, disloyalty." Criminisi pointed to his chest. "I would see it as disloyalty. And this would cause all of us problems. Problems that must be avoided. Give him time. Give yourself time. Earn for me, and earn for yourself. In time, I know, your brother will come around. Each of us can have our respective businesses and not cause one another harm."

Dominic said, "How do I earn my own restoration shop?"

"You will own your business on paper. But for the first year, it will really be my business. I am sorry Dominic, but it has to be this way. It's my money and I need to see that you can sort out this thing with your brother and get the business started. This way, if you fail, I can take back the building, the equipment, everything. If I have to, I could always put someone else in it.

"But this is only for my security. The building, the cost of supplying you with equipment for your shop, represents a lot of money. I will let you in on a secret: it won't all be mine. We all have bosses, my young friend. Even the Pope has to report to God.

Criminisi motioned for them to walk further into the alleyway, out of earshot of his bodyguards.

"You chop cars for me, separate the parts, and I will pay you one thousand dollars a car. You do this for six months and you will own half the business with me."

Dominic shook Alfonso Criminisi's hand in the full knowledge that he was trading the devil he knew for one he'd just met. There was no warmth in the old man's hands, but neither was there false pride, or the pressure of a future that appeared no different from the present.

"Good," Criminisi said. "Let's go back to the restaurant and see if Magilla has left us any cheesecake."

"No, thank you," Dominic said. "I really need to get back to Tony's. I am still working for him."

"Good. You are learning. We will do this again." Criminisi reached into his pocket and pulled out a key. There was a white tag tied to it. "The shop is on Brampton Street, number 412, unit 6." Dominic took the key, feeling as he did so the underlying anxiety of his choice. The key in his pocket led back to City-Wide. The key in his hand led only forward.

Criminisi handed Dominic a business card. "I want you to see this man tomorrow. He'll have some papers for you to sign — the lease on the building, insurance, that sort of thing."

Dominic looked at the card. It read Malatesta Insurance. "Papers?"

"Yes. We need a paper trail, for the government. Don't worry about it. I will teach you everything you need to know. Right now, trust me. The business plaza and everything in it is above board. It keeps nosy bureaucrats away, and the police."

Criminisi and Dominic walked out of the alley. "I will have Bela come by tonight, some time around midnight. He will bring you the first cars and some equipment to start." He shook Dominic's hand again. "This is a good thing you're doing. A man your age, you should start to take control of your own life, not live under the shadow of your brother."

Criminisi turned towards the restaurant, followed by Nastasi and Spagnoli. Dominic turned in the opposite direction and walked slowly away. When Criminisi and his cohorts disappeared inside the deli, Dominic turned around and ran back into the alleyway. Behind a dumpster, he quickly unzipped his pants and closed his eyes as the stream of relief splashed against the wall.

"You got a problem with toilets?" A strong voice echoed down the alleyway. It was a police officer, framed in silhouette against the darkening afternoon sky.

"Sorry, officer," Dominic said, zipping up his trousers.

"I could fine you, you know," the policeman said. Dominic came out of the alley and continued to walk past him.

"Sorry, officer," he said again. "Emergency measure."

"Wait there." The officer walked into the alleyway and looked around. He pulled out a ticket book from his back pocket. "Let me see some ID."

Dominic handed the policeman his suspended driver's license. He cursed himself and the officer under this breath. The officer wrote up the ticket. Public mischief. One hundred dollars.

"Be grateful, kid," the officer said. "I could have written you up for indecent exposure or lewd behaviour, both sexual offences."

"Thank you." Dominic took the ticket. He watched as the officer walked away. As soon as he turned the corner, Dominic crumpled the ticket in his hand and tossed it into the alley.

# 13

Dominic hung back in a corner of the shop that had a clear view of the office. When he arrived, Tony was at Lisa's desk, speaking to her in an agitated manner. Dominic waited for Tony to ascend the stairs to his perch and close his door behind him, then he walked across the shop floor.

"Sorry I'm late," he said to Lisa. "Got kinda held up."

"Tony's steaming. He's been down here twice in the last hour asking where you were."

"Like I said, sorry." Dominic hung his blazer on a hook by the door. He never planned to wear it again. Except maybe to a funeral.

Lisa always waffled between the roles of co-conspirator and mother. "I'd cover for you, " she said, "if you gave me a heads-up. But you're your own worst enemy. You know, if you just did what he asked you to do, for a *little* while, he might let up a bit."

Dominic didn't always trust her. But Lisa had become the best friend he had at City-Wide.

"Tony's not going to lighten up until someone takes his fat fucking head off," he told her. "If I had somewhere else to go, I'd be gone in heartbeat. But there isn't a body shop owner in town who'd hire me — not when they hear my last name."

"Dominic, this is a family business. You working somewhere else would break Tony's heart. He's got big plans for this business. His success is our success."

"I don't care about his business, and I wish he'd stay out of mine."

"He's only got your best interest at heart. When your father died, he left the whole business on Tony's shoulders. He's had to take care of all of us. Even me, and I'm only a cousin."

"I'd be happier if he and I weren't even related. But last I heard, brothers can't get divorced."

"You know, he really loves you."

"Then I wish he'd stop. It'd be better for both of us." Dominic went over to his desk, where Lisa had arranged a large pile of file folders. "I see that the business has carried on nicely, even in my absence."

"It's a simple job, really." Dominic was to take the insurance company's purchase order and match it against a work order. He was to make sure the hours approved by the insurance company matched the job estimate, then check the parts, paint, and supplies requirements to ensure that everything was on hand when the technicians started the collision service.

Dominic was happier being on the user end of the supply chain. "It seemed a lot easier when all I had to do was colour-match the paint and make sure there weren't any drips or splatters."

"If our end of the work gets screwed up, then the whole repair line goes down. No insurance company paperwork means no money. No purchase orders for parts means no replacement parts for the cars. No paint means ..."

"All the idiot who replaced me has to work with is high-pressure air." Dominic forced a smile.

"Right. You see? The power is in the paperwork." Lisa dropped another dozen file folders on top of the original pile. "Everything that runs this business comes through this office. When you're finished with a file, put it away in the proper insurance company folder over here." She walked over to a large wall-sized cabinet, which contained hundreds of file folders marked alphabetically. Many of the files were devoted to companies that Dominic was familiar with, like Allstate, Prudential, Pilot, and Maritime. Other files were marked with names that were as foreign to him as a concert hall full of opera singers.

Lisa said, "Five shops, twenty years worth of customers and a hundred-and-fifty-odd insurance companies. That makes for a lot of paper work."

"A hundred and fifty? I didn't think there were that many in the world."

"There are a dozen or so that we do a lot of business with. Some smaller companies only send us one car a year. Don't forget, we handle the insurance claims and billings for all of Tony's shops, not just this one. That's where our money comes from: the insurance companies. Less than one customer in a hundred comes in here with their own money to pay for a job.

"Sometimes I feel like I'm running my own bank. I send a finalized claim form and repair order into the proper insurance company and they send us a cheque. Ninety percent of the time we never even see an insurance adjustor. They just call. Most of the time, we send in the paperwork and they send off the cheque. There are some companies that have never had anybody visit us. But they do send us a lot of money."

"Frankly, I don't care anymore. I'm just gonna do my job, then go home."

"Get used to it." Lisa was sorting files in the wall cabinet. She closed a large steel drawer. "There's a lot more where these came from, every day."

Dominic wanted to pick up the pile on his desk and toss it across the room. Then he remembered Criminisi's words of warning. He knew he was going to have to find a way to survive at City-Wide.

"This can work okay for both of us," Lisa said. "Tony wants to put you in charge here."

"You're kidding me."

"No. He wants me to go work for Constantine's campaign. Run

the office there. But he needs me to be able to tell him that you can run things here while I'm gone."

Dominic took a file folder off of the pile and opened it. He wished that his own opportunity for freedom was so clear, so simple. "Alright. For you, I'll do my best. But if it weren't for you I might end up faxing these files off to China or something."

Lisa gave him a kiss on the cheek. "Thanks. If Constantine wins, maybe I can get you some extra work for him as a driver."

"My license is suspended, remember? The mayor's not gonna want a driver with a couple of drinking and driving convictions. I'm here for the duration. But that doesn't mean you have to be."

Dominic started to scan the file. The client's name and address were listed on the form, along with the car's make and year, its VIN, and a diagram detailing the extent and location of damage to the vehicle. Attached to this was a form from Ostander Insurance. Dominic's job was to fill out the insurance form and fax it with the other paper work for approval. It wasn't such a bad job, and it didn't aggravate the ache in his shoulder. He realized that since he'd started working in the office, his Advil consumption had dropped considerably. But he'd cheerfully swallow a whole bottle if it got him back to painting.

He opened another folder, but was distracted by Walter Janowitz breezing into the office.

"Lisa, my dear, you are as radiant as always. When is someone going to sweep you away from this place and put you on the pedestal you deserve?"

Lisa blushed. "One day," she said. "I keep hoping that my prince is going to walk through these doors, in agony because his brand new Mercedes been crushed like a can of tuna fish. Then he takes one look at me and forgets about all his problems."

"I only wish that I could be that prince," Walter said.

"You're driving a Chrysler and wearing a wedding ring, so I think you're out of the running."

"I thought it was just because I'm Polish."

"That too, but I didn't want to hurt your feelings. What's up?"

"Nothing, really. I came by to see Tony. I need to arrange a time to show him some new equipment we'd like to put in the shop."

"He's upstairs. You can just go up."

"I tell you, Lisa, he's been kinda grumpy lately. We had to raise the price of paint — not by much, but ever since, I can't even get him to return my phone calls."

"Yeah, he told me."

"That's why I'm here. I convinced my bosses that we should be putting some new equipment in here at no charge, to keep him happy. Could you, ah, go upstairs and convince him to see me? I don't think I should just barge in. It's about a twenty-foot drop from his office to the shop floor and that concrete looks pretty hard."

"Chicken," she said.

"Colour me Kentucky Fried."

"Okay," Lisa picked up the phone.

"No, please. Go up in person."

"Alright. But there better be something for me in all this." Lisa got up from her desk and left the office. As soon as the door closed, Walter headed for Dominic's desk.

"I'm really sorry."

"What do you mean?" Dominic peered over a pile of file folders.

"About selling Nicky's shop to Tony."

Dominic got up from behind his wall of files and walked around his desk. He had wanted to forget about the shop on Cannon Street from the moment that football flew right of the goal post. "It's alright Walter. I tried to sell my soul, but I'm afraid Tony's already laid claim to it." He extended his hand. "Thanks for at least giving me the opportunity. I know you had to do what you had to do." Dominic returned to his desk. "Tony's not a guy to take no for an answer."

Walter looked as defeated as the younger DiPietro felt. But

Dominic was wise to the salesman's strategies of false empathy. He liked Walter, but the act went down like skunky beer.

Lisa came back into the office. Walter drew a brochure out of his briefcase and handed it to Dominic.

"Hope you get back in the paint booth," Walter said. "These new spray guns are incredible. They'll give you the touch of a da Vinci."

Dominic handed the brochure back to Walter. "Save the pretty pictures for Tony."

"He'll see you now," Lisa said.

Walter snapped his briefcase shut and headed out the door. "I owe you," he whispered to Lisa as he passed.

"It's not me you owe, it's Tony. I told him you were coming up to talk about a campaign contribution for Sal Constantine."

# 14

Sammy drove Dominic to the Brampton Street shop. The industrial plaza was nondescript; it lay back from the dark street like a cat sleeping in the shadows. The body shop was at one end, taking up about a third of the plaza's space. The other businesses were unmarked save for unit numbers. Outside unit six, Dominic explained to Sammy the kind of work he planned on doing.

"You gotta be kidding me," Sammy said.

"It won't be for long," Dominic said. "Just a few months, maybe half a year."

Dominic trembled as he slipped the key in the lock. He paused for a moment as though if he never opened the door he might still be able to walk away.

"What's the matter?" Sammy was staring over Dominic's shoulder. "It's freezing out here. Open the door!"

Dominic turned the key and entered his new life. Light from street spilled into the shop through the open door. Sammy fumbled along one wall and found a series of light switches. The overhead fluorescents came on one by one from front to back as if illuminating a tunnel that had been sealed off at both ends.

"It stinks," Sammy said. "Who was in here before, a garbage collector?"

"I don't know, but you're right." Dominic sniffed the air. "It smells like something's gone bad."

The Romanian was scheduled to arrive at midnight. Dominic had brought along a couple of power washers from City-Wide Collision. He and Sammy set to work wet-washing a couple of decades of neglect off the walls and floor.

"You know," Dominic said, looking at the shine on the walls, "this is going to work."

"Leo know what you're asking him to do?"

"Not yet. I was hoping you'd help me explain it to him. He trusts you."

"Trusts me? You're dreaming in surround sound, man. Leo don't trust anybody that don't eat meat."

"We need him. He's strong, and good with his hands. If we're gonna get this done, we're gonna need a guy who can pull more than his weight."

"Who's we?"

"Me, you. You're in this too, you know."

"All I know is that you need me for my cutting torch."

"Sure, yeah, I need you *and* your tools. These cars don't come apart like IKEA furniture. But we'll be restoring cars, soon. First for Criminisi. Then for me."

"I'm happy welding steel for Stelco. Pays well and keeps me outta reach of several undesirable people, like the goombahs you're hanging with. I'll help you set the place up, but as far as doing any actual criminal work, that's another story."

"How much of a life do you have working for the steel company? Shift work? Nights? Working around all that heat? And you tell me that paint fumes are bad for my health, but what about coke and coal gas fumes?

"I wear protective clothing. The steel company provides it, for free. It's not too bad."

"What about the guys you're working with? They don't strike me as really your type."

"And you are?"

100

"I'm your friend. Here we can work together. It'll be nights to start, for a couple of months. I've done this kind of work before. It's no big deal. It's not like *we're* stealing the cars. After a couple of weeks, Criminisi will have the equipment put in here to really fix up some great cars. He promised." Dominic put his arm around Sammy. "Come on. We'll have some fun, and you'll be making more than welding wages."

Sammy shrugged Dominic's arm away. "I do okay. If I stick it out at the steel company, I'll have a pension.

"You don't have to quit anything. Just help me out when you can. You can change your mind later, if that's what you want." Dominic lit a cigarette. "You know what I'm looking forward to? Not the money. The cars. '57 T-Birds. '68 Camaros. Maybe a bull-wing Benz. These are the kind of cars I can't wait to lay my hands on. If we can do just a few of them, word will spread."

"I can see the ads now," Sammy said. "Maybe you can put your face on the side of a bus, like your brother."

The mention of Tony's name sounded to Dominic like an ax against a grindstone. "There will be no comparison between our business and Tony's. Ours will be art."

"And in the meantime, we're operating a chop shop for the mob."

"Temporarily. For now, we just pull apart a couple of cars a week and the Romanian comes by with a truck and hauls the pieces away. It's easy money."

Sammy shook his head. "No such thing, man."

"Maybe, but there's no risk on your part."

"You consider jail time a no-risk proposition?"

"Not for you. This'll be my business. You don't know where the cars come from. I pay you to come in on your off hours to cut up steel. That's only until I've earned enough cash to buy Criminisi out. I figure six months, maybe less, we're free and clear."

"I'm hearing the word *we* a lot."

"You're right. Me. But as soon as we start doing restorations full-time, you're a full partner. I can't do this without you."

"You really think Leo's gonna help you?"

"God, I hope so." Dominic ran his fingers through his hair. "He grumbles a lot, but that wife of his is looking to buy a house in Burlington, on the North Shore. That's Tony's rent district. Ain't no way a butcher is gonna pull in that kind of dough, not unless he's prepared to do something a little less than street legal."

"Still …" Sammy sat down on an old couch that had been left by the previous tenants. He relaxed for a moment, until he noticed the stains and torn upholstery. He was back on his feet and pacing in a flash.

Dominic tried his best to convince him. "Yeah, I know what you're saying. But nobody's getting hurt."

"So all I got to do is cut 'em up for you?" Sammy looked back at the couch and used his hands to brush off whatever bacteria he might have picked up on his clothes.

"That, and some of the mechanical work. The parts gotta get taken off clean. We can't strip the bolts or anything, and we have to keep the wiring in place. That sort of stuff."

"I thought you didn't know anything about engines?"

"Just enough to take them apart. But don't be asking me to put them back together again."

"Where does Criminisi send the parts to?" Sammy was still looking for a place to sit down. He found a workbench running along one wall. He took out a large handkerchief from his pocket and wiped off a space on the bench.

Dominic dropped the remains of his cigarette on the ground. "I didn't ask. I don't want to know. Neither do you. Safer that way, for everyone."

Sammy picked up the butt and dropped it into a garbage can. "If I'm gonna work here, let's at least try to keep the place clean. Okay?"

★  ★  ★

102

Leo came by after the work, as arranged. He looked larger out of his butcher's whites. As soon as he walked in the shop, Dominic realized he'd made a mistake.

"What kind of fucking *merdaio* is this?" Leo covered his nose with his hand. "I've smelled better slaughterhouses."

"It's not pristine, but we can fix it up," Dominic said. He told Leo about his plans for the shop.

"You're shitting me," Leo said. "Even you are not that stupid."

"I'm not the first guy in town to exchange a few favours with the mob, and I won't be the last."

Leo looked around the shop. Less than half the fluorescent lights were working, and several of the others were flickering. "You want *me* to work here, with you, for the mob?"

Dominic nodded.

Leo said to Sammy, "You're not going along with this, are you?"

Sammy shrugged. "Yeah, I am. Dominic's promised me a partnership in the restoration business."

"You guys deserve each other. I hope they let you share a cell."

Dominic said to Leo, "I'm the only one with my neck on the line."

"Like I said, a head fuck. I'd never get involved with those shits, or you. There's no way out, understand? This isn't some kind of social club you're joining. Once you're in, you're in until you're dead. Which in your case could be very soon."

"You know why I have to do this, don't you?"

"Yeah, I know, and I don't care. Your brother's given you a job and he's built this great business. Hell, Dominic, you don't know where City-Wide's going. Tony could take it nationally. Maybe franchise it. Your brother is trying to get you to learn the whole collision business, not just the paint side, and now you are going to fuck with him."

"No more than he's fucked with me."

"Patience, man. You don't get it. You think you should be king or something just because you're good with a paint gun? Well, I'm just

103

as good as you with a butcher knife but it's taken me four years to make assistant meat manager. Another four and I could make manager. Time, Dominic. You gotta put in the time. There's no skipping steps."

"I'm gonna do this."

"Then you're doing it without me. I can't have anything to do with you."

Dominic closed his eyes and let out a deep breath. "Then you should leave. And do me a favour: forget you ever came here."

"Don't worry, Dominic. I'm going forget I ever knew you."

As Leo left, Dominic kicked an old garbage can so hard it went airborne and cracked a window at the rear of the shop.

Sammy chuckled. "If only Scott Norwood had been able to do that, you wouldn't have needed Leo's help in the first place."

A half hour later, Gino came around with his tow truck. There was a car on the back, the front end of which looked as if someone had blasted it apart with a pair of bazookas. Gino was towing the injured car back to the company's lot until City-Wide reopened in the morning. He listened as Dominic outlined his plans.

"Man, you got bigger balls than I thought. Cool! When can I start dropping cars off? Tony pays me a hundred bucks a hook. You up for that?"

"Your cars are going to have to wait," Dominic said. Gino's eye wasn't the only thing that was lazy. So was his attention span. But if there was a chance for him to help and have a good time doing it, Dominic knew he'd be there.


The first two cars arrived at one-thirty. Gino had gone home. Sammy and Dominic were dozing on the couch. Sammy had stretched out a pair of coats to cover the stains. Banging on the front bay door awakened them. Sammy opened the door.

"I am Nastasi. Who are you?"

Sammy pointed to Dominic. "I'm with him."

There were three vehicles outside, a Mercedes-Benz C220, a Pontiac Firebird, and a black Chevy Suburban. Dominic figured the Mercedes to be about four years old. The Firebird, like the Mercedes, was hot. The Suburban belonged to the Romanian. Dominic had seen it parked in front of other job sites. Paulie and Zeno, two of the bikers Dominic had worked with before, drove the stolen cars inside. They looked around the shop and cast their eyes at Dominic and Sammy with all the respect they'd give to a 7-11 clerk. They went out and got into the back seat of the Romanian's Suburban.

Nastasi looked Sammy up and down. "This all you got? He doesn't look like he could lift a hammer."

"He's strong enough, and he's better with a torch than I am. I'll have more guys in a few days. Give me time."

"We bring you two more cars, tomorrow," Nastasi said. "That is all the time you have."

"Two more, tomorrow night?" Dominic said.

"Yes. Same time."

"What kind of cars?"

"Don't know yet. You got some kind of special order?" The Romanian took a large envelope out from inside his jacket. He handed it to Dominic. It was bulky and heavy. Dominic opened it. It was a gun.

"The boss told me to give this to you."

The gun was an old police style revolver. There was also a box of ammunition, half full.

Dominic handed the envelope and its contents back to the Romanian. "I don't want anything like that in here."

Nastasi refused to take the package. "Boss say give it to you. I give it to you. He told me nothing about taking it back. You learn, DiPietro. You do what you are told."

Dominic took another look inside the envelope. In addition to the gun and the ammunition was a note. It was from Criminisi.

*This is to protect my investment. Put it in a safe place. May God grant you the wisdom never to have to use it.*

Nastasi got behind the wheel of the Suburban and drove off along Brampton Street. Sammy dragged the acetylene and oxygen tanks out from one corner. He connected the gas tubes to the tanks and his cutting torch to the tubes Dominic and Sammy stood beside the Firebird. It was a few months old, bright and clean despite the dirt and salt from the short drive on Hamilton's winter streets. Dominic laid both of his hands on the roof, moving them along the top, down the windshield, and up to the front bumper.

"Let's do it," he said.

Sammy dropped his visor over his face and lit his cutting torch. Two thousand degrees of fire burst out of the end with enough focused heat to cut through a car as if it were made of aluminum foil.

# 15

Nastasi left the Brampton Street shop and was about to head back into the city's core.

"Go left here," Paulie said from the back seat. "Last couple of days, I seen a really nice Range Rover parked at the far end of Pier 24, by bridge. It's been there every night."

"You want to boost it?" Nastasi said.

"I could use the dough."

"I'll give him a hand," Zeno said.

"I tell my boys to get it. Is not your job." Nastasi turned left and drove towards the port. "You show me where car is."

"Why can't we do it?" Paulie asked. "Christ, it's not fair your Bulgarian buddies are getting all that sweet boost cash. Leaves nothing for us."

"They are Romanians," Nastasi corrected. "And is boss's decision, not mine. You got your job. I got mine."

"Come on, Bela," Zeno said. "Paulie and I can do it just as well as some fucking immigrant, and faster. Just watch us. You got a slider?"

"I am fucking immigrant. You will never be faster than me." Nastasi turned into the dark, empty parking lot that ran alongside Hamilton's easternmost pier. Paulie was right. Nastasi could see a dark green Range Rover sitting there just as pretty and lonely as a street corner whore at high noon. He stopped the Suburban and scanned the parking lot.

"It's clean, I tell ya," Paulie said. "Just give us this chance."

"Alright. Let's see how you do. But as far as the boss is concerned, I boosted it, and money is mine. I pay you a third."

"Half," Zeno said.

"A third, or I walk over and take it myself. You get nothing."

Zeno spoke for the partnership. "A third."

"I will drop you off. You take car directly to the DiPietro kid. There is a slider underneath passenger seat."

Nastasi drove alongside the Range Rover. It was hard to tell how old it was; the model hadn't changed in a decade. Snow had collected on the windshield along with a scattering of road salt and mud. Judging by the condition of the chrome wheels, Nastasi thought it would be worth the risk. Paulie got out of the Suburban. He used the sleeve of his jacket to wipe the window and peer inside.

"Full leather interior," he said. "Plus a CD player, and phone. This is great!"

Zeno went around the back of the Suburban and opened the rear door. He found the slider and met Paulie at the Rover.

"Be quick, or I never know you." Nastasi drove across the parking lot toward Eastport Avenue, then stopped. He turned off the Suburban's lights and backed into an area reserved for the Port's garbage. He parked between two blue dumpsters and a concrete retaining wall. The position gave him a full view of his rookie car thieves. He lit a cigarette and watched.

The bikers were brawny, hired for their muscle and their talent with knives, guns, and chains. Nastasi watched as they tried to use that muscle to open the Rover's solid British-made door, failing repeatedly. An experienced booster could have the Rover open in five seconds or less. Nastasi checked the clock on the Suburban's dash. His bikers had already been at it long enough for Nastasi to finish his smoke down to the filter.

He watched as both of them stood back from vehicle. Paulie held the slider in his hand and appeared to be deciding whether or not to give it one more go. He slipped the bar into the window seal and drove it down into the doorframe. But he made a muscle man's mistake — he pushed too hard. The bar was now stuck in the doorframe, welded by excessive pressure into the door just as surely as if he'd used a blowtorch. Nastasi watched as Paulie pulled and pulled and pulled at the slider with no success. In frustration, he kicked the side of the Rover's door, leaving a dent twice the size of his boot. Nastasi had had enough. He restarted the Suburban's engine.

Paulie wasn't finished. He raised his leg and kicked the sole of his boot into the driver's side window. The tempered glass cracked but held. He kicked it again, shattering the glass. Nastasi kept his foot on the Suburban's brake for a moment.

The bikers pulled away sections of broken glass and reached inside to open the lock. Paulie climbed into the driver's seat. The other biker ran around to enter through the passenger side door. Nastasi watched as Paulie took out his knife and used it to cut the ignition wires. In a moment, cold white exhaust ejected from the Rover's tailpipe and its running lights ignited.

From across the street a Hamilton Port Police car made a U-turn across the divided road, bumping its way over the concrete as it fired up its lights and sirens. Another port police car had been parked and waiting, like Nastasi. It powered up its lights and skidded across the frozen parking lot towards the Rover. Both cars crossed the pier with as much speed as the frozen surface would allow. They stopped in a V-formation beside the Rover, their lights flashing and their headlamps on high to blind the two bikers.

"Anglos," Nastasi muttered to himself as he took his foot off the brake. Leaving his headlights off, he began to sneak his Suburban away from the crime scene, being extra careful to avoid touching his brake pedal. In his rear-view mirror, he saw that the port police had yet to leave their cars. They weren't acting as aggressively as the city police, who would have already had their guns trained on the car thieves. Nastasi turned the Suburban a hundred and eighty degrees and tightened his seat and shoulder belt.

He pointed the Suburban at the port police cars and put his foot to the floor. With his arms outstretched and his back pushed into the seat, he sped across the ice of the empty parking lot pushing the four tons of steel to eighty miles per hour before reaching the pair of parked Crown Victorias.

There was a look of fear in the port police officer's face as he saw the heaviest passenger vehicle ever built by General Motors hurtling towards him. Nastasi grinned and bared his crooked teeth. He hit the first cruiser on the driver's side. There were no squealing tires, just the crash of metal meeting metal and muffling the screams of the port officer. The second port officer, holding his radio transmitter to his mouth, had it little better. The first Crown Victoria acted as a buffer between him and the crushing weight of the Suburban. Nastasi never took his foot off the gas pedal. He pushed both cars along the parking lot.

The officer in the first car was unconscious. Nastasi glared past him at the officer in the second car, feeding off of his fear. The Romanian eased up on the gas pedal of his steaming Suburban. The second port officer was still clutching the radio transmitter. The Romanian gave the Suburban a little more gas and both port police cars slipped off the pier and into the forty-foot depth of dark industrial harbour water.

Nastasi shook off the shock of the collision. He got out of Suburban to let the winter air clear his head and walked around the truck to inspect the damage to the front end. He looked over the edge of the pier. It was too dark to see any air bubbles escaping from the black depths. The harbour had swallowed the two cars whole. It was like the port police cars had never existed.

The Suburban's grille was smashed and the bumper askew, the hood peaked like a mountain range. But it was drivable. The Romanian headed towards the two bikers in the Rover. Paulie rolled down the window. Nastasi didn't give him a chance to utter a word.

"Get this thing over to DiPietro's," Nastasi said. "I'll follow you."

They found Dominic sorting parts into bins and applying labels. Zeno opened the bay doors and two cars pulled into the shop: one nearly new Range Rover with a broken driver's side window and a Suburban that appeared to have been dragged from a demolition derby.

"You chop this one," Nastasi said, pointing to the Rover, "and fix this one." He pointed to the Suburban. "Where's your phone?"

"I don't have one," Dominic said. He had dropped the parts and was looking closely at the Suburban. "You gotta use the one at the coffee shop across the street. What the hell happened here?"

Nastasi ignored the question and addressed Paulie. "Call Spagnoli and tell him to pick us up. Tell him we had an accident and can't use the truck. Nothing else. You hear me?"

Paulie nodded and left the shop. Nastasi was bleeding from his forehead. "You better get that looked at," Dominic said.

Nastasi wiped his fingers across the cut. "Is not your business," he said. "You fix this car. You repaint, change colour."

"Sure, I guess so. I'm not really set up for this. Not yet."

"Get set up. I'll be back with new ownership papers, plates, and VIN. Paint it white. And say nothing of this to Criminisi or I bury you in the harbour."

# 16

Dominic held Malatesta's business card in his hand and checked the address, 342 King Street East. He expected an office building, or perhaps an older home, like the ones he'd seen in Westdale, gentrified buildings that had been renovated into offices, the kind that a doctor might use. He saw neither. He stood at the doorway of a bedraggled convenience store. Branded posters for cigarettes and newspapers had faded behind the window. The price of jug milk was displayed, along with notices for lotteries, skin magazines, and a giant chocolate bar that looked like a club ready to strike the next customer that entered. Dominic looked to the left and saw 340 King Street East. He looked over the doorway and saw 344. No 342. He counted himself lucky and decided to press it by going into the convenience store for a pack of smokes. Three steps inside he found another doorway, unmarked except for the number 342. A stairway led to the second and third floor of the building. He ascended the stairs, which creaked loudly at every step as if they were talking to him, urging him to walk away. Dominic wasn't listening.

He reached a small landing, big enough for two people to stand uncomfortably close, where he was faced with still another unnumbered door. Dominic turned the handle. The door was locked, but there was a buzzer on the wall beside it. Dominic pushed the button and in a moment heard the click of the lock opening. He turned the doorknob again and the door gave way. Dominic walked into a large room and was immediately greeted by the overwhelming smell of stale cigar smoke. Four men and a woman were working behind heavy wooden desks that looked like they had been borrowed from an old movie set. Pale winter light scattered the room from windows overlooking the rear of the building.

"What the fuck do you want?" one of the men said. He threw down his newspaper. His feet were propped up on the desk, a stubby cigar sticking out of his mouth. The others in the room ignored him. They were on the telephone, smoking, or casting their eyes across huge books that reminded Dominic of auto repair manuals, each one large and unwieldy. The woman read a newspaper and glanced past the pages to see Dominic come in before returning to whatever had originally drawn her attention. Her ashtray was clean, her desk orderly with pens lined up in rows, by colour and size. There wasn't a stray file or paper on her desk.

"You better not be selling something," the man said. His head was large and dark, with eyebrows as black and thick as brushes. "The last guy who came here selling something ended up with his face sliding down those stairs."

"No," Dominic said. "I … I'm not selling anything."

"Then whaddya want?" the man said. He took the cigar out of his mouth a placed it on the edge of a large black ashtray on his desk.

"To see Mr. Malatesta."

"What for?"

"Mr. Criminisi sent me."

"Oh, well, that's different. You shoulda said something," the man said. "I'm Malatesta, but you can call me Louie."

The man stood up. Dominic recognized the former football player. He had retained the oversized head and long body that had made him an easy target for quarterbacks. He was tall, but the days of twice daily practices and forty-yard sprints were well behind him. His belly hung over his belt like a loaf of unbaked bread. Dominic could see the pain in his eyes from several too many tackles.

Malatesta extended his hand. "Sit down," he said, directing Dominic's attention to a wooden chair opposite the desk. Dominic shook the ex-footballer's melon-sized hand. What is it about big guys, Dominic wondered.

Dominic pointed to a Canadian Football League ball perched on a kicking tee at the corner of Malatesta's desk. "Is that the ball?" It was a Spalding, a J5V, with Commissioner Gaudaur's signature splayed across the bottom below the seams. The painted white bands at each end had lost their lustre and faded into the brown pebble grain leather of the pigskin.

"Sure is," he said. He took the ball from its perch and handed it to Dominic. Dominic inspected the ball as though he were holding the crown jewels.

"I was there, you know, at the '72 Grey Cup. Dominic sat down, still holding on to the ball, fondling it. "I was ten and my dad took me to the game. It was amazing."

Malatesta reached over and took the football from Dominic. "I was lucky."

"Lucky? Shit. No way, you were great. With one hand, you reached right over the defender's shoulder, just like you did with me now. You took a sure interception and turned it into the game-winning touchdown."

"It was luck," Malatesta repeated, placing the ball back on the kicking tee. "Maybe divine providence. I don't know. But it wasn't me. I was just trying to knock the ball away from him. Next thing I know, the ball is my hand and forty thousand people are cheering."

"It's an honour to meet you, Mr. Malatesta."

"I said call me Louie. The only people that call me Mr. Malatesta are loan officers and judges. What can I do for you?"

"Mr. Criminisi told me to come by and sign some papers for my business."

"Oh, right, you're the DiPietro kid. How's your brother doing?"

Dominic lost the air from his lungs. "You know my brother?" Christ, he thought, where didn't Tony's hand reach?

"Nah, not really. I send some of my clients to you guys over at City-Wide, sometimes. I've been by, a couple times. Hey, you still got that hot little *donnina* working in claims? What was her name ... Linda. That's right Linda. Or was it Louise?"

"Lisa."

"That's it, Lisa." Malatesta got a twinkle his eye. "Tell me ..."

"Dominic."

"Yeah, Dominic, tell me," Malatesta leaned over the desk and lowered his large voice. "You done her?"

"What?"

"You know, done her. Screwed her. Put her over the back of the desk and pounded her."

Dominic shook his head. "She's my cousin."

"Guess I spent too much time playing in Tennessee, 'cause if she was my cousin, she'd be a kissin' cousin."

"She's cute, but like I said, she's family. About those papers?"

"Oh, right. I got it all written up here." He pulled a file folder from his desk drawer. "It's your standard property insurance policy. It states the replacement capital value of your auto collision repair business is half a million dollars."

"It's an auto restoration business. We restore classic cars."

"That's nice. If your car restoration business, or whatever, is destroyed by fire or something, you and Mr. Criminisi's holding company," he looked at the policy, "Palestra Enterprises, split the proceeds fifty-fifty."

"How much does that cost?"

"Oh, I wouldn't worry about that. Alfonso is footing the bill for the premiums. All you have to do is sign." He handed to policy to Dominic, who flipped through the pages.

"The policy also covers you for up to two million dollars in liability, should someone get hurt in your building, or maybe one of those fancy cars you're working on gets banged up. You got no worries, insurance-wise at least."

"It says here that Malatesta Insurance is the beneficiary."

"That's right. In this policy, that's what it says. I have another piece of paper for you to sign. It's called a binder. It directs me to pay out half the proceeds to Palestra Enterprises and the other half to you."

"Oh." The familiar sense of being treated like prey was starting to tingle the hairs on the back of Dominic's neck.

"The policy gets filed with the Insurance Bureau of Canada, so this keeps you and Mr. Criminisi off the public record, if you know what I mean."

"I guess so." Dominic closed his eyes. The price of doing business. What choice did he have? He signed the paper and handed it back to Malatesta, who tore off the bottom sheet and gave it back to Dominic.

"This is your copy. Now I need you to sign the binder agreement." Another piece of paper, another signature. His neck hairs were ready to get up and leave.

"As for the premium," Malatesta said, "I don't get the feeling you're in a position to write me a cheque today."

"I thought you said Mr. Criminisi was paying for this?"

"He's agreed to pay for the basic premium but not the cost of the binder."

Dominic frowned and exhaled. "You got some kind of month-to-month plan?" He was beginning to wonder how much Ciminisi's investment was going to cost him.

"That's not the kind of thing we usually write up. We're a cash business. I tell you what. Since you're working with our mutual acquaintance, and he's the real beneficiary, why don't I take this back to him and see if I can work out a payment plan?"

"You sure?"

"We done this kind of deal before, on occasion. I wouldn't worry about it. Now, what can I do for you?"

"For me?" Dominic was of the opinion he'd already been done.

"Yeah, like car insurance, home insurance, maybe a retirement savings program. I got some great places to put your money. Clean too. Keep those sticky federal tax fingers away. I gotta at least be able to take on your car insurance? Everyone needs that."

"Yeah, you'd think so. But not me. I don't drive, at least right now."

"A car guy who doesn't drive? What the hell is that about?"

"I lost my license."

"Lost your license?"

"Yeah. Suspended. A few months back."

"What for, lead foot?"

"Nothing like that. Drinking and driving."

"Oh, man, been there myself." Malatesta took a sip from what looked like a coffee cup. It must have been cold, because he grimaced and put it down. "You get to drinking, watching a few girls take their clothes off, and then you got to drive home. Right? The laws are getting so screwed up, the only folks that are going to able to have a good time are the ones that don't know how to. Next thing you know, they won't be letting us smoke, either." Malatesta pulled out a fresh cigar and offered one to Dominic. He declined.

"I can help," Malatesta unwrapped the cellophane on the cigar. He didn't inspect it, like Tony did. He just clipped the end, fired up his lighter, and puffed.

"How?" Dominic knew he was getting in deeper, but he had to admit that he was attracted to some of the people he was doing business with, like Malatesta. Or maybe this was how prey was supposed to feel just before it got swallowed.

"When the authorities give you your license back," Malatesta slid the pack of cigarettes into his desk drawer, "in, say, three four month months, you're gonna go somewhere and get some insurance so you can drive again, right?"

"Yeah ..."

"And that insurance is gonna cost you a bundle. You're what, twenty-eight?"

"Twenty-four." Dominic felt sixty-eight.

"Oh, man, are you in big trouble then. You're looking at four, five, maybe six grand a year for basic insurance, let alone collision coverage and any decent amount of liability."

"Looks like I'll be taking a bus for quite a while."

"Doesn't have to be that way. I can set you up with a second driver's license, one with a clean record." The insurance agent gave him a wide grin, the kind a cat has when its got a bird in it sights.

"A second license?"

"Yeah. I can get you one now, if you want." He waved the cigar in the air, like he was telling a story. "When the cops pull you over, it'll come up on their computers as your license and you won't ever have had so much as a parking ticket."

"That's gotta cost a bundle."

"Seeing as you're in business with the Lip, I'm sure we could work something out."

"I'd have to think about it."

"You do that, Dominic. I can save you a ton of money." Malatesta stood up. "Say ... are you working with that Nastasi character?"

Dominic nodded, hesitantly.

"He left me some garbled message on the answering machine, this morning. Something about his Suburban and needing new papers. For a white one, I think." Malatesta ran his hand through his hair. "I can't figure him out, with that accent and all."

"It takes some getting used to."

"Next time you see him, tell him the new papers will be ready in a week." He shook Dominic's hand. "Thanks. He's the hardest guy to get a hold of, and I don't wanna be sitting on a set of phony VINs for longer than I have to."

# 17

A pair of tugs plodded the inland waters of the harbour in a slow and steady crisscross pattern. Through the night they'd pulled a dredger, a monster of a machine that hauled twenty tons of debris up from the harbour's grimiest depths with every scoop of its iron jaws. Like twin oxen dragging an underwater plow, the tugboats strained against the weight of the dredger.

The barge was a rectangular hulk the size of three football fields and just as seaworthy. It was large enough to require a crew of three and housed a pair of bulldozers that were capable of building an eight-lane highway. Yet on the harbour, floating in the dark, the tugs, the dredger, the barge, and its bulldozers seemed like a set of children's toys left out too long in a sandbox, the rain rusting away their colour.

Vinnie Carbone monitored the progress of his commercial disposal crew from his Jeep on the barge. The process of removing the area's contaminants and ancient debris was going much too slow. The bulldozers pushed the sludge into heaping piles, like snowplow drivers, taking great care to pile the night's load evenly. If the workers weren't careful in their distribution, the three hundred thousand tons of sludge could tip the great barge like a canoe, returning its toxic contents back to the grave they were exhumed from.

Vinnie monitored the progress through the curtain of lights from the steel companies, the neighbourhood homes, and the city towers that framed the harbour. He'd expected to get as far as the foot of Bay Street, but he could see they wouldn't make it that far tonight. The dredger had pulled its full shift's worth of harbour silt as the sun started to pierce the black sky. *Good pickings,* he thought. Each bucket was coming out of the water fully loaded. If he had any luck, there'd be a few choice additions to his spring garage sale. Each barge had a little treasure in it — a discarded bike, a vintage dishwasher. Once, he rescued a full set of railway china from the muck. He'd sold those to an antique store for enough money to keep him in beer for a month.

He had scheduled the dredgers to be on the water until ten a.m., but he was sure he'd have to call a stop soon.

He radioed ahead to the tugboat captains.

"Harbour One. Harbour Two. This is the Sandbox. Do you read me?"

The radio squeaked back at him.

"Sandbox, this is Harbour One. I read you."

"Harbour Two, check on that, Sandbox."

"On my mark, go to full stop."

"Roger that," came the response from the first tugboat. "A-okay," sounded the second.

"Mudslinger, this is Sandbox, do you read?"

"Hello, Sandbox. This is Mudslinger." Mudslinger was an Italian refugee who came to Canada in the early sixties and had taken to the harbour's dredging operations with the skill of a gravedigger.

"Mudslinger, prepare for full stop. Once the tugs stop pulling you, finish up your plot and make ready for an early breakfast."

"That's good, Sandbox. This monster is getting tired."

"Roger that, Mudslinger. What do you figure for time?"

"After the full stop, give me another two bites. That'll give us a head start tomorrow."

"Ten-four, Mudslinger. Two bites, then breakfast."

120

Vinnie gave the order and the tugboats slowed from a dead crawl to a dead stop. The daisy-chain beast bumped its parts together and ground to a halt in the west end of the harbour. Vinnie ordered the bulldozers at the rear of the barge to clear off the last two pulls.

The harbour doesn't give up much. She keeps her treasures hidden, far away from the prying eyes of admirers and thieves. As the tug pushed the barge homeward, the icy wind gave birth to a rare winter rain, which came down like a river from the sky. Creeks began to form in the mounds of mud, and the rain began to wash some of the night's work back to harbour's muddy bottom.

The only way for Vinnie to direct the bulldozers would be to walk the length of the barge and find the places where the rain was washing the most mud back into the harbour. Reluctantly he stepped down from the comforting heat of the Jeep and waded into the rain and the wind. Vinnie walked the barge with his walkie-talkie in hand, the hood of his parka up, his eyeglasses streaked with rain. Now and then he'd stop, stoop to inspect the rivulets of rain, and notify a bulldozer to push up a particularly dangerous mound or create a new barrier altogether. At the far corner of the barge, Vinnie's eye was caught by a flash of light coming from near the base of a large pile of mud. Lightning was rare for a winter storm, but he turned his face to the horizon to see if the light was being reflected from out of the clouds. He saw nothing, but the direct rain on his face started to freeze his cheeks.

He walked closer to the pile, the mud knee-deep around him. He caught another flash of light and noticed that it came from behind him, where the bright lights of a bulldozer's halogens cast a beam through an open fissure. The light that he'd seen in front of him, Vinnie realized, had been a reflection from the bulldozer's headlights. In two years of dredging, he'd seen nothing in the mud that would do that.

Vinnie turned on his flashlight. He pointed it at the pile and scanned from side to side, searching not for the light of the object but for light reflected from a distant source.

His eye once again caught the reflected light and he directed the flashlight beam towards it. The object in the mud was flat, like glass, about a foot across and eight feet from the barge's floor. He scrambled through the mud, oblivious to the deepening river around him and inched closer for inspection.

He was swimming now, using his arms as much as his legs for propulsion. Vinnie was now chest-deep in mud and momentarily considered returning to the dry warmth of his Jeep, but thought that since he'd come this far, he might as well carry on. He would not tell them what he found.

The wind changed and directed the full force of the rain against the reflective object. The fresh run of water cleared more of the mud away. The object glared back at him, challenging him to reach out and touch it. It was a clear pane of glass, at least three feet wide, one edge of which was not quite as reflective as the rest. He moved closer. The object was a metre away and just as far above his head. He saw it. He was sure.

It was a car window.

Vinnie reached out and scrubbed with one hand, the other holding the flashlight aloft. He couldn't reach the window, but he could get his hand inches below it. More mud. After a few wipes of his hand, he felt the mud give way the car window slid down to meet him.

It missed him by millimetres, stopping so close to his face that his breath cast a ghostly mist upon it. The reflection of his eyes stared back at him like some delusional beast, his glasses streaked by freezing rain and fear. He moved away with the care of a burglar stealing through a house in which owners slept soundly in their beds.

# 18

The banging of the auto bay doors awakened Dominic. The noise reverberated through the steel girders. Dominic thought he heard shouting.

It was still dark; the midwinter morning had yet to see the sun. He threw on a pair of City-Wide Collision overalls — Dominic's version of a bathrobe — and wandered barefoot from the old employee lounge, now his bedroom, to the auto bay, neglecting to turn on the overhead lights. He weaved his way through darkness past the carcasses of a half-dozen old Mercedes and two Honda Accords stripped past their usefulness. A few times, his bare feet found the sharpness of a couple of freshly cut bolts and a few shards of tempered glass.

He pulled down the chain that operated the bay door and saw Gino standing in the winter air. The tow truck driver's lazy eye was cast to the ground while his good eye met Dominic's face.

"Where have you ... been hiding?" he said, trying to catch his breath.

Dominic pulled him in from the cold and led him back to his freshly minted living quarters. He sat down on the couch and inspected the soles of his feet.

"I moved in here a few days ago," he said, picking bits of steel and glass from his cold soles. "It seemed to make more sense."

Gino shook the rain off his jacket and took off his baseball cap.

"I've been trying ... to phone you ... for hours. All night practically."

Dominic glanced at his watch. "I haven't got a phone hooked up here. I wasn't figuring on anyone needing to call me at five o'clock in the fucking morning." He fell back into the sofa bed and pretended to go back to sleep.

"I need you to ... to come with me," Gino said.

"Now? Where the fuck do you want me to go at this time of the night?"

"You remember my cousin, Vinnie Carbone."

"Yeah, the boxer."

"That was a few years ago. He's working on the harbour now."

"And this needs my attention, how?"

"He asked me bring you down to the sewage treatment plant."

"The sewage treatment plant?"

"Yeah ... right away."

"I am telling myself I didn't hear you say that," said Dominic, his head buried under the sheets. "You didn't ask me to get out of my warm bed to go with you and visit the goddamn shithouse."

"You have to come with me, Dominic. Get dressed. There's something there you got to see."


Vinnie stepped out of his Jeep when he saw his cousin's tow truck arrive. Wet snow blew off the harbour and covered his glasses. He didn't bother cleaning them, he just peered over the rims. The rest of the parking lot was empty, the winter sun still an hour away from rising.

"Sorry we took so long," Gino said to Vinnie. "I had to pull a few people out of the ditch on the way over here."

Dominic was groggy. Gino had refused to stop for coffee. Only disabled cars drew his attention.

Dominic said, "He thinks he's the fucking Red Cross."

"We had to stop," said Gino. "Those emergency lights on top of my truck aren't there for show. They come with a responsibility."

"The next responsibility you've got is to get me to City-Wide in time for work." Dominic pulled a pair of Advils from his jacket and cracked them between his teeth.

"Phew," Dominic said, curling away from Vinnie. "You smell like you just took a swim in the harbour."

"Sorry, can't smell a thing," Vinnie said. "But I think the swim was worth it."

"It better be," said Dominic.

"That depends on how much you know about old cars. Follow me."

Dominic and Gino returned to the tow truck and followed Vinnie's Jeep through the parking lot. They drove around the south end of the sewage treatment plant and weaved through the futuristic domes that capped the cleaning pools and wastewater treatment tanks. Dominic thought the place looked alien and surprisingly clean. Vinnie stopped just before a long, flat barge docked at the edge of the harbour. As they pulled up behind him, he drove forward and down a ramp that connected the road to the barge. They followed, finding themselves on a huge barge, barren as a brown desert save for the large dark mound at the far end. Vinnie pulled up in front of the mound. He stepped out of his Jeep, but left the engine running. The headlamps were still on and focused on the mound of mud. He motioned for Gino to park in a spot a few yards away from his Jeep, directing his cousin to angle the tow truck to align its headlights at the same spot as the Jeep. The headlamps of two vehicles were triangulated on a place on the mound where the mud had smoothed itself out to a long, flat spot.

Dominic opened the passenger door. The wall of putrid air and harbour grease hit him in the face with force of heavyweight punch, pressing him back into his seat. He slammed the door shut and said, "Jesus, Gino. I've had my face in better toilet bowls."

Gino opened his door and sniffed the air like a hound in search of a scent.

"I've smelled worse," he said.

They both exited the tow truck and stood between the two vehicles, saying nothing. Dominic kept his nose tucked under the collar of his jacket while Gino stood full against the wind, the chill, and the odour. Dominic turned his back to the wind and lit a cigarette, hoping that the familiar smell of tobacco would overpower the air. It didn't.

Vinnie reappeared on the other side of the mound. He was pulling a long hose. It looked a little smaller than a fire hose.

"I want you to have a look at this and tell me what you think," he said. He opened the valve on the hose and high-pressure water began to cover the corner of the barge's deck. Dominic's sneakers were washed by a wave of harbour sludge. He danced away from the flow.

"Sorry," Vinnie said. "I guess I should have told you to wear rubber boots." He directed the flow from the hose toward the mound.

"Stand back. This is going to get messy."

Vinnie opened a valve on the hose and managed to get more pressure. He held the nozzle with both hands and directed the spray at the mound.

Dominic and Gino stood in the dark staring at the focal point of the spray. At first they saw nothing but mud, mud, and more mud as the jet stream of water pushed the sludge away from the mound and scattered it around their feet.

Like an exotic dancer, the miracle within the mud began to reveal herself with the deft touch of experience, beauty, and an intimate knowledge of herself, baring her body in response to the cleansing shower of fresh water on her frame. Dominic was first to recognize one of her eyes. It was dim and foggy, its whites turned grey from its burial, but an eye it surely was. He saw the pitted chrome ring that encircled it. The water continued to shower down and the dancer flashed her smile.

"They don't make grilles like that anymore," said Dominic.

The lady smiled back at him in the light from the tow truck and the Jeep. Unconsciously, Dominic moved forward, slowly, like he didn't want to wake her from her sleep.

"Turn the water off," he said. Vinnie closed the nozzle.

Dominic moved closer and reached out to touch her grille. He hesitated for a moment, then placed his hand on her. She was cold, dead cold, like she'd been dug up from an old grave. He brushed away more mud from her grille then reached out and took the hose from Vinnie. He opened the nozzle and directed the spray at her from a tighter angle. He was only inches away.

"There it is," he said, shutting off the nozzle again. He let it drop to the deck. "Look at that. Do you know what it is?"

The three of them stared at her tattoo, the brand placed squarely between her eyes. It was a silver horse running at full stride.

"It's a Mustang," said Gino.

"It sure is," said Dominic, brushing away more mud from the grille with his bare hand, like he was fixing the hair on a baby girl. Vinnie picked up the hose and directed the powerful shower back at the car. The dancer revealed herself one veil at a time until all her old beauty was on display.

The three men stood in silence, staring at the old girl standing before them. Like an automobile sized diamond in the rough, the ancient Mustang's beauty was barely discernible. Only the odd glimmer of old paint and the sharp edges of battered fenders betrayed her heritage. She was dented, scratched, and pitted. Her chrome bumpers were chipped from the harbour water, leaving them raw and exposed. Her driver's side window was gone. Some of the harbour's grim mud had filled her insides so that barely a headrest could be seen. She was cemented up and sealed.

"Fucking amazing," said Dominic.

"What are you going to do with it?" said Gino.

Vinnie looked over his shoulder towards the main buildings and the parking lot.

"In about fifteen minutes, it becomes the property of Commercial Disposal Incorporated," he said. "And all they're gonna do is throw it in the scrap heap."

Dominic knelt down beside the rear fender. He ran his hand along it. "What a shame, man."

"Get it out of here," said Vinnie.

"Just like that," said Dominic. "Just take it and do what?"

"Fix it up. Put it back on the road."

"You don't know what you're talking about."

"That's why I asked Gino to bring you. I don't know a thing about fixing up a car like this."

"And I do?" said Dominic. He stood up and walked around the car. "I don't know anyone who knows how to restore a car like this. You're talking major work, and a lot of money."

Vinnie said, "But Dominic, you've got our own shop now, right? This could be the start of your business."

Dominic shot an accusatory glance at Gino. "I'm not starting any business. I don't have any business. I work for Tony." Dominic thought of the remains of five cars littering his shop and the trac-tor-trailer parked out back ready to receive the parts from another thirty cars.

Vinnie said, "Your brother, then … you think he'd want to work on it?"

"Not a fucking chance. Not unless you rolled this pile of rust into his shop and handed him a blank cheque. And he'd be right."

"Then you could do it, at your shop," Gino said.

"You're not hearing me, Gino," said Dominic. "I don't have a shop. I work for City-Wide Collision. I might have my own business one day, but not right now."

Gino looked over his shoulder again. A car was pulling into the parking lot. His glance drew Vinnie's attention. The sight of the approaching vehicle made him nervous.

"Listen, Dominic. Gino's told me what you're up to. I'm cool with it. You don't spend most of your life in the boxing ring without knowing that there are times when you gotta do business with these guys."

Dominic took the bottle of Advil from his pocket and rolled four pills out into his hand. His knee throbbed like someone had dropped the whole car on it. He crunched the pills hard and swallowed. They felt as hot as the acid in his stomach.

"Alright. Let's take the car, or whatever's left of it, back to Brampton Street. We can have a better look at it there, away from any prying eyes."

Vinnie thanked him and left, returning his Jeep to the parking lot to distract any early arrivals. Dominic watched Gino hitch the hidden harbour jewel to his truck and pull away. Gino waved to him to run up and jump in the truck.

"You got a place where you can stash this thing until tonight?" Dominic asked.

Gino agreed to hide the car at Ace Towing's locked storage yard for the day. He'd tow it to Brampton Street after City-Wide closed for business.

# 19

It was after eight by the time Gino arrived at the Brampton Street shop. Vinnie was with him, dressed for another night on the harbour, but knowing full well the coming shift would not be as rewarding as the previous one. With his weatherproof parka open and thick glasses he looked like an overweight polar explorer. He jumped out of the passenger seat.

Dominic came up to the driver's side window of the tow truck. He hoisted himself up by the side-view mirror and perched on the running bar. Sammy was keeping warm at the rear of the shop. His back was against a wall of old tools and workbenches, his arms wrapped around his pencil-thin body. He'd come by earlier to help Dominic clear just enough room in the cramped shop to park another car.

"Shut the door," he said. "Jesus, Dominic, living here is gonna lead you to an early grave."

Steam began to rise from the Mustang's bulk as the icy mud that encased it met the warmer air of the shop. They cast the blue tarp aside, and the car seemed to breathe. They gathered around the car, awash in awe.

"You know." Sammy said, "there's enough chemical shit in all that mud to burn your eyes out. My chances of getting cancer have gone up exponentially just by being in the same room with the thing."

Dominic said, "Sammy's right. It's starting to stink up the place."

Vinnie just smiled. "Yeah, it's filthy," he said. "Spend a few years at the bottom of a cesspool — you'll start to stink, too."

They gathered the power washers along with some old tools that Dominic had taken from his mother's gardening shed and started to clean off the Mustang. Vinnie approached from the rear with a shovel, gently pushing it into the thick cake of mud at what looked like the roofline above the passenger seat.

"Don't be afraid of it," Dominic said as he hooked up the pressure washers. "It won't fight back."

"It's not that," Vinnie said. "I just don't want to damage it." He gingerly pushed the shovel down into the mud, but the blade sank only a few millimetres.

Dominic grabbed the handle of the shovel and crawled up on the heap like a kid playing king of the mountain. "Let me get this started." Dominic shoved the spade deep. Sammy winced. "Christ," Dominic said. "I should've hit the roof." He pried the shovel out and pushed down harder in the same spot. The mud swallowed the blade up to the handle. "Shit. I bet this thing's rusted out clear to the floorboard."

Sammy carried out his supervision duties with a beer in his hand. "Shouldn't be a lot of rust on that thing."

"It's been on the bottom of the harbour," Gino said. "It's probably nothing but a ball of rust."

Sammy shook his head. "Rust needs oxygen. There's isn't very much of it at the bottom of the harbour."

"Sammy's right," Vinnie said. "That's why there's no fish or plant life, at least for most of the year. Not enough oxygen in the water to breathe."

Dominic knelt on the five-foot-high pile of mud and steel.

"This shovel went through something."

"Boys, I think what you've got there is a convertible." Sammy walked over to the cooler. "I definitely need another beer." He cracked open the bottle on the side of a work bench and tossed one over to Dominic.

The rain dance began in earnest and didn't let up until the last speck of harbour mud was washed from car. The pressure washers blew away surface mud like it was beach sand. Sammy hid behind a doorway in an effort to keep the toxic spray off him.

Some of the surface mud had petrified into stone that at points was indistinguishable from the car. With the thrill of a prospector, Vinnie leapt into the emerging back seat and began to throw mud out of the car with righteous abandon. The spray from the pressure washers filled the interior cavity as fast as Vinnie could empty it. Ignoring the fact that he had to go to work in the clothes he was wearing, Vinnie got down on his knees and grabbed handfuls of harbour mud as fast as he could.

Dominic directed his washer at the driver's side door. Slowly, like layers of dirt falling off a Renaissance masterpiece, some colour began to peek out. White. Bone white. The paint was dirty, faded, and scratched, but it was there.

"Wimbledon white," Dominic said.

"What?" Gino stopped spraying for a moment.

"The colour. It's an old version of the off-white that Ford uses." Dominic and Gino blasted away another dozen layers of silt. The dull chrome of the door handle and a lock came into view.

Gino pointed at Vinnie. "See if you can give the door a push from the inside. I'll pull from out here."

"We've got to get inside the door jamb," Dominic said. "Whatever's in there has locked the door up solid."

They aimed their pressure washers at the tiny space left between the door and the rear quarter-panel. Nothing but clear water came back for a few seconds then a river of mud started flowing from the bottom of the car.

"Vinnie," Dominic yelled over the sound of the washers, "start pushing. Gino, you start pulling and push down on that handle lock.

132

I'll keep the water flowing."

Dominic shot clean high-pressure water in the door jamb. Gino and Vinnie pushed and pulled at the door with the ferocity of two boys fighting over a loose football. Vinnie, still sloshing around the car's water-filled interior, crouched down in the pool to use his legs for leverage.

"Dominic. Lend a hand. I think it's starting to give."

Dominic stood beside Gino and gripped what he thought would have been the top of the door. Leaning back and pulling hard with both arms, Dominic strained against the unyielding weld of mud and metal.

In an instant, Dominic and Gino found themselves on their backs holding what looked like a car door on their stomachs. A river of water flowed out from the car's interior leaving Vinnie sitting awkwardly on a mound of mud where the transmission shifter should have been.

All of them were muddy almost beyond recognition. Dominic's hair drooped straight over his forehead like a tattered corn broom. Vinnie crawled out of the car and pulled the door off Gino. The water on the floor was ankle deep. Dominic trudged through it and sat in the car's cockpit. The smile on his face burst through the dirty straw on his head.

"Now this is a car," he said, using the back of his shirtsleeve to wipe mud and water off the instrument panel. "And it's nearly new."

The boys gathered around their muddy Buddha and stared over Dominic's shoulder at the driver's gauges. Dominic pointed to the odometer at the bottom of the dashboard panel.

"Thirty-two miles," he said. "This baby is just a baby. Barely off the lot."

Sammy said, "Remind me never to buy a used car from you. This is a piece of shit. Look at the front fender."

Dominic leaned out looked down driver's side of the car. The front fender had been torn completely away. All that was left was the mud-slicked wheel well and surrounding metal.

Vinnie said, "Thirty-two miles. How can that be? And in the harbour. Someone threw it away like a beer can."

"Fucked if I know. But it's our beer can now," Gino said.

"I've heard about that sort of thing," Sammy said. "Cars get transported on railway trains. Right? Yeah, railway trains. Sometimes the cars fall off. I remember a scam a few years ago, cars falling off trains and the company trying to resell them as new."

Gino was about to open a beer, but thought better of it. He passed the unopened bottle to Dominic. "That doesn't explain how this new car found its way into the harbour," he said.

"There's a rail line running around the harbour isn't there, Vinnie?"

"Yeah, on the west side."

"Where'd you find the car?"

"In the west side of the harbour, by the yacht club."

"There you go. So you're the engineer of the train, right, and you're pulling these cars to Oakville, where Ford has its Canadian headquarters. You're pulling through Hamilton and you hit something. The cars shift, one falls off, hits the ground on the driver's side, smashes up the fender and rolls into the harbour."

Dominic said, "You sound like some idiot describing his accident to an insurance investigator."

"Well, if I'm this engineer, I say nothing. Hell, I might not even know there was a car missing. You got another idea where this car came from?"

Gino said, "It had to come from somewhere. How old is this car?"

Dominic said, "Sometime in the mid-sixties, '65 or so. Maybe even '64 ½."

Gino said, "And a half?"

"Yeah," Dominic said. He got out of the car. "Used to be that all new cars were introduced in the fall of the previous year. So a new

'64 would be introduced in the fall of '63. Now they don't do that; new cars get introduced all year round. Ford was the first company to introduce a car in the spring, in mid-1964. The Mustang. They put it out in the spring to catch the competition off guard and so they could sell a shitload of convertibles."

"Like this one?" Vinnie said.

Dominic said, "Maybe, only there aren't many of them anymore. Maybe one or two."

Vinnie said, "Or three ... Sammy, I don't think this call fell off a railway car."

"Why's that?" Sammy said.

"Not unless it fell off with a license plate attached."

The others joined Vinnie behind the car. Dominic grabbed a power washer and directed it at the place where the license plate would be attached. It was dark blue, so dirty and dark it almost looked black, and the bolts that attached it to the chassis were rusted brown. Vinnie scrubbed hard. The year appeared. 1964.

"Shit," Dominic said. "We're fucked."

Vinnie turned to Gino. "What's he talking about? What's he mean we're fucked?"

"I don't know. I don't know what he means. What do you mean Dominic? How are we fucked?"

"Somebody already owns this car," Dominic said. "This baby's plated ... The plates haven't been renewed since '64, but it's plated. Dig around long enough and we're gonna come up with a VIN, maybe even a set of ownership papers." Dominic walked around the car like he was hoping the papers would somehow appear before his eyes.

"Then again," he said, "if the papers were in the car I'm sure they've rotted away. Makes no difference anywhere. In the Licensing Bureau, somewhere, there's a file with this car's number on it, and the name of the owner, whoever he or she is."

"Or was," said Gino. "The car's twenty-seven years old. Whoever owned it may be dead."

"Someone owns it, that's for sure." Dominic lit a cigarette.

"That's crap," Vinnie said. "I drag this piece of shit from the bottom of the harbour and now your telling me we don't own it."

"We might even have to give it back."

"Oh Jesus, you got to be fucking with me," Vinnie said. "Give it back! I'd rather give it back to the harbour! For Chrissakes, Dominic, there's got to be another way."

"I know a guy. He's hooked up with Criminisi. He may be able to help us, but I suspect its gonna cost big bucks. Forged ownership papers can't come cheap."

"Un-fucking-believable," said Sammy.

Vinnie sat on the floor and stared. Gino reached over his shoulder and touched the numbers one, nine, six, and four, like he was reading Braille.

# 20

The party began there on the cement floor and carried on through the night. Hour after hour a little more of the mud fell away. One man would hug the car and take a pound or two with him. They sprayed beer on the fenders and the hood like Stanley Cup champions, shaking their beers as if they were bottles of champagne and dousing the car. The smell of the harbour, the toxicity of the mud, and the brewer's yeast of the beer combined to create an odour previously unknown to mankind. It was indescribable, part earthy and familiar, part foreign and manufactured.

Vinnie called in sick. Gino turned off his pager. Sammy returned to his apartment to retrieve a full case of Molson and a bottle of whiskey. Dominic called out for pizzas. All that was missing were women, but the Mustang was a more than acceptable substitute. Passion lay within, buried like her body under the weight of a hundred-year-old harbour. She cast enough love around the old body shop to wet the dreams of a hundred boys.

In the morning, the winter light came through the bay windows like high beams pointed directly at Dominic's eyes.

Sammy sat in a car seat that had been extracted from a Toyota Supra several nights before. His feet propped on a car battery, he was sleeping off the activity of the night before. Vinnie slept on Dominic's couch. Gino had managed to curl up in the back seat of the muddy Mustang, his feet hanging over the side.

Dominic walked around the car. The floor was a sea of mud and car parts. He squatted down at the front of the Mustang.

"You know, we can't just start hacking away at this thing like some boosted Honda the Romanian dragged in here. This car's a gem, and worth a lot of money took another dig, but only by millimeters. If we can fix it up right."

Gino sat up in the car. "Really? You think it's worth something?"

"Maybe ... What we got here is a lump of coal. As it is, it ain't worth much more than scrap. But if, and this is a big if, we could fix her up, make her like showroom new, that combined with the low mileage could turn it into a diamond."

Vinnie said, "What good would that do us?"

"I figure that all of us getting together to fix up this car then share it between us is kind of stupid. What are we gonna do once we're through? Vinnie, you have it one day a week? Me, another. Sammy, on Tuesdays. That's lame." Dominic never took his eyes off the car. "You know what this could be worth, if we restore it completely? I've been reading about cars like this for years. I know there's a guy, somewhere, who'll pay seventy-five, maybe eighty-five grand or more, US, for this car, if it's in showroom condition."

"Holy shit," said Sammy, who had awoken from his nap.

"Damn right. And that's not for a stored original. We might get twice that much. I don't know."

"Where you gonna tell people you stored it? In the harbour?" Vinnie asked.

"We're not gonna tell them anything. When we're done, all people are gonna know is that they'll be buying a fully restored 1964 ½ Mustang with thirty-two miles on it."

"Who's gonna buy it?" Gino said.

"A car like that will sell itself." Dominic lit a cigarette and looked across the room. "Here's my idea. Together, we restore this car. I figure that if we beg, borrow, or steal the parts we need, we can get it on the road for about ten, maybe twenty grand. We fix up the car, sell it, then use the cash to buy out Criminisi."

Vinnie said, "I see how this works for you, but not for us."

"We'll all be partners. This car represents the only work I've ever wanted to do. Painting wrecks is one thing, but restoring a classic, that's another. Restoring this car will not just fund the business, it'll advertise it." Dominic waved his cigarette in the air and walked around the garage. "I have to do this. I'm the best guy with a paint gun in this city, I know that, but I haven't painted a car in weeks."

Sammy crouched beside the car and ran his hand along the bumper, "I don't know, Dominic. Maybe we could just track down the insurance company, or whoever owns the car, and negotiate a reward for finding it. They might even pay you to restore it."

"Too many maybes," Dominic said. "I know this will work. What do we have to lose, anyway?" He looked at Vinnie. "You got fifteen or twenty grand lying around?" He looked at Gino. "You? Sammy? I already know your answer."

"You told me once that you were a lousy investment," Sammy said.

"I know I did," Dominic said. "And at the time, I was right. But I've changed. I'll make you this promise: as long as we're working together to restore this car, I won't take a drink."

Sammy looked serious. "Or," he said, "make a bet."

"You're on." Dominic sat down in a discarded car seat. "None of us has the money to put this car back on the road, and we couldn't share the finished car if we did. So, in my mind, we either turn this into a business opportunity, or Vinnie should drop this thing back in the harbour, where it came from. It's your call."

"I guess having a piece of a body shop business is better than owning all of a car I can't do a thing with," he said.

Dominic knew there were more problems than whether to fix the car or toss it. They had to raise money, a lot of it, and no one in the shop had the experience to restore the power train.

"We're gonna need a mechanic." He cleared both sides of the hood, tried to lift it up again, and failed. "A real one. Not some guy who changes parts for a living. He has to know his stuff, and, given how we make our money around here, he has to be someone we can trust."

"You must know someone?" Sammy said.

"Not really, just a few guys that Tony's done some business with, and I wouldn't go near 'em."

"I know someone," Gino said. "Real good with a wrench, and really experienced around engines. Even did some time in the States on the racecar circuit."

Dominic tried to pull up the hood one more time. It gave an inch, then froze. "There must be a ton of mud wrapped around that engine. Think he could handle this?"

"No problem. A real genius."

"He's gonna have to be," Dominic said. "This piece of steel is gonna need a miracle worker to turn her over. Ask him to come down here and have a look."

Sammy looked at his watch. "I'm out of here. I got just enough time to get home and change for Mass."

A look of shock crossed Dominic's face. "It's Sunday?"

"Yeah. But what do you care? Unless you're supposed to be taking your mother to church today."

"It's my nephew Aldo's christening. If I don't show up, Tony'll have me buried."

# 21

Sammy swerved in and out of the early morning traffic like a stock car racer. He and Dominic had washed up in the garage's sink, but neither had had time to shave. Dominic loaned Sammy an almost-clean shirt. Dominic wore his cleanest dirty one, but had to do without his blazer, which was still on the back of the office door at City-Wide.

"I'm gonna do it," Dominic said as Sammy negotiated the Sunday morning traffic.

"Do what?"

"Tell Tony to take his job and shove it up his ass."

"Not today you're not. We're going to witness the blessing of your nephew. This is not something you mess with."

"Aldo's christening has nothing to do with getting him blessed. It's all about Tony. I guarantee you the place will be filled with people all puckered up for Tony. Every employee. Everybody he's ever paid off, everybody who wants to be paid off. Especially that crook, Constantine. This ceremony has nothing to do with God."

Sammy turned onto King Street the large one-way street acting like a five-mile driveway to Hamilton's Cathedral of Christ the King. "Don't talk that way about the Church. It doesn't matter what Tony's using it for. That's his cross to bear. You should give it respect."

"Respect? We *are* going to the same church that believes that you're gonna spend eternity in purgatory."

"They may be right," Sammy said. "But that doesn't change who I am or that I believe in the Holy Trinity."

"Yeah. So does Tony. As in, me, myself, and I."

They were running late. Sammy pushed the speed limit and raced through a yellow light. "You know, you might not feel so bad about yourself if you took the spiritual side of life more seriously."

"I feel fine. As for God, I wore out my welcome a long time ago."

"Your nephew's just starting out in life. Don't fuck it up for him."

Dominic took a deep breath and put one of his hands on the dashboard. "I promise, I won't say a thing at the christening. I'll wait to talk to Tony alone, at his house."

"Get the Mustang on the road. He'll be envious enough of that."

"I don't want him to be envious. I want him to regret the day he ever pushed me around."

"What if he never does?"

"He will." Dominic was looking out the window, staring at the cars as they passed. "Tony will know my work as soon as he sees it. On every street. In every parking lot. Even in his dreams. I'll be his worst nightmare."


Five minutes into Sunday service was not the best time to find parking at the city's most popular Catholic church. On Sunday mornings, a parking space was scarce as an unrepentant soul, leaving Sammy no choice but to park his car behind one of the church's dumpsters. Dominic left his sweat-lined baseball cap in the car, combed his hair straight back, and began to walk around to the front of the church. Sammy directed him to an open back door. It led into a large kitchen.

Sammy appeared to know his way around. They navigated among the pots and pans and empty soup bowls. All was quiet until Dominic bumped a corner of the large kitchen table, drawing an accusatory glance from Sammy. *What is about churches that make everyone so goddamn judgmental?* The table acted as a chopping block, prep table, and serving area for the seminary's kitchen help. It was lined from tip to tail with glassware and cutlery. Dominic and Sammy watched helplessly as the glassware rocked like upright eggshells, making its own morning music to greet the latecomers. They stood still, their eyes hungover from the hours before, as the glasses and the knives and the forks decided whether to come to life or rest quietly until lunch. Everything stilled. Sammy let go a self-chastising breath and walked on.

He led them through crooked halls lined with paintings of past bishops and long-dead saints, following the rumble of prayer and the ever-stronger smell of incense and burning candles. The church was wide, and reminded Dominic of a large plane, with the priests looking back from the cockpit over a congregation spread from wing-tip to wing-tip on both sides of the center aisle.

From a doorway, they could see that they were behind the pulpit. Rows of choirboys with Santa Maria collars ringing their necks sat stiffly, waiting for their next turn to sing. Dominic spotted a space between the last row of the choir and the wall. He motioned for Sammy to follow him. They crouched and ran like soldiers slipping past enemy sentries. Sammy stopped, turned to face the crucifix, and crossed himself.

The Mass was well underway by the time Dominic slipped into the DiPietro family pew, entering from the outside aisle. He spotted Leo and Christine sitting a few pews away. He made eye contact with Leo, who looked away quickly and focused on the altar. Sammy found his own place alongside some people Dominic had never met before. They greeted Sammy, which confused Dominic for a moment. He thought he knew everyone in his friend's life, but clearly the welder had secrets even from him.

Dominic slid past his sister's husband and nodded a greeting. His sister, Angelina, gave him a look of mild relief. She opened a space for Dominic between her and their mother.

"Mama, sorry to be so late," he whispered.

Mrs. DiPietro placed her hand on his and gave it a gentle squeeze. At his mother's movement, Tony's attention was drawn from the priest to his brother. The expression on his face was silent, but clear. It said something like *you miserable son of a bitch*.

Tony stood and accompanied his wife, who carried the newborn Aldo in her arms, and their young daughter to the baptismal font.

Angelina leaned over to Dominic and said, "You smell like a barroom toilet."

Dominic took a deep breath of himself and shrugged at his sister. "Celebrating last night."

"Celebrating what?"

"Can't tell you right now."

"Dominic," Angelina said, "what have you got going on?"

"Later," Dominic said. "I'll tell you later, after the christening."

Tony DiPietro and family stood tall by the baptismal font. Sal Constantine and his wife stood beside them. Godfather and mother. The priest rolled water from his hand onto the forehead of the newest member of the DiPietro family, Aldo Raphael DiPietro. He didn't cry. He was a DiPietro. DiPietros didn't cry about their situation, they dealt with it.

# 22

Hamilton Harbour is all that separates the cities of Hamilton and Burlington. It might as well be an ocean. Hamilton's side of it is a post-industrial Mechano set of belching fires and interconnected pipes and sewers punctuated by buildings large enough to hold a dozen space shuttles; Burlington's side is pastoral. Eighty-three houses dot the tree-lined shore, competing with each other for magnificence and style. Tony DiPietro's home was one of them.

Dominic sat in the enclosed patio area that overlooked the harbour, chain smoking du Mauriers, and sipping on colas in the hope that the sugar and caffeine would dull his urge for alcohol. It wasn't working. From his vantage point on the Burlington side, he could see Hamilton's harbour piers, the flaming towers of the city's two steel companies, and a latticework of pipe, rusted from rain and overuse, that connected the hard metal industry to the port that carried its products away. To Dominic, the view was only a distraction.

Jackie Constantine walked over, popping nuts into his mouth. He talked quickly. Staccato-like. He pumped words out of his mouth in counterpoint is the cashews he popped in.

"DiPietro, you look like shit," he said. A cashew flew from his hand. Dominic looked up from his drink but gave no further response.

"How's life in the office?" Another cashew. Still no response from Dominic.

"What's up? Paint fumes fried your brain?" Another cashew, and another. Two at a time. "I hear it does that, you know. Gets in your head. Real bad shit. Chemicals get in there, coat your grey cells blue. We have to get Sal to pass a by-law or something. You know, get you guys to work cleaner. Healthier, you know?"

"I'm fine." Dominic wished for a tumbler of rye in his cola.

"You wear a mask, one of those paper things, you know, when you're painting?"

"No, it's a respirator."

"That's good. Better." Another cashew. "You have to take care of yourself. Nice talking to you. I have to go work the room. Hustle up some bucks, you know? We need a quarter million bucks to get the mayor's job. You know?"

"I didn't know it was for sale. But what the fuck? It's Hamilton, so I guess anything is possible." Dominic downed the rest of his cola and went in search of a refill.


"I don't like this kitchen," Dominic's mother, Sophia, said. "I can't find anything. What does this do?" Sophia picked up a large aluminum cylinder from the granite countertop. She had yet to take her winter coat off. It was woolen and heavy.

"It's a pepper grinder," Rosemary said.

"Nice. Very nice. It must make the pepper taste much better than mine does."

"You don't need to do this Mama. I've hired a caterer. All the food we need is set up in the dining room."

"That's good. Very good. But I think my newest grandchild and his guests deserve a little real food. Where's the oven?"

"Mama, let me take your coat first. You'll be too hot." Tony's wife started to help Sophia out of her coat. The elder DiPietro said nothing, but looked around the kitchen, running her old eyes over the counters.

"Angelina, did she bring in the manicotti?"

A soft voice came from the entrance to the dining room. It was Angelina. "In the refrigerator, Mama, on the second shelf."

"And this refrigerator, where would it be? I must be going blind."

Rosemary guided Sophia to the far right of the kitchen. There were two refrigerators, one for food with an attached freezer, and another for wine and cold beverages. Sophia stood in front of them as if they were Easter Island statues.

"Let me help you, Mama," Rosemary said. "You sit over here, at the counter, and tell me what to do. I'll get the manicotti out of the fridge. How hot do you want the oven? Four hundred degrees?"

"Four twenty-five is better. But not too long. This was my grandmother's recipe and her wood stove was much hotter. Just twenty minutes to heat and it will be fine."

Rosemary took the trays of rolled pasta, ricotta cheese, and tomato sauce and placed them in the oven. She programmed the touchpad to four hundred degrees, the timer to thirty minutes. "There," she said. "Now, Mama, can I get you some wine? Maybe you want to come into the living room with me and talk to some of our friends?"

"No, I'll sit here. I am more comfortable. Too many people out there. Where's my Dominic?"

"I don't know, Mama. I didn't see him after he left the church. Angelina, is Dominic here?"

Angelina was laying out dishes and cutlery on the dining room table and supervising the caterers. She came into the kitchen. "I need hot water for the steam trays. Can I boil some water?"

"No need," Rosemary said. She walked over the sink, where a second tap sat askew to the main faucet. She pushed down on it. Steaming water poured out into the sink. "This is a hot tap. Boiling water is kept ready here all the time. Just fill up a pot and you're set."

"My Dominic, has anyone seen my Dominic?"

Angelina said, "Last time I saw him he was leaving the church. I told him to go home and clean up. He smelled like a garbage can."

"He works too hard, my Dominic. It's not good for him."

Rosemary shot a withering glare at Angelina, who only shrugged and filled a pot with boiling water.

"Tony sets a good example," Rosemary said. "Dominic knows that he has to work hard to make something of himself." She poured Sophia a glass of red wine and placed it in front of her.

"He's a sweet boy," Sophia said. She tried to take a sip of the wine, but her shaking hand caused the wine to spill.

Angelina took the glass from her. "You've got too much there, Mama." She turned her back to her mother and took a deep swig from the glass. She looked at the new quantity of wine in the glass and returned it to the counter in front of her mother. Rosemary used a dishcloth to wipe her mother-in-law's hands.

"He just needs to find something he can get excited about," Sophia said.

"Come on, Mama," Rosemary said. "Let's let everyone pay their respects to the proud grandmother."

Angelina followed behind them. She was carrying a steam tray half full of boiling water intended to keep the veal warm and at the ready.

"Let me take that," Rosemary said to Angelina. She took the steaming tray from Dominic's sister and placed it on the table. "Now," she said, "what was I going to put in it? Right, the veal. I'll find the caterers."

Sammy stalked the buffet table, loading up on whatever food he thought was pristine enough for his body. There were a lot of green leafy items on his plate. He sat down next to Dominic and offered him a zucchini stick. Dominic pushed the plate away.

"You're not eating," said Sammy.

"Doesn't look like you are either."

"If I haven't cooked it, I don't know what's in it, or how its been handled. How do I know those cretins washed their hands, or didn't drop anything on the floor. They spit on stuff when we're not looking, you know. I saw a show about it a couple of months ago. Half the food in here could have been handled by a guy with TB for all I know."

"This is Tony's house. I wouldn't wanna be the caterer that got one of his guests sick." Sammy took another look at the food and set the plate on the floor.

Tony emerged from another room. Dominic stood up from his chair and wobbled a bit. He leaned on Sammy for support.

"Maybe you better rethink this. Monday morning's not that far away."

Dominic ignored him and moved towards the centre of the room. He stumbled a bit through the maze of well-wishers. Tony saw him coming but maintained his public face.

"There's my Dominic," Sophia said. She was holding onto Angelina's arm. She came over to Dominic and gave him a hug. "How long have you been here? Why you don't come and see your mother as soon as you get here?"

"Only a few minutes, Mama." Dominic was struggling to be polite. "You're looking good. Is that a new dress?"

"Rosemary made me buy it. She thinks I need new things. But I don't like this."

"It's nice, Mama. You should like it."

Tony came up to Dominic, Angelina, and his mother in the centre of the living room. A hundred or more extended family, friends, and employees of City-Wide surrounded them, scattered throughout the house. Aldo remained passive in his playpen, tired from the attention.

"You can't get yourself cleaned up for my son's christening?" Tony said to Dominic.

"We need to talk, Tony."

"If it's important, it can wait until Monday. I'm here now for my guests."

"Now, Tony. I have to talk with you. Now." Dominic raised his voice. Tony stared back at him.

"Not now. I got business to take care of." His words shut Dominic down as surely as if he'd used the back of his hand. "Ladies and gentlemen. Please, gather around." Tony raised his arm and waved it in the air. The attention of his guests was drawn to the centre of the room. Leo Deluca and his wife Christine appeared from the back of the crowd. Leo looked briefly over at Dominic then focused his attention on Tony.

"Thank you, all of you, for coming here today. Rosemary and I are very fortunate to call everyone in this house our friends and part of our very dear family. You've made this day very special. And even though Aldo won't remember a thing about today, I can assure you that your presence here and at his christening will be carried forward with him all his life.

"Since this is my house, and we're all gathered here enjoying the fine food ..." Rosemary pointed to Sophia. "And, oh yes, my mother's manicotti, which made me the man I am today ..." Tony patted his stomach. "I want to talk to you about the future of the city across the harbour.

"Most of you live in Hamilton. I was born there and all of my family, except me, still lives there. I own and operate six collision centres within its borders. I owe the city my family, my heritage, and my future. That's why I'm going to ask you today to help Sal Constantine become the next mayor of Hamilton."

Polite applause rumbled through the house, muffled and hesitant, as if Tony's guests were unsure whether the political message was going to go on much longer.

"Friends," Tony continued, "family, I'd like to introduce you to Councillor Sal Constantine, the next mayor of Hamilton."

The applause got a little louder.

"Thank you," Constantine said. He crossed his hands. Tony stood beside him, beaming like the owner of a winning racehorse. "As a politician, I never turn down a chance to speak, but this is the first time I've been the guest speaker at a christening. Good thing Tony's not Jewish. I don't know what I'd say if this were a briss."

The laughter, like the applause, was polite and short. Constantine could judge the mood.

"Most of you know my family's deep and long-held love for the city of Hamilton. In many ways, the Constantines are not that different from the DiPietros. My old friend Angelo came to me about thirty years ago and told me he wanted to start a body shop business. I told him he was crazy, but he wouldn't listen. Stubbornness seems to run in both our families.

"Of course the Constantines were known in Hamilton as jewellers, not lawyers. I fell pretty far from my family tree. Not like Tony. But there is one difference between us, and it's something I have to rectify. If I run for mayor, and if I win, Tony, you have to promise me that you'll move back to Hamilton and stop building your dreams out here in the suburbs."

Laughter and applause rolled through house. Tony smiled and nodded.

"In a few weeks, I intend to announce my candidacy for mayor. The campaign will be long and expensive. I hope I can count on your support. Thank you."

The applause was louder, whether out of appreciation for the speech or its termination, it was hard to tell. The Constantines began working the room, asking the harder questions of how much money the campaign could count on 'and when they would get it. As the group dispersed, Dominic resumed his path towards Tony, nearly bowling over his sister Angelina in the process.

"Let's not have any trouble," Angelina said. "Not today."

"No trouble, Angie." Dominic gave her a kiss on the cheek. "Just some good news. I'm not going to be working at City-Wide anymore."

Tony looked hard at him. "What?"

"Yeah, me and Sammy, a couple of other guys, we're starting a car restoration shop. You know, old cars, fancy cars. We're gonna rebuild them."

"You've lost your fucking mind," Tony said.

"No, Tony, I've found my mind. I told you: I want to paint cars, not push paper." Dominic set his hand on Tony's chest. Tony pushed it away.

"This is our family business. You can't just leave it."

"Don't give me that line of crap. This is your business, and everyone else in the family is here to serve you." Dominic's voice was growing louder. The party noise in the living room, which had begun to build after the speech, lowered again.

Angelina moved closer to Tony. "That's not fair, Dominic. You don't know what you're saying."

"I do know what I'm saying. You don't have to work for this asshole. You get to suck off the teat and do nothing for it. What's that pay you? Thirty thousand a year? Fifty? What do you do for it? Have you ever actually gone to work?"

Tony stepped between Angelina and Dominic. "You leave your sister out of this. You got a problem, you deal with me."

"Oh, I got a problem, alright. And I am doing something about it. I quit."

Sal Constantine looked over at Dominic and Tony. His eyes urged Tony to postpone the family feud. Tony ignored them.

"Our father started this business with ten dollars in his pocket," he said, pointing his finger in Dominic's face. "He used it to feed and clothe us. Now we do the same, for our children. Maybe if you'd grow up and start a family of your own, then you'd understand."

"I understand, Tony. I understand everything. I'm no more than an employee to you. All of us, we're all just employees of the great Tony DiPietro. The people in this room, all of us, our backs are broken from bending over to kiss your ass."

Tony stepped closer to Dominic. "So you and your little boy-

152

friends," he glanced at Sammy, "you gonna put your pennies together and start painting cars? You think it's like selling lemonade on a street corner, do you? Well, you know nothing. Absolutely fucking nothing."

"We know enough."

"You'll be broke before you even open the door. Hell, you're broke now."

"Papa started with ten bucks."

"You're not our father. You haven't got his brains or his work ethic. You're just a drunk who needs his big brother to take care of him."

"I don't need you. I don't need anyone."

Leo came over and took Dominic's arm. "Dominic, calm down."

Dominic shook off Leo's grip. Tony stared at him, breathing hard. "Give this up, Dominic. Forget about this."

"Like we all forgot about how you stole the business from Dad and me?"

"All you had to do was write the big check, Dominic, and you could have had your piece of the business."

"And I'd still be stuck with you. Not a fucking chance."

"Come on, Dominic." Leo said. "Let me take you home."

Dominic pushed Leo aside and addressed the room. "I want everyone here to know that you robbed me, you robbed Mom, you robbed us all. You didn't use a gun. You did it with your lawyers, like this asshole Constantine." He pointed at the mayoral candidate. "All of them. They're still sitting here sucking at your tit, Tony. You paid them off to look the other way and sold your family into slavery with you as our fucking master."

"Get out of my house." Tony pushed Dominic with both hands, more as a gesture of power than force. Dominic stumbled backward towards the buffet table. He tripped over an area rug and landed on his backside. Grabbing the buffet table for support, he pulled himself up. The top of the table was wet, slick with olive oil from a tray

153

of salad. The hand that held the weight of his body slipped, his arm caught the water-filled steam tray and sent it flying off the table.

The room was silent as the aluminum tray tumbled off the table and banged mercilessly on the hardwood floor. Boiling water splashed. Dominic felt the burning heat on his hand as spray from the spill leapt back at him. Then there was a wail.

Aldo — quiet submissive Aldo — got caught in the flood from the falling steam tray. He screamed. Then Angelina and Sophia screamed. Rosemary left her mother-in-law's arm and dove for Aldo. Boiling water soaked the back of his clothes. She ripped them off him while he continued to wail and cry. Guests from all around the house ran towards Aldo's shrieking cries. Muffled shouts filled the halls. Rosemary grabbed her baby and ran into the kitchen.

"Call 911," a voice said.

"No, don't," said another voice. "Get him in a car and over to emergency."

"I ... I'm sorry..." Dominic pleaded. He stood by the table, his feet locked.

Tony ran at Dominic, his hands reaching for his brother's neck. Constantine and Jackie stepped between the two brothers.

"Get out of here, Dominic," Al said.

Tony tried to push his way through them. "Let me go! I'm gonna kill him. I'm gonna break every bone in his body and grind him up for fertilizer."

Sammy pulled Dominic away. The elder Constantine turned to him. "I said get of here, now." He grabbed Tony by the shoulders. "You do nothing. You hear me?"

"I want him dead."

Constantine talked to Tony with a tone of authority that Dominic had not heard from anyone but his father. "Get him out of your life, now. Put as much distance between you and your brother as possible. But if you hurt him, you hurt me. You'll kill this campaign before we ever get it started."

Over Constantine's shoulder, Tony shouted at Dominic, "Get the fuck out of my house, Dominic. Get out of City-Wide. Get out of Hamilton. I don't want to ever see your face again." He followed his wife into the kitchen.

Sammy led Dominic out of the house. Jackie caught them before the got through the front door. "If you ever so much as breathe in the direction of my uncle or Tony," he said, his breath heavy with adrenaline, "your life won't be worth shit."

# 23

Dominic woke to the taste of cigarette butts coating the inside of his mouth and a headache that wrapped around his skull like a band of steel. He opened his eyes, the light assaulting his pupils and drawing the steel band tighter about his head. Sammy had brought him home to the Brampton Street shop after the reception at Tony's, this much he remembered. And Aldo, he remembered Aldo wailing, the pain of the boiling water that splashed onto his back.

Dominic sat up on his couch and buried his head in his hands. Nothing would loosen the grip of his headache.

"How are you feeling? I thought you were going to puke." It was Sammy.

"I'd feel better if I did. How's Aldo?"

"He'll be okay. I called your sister after we got back. His cotton sleeper had a dual effect. It kept some of the heat from the water off his skin, but it also kept what heat there was on his skin longer. It looks like second degree burns."

"What does that mean?"

"It means he'll be in pain for a while and there may be some long-term scarring. Plastic surgery could help, later, if it's necessary."

Dominic cried into his hands. "Jesus, what have I done?"

"It's not your fault. Tony pushed you down. You were just getting up off the ground and you slipped."

"I went there looking for trouble with Tony. I wanted a confrontation."

"Well, you got that, alright." Sammy got up from his chair and came over to Dominic. He offered him a cigarette.

"Thanks. But what I really need is an Advil, a bucket of them. Do you mind? They're in washroom, under the sink."

Sammy left the room and came back with the pain killers, a glass of water and a forty-ounce bottle of Smirnoff Vodka. "What's with this?" He said, holding out the bottle. Dominic took the Advil and water from his other hand.

"My toolbox was full."

Sammy rolled the bottle in his hand and looked carefully at the label. "I'm pouring it down the sink. You got a lot of work to do."

"I guess I do now. There's no going back to Tony's now."

"Oh, you'd be right about that."

"But I should go by, just to see how Aldo's doing."

"I wouldn't be heading down to the hospital. Stay away, for now. Talk to your sister if you want to find out how Aldo's holding up, but keep away from Tony. You've wounded that dog pretty good. He'll bite the first chance he gets."

A loud noise came from the garage. Dominic could feel the band tightening with every echo.

"Who's working in there at this time of night?" It was still Sunday, about nine o'clock, but the March night was as black as Dominic's mood.

"Gino brought Andy over to look at the car. I guess they're working on it."

Dominic stood up slowly, as if every movement tightened the band around his head a bit more. "At least that's some good news. I should go meet him."

"Go on," Sammy said. "You'll get quite a kick out of our new mechanic."

Gino had pried the hood off the Mustang after Sammy discon-
nected a few of the mechanical parts that were impeding its movement. He held a large flashlight over the open engine area so that
Andy, the freelance mechanic, could get a better look.

"What do you think?"

"Well, once we pull it out, take it apart and put it back together
again, you've either got yourself one beauty of a 289-cubic-inch
Ford engine, or a 600-pound piece of cast iron."

Dominic walked into the garage bay, stepping gingerly toward
the Mustang. The mechanic was bent over the front quarter-panel;
all Dominic could see of him was a pair of wide-leg jeans, worn
skateboarder style and giving no indication as to the wearer's body
shape or size.

"Hey, Dominic," Gino said. "Glad to see you're up and around."
As he turned, Gino pulled the flashlight away from the Mustang's
engine.

"Give me some light down here," the mechanic said.

"Oh, Dominic, this is Andy Montecalvo, the mechanic I told you
about."

Dominic came closer to the car, "Yeah, so I heard. I wanted to
meet —"

The mechanic rose up from the car. Medusa dreadlocks covered
her head. Andy was a woman, with small and striking features. She
used the back of her hand to wipe the dreadlocks from her face,
revealing eyes that were as black as her hair, strong and intense. She
looked like she knew everything there was to know about this car.
She extended her hand. It was covered in harbour mud.

"Hi. I'm Adrienne Montecalvo. But my friends call me Andy."

"Shit," Dominic said. He shook her hand, cautiously. She
squeezed it hard. Her hands were small but had the strength of
someone who worked with them every day.

"Gino didn't tell you?" she said.

"No. He ... neglected to fill me in on a few important details."

Gino was defensive. "Hey, I thought it might prejudice you."

"You thought right," Dominic said, wanting to be angry but not finding the strength. "I've never met a woman who knew a thing about cars."

Andy wiped her hands on a rag. "I've been fixing cars and rebuilding engines since my daddy was driving pro-stock at Cayuga."

"Pro-stock?"

"That's right. He was just a ride away from the Winston Cup circuit. I've been around hot grease and wrenches since I was old enough to hold a screwdriver."

The hot grease comment made Dominic queasy. He heard Aldo screaming in his ear. The band around his head tightened. He had no energy to argue. "The job pays lousy, if at all, and when you do get paid it's a share of the revenue. If we sell this thing."

"Oh, you'll sell it," Andy said, looking back at the car. "You'll sell this car for a boatload of money when I'm done with it."

"You can get it running?" Dominic asked.

"I think so. Like I said, I won't know for sure until we haul the power train out and take it all apart." Andy shook her head and smiled. There was a sense of mischief in her eyes. "When Gino told me you dragged it out the harbour, after I stopped laughing all I could think of is that there is gonna be dirt in places we never thought possible."

Dominic walked over to the car. "I figure we gotta strip it the bone, rebuild it piece-by-piece, like it was brand new from the factory."

Andy followed him step for step. She reached into Dominic's top pocket and snatched his pack of cigarettes, lighting one with a Zippo she had drawn from the hip pocket of her overalls.

"That's the only way," she told him. "We're gonna have to disassemble and clean every part before we put it back together."

The body man and the mechanic paced around the car like two surgeons discussing a seriously ill patient. Neither one could save the car's life without the other. The pair of them knew it.

"It's the organic materials that have me the most concerned," said Dominic. "The hoses, high tension wires, shit like that."

"Don't worry about 'em," Andy said. "They won't be worth crap. It was underwater for what, twenty-five years? They'll all have to be replaced. If it's not made of steel, it'll be worthless."

Dominic waved Gino and Sammy over to the car. They had been standing back, watching the body man and the mechanic dance around their respective roles.

"I suppose you told your friend how we're paying the bills around here?" Dominic asked.

"Kinda," Gino said. "Well, yes, I told her."

Dominic frowned. Another flaw in his plan. He hadn't figured on this many people being involved in the underside of his business. But he resigned himself to the fact that he was so far over his head that if it took a legion of mechanics to drag him out he was going to use them. "What do you know about this car?" he said.

Andy perched herself on a workbench. She was eye-to-eye with the men in the garage now, but her feet dangled off the floor.

"The '64 ½ Mustang is the car that revolutionized the automotive business. Lee Iacocca, the guy who's heading up Chrysler right now, pretty near invented this car to save Ford from bankruptcy."

"No shit," Gino said.

"You see," Andy said, "even though it's called a Mustang, it's really just a Ford Fairlane with a groovier body and engine."

"A shitty little suburban Fairlane," said Dominic. "The perfect car for the soccer mom of the sixties."

"That's right. Iacocca convinced Ford that they should be building more than one car on a frame. He told them it would be cheaper and they could get more and different cars to market faster. What you have here isn't just car. It isn't even a great car. It's like finding Lucy in Africa, or the Rosetta Stone. This is the mother of all cars. There isn't a vehicle on the road that doesn't owe part of its existence to Lee Iacocca and this '64 ½ Mustang."

"How'd you get to know all this?" Sammy said.

"Just interested. Plus I did some time a few years ago at the Ford plant in Oakville. Building Crown Vics. The money was good, but you can only install the engine component in the same car every day for so long. I need a little more challenge in my life."

"This should answer that calling." Dominic said.

"You bet. Give me a wrench and let's get to work."

The restoration of the Mustang was an exercise in patience unlike Dominic had ever experienced. Vinnie took on the role of chronologist, examining each piece of the car as Dominic and Sammy extracted them. Gino handled the cleaning, bathing each part in water, then etching each piece first in muriatic acid, next in alcohol, before passing them off to Sammy for labelling and storage. It was as if they were taking apart a completed jigsaw puzzle and examining each piece to ensure that it would stand up to scrutiny once the whole thing was put back together. Andy took charge of the power train, working with Gino to clean the parts when they were ready. She had brought with her a large tabletop magnifying glass, with a fluorescent lamp ringing the exterior. She used it to examine every engine part with a health inspector's eye for dirt and corrosion. She tossed as many parts as she kept.

Dominic felt the financial weight of the discards with a poor man's hand. "This looks good enough to me." He was holding the remains of a four-barrel carburetor that looked like a rusted salad of iron and aluminum. "Can't we just take some steel wool to it?"

Andy lifted her eyes from the magnifying glass and glared at him. "That might work for the body, but this engine is as rare as the whole car. It's a high-performance V-8 that runs at two hundred and seventy-one horses out of the factory. With a little polishing of the valves, I'm going to get her up to two eighty-five, maybe three hundred. That means the fuel and air mixture has to fry at just the right temperature and ratios." She grabbed a piece of the salad from his hand.

"See this?" She shoved the four-inch-long piece under the magnifying glass. Dominic could see craters and pock marks on the surface of the steel as if an Apollo astronaut had brought it back from the moon.

"Looks like it just needs a good sanding."

"Good sanding? You are not listening to me." She poked him in the chest. "This is not some body part that you can just sand, mask, and paint to cover up its flaws. It's an integral piece of high-octane machinery that no one has figured out how to make better in twenty-seven years. If we do this your way this engine will be lucky to turn over. I need new parts, or refurbished parts. At worst, we'll have to send these to a place I know in St. Catharines. There's a guy there who will rebuild whatever we need."

The balance of the evening was a concert of blowtorches and scraped knuckles as the chop shop team pulled apart the body of their beast from the harbour. This one, unlike any other of their work, became an immediate labour of love; each piece was cleaned, inspected, and labelled for re-assembly.

Some of the parts were beyond hope. The seat cushions were rotted, so Vinnie volunteered a marine upholsterer to reconstruct them. All the hard components, engine parts, body mouldings, frame, and transmission, had to be sandblasted clean. Sammy had an idea to sneak the parts into the steel company and use some of the machinery that was reserved for specialty metals and finishes. Andy handed Dominic a list of what would have to be replaced. She estimated the cost of replacement parts at six to eight thousand dollars. Dominic figured that the Mustang would cost at least fifteen grand all in. He was guessing at the cost of rechroming the bumpers and rebuilding the convertible top. His crew of mechanics and help were draining his meagre cash reserves with every cry of *send it out, we need to rent this,* and *we have to buy a whole lot of that.* The rest of his money was either somewhere in Nastasi's pocket, as a paid-off debt, or in Magilla's, as a negative in his ledger of losses yet to covered.

# 24

The silver Mercedes S500, with the vanity plate HITFIXER, pulled into a low-lying industrial plaza on Hamilton's east side. From behind the wheel, Tony could see the familiar snakes-and-ladders pipe work of the soap factory that, over the years, had grown to surround the plaza in an iron jungle. A palate of grays and browns punctuated only by passing trucks bearing corporate colours and mechanical names, each fuelled the gray air with every shift of their diesel-powered transmissions. Tony bypassed the parking stalls at the front of the plaza, driving around to the back instead. Past a dozen garbage dumpsters, four or five trucks backed into loading docks, scattered wooden pallets and discarded cardboard boxes and garbage, he navigated the Mercedes into a parking space alongside a large unmarked tractor trailer.

Tony killed the car's engine and let is sit quiet and still, like him, unmoved by the traffic noise swirling around him.

From the passenger seat beside him, he opened a small leather portfolio. It was oxblood red and sufficiently impractical to carry anything but a notepad, a Cross pen, and a chequebook — the commercial variety with pairs of cheques and perforated stubs for the bean counters. The pen was twenty-four karat gold and engraved with his father's name: Angelo Sebastian DiPietro. He tucked the leather portfolio under his arm and got out of the vehicle.

He followed the line of trailers to a set of concrete stairs that led to a locked steel door. Tony pressed a buzzer and turned his face upwards. There was a small video camera secured to the exterior wall near the roofline. Tony heard a loud click and opened the door.

A wall of soft drink cases greeted him. It created a path that he followed like a mouse towards the cheese. Behind a large, ornately carved desk, pair of black telephones, and a large ashtray waited Alfonso "The Lip" Criminisi.

Hamilton's mob boss sat at his desk — elegant, regal and rectangular — like it should be, and large like he demanded it be, as if he had to have a working stage large enough to both protect the body behind it and, if necessary, hide one.

"Marconi owned this desk," Criminisi told Tony. As he spoke, he passed his hands along the desk's surface, following its trim edges with his fingers. "Before he sent that first telegraph message across the Atlantic, he conceived of the whole process right here." He pointed down at the desktop with an antique letter opener. "And later, he used *this* to stab his wife's lover. Put it through his neck like that son of a bitch was a chicken." Criminisi demonstrated Marconi's skill with twist of his own arthritic hand.

"That's how he ended up in jail," he told Tony, "and why I bought this desk. It reminds me that even the smartest Italians have more strength in their balls than in their brains." He emphasized the point by grabbing his groin. "Passion is our ruler."

Spagnoli and Nastasi, who had both heard the story many times before, shared a leather couch across from the desk. Spagnoli looked relaxed, his arm across the back of the sofa. His legs would have been up on a stool, if such a stray piece of furniture could be found in the cluttered office. In the absence of a proper footstool, he'd stacked four flats of Coca-Cola on top of one another. He occupied himself for the duration of his boss's speech by admiring the shine on his loafers. Nastasi perched himself on the opposite edge of the couch. There was enough room between them for another body, to lie prone, either in repose or death.

Criminisi stood up to greet Tony. "Antonio. To what do I owe the pleasure of your company?"

Tony placed his portfolio on the desk and stood off to one side. "It's that time of the month."

Criminisi opened the portfolio. "Yes. So it is." He removed several stacks of hundred and fifty dollar bills, each wrapped in a rubber band. An accounting had been jotted on a stray piece of paper. Ignoring the cash, Criminisi scanned the accounting. "A good month, too. I needed it."

Tony smiled for a moment. "Same as always."

Nastasi pretended as best he could to follow along, his eyes more on the cash than his ears were tuned to the conversation.

The Lip opened a drawer in his desk and slid the cash inside it, placing the accounting on top. Before closing the drawer, he removed a banded stack of hundreds and handed them back to Tony.

"For Aldo," he said. "I am sorry that I was unable to attend his christening."

Tony took the bills and put them back in the portfolio. "Thank you. But, of course, it would have been inappropriate."

"Yes, I understand. I hope it went well?"

Tony grimaced, then related the story of Aldo's accident, emphasizing Dominic's responsibility. "Constantine had to stop me from killing him on the spot."

Criminisi listened, giving away little emotion during Tony's story.

"Please, Antonio, sit."

Tony sat between Spagnoli and the Romanian.

Criminisi came around to the front of the desk, his hands in his pockets. "I had truly hoped that we could maintain a sense of cordiality between you and Dominic. I don't like family feuds."

"There is no feud," Tony said. "It's over. He's your problem now."

Criminisi pointed at Nastasi, then at a bookcase. The Romanian got up and opened a door in the bookcase, withdrawing a bottle of scotch. He put out four shot glasses and filled each one.

"A Scotsman may have invented scotch, but an Italian perfected it," Criminisi said. "Salute." He raised his glass. "Salute," they said in unison, and drank back the shots.

Nastasi refilled the glasses. "He thinks everything was invented by Italians."

"Italy is the greatest country in the world," Criminisi said. "You Romanians even stole the name of your country from us." He laughed. "Oh, I correct myself. When we conquered your country, centuries ago, we named it after ourselves."

"Thank you, but I should go." Tony said.

"Please stay. Just for a few more minutes. Your family is in crisis, Antonio. Ignoring it won't help. But, relaxing for a few moments, with friends, may at least lighten your burdens." Criminisi picked up the bottle of J&B and topped up all the glasses. "You see, it used to be that all scotch was single malt, a drink that many today consider exceptional. But years ago, single malt scotch could either be putrid or wonderful, you could never tell. Consistency, as you know, Antonio, is the key to long-term success.

"It took an Italian by the name of Giacomo Justerini to come up with the idea of blending different kinds of scotches to make a good scotch a great scotch, and to make every bottle of the same quality. Justerini was a liqueur maker. His specialty was mixing many types alcohols and flavourings to make fine liqueurs. He learned his trade at the knee of his uncle, a liqueur maker of some renown from Genoa. Justerini and brought this experience to London in the mid-seventeen hundreds.

Tony held onto his empty glass.

"You don't believe me, do you?"

"It's not that," Tony said. "I just never thought about it. Goes to prove that Italians are everywhere."

Criminisi's face grew expansive, his eyes delighting in his subject.

166

"Justerini, of course, was inflicted by the sickness that plagues all Italians: passion. Like Marconi who used that letter opener to kill his wife's lover, Justerini followed an opera singer from Milan to London, chasing love like a dog in heat. And poor, oh how he was poor! His only wealth was that which he stole from his uncle: a book of secret liqueur recipes."

"Then you can let Dominic know that he has an Italian to thank for his hangovers."

"Oh, yes. Because our Italian liqueur maker Mr. Justerini went into partnership with a British fellow by the name of Brooks, and the rest is history. We're drinking Justerini and Brooks's scotch, J&B."

"No shit," said Spagnoli.

"Italians have been changing the world for centuries. Some you know, like Columbus, some you do not, like Justerini. All of them different but all the same in one way." Criminisi paused. "They all had partners. Some were kings, some were queens, some were peasants with access to a good still, but all of them had partners. We are partners, you and I. So you must remember, I will never let you down."

"I know that," Tony said.

Criminisi pushed himself away from the desk. "Then why do you fight with your brother? What is this between you two? Why could you not bring him into your business as a partner, with us, rather than forcing me to recruit him, like he was one of Bela's refugees?"

"The less Dominic knows about my business, the better."

Criminisi shook his hand, as if swatting a fly. "So foolish, but I respect your decision. Still, none of this would have had to happen had you agreed to do the work."

"Not possible and you know it. The risks are too great. City-Wide can't be associated with hot cars. A discarded, no-good brother, yes. But not my company."

"You are right," Criminisi said. "I miss the days when ours was more of a family business. And me? I have no children to hand all this over to." Criminisi looked at his desk like he was trying to imagine pictures of the family he never had. "I was hoping for more from you."

"Dominic is yours to deal with now. Use him as you see fit, just keep him away from me."

Spagnoli, sipping on the scotch like it was rubbing alcohol, said, "We'll keep him busy. In a couple of weeks, he'll be painting more cars in a hour than you had him doing in day."

"Good luck with that," Tony said. "I wish I could see it." He got up from the couch. "I really do have to go. I'm planning a fundraiser for Constantine."

"You won't be getting a cheque from me." Criminisi said. "An Italian in the mayor's office is a good thing, but Constantine? No. That is too high a price."

"This city's gotta grow up and embrace its heritage," Tony said. "Italians built this city. We paved the roads, put up the houses, dug the sewer lines. Most everything that everyone takes for granted came off the back of some poor *paisan* like us. But do we elect an Italian mayor, ever? No. We'll elect a WASP in a heartbeat. We'll elect a Jamaican immigrant as our representative in government and even name an expressway after him, but where's DiPietro Highway, or Angostino Boulevard? Nowhere. Not even a goddamn Constantine Crescent! Sometimes I feel like I know what it would have been like being some kind of sharecropper in Alabama. It's about time Italians in this town got some respect!"

"Respect comes first from respecting ourselves," Criminisi said. "Constantine, I think, is a Catholic of convenience and a fraud. He hasn't changed one iota since his days as a defence lawyer. Sure, he'll get his client off. But at what price? That con artist should have enough money now to buy the mayor's office."

"Possibly," Tony said. "But we live in a democracy. People still have to vote for him. Italians, Anglos, Portuguese, everyone."

"You don't have to worry about me," Criminisi said. "Can't vote. Your Canadian government has yet to grace me with the privilege of citizenship."

"All it takes is a little test," Tony said.

"Italian history, I know. But Canadian? Damned if I'm gonna take the time to study for an exam. Stopped doing that the day I dropped out of school, in the seventh grade." Nastasi, himself not even listed as a legal immigrant, said, "We could always find someone to take the test for you."

Criminisi pretended to inspect his letter opener. "True. But if they failed, I could not take the embarrassment. Nor, I suspect, could they."

"Then I'll just consider you a consultant to the campaign, though not a positive one." Tony said. He walked towards the door. "Alfons, did Justerini get the girl? You know, the opera singer?"

"In a fashion," Criminisi said, tapping the rim of his glass with the letter opener. "She spurned his affections for many years, until he prepared for her a special liqueur blended from rare ingredients and of his own secret recipe."

"And they lived happily ever after," Tony said.

"No, that would not be the way of an Italian man," Criminisi said. "I thought you would know this. The liqueur was both addictive and poisonous. The object of his affection was dead before she finished the bottle."

"Italians," Nastasi grumbled. "Everything has to be fucking opera."

After Tony left, Criminisi poured himself another shot of J&B. "We need to keep a closer watch now, on both of these DiPietros. Teddy, assign someone to Antonio. Bela, let you and I set up a little test for young Dominic. I want to make sure he's on our side."

"Sure, boss," the Romanian replied.

"Start by slowing down the flow of cars to our little business with him. Now that's he's made his bed without Tony, let's see how much he really needs us."

# 25

The Barton Street coffee shop was filled with smoke. The air was rich with nicotine. It saturated the donuts and would, no doubt, be responsible for early addictions in twelve-year-olds who got their first taste of the chemical inside a honey dip. That's likely where Dominic got his first hit, but his addictions evolved through the years. It started with colas, packed with sugar and caffeine. He had his first cigarette at the age of ten; he stole it from the pack he knew his brother kept in the pocket of his leather bomber jacket. Dominic remembered loving the intoxicating aroma of old leather and smoke and the secret scent of sex that his brother came home with after a Saturday night. The mélange of perfume, sweat, and ingrained smoke fired his imagination: what was it like to be twenty-one, driving your own car, the girls all wanting a piece of you?

He'd left the colas behind, except as mixer, but brought the cigarettes along with him for life. He added alcohol before he reached his teens. Picking the lock to his father's liquor cabinet, clearing up the dregs of an evening's adult partying, swigging stale gin and tonics, old Campari and sodas, and sneaking shots of Canadian Club before the adults rose in the morning. "Such a good boy," his mother would tell him. "You started cleaning up for us." She'd give him five dollars, or, when times were better, ten. He'd trade the bills for beer from a neighbour's older brother down the street.

Painkillers came soon after he started working at his brother's shop. He was working on a fender, trying to pull out a dent when he rocked the car so hard it slipped off its supporting stanchions. The car rolled over on his right shoulder, crushing it. Four months in a cast, another year in physiotherapy, none of which helped him as much as the Tylenol 3's, then the aspirins with codeine, then, as an everyday fix, Advils — sugar coated like Smarties. They were as constant in his pocket as a pack of cigarettes and better than booze when it came to putting distance between Dominic and what pained him.

He'd promised himself that he'd keep away from alcohol until after the Mustang was restored. It wasn't the need for a clear head to complete the task that motivated him — he'd worked on hundreds of cars with more booze in his blood than would be legal for him to drive. No, it was Aldo. Tiny screaming Aldo.

The Advils kept him company this morning and this time the pain was real. He'd slept off the night after Andy, Sammy, and Gino left the body shop. The steel band around his head hadn't let up much and the March morning was especially bright. The sun reflected off the ice and snow with aching clarity. A pair of mirrored aviator sunglasses and a handful of sugar-coated acetaminophens guarded what was left of his spirit.

When Dominic entered the coffee shop, Magilla was in his usual spot, occupying a pair of stools, hunched over a cup of coffee and the sports sections of that morning's *Hamilton Spectator* and *USA Today*. Dominic sat beside him and saw that he was comparing betting lines and point spreads. A waitress in a uniform that needed pressing approached him from the other side of the counter.

"What can I get you?" she said. Her hair was in a net and a paper tiara-like cone stuck out of the top of her head. It had the shop's name and logo on it.

"Coffee, black, and two honey dips," Dominic said. Magilla looked over at him. His head looked like Dominic's felt — fat, puffy, and ready to burst. "And a double-double for my friend here."

"What's your pleasure?" Magilla said, wiping his nose with the back of his index finger.

"A yard on the Bulls tonight, three on the Bucks tomorrow, and Wednesday … what's on Wednesday?"

Magilla scanned the *USA Today*. "Lakers/Kings, Knicks/Celtics, and the Magic are at home against the Heat."

Dominic gave up a pensive frown.

"I'll go a yard each on the home teams."

"That's six grand, not including the action you called in on the Leafs. I didn't know the Romanian was treating you that good?"

"Could be better, but you know that."

"Doesn't matter to me, DiPietro. Your credit's good. Criminisi's guaranteed it. Bet the house on the colour of the next car coming around the corner if you want." Magilla opened his notebook to the day's date and wrote down Dominic's action.

Dominic stopped him. "No. Cancel that."

Magilla peered at him through eyes thick with a fatty sheen. "You fucking with me?"

"No. I'm out of the betting business, for now."

"There goes the money for my Florida vacation. What'd you do, find God?"

The waitress put a cup of black coffee down in front of Dominic along with two donuts glistening in a sugar glaze. Dominic took a large bite out of one of them while pouring sugar into his coffee from a dispenser on the counter. It took about a minute for enough sugar to come out of the container to satisfy Dominic.

"Careful kid," Magilla said. "Don't want you going diabetic on me."

"I need more cars."

"I know you do. You take another run of bad luck like you did last month and you're gonna need to chop up the whole goddamn Ford plant to get even."

"That's personal. The cars are business. I got people to pay and I'm trying to raise as much cash as I can."

"Then it's the Romanian you should be talking to, not me."

"I can't stand that thug, and I don't trust him." The sugar and caffeine were starting to hit Dominic's brain. He could feel himself beginning to breathe again. "He's shaking me down, you know. Two hundred dollars a car. Asking him for more cars would be like sticking a gun to my own head."

"He won't be very happy, you not going through him about that part of the business."

"He's only happy when he's laying a hurt on somebody. I'll worry about him later."

"Alright. I'll do what I can to get a message to Criminisi for you."

"Tell you what. Try to make it sound like Criminisi's idea, or even your idea. Tell him I'm over my head with you and need more cars to get out of it."

"That would be the truth."

"The best lies are."

"I'll do what I can. But what's this all about? How are you going to be able to handle the work and everything?"

"I'm not working for Tony anymore. The Brampton Street shop's got my full-time attention."

Magilla lit a cigarette. It looked like a toothpick in his sausage-sized fingers. "That's not good news."

"It's done. Nothing to go back to." Dominic tossed back the rest of his coffee. The donuts weren't looking that good anymore.

"Another cup, hon?" the waitress said.

"Yeah. To go."

Magilla flicked ash onto the floor. "I'll do what I can, but no guarantees."

"Since when did you ever give guarantees?" The waitress brought over the take-out coffee. Dominic left her a five-dollar bill.

"You just gonna leave those?" Magilla said, looking at the donuts with the kind of gaze most men reserve for naked women. Dominic didn't answer him. He had another commitment to make for the Mustang's restoration.

The woman wore the same bedraggled dress she'd had on the first time Dominic had visited the King Street insurance office. He remembered it because it seemed so out of place. She was orderly, her life was stacked in neat little rows. Her dishevelled dress was out of context, but, then again, so was Dominic.

"Louie's ... occupied," she said. "You can take a seat. He shouldn't be much longer. You want a cup of coffee or something? There's a machine just over there." She pointed to vending machine, the same kind that dropped cups covered in poker hands at his brother's place.

The office had a quiet hum, that mirrored the slow pace of steady work. All the desks were occupied except Louie's. An old man slept sitting up behind one of them. A steady stream of smoke rose from a lit cigarette sitting in the ashtray on his desk. A door opened and Louie appeared. He carried a copy of the *Hamilton Spectator*, rolled up tight like a police baton.

"Dominic," he said. "What brings you here? Haven't had an accident or nothing, I hope?"

"I was hoping you could help me with something."

"Sit down. What can I do for you?" Louie tossed the rolled newspaper onto the corner of his desk.

"It's a long story, but I need some ownership papers for a car."

"Give me the *Reader's Digest* version."

"I've come into possession of an old car, a Mustang."

Louie flipped open a notepad and clicked a pen. "What year?"

"'64 ½?"

"Half?"

"Yeah, you know, like when a car company —"

174

"I know about half years and car companies, but the licensing bureau don't give jack shit about it. It's either a sixty-four or a sixty-five."

"I don't know, then. I guess it would be a sixty-four."

"That settles that. How did this car come to be in your possession? Did you steal it?"

"No! Christ, no. I'm not a car thief."

"Well, you're not here because you bought the thing out of the classifieds? How'd you get this car?"

"I found it."

"Found it. How?"

"That's the long part of the story."

"OK, let's get this thing down to a two-minute drill. Who used to own the car?"

"I don't know."

"Alright. When was the last time the car was on the road?"

"I'd say sometime in 1964."

"It hasn't been on the road in twenty-seven years?"

"That's right."

"Then it's either gorgeous or a piece of junk."

"Right now it's closer to junk than gorgeous."

Malatesta pretended to be taking notes, but Dominic could tell he was only doodling.

"You found this car abandoned, in a farmer's field, or a forest, or something like that?"

Dominic paused. "I guess that's about right. We did find it."

"We? Who's we?"

"Let's just say me."

"Okay. That's a better answer anyway." He make a check mark on his pad. Then he circled it. "You got a VIN?"

"Yeah, I do, as well as the original plate number from 1964."

"Well let's forget about the latter and focus on the former."

"What?"

175

"Just give me the VIN."

Dominic took a piece of paper out from his pocket. He had the number written down on it. He showed it to Malatesta who copied it into his pad.

"Well," Malatesta put down his pen, "we got a couple of options here. I got some people inside the bureau who can get you a certifiable set of ownership papers. The age of the car makes it harder, as does the model. The papers today are a lot different from what they were in the sixties. It's not impossible, just more work, and you know what that means …"

"More money."

"Yesiree, Dominic, you do have a knack for business. My usual fee for this kind of thing is ten grand, but this car would need some extra attention to detail from my people. You're probably looking at around fifteen thousand. And I couldn't guarantee that price, not today."

"There's no way I can come up with that kind of cash. I'd be better off chopping the car up for scrap."

Malatesta looked disappointed, but undefeated. "There is another way. It's a little riskier, but a lot cheaper."

"What would that be?"

"It's not usual for cars to get abandoned. A guy's got too many parking tickets and he's driving a junker, so he just leaves it at the side of the road. He figures the cost of paying out the tickets is more than the car's worth. Or say you buy a farm with an old barn. You open the door to let in your first herd of chickens and voilà, you find a vintage car under the hay. Trust me, it happens. Our local automobile licensing bureau has a procedure for just such an occasion."

"They do?"

"Shit, they're government. They got guys sitting around drinking coffee and thinking about every possible situation for every possible thing everywhere in this country. So yes, they got a procedure. They even got forms to fill out."

"What do I do?"

"We'll handle the paperwork for you. That's our job. We just fill out an application for ownership papers for an abandoned vehicle and in about thirty days, you got yourself paperwork. Best of all, it's perfectly legal. Only gonna cost you about a hundred bucks."

"Shit. That's fabulous!"

"There is only one problem, and I'm sure it's not going to affect you. The government's gonna run that VIN against any stolen vehicle files, police files, that sort of thing."

"Why?"

"In case somebody really owns it. But I wouldn't lose any sleep over it. Besides, its either that or spend fifteen grand on paperwork that will only hold up for so long. And the car's what, twenty-five years old?"

"Older."

"Then whoever owned that car is dead or long forgotten."

# 26

Dominic returned to the shop, his head a little clearer. There was a spring breeze in the air, the first of the year. It fought with the clear bright light of the afternoon, the young season anxious to put the winter behind it. It was time to begin the task at hand Dominic's Restoration Services, Job Number One, Year One.

Andy had beaten him back to the shop. He found her neck-deep in the Mustang's hood, pulling out parts like she'd been working there forever. But her early arrival was not what surprised Dominic — it was the shop. The day before the shop was littered with the remains of several dozen cars; the parts deemed unfit for the Romanian's criminal consumption. Fenders too bent to be repaired, plastic cracked and broken during the process of surgery, door handles, windows, bolts, screws, and wires — the shop had been a junkyard.

Now the floor had been swept clean. Stray auto parts had been placed in a series of large tin garbage cans, one marked steel, another plastic, another glass, still another wiring. The overhead lights, once bare-bulb affairs whose light cast shadows and spoiled both colours and surfaces, had been replaced by white-hot halogens in frames that eliminated the darkness in all the shop's corners and made even the muddy Mustang's pale white finish seem frightfully unforgiving. A series of three new vending machines hummed in the corner, one for cold drinks, one for hot, and a third that could fuel the junk food cravings of an entire legion of parts pullers.

"I spend a day away from this place and look what you've done," Dominic said. "This place is clean enough to paint in."

Andy pulled her head out of the Mustang. Gino came out of the back room, with a roll of clear heavy-weight vinyl over his shoulder. Vinnie held up the other end. They dropped it on the newly cleared floor. The noise caused Sammy's head to snap up from a barrel of parts he was sorting.

"I didn't clean it," Andy said. "I don't clean. You want things clean, get yourself a cleaning lady. I just got the place better organized. That's all."

"Where'd all the shit go?"

"I packaged it up and had Gino and Vinnie haul it out to a metal recycler. Got you a couple hundred bucks cash." She was wearing a pair of City-Wide Collision overalls. She swam inside them. She had tied a piece of ignition wire around her waist to keep some semblance of order and rolled up the pant legs and sleeves. Dominic had never seen a pair of his brother's overalls look so good. Andy handed him a wad of five and ten dollar bills.

"Thanks," Dominic grinned in both surprise and delight.

"Good steel gets good money. Looks German, like you been cutting up a lot of Mercedes and Beemers."

"Mercedes, mostly. A lot of them seem to have found their way here recently."

Dominic looked around the shop. There wasn't a shadow anywhere.

"Where'd these lights come from?" Dominic said.

Gino was climbing a ladder with one end of the roll of vinyl perched on his shoulder. "Andy had me pick those up this morning," he said. He hooked his end of the roll to a hook he'd installed earlier that morning. With Vinnie on the other end, they hung the vinyl roll like there were putting a set of clear plastic blinds on a twenty-foot-wide window. The drapery separated the Mustang from the rest of the shop, making the vintage car appear as though it were on a stage.

"Can't fix what I can't see," Andy said. "And I have a shitload of problems to look at."

"That's fine," Dominic said. "Must have set you back a few bucks, though."

Gino jumped down from the ladder. "I paid for them, actually." He fished a receipt out of the chest pocket of shirt. "It was ... ah .... three hundred and seventy-five dollars."

Dominic took the wad of bills that Andy had just given him and slapped them into Gino's outstretched hands. "If that doesn't cover it, let me know." He strolled over to the vending machines.

"Some guy dropped those off this morning," Sammy said. "Set them up, too. Said you ordered them."

"I didn't order any vending machines." Dominic inspected the menu of brands.

Gino sucked back a Coke. "Well, it's not like it costs you anything, other than seventy-five cents for a drink."

"Which reminds me," Vinnie said, "I think you're taking advantage of us." He picked up a cup of coffee that he'd left steaming before setting up the vinyl barrier.

"What?"

"Sure are," said Andy. She was drinking a diet Coke and munching on some potato chips.

Vinnie put his cup of coffee down on an overturned box. The paper cup had a full house on the side, three Jacks and a pair of threes. "Seventy-five cents is way too much for a Coke, and this coffee, too. You gotta roll back the prices."

"What do I have to do with this?"

"Hey, man, they're your machines."

Dominic stood back from machines and stared. They glowed back at him, begging for change. He looked over at a series of labels that was on each machine. They read *Queenston Vending*. There was a phone number.

"I'll call them tomorrow."

Gino said, "I guess that means you'll be getting a phone, then."

Dominic smiled. "Yes, as soon as I get a phone in here, I'll call whoever dropped these machines into my shop and tell them to haul 'em the fuck out."

"Good idea," Sammy said. "Eating that stuff'll kill ya."

As the days wore on, Dominic found it increasingly hard to concentrate. He could see the beauty of the Mustang taking shape but he had neither the tools nor the money to complete the job. It was becoming increasingly frustrating. Several days had passed since his conversation with Magilla, which looked to have backfired on him. Before the exchange at the donut shop, a car or two was arriving each night; after, not a one. He'd spoken with Magilla several times by phone, each time fighting his instinct to lay a bet down, instead prodding the bookie for information. All he ever heard were grunts and, "I'm doing what I can." Before the Mustang had come out of the water, Dominic had been doing eight hours a day at City-Wide, then chopping cars for the Romanian into the wee hours of the morning. Now, he felt practically unemployed. His life had lost its frenetic pace, and he was unable to cope with the monotony of hour after hour of rubbing steel wool against mud-stained body parts. He'd promised himself he wouldn't drink, but the boredom and the waiting made the idea of reaching for a bottle very tempting.

Andy didn't appear similarly afflicted. She kept odd hours: she'd appear a few hours one day, then she'd stay for the entire day the next. She said she held down another job. Dominic wasn't paying her, and until he put the money together for the parts and equipment they needed, there was only so much work they could do on the Mustang. Sammy, Gino, and Vinnie came by regularly. No one seemed to want to be too far from the Mustang, even if there wasn't a lot happening.

Dominic was going over the list of items Andy needed when the Romanian finally arrived. Nastasi had three cars with him ready to be chopped.

181

"I was beginning to think you'd forgotten about us," Dominic said.

"Never worry about that." Nastasi looked around at the orderly piles of Mustang parts. "Why are these not in the trailer?"

"They're not yours," Dominic said. "We're doing a restoration job."

"What about my Suburban?"

"We're working on it. I don't know what you did to it, but it's no simple front-end job. You twisted the frame into licorice."

Nastasi handed him an envelope. Dominic expected it to contain cash but there was only paperwork inside.

"Is new ownership papers," Nastasi said. "Says truck is white now."

"I see that," Dominic said. "And it says your name is something unpronounceable."

"When will Suburban be finished?"

"Weeks. We got a lot of work to do. The frame needs realignment, and colour changes are especially hard."

"Criminisi told me to bring you more cars. He said you could handle the work. If you can't do my work, how can you do more work for boss?"

"You let us worry about whether we can handle it. Okay?"

Nastasi pulled another envelope from the interior pocket of his black leather jacket. He handed it to Dominic.

"Four thousand dollars," he said. "Less my end of deal."

"Of course," Dominic said. He opened the envelope. There were several fifty-dollar bills inside. Dominic could tell immediately that the Romanian had shorted him. He removed the cash and gave it a cursory count. "There's only a grand here."

"I run into Magilla this morning. Fat man make claim. Says you having bad luck, lately." Nastasi smiled through dirty teeth.

Dominic was still carrying red on the bookie's ledger. "He can't do that," Dominic said.

"Yes he can," the Romanian said. "We both work for same boss. Is same boss's money. Boss owes you, you owe Magilla, boss owe you. Me? I just accountant in the middle."

Gino grabbed the envelope. "What do mean there's only a grand? What kind of shit of this? Where's our money, Dominic?"

"You guys are getting what you're due." Dominic counted out five hundred for Gino, and another five hundred for Sammy. "As for the rest, there's been some kind of foul up." He turned to Nastasi. "When am I getting more cars?"

"You get cars. For these three and for all the rest, you pay me kick-back, two hundred and fifty a car."

Dominic shook his head. "You're already robbing me."

"My costs go up. I need more drivers, more people with fast hands and slow brains." He pointed at his temple. "They are hard to find, now that most of them are working here."

Dominic knew that he was going to have to do the thing he'd been avoiding: meet with Criminisi directly. "We'll take whatever cars you can send us for the next six weeks. And I'll pay you your two hundred and fifty dollars a car. But I want to talk to Criminisi about this."

Nastasi ignored him. He was looking at the skeletal frame sitting naked on the floor. "What kind of car is this? I did not bring it here."

"It's an old Ford," said Dominic.

Nastasi scanned the empty frame. He spotted the chrome icon of a running horse. "Moostang, yes?"

"Yes, it's a Mustang," Dominic said.

"Do good job, DiPietro. I come back and steal it from you one day."

Sammy said, "I thought you only dealt in cars worthy of their parts."

"No, I am always open to cars for my friends in Europe. Good cars, they pay good money."

Andy came around and stood between the open frame and Nastasi. "This car isn't for sale, not to you."

Nastasi hit her with the back of his hand, a full-force sweep that threw Andy to the concrete floor. Dominic and Sammy ran to help her up. She spat blood out of her mouth.

"It is not for a woman to talk to me that way."

Dominic grabbed a wrench and ran at Nastasi, but the Romanian was too big and fast. He knocked the wrench away and twisted Dominic's wrist between his hands. "I break your wrist, but you need it for my Suburban, do you not?"

"Get out of here," Dominic said.

"I go when I please. My business is not finished." He let Dominic go.

Dominic rubbed his wrist as Sammy helped Andy over the washroom where she could tend to her face. He looked at the Romanian. "What else do you want?"

"Criminisi wants to see you."

"When?" It was a summons. Dominic had expected it. The mob patrician probably wanted to talk about Dominic's abandonment of City-White Collision. The meeting was a necessary evil, and would give Dominic the chance to press Criminisi about getting him more cars.

"You come with me." Nastasi looked at his watch. "The boss wants to see you at two o'clock." It was already well past one-thirty.

"Give me a minute." Dominic walked to the washroom. Andy was washing her face in the sink, her dreadlocks hanging down and clinking on the porcelain edges. Sammy sat on the toilet, an over-cautious observer.

"How are you doing?" Dominic said.

Andy lifted her head. A bruise was starting to swell on the right side of her mouth.

"It's not like it's the first time." She looked away.

"What was that all about, anyway?" Dominic asked. He put his hand on her shoulder.

Andy shrugged it off. "Don't touch me. Not less you're invited."

"Alright. I'm sorry. It's a little strange, though. You were protecting that car like a mother bear."

Andy straightened up and put her hands on Dominic's wrist. "Did he break anything?" Dominic shook his head. "Next time," she said, "leave him alone. That guy kills with less thought than he takes to put on his pants."

Dominic went to the sink and washed his own face. "How do you know so much about him?"

"Some guys like to kiss women. Others like to hit them."

Dominic grabbed a comb from the medicine case above the sink. "We have to talk about this," he said, dragging the comb through his hair. "Right now, I got to go with the Romanian. But when I get back, we're going to talk."

Andy murmured her reluctant assent. There was pain in her eyes that wasn't the result of Nastasi's blow. It was too old, like she'd been born with it. "Be careful," she told him. "Don't believe a word he says."

Dominic left the building by the rear doors. Nastasi was waiting for him outside, standing in front of a Cadillac Seville. Paulie and Zeno were with him. The thought of climbing inside the Cadillac with the two gigantic bikers was enough to make Dominic's knees quake. He bit his lip in an effort to hold himself together.

"Nice wheels," Dominic stuttered. "What's your hurry for the Suburban?"

"You tell that whore of yours, unless she is sucking my dick, she should keep her mouth shut around me."

Dominic didn't respond. He walked slowly to the passenger side door, where Nastasi and his muscle were standing. Dominic came to within a few feet of them and stopped. They blocked the way.

"And you, DiPietro, you no talk to that fat Jew about our business. You want to talk cars, you want to talk with the boss, talk to me."

"Sorry," Dominic said. "I was placing a bet and the subject came up."

Zeno said, "I don't think he's that sorry, Bela." The biker had a purple tattoo that climbed up from his collar along the right side of his face. It looked like the tail of a dragon. The dragon's tail had a spike driven through it. Blood spewed from the wound. Zeno said, "I don't think he's that sorry, Bela."

"Yeah, I don't think he understands the embarrassment he caused you," Paulie said.

"DiPietro, we are supposed to partners in this operation. Partners, you understand. But when you talk to the Jew and not me, the boss thinks that I not manage my business well, and I care very much what the boss thinks."

"I am sorry. I meant no disrespect." The bikers looked hungry for a fight.

"You will remember," Nastasi said. "Next time, yes?"

Dominic held up his arms, defensively. "I will remember. Absolutely. You're the boss of the car business."

"That's good. But, you will need a reminder, I think." The Romanian turned and got into the Cadillac. Zeno took two rolls of quarters from his pocket. They were wrapped in tape, tight and heavy. He put one in each hand, closing his fists around them.

Dominic's brain couldn't get a message to his feet. All he could do was stand there and wait for it. Paulie turned him around and pinned his arms back, acting as brace. Zeno, the bleeding dragon, delivered each blow. Six to the chest, three to stomach, and two slaps to the face with both fists together. With the final blow, one of the rolls of coins exploded in Zeno's hand, sending quarters spewing over the alley.

Paulie released Dominic, who dropped to his hands and knees, silver pieces scattered on the ground around him. Zeno whispered, "You owe me ten bucks." They rolled Dominic into the back seat of the Cadillac. Nastasi leaned over from the driver's seat. "Next time, the reminder will come from me, and I won't be as gentle as these Canadian boys."

# 27

"Sit down, my young friend." Criminisi was seated behind his desk. He stubbed out a cigar in the remains of hubcap.

"You want something, some chips, maybe a chocolate bar?" Criminisi offered.

"No, thank you."

"Bela, get Dominic a chocolate bar. You're so skinny, my little friend. You are working too hard. You have to take care of yourself. We're partners, you remember. I need you healthy."

Nastasi raised an eyebrow but said nothing. He reached behind a freestanding pillar of Seven-Up cases and brought out a box of Oh Henry! bars. He opened the box and presented a wrapped chocolate to Dominic. Dominic took it and nervously played with the wrapper. In Tony's house, hospitality came with a price. It would be no different here.

"You will have to excuse my office," Criminisi said. "We had an unexpected delivery from one of our new suppliers. It will take us a few days to get the product into the market. so we need to use any space we can for storage."

Dominic opened the chocolate bar. "I need more cars to work on." He took a bite.

"And why would that be?"

"I've decided to work at the shop full-time."

"So I understand. This is not what we agreed."

"I know. But it had to be done. I can't work for my brother. Not anymore."

"You know my feelings about this. Bad blood in a family is like a virus. It infects everyone who comes into contact with it."

"I'm sorry. But some things just have to happen."

"Yes, I am well aware of that. Unfortunately, all of us are forced into such decisions from time to time."

"I wish it could be some other way, but I can't make it work with Tony anymore." Dominic finished the chocolate bar and looked for a place to toss the wrapper. He fidgeted for a moment, and held the wrapper between his hands.

"I see," Criminisi said. "And you expect me to solve this problem for you?"

"Problem?"

"Yes, my young partner. You have decided not to work for your brother and so you need more cars. Why is this my problem? I was very pleased with the way our arrangement was going."

"I only want to make it more profitable for both of us." Dominic twisted the empty wrapper in his fingers.

Criminisi stood up and leaned his right fist on the desk. His upper lip started to quiver. "It is not a decision for you to make! Who do you think you are, you little piece of shit?" He picked up the antique letter opener and flipped it in the air like a knife, catching it on the handle.

"We have been in business together for, what, two months? Do you think I am stupid? You want me to send you more cars so that you will have enough money to buy me out of my own business. Well, I am not a stupid man, young DiPietro! Not stupid at all! Is that what you think of me? You think me stupid? You think that I am old and weak and you can come in here and tell me to change the way I do business because ... because?" He drove the tip of the letter opener into the desk.

Criminisi's face was as red as his hair. He pushed himself away from the desk and stood back, daring Dominic to rise and defend himself. DiPietro sat with his hands on his lap, the Oh Henry! wrapper twisted and torn. A patch of yellow confetti had gathered between his shoes. He looked up at Criminisi from his subservient position. He knew that if he stood he might not make it out of the building alive.

"I do not think you're stupid, sir. You're right: I do wish to earn more money to make this business my own. That's my error. I am the stupid one. I beg your forgiveness. I realize that I am fortunate to have you as a partner. It's not something I'd ever want to change."

Criminisi walked around the room slowly, as if thinking. Finally, he stopped pacing and sat back down at his desk. "Thank you. I do not think I could continue to do business with a man who thinks me stupid."

"I am sorry, Mr. Criminisi. The foolishness is all mine."

"Yes. But young men are prone to mistakes. Experience is a good teacher. May you live long enough to learn from it."

"Thank you." Dominic took a breath. He felt the air returning to his lungs.

"You know, Dominic, I would like to help you. I have great hopes for you. If you want to earn more money, I can always find you a way."

That was exactly what Dominic feared in his dealings with Criminisi: the help he was asked to give would steadily increase. Soon, he feared, the mob boss would make him kill someone, or worse.

"There is a way for you to get the money you need," Criminisi said. "You could do me a favour."

"Anything." Despite his anxiety, Dominic thought that he was prepared to do just about anything Criminisi might ask of him if only to get out of the building. Immediately. The favour Criminisi asked was simple enough, if a little strange. Dominic wasn't about to ask any stupid questions. He did, however, have one condition, which he requested through teeth that were clenched in a very real fear of reprisal.

"I need the Romanian to keep his hands off my people," he told Criminisi. "He's been roughing them up. He hit my mechanic, pretty hard." Receiving no reaction from Ciminisi, he pressed as far as he dared. "I can't keep up my end of our deal if half my crew is in the emergency ward."

"Is this true, Bela?"

"I not even know he had a mechanic."

"The girl," Dominic hissed. "This afternoon. I think you broke her fucking nose."

"You hire whores," the Romanian said, "you get diseases. I was doing you favour."

Criminisi frowned. "Stop with the favours, Bela. Dominic's got good people. We need them." He looked at Dominic. "Alright? Are you satisfied?"

Dominic nodded his assent and rose from his chair. "I've got work to do."

"Yes, you do," Criminisi said. "I will have Bela take you back."

Dominic followed Bela, Zeno, and Paulie through the maze of confectionaries and colas, through the back door to the top of the concrete stairs that lead to back lot. Nastasi was in the lead. The two bikers were on the stairs, with Dominic a step behind them. He put the flat of his hand on Paulie's upper back and pushed him into Zeno. The pair of burly bikers tumbled down the stairway and landed in a lump on the pavement, bruised but not broken.

Dominic tossed a ten-dollar bill onto Zeno's chest. "We're even."

He turned to Nastasi, whose eyes had widened like a cornered animal. "You, Bela," Dominic said. "I got no time for anyone who beats up on women."

Nastasi glared back. "The boss won't always be protecting you."

"Well, until he stops, hands the fuck off." Dominic walked away, waiting for the gunshot that was due to pierce his back as he left parking lot. Once he was out of sight of Queenston Vending, he ducked behind a dumpster and took a series of deep, hard breaths. *Christ, I want a drink.*

# 28

Constantine left the council chamber a little past eleven p.m. It had been a long night of debate. The city's budget was on the table, as was a proposal to fund a shelter for homeless men. Something had to give, but the twenty-year veteran of municipal politics was sure that putting men out on the street was not the best path to the mayor's office.

The hallway lighting was dim. The councillor had his head down, his thoughts a chaotic jumble born of physical weariness and the eagerness required to begin another political campaign. He didn't hear his name being called nor did he see the man who blocked his route to the parking lot. It wasn't until he felt the firm hand on his shoulder that his attention was roused.

"Shit. You scared the life out of me," he said to the figure. He was startled, but felt safe. The man was wearing a wrinkled sports jacket over a pair of faded jeans. His aggressor was out of place, but didn't look dangerous.

"Sorry, councillor," he said. "My name is Eric Batista. I'm with the *Spectator*."

"What the hell are you doing down here? The media gallery is at the back of the council chambers. You know the rules. You want to talk to me, meet me there."

"I'm not on the City Hall beat. I'm assigned to fires, burglaries, and murders. Things like that."

Constantine started to walk again. "Then what do you want with me? It's late. I'd like to get home and reintroduce myself to my wife."

"I want to talk to you about your brother's murder."


Dominic felt shaky when he returned to the Brampton Street Shop. Andy noticed his staggering gait as he walked in.

"Christ, what happened to you?" she asked.

"Had to take one for the team," Dominic lay on his stomach on the couch, burying his face in a musty pillow. A loud grinding noise brought him to attention.

"Who's working?" he said.

"Pretty much everybody's here," said Andy. Her eye was black and blue. "Sammy's cutting up a car, Vinnie and Gino are grinding out some rough spots on the Mustang. It's looking better than I thought it would. The harbour has been kind."

Dominic rolled over and looked at Andy. "Jesus, woman, you look like I feel."

"I'm alright." Andy touched her cheekbone. "Had worse."

"You won't have to worry about the Romanian ... not for a while. I asked Criminisi to get him to back off. For some reason, he agreed."

Andy glanced down at the floor. When she looked back at him, Dominic saw the faintest sign of a tear in her eyes, emerging as if the full stream ran constantly under the surface, her emotions, a well-constructed dike between them and her outward reflection. Her bruises, purple with pain, were deep. And it wasn't the Romanian who had inflicted them.

"How did it go with Criminisi, or should I even ask?"

Dominic sat up and held his own bruised head in his hands. "I found out where the vending machines came from. They're his."

"So I guess they're staying."

"But I'm not. I've been sent on a mission."

"A mission?"

"I'll tell you all about it. Toss me a Coke will you?"

Andy threw a can of cola across the room and Dominic caught it. It exploded in his hands when he opened it, though he didn't seem bothered. He let the sweet fluid drip over his hands and onto his lap, slurping the pool of cola from the top of can.

Andy got caught in the spray. She wiped cola from her eyes and hair.

"What's going on between you and the Romanian?" Dominic asked.

"We've crossed paths. It's a small city."

"That was a pretty good swipe you took just for coming across his path."

"I really don't want to talk about it." She wiped more of the cola from her hair. "Come with me and take a look at the power train. It's gonna be a beast."

Dominic stood up. "When will it be ready?"

"Not long. All it needs is some cash for the electrics and I'll have it singing for you." She tied the braids of her dreadlocks in a knot to keep them out of her face.

"Cash is what everybody seems to be after right now." Once he completed Criminisi's favour, he hoped he'd have enough money to fund the rest of the work.


"My brother's been dead for decades," Constantine said. "What could you possibly want to talk about now?"

"I'm working up a story on your mayoralty campaign. This is just background stuff for the piece."

Constantine shook his head. "You little fuckers. If your newspaper doesn't want me to be mayor, you should just run a goddamn editorial. Don't go muckraking around in a past that I didn't have any control over."

194

Batista took out a notepad. "It's nothing like that at all, councillor. I think the editorial board wants to endorse you."

Constantine started to walk towards his car. "Just leave my family alone. You can write about me and my politics all you want. But let my brother rest in peace."

"Well, there's a problem there," Batista said, hustling to keep up. "Part of this story looks like it's come back from the dead."

Constantine stopped and looked at the reporter.

Batista said, "I was wondering if you could help me check into something."

"What?"

"I have a couple contacts in the Ministry of Transport. One of them gave me some interesting information that your brother's car, the one that was stolen around the time of his murder? It would appear that someone is trying to take possession of it."

"What car?"

"His Mustang."

"That's impossible. No one's seen that car since he died."

"Be that as it may, my source tells me that in a few days the estate of Roberto Constantine Jr. is going to be receiving a letter from the licensing bureau requesting proof of ownership of a 1964 Mustang."

"It's got to be some kind of mistake."

"I don't think so, councillor. Regardless of who takes ownership of that car, it's going to make one hell of a story. Great photograph, too. Murdered by the mob, his Mustang comes back to life! I'm not a headline writer, but you get the idea."

"How old are you, Batista?"

"Thirty-two."

"That would make you five years old when my brother died. Get your facts straight. There was no mob hit, no nothing. My brother was killed during a jewellery store robbery. That's right there in the coroner's report. The suggestion of anything else is libellous. You print a word of it and I'll come down on you and your newspaper so hard that it'll cost you your house and every penny you'll ever make for the rest of your life."

"Take it easy. I don't have anything, yet. My editor says no car, no story. So until that Wimbledon-white Mustang shows up in somebody's driveway, I got nothing."

"That's all you're ever going to have, too." Constantine turned and stormed away.

Sammy was firing his torch at an angry ball joint. Dominic tapped his friend on the shoulder. Sammy lifted his face shield, and Dominic beckoned him over to the restoration area where the others were already gathered.

"Criminisi is giving me the money to finish the car," said Dominic.

"Who do you have to kill?" said Sammy.

"Nothing like that," Dominic said. "Well, maybe it's a little like that. I have to go to Buffalo tomorrow night and bring some kind of package back."

"That little bastard's turning you into drug courier," Andy said.

"I have no idea what's in the package. Criminisi gave me tickets to a hockey game. Somebody at the arena will give me the package and I bring it back. It's simple."

"It's stupid is what it is," said Sammy.

"Maybe. But I felt like my choice was either say yes or end up at the bottom of the harbour."

Vinnie put his pudgy hands together. "Well, what can you do? My mother always said if you sleep with snakes you shouldn't complaint about the odd bite."

"True enough. The thing is, I need someone to come along with me. Criminisi wants two guys to go to the game. He says it's a better cover story at the border, and I'd have to agree with him. Besides, I need a ride."

"I'm working on the engine," Andy said.

"I'm doing the night shift at the steel plant," Sammy said.

"My wife would kill me if we got caught," Gino said.

All eyes focused on Vinnie. "What about Leo?" he said. "The trip could be some kind of peace offering between the two of you." There was no reaction from the assembled group.

"Alright," Vinnie said. "I was just shitting you anyway. I'll go along. As long as we get there early enough to get down to Main Street. It's the home of Duff's Wings and I am not going all the way to Buffalo without getting a belly full."

When Constantine got home he headed straight for his den. He turned on a lamp over his oak desk and withdrew a small black book from the top drawer. His finger followed the pages to the D's, and he picked up the telephone. He dialled Tony DiPietro's home number. He neglected to apologize for calling so late.

There was a short pause. "No problem. What's got you up at this hour?"

"Nothing I can talk about right now. It's got to be in person. Can you meet tomorrow? Dinner."

"Sure, whenever you want."

"I'm at a committee meeting until after seven. Let's make it eight, at La Pergola."

"OK, Sal. What's this about?"

"Tomorrow, Tony." Constantine hung up the phone.

Dominic and Vinnie passed across the border into Buffalo without incident. Vinnie had decided to take his Harley Davidson instead of the Jeep.

"We're riding all the way to Buffalo on that?" Dominic had said.

"It's the first decent day of spring. It'll be blast. If we're gonna go, let's go all the way."

"I was hoping we could just slip across the border like a couple of regular guys going to see a Sabres game, and you turn us into a pair of refugees from the Hell's Angels."

"Don't shit on my buds, man. And don't worry so much. It's not like were wearing colours. Plus, you'd never see two club bikers on the same machine. We're wannabes, man. That's all the border guards are going to see."

"You know some Hells Angels?"

"Sure," Vinnie handed Dominic a helmet and a leather jacket. "I trained a couple of them as boxers when I was coaching at Duncan's. They invited me over to their clubhouse on the Beach Strip to do some personal training. Nice fellas."

"Nice fellas?"

"It's not like I'd want to join up or nothing. It's too much of a lifestyle commitment for me. I'm strictly a weekend biker. To those guys it's a life. But I'd rather have them as friends than enemies."

Dominic put on the helmet and jacket. He threw his leg over the bike and settled into the tiny rear jump seat. Vinnie took up the pilot's position.

"Have you met any of the goons the Romanian is using?" Dominic said.

"Not that I know of. They may be from another gang. Maybe Banditos. Maybe freelancers."

Vinnie fired up the Harley. The boxer turned his head around to yell at Dominic over the rising and falling roar of the engine.

"Hold on, DiPietro. My best time to the Peace Bridge is forty minutes. Let's see if we can break it."


Constantine ordered the veal piccata, but spent more time pushing the food around on his plate than putting it in his mouth. Tony had ordered a Caesar salad and the grilled sea bass.

"If my brother was alive, I'd kill him," Constantine said. "For twenty-seven years I've raised his kids like my own and put as much distance between me and his past as possible."

"You should avoid words like kill, even in private," Tony said.

"Everything I am I owe to this city. It gave me an education. It gave me a heritage. Christ, after Roberto died, it gave Julie and me a family. We couldn't have kids. Us having Jackie and Marsha to care for was a blessing for everyone. Can you imagine what it would have been like for those kids to have been raised by their father? I can't comprehend what Jackie would have got into. It was hard enough getting him through law school. As a teenager he was more interested in breaking the law than learning it. Now he's running the whole show for me. If my brother had raised him ... it scares me to think about it."

"Brothers are God's curse," Tony said. "That's why He had the good sense not to give Jesus one. I wish He'd extended us the same courtesy."

"Jesus had James."

"Half brother," Tony said. "Doesn't count."

"Mine's come back to haunt me."

Constantine related the story about the *Spectator* reporter.

"I get to the office this morning and there's a letter on my desk. It's addressed to the Estate of Roberto Constantine. Twenty-seven years later I'm still acting as executor. So I open it, and there it is. The reporter isn't shitting me. It's a letter from the Vehicle Licensing Bureau telling me I have thirty days to prove ownership of Roberto's '64 Mustang or it will be declared abandoned and the ownership transferred to an unnamed applicant."

Tony took a sip of red wine. "So let it go. It's not your business anymore."

"That's not the point. Now that the newspaper's gotten wind of it, they're going to find whoever has that car and drudge up the story of the my brother's murder. All that speculation about his involvement in the mob, those photographs of him and his wife with their throats cut from ear to ear."

"That'll kill the campaign," Tony said. He took a roll of antacids out of his pocket and put two of them into his mouth.

"If this story comes back, we won't even have a chance to

announce," Constantine said. "If any speculation surfaces that any member of my family is mobbed-up, I won't be able to run for garbage collector."

"Every Italian in Hamilton will be painted with the same brush," Tony said. A tuxedoed waiter brought him a cappuccino.

"What about Jackie and Marsha? They don't need a past they had no part in coming back to destroy their future."

Tony took a sip. "What can I do to help?"

Constantine lowered his voice to a conspiratorial whisper. "You have this huge collision business, right?"

"Yeah ..."

"Well, we got to find out who's trying to take ownership of Bobby's car. I know the police chief and his staff. Hell, I hired half of them. But I can't ask them to get this kind of information for me. I've got to stay as far away from this as possible."

"Where do I fit in?"

"You must know some policemen, don't you, Tony? You must have done business with a fair number of them, vehicle investigations, that sort of thing?"

Tony nodded.

"I need you to find out who's trying to take possession of that car. I need you to pull in some favours and get the information. Very quietly."

"Let's say for a moment that I can do this. What then?"

Constantine took a long drink of water. "We get the car back and get rid of it."

"What if this guy, whoever he is, doesn't want to sell it?"

Constantine said, "Tony, that car has got to be a piece of junk by now. It was reported after the murder, probably by the guys who killed Bobby and his wife. I figured it was long gone. And I can't be the one to go after it. That's why I need you. If the guy who's got the car figures out where it came from or what it could do to my campaign, I'm finished."

"Really, Sal. Do you think anyone is gonna care about the history of a twenty-seven-year-old Mustang?

"This is politics, Tony. We're talking about my life, and my family. I can't afford to fuck with this." The councillor handed Tony a copy of the letter from the Vehicle License Bureau. "The VIN is on the letter. It's the only information I have."

"Alright," Tony said. "I'll do what I can. No promises, though. This is not the kind of thing I usually get involved in. If I can find the person who has your brother's car, I'll try to buy it back."

"Thanks, Tony. I'll feel a lot better when that car is in your hands."

"I'm sure you will."


The bleacher seats were just as Criminisi had described them. Great seats with a blue line view of the whole ice surface. Vinnie sat beside Dominic and negotiated two chili dogs and a beer. A half-eaten barrel of popcorn sat on the floor between his legs. Dominic had only beer. Four empty cups were scattered around him; some of them had rolled onto the floor in front of the empty seat beside him.

"How can you eat all that?" Dominic said. "We put back four pounds of wings less than an hour ago."

"I don't know. I think riding a motorcycle burns calories or something," He shoved the remnants of the first chili dog into his mouth and waved the second dog in Dominic's face as an offering. Dominic declined and put back half of his fifth beer.

It was mid-way through the second period. The Sabres where leading the Rangers 3 to 2, but Dominic took no enjoyment in the game, despite the grand he'd laid down on Buffalo. Every time a fresh face came walking up the centre aisle to his right, Dominic thought it was Criminisi's courier.

"Christ, where is this bastard?"

"Hey, man, the best thing that could happen might be for this guy to be a no show," said Vinnie. "Maybe something scared him away or went wrong on his end."

"I never thought of that."

"I say we relax, watch the game and have a few more beers. Once the final whistle blows, we're off the hook. Nothing Criminisi can do to you about that. You held up your end of the deal."

"I don't think that will mean a thing to Criminisi." Dominic waved over a beer vendor and held up four fingers.

There were several police officers that Tony could have called on. Sergeant Benedict was a twenty-year veteran of the Hamilton Police Department. His career path had come to a halt after a decade spent cleaning up vehicular accidents and directing traffic when the power when out. Over the years, Benedict had followed hundreds of vehicles from accident sites on the highways around the city to the hoists at City-Wide Collision. Benedict was the only cop Tony completely trusted, and that was only because he had directed enough money in graft and kickbacks the sergeant's way to put him behind bars and Benedict knew it.

When Tony got the sergeant on the phone he gave him the particulars of the situation. Benedict promised to get back to Tony within the hour. Tony's phone rang twenty-eight minutes later.

"You're not going to like the answer to your question."

Seconds later, Tony hung up the phone and lifted the lid of his humidor. He took out a Montecristo, cut off the tip, and lit the six-inch cigar. With his feet on the desk, he smiled then shook his head. *Brothers are God's curse.*

Dominic's energy was waning. Two hours of sitting watching a hockey game and sucking back beers had finally slowed his heart rate. He was starting to think that Vinnie must be right: the exchange was off and he could go home and sleep. Until a man in a long, black overcoat and a natty, blue suit underneath came and sat beside him. He held a schoolboy's knapsack in his hand.

"Did I miss much?" he said.

The man was as normal as could be; he looked like someone you'd hire to do your taxes or buy insurance from.

"Game's been kinda slow," Vinnie said.

"You want a beer?" Dominic said.

"No, but I am kind of hungry. I think I'll take a walk down to the concourse and get myself a hot dog." He stood up and walked away, leaving the knapsack on the concrete floor. It had a zipper with a small padlock on it. Dominic and Vinnie stared at the bag as if they were waiting for it to get up and walk away too.

The courier never returned. For the next twenty minutes of hockey, which translated into forty-three minutes of real time, Dominic and Vinnie never took their eyes off of the knapsack. They didn't watch the game. They just stared at the knapsack hoping against hope that the man in the long, black overcoat would come back to retrieve it. When the final whistle blew, Dominic reached down and slung the knapsack over his shoulder.

"It's now or never," he said.

"Never is looking better all the time," Vinnie said.

Vinnie stopped the motorcycle at the river's end of downtown Buffalo. A fine rain had begun to mist around them, leaving a film of dew on their leathers. The highway entrance to the Peace Bridge was one hundred yards away. This was their last chance to change their minds.

"Whose wrath would you rather face," Vinnie said, "the border police or Criminisi's?"

Dominic paused for a moment. "Let's go." Rain began to mist their helmets.

"Hold on then," Vinnie said. He got off the motorcycle and using the light of the towering street lamps as guides, walked over to a pool of melted snow, salt, and dirt. He picked up a pile in this gloved hands and returned to the bike.

"Here," he said. He placed a small amount of mud in Dominic's hands. "Rub some lightly on my helmet and visor." He did the same to Dominic. Vinnie took the remainder of the mud and smudged it over motorcycle, taking extra care to obscure the license plates. He stood back from his work like an artist. He touched up the head-lamp with dirt and mud from the road. "Okay. We're good to go."

The pair of Italian boys from Hamilton started their journey home. Their only impediment the waiting arms of the Canada Customs and Immigration inspectors a half-mile away over a bridge spanning a river that ended in a torrent of destruction called Niagara Falls.

The motorcycle took up a place in the customs line behind four cars. An alternating red and green light signalled traffic to move through.

"Let me do the talking," Vinnie said. "You were so nervous coming down here that they barely let us into the States."

At the green light, Vinnie pulled the motorcycle beside the booth. A woman not much older than Dominic leaned over and said, "Citizenship?" Her voice had a bureaucratic flatness that came from asking too many drivers the same questions.

"Canadian, both of us." Vinnie said.

"How long in the United States?"

"About five hours."

"Purpose of your visit?"

"Pleasure. We went to the Sabres game."

"Not much of a pleasure though," Dominic said. "Sabres lost."

Vinnie poked him in the ribs.

"Did you acquire any goods while in the United States?"

"None," said Vinnie.

The customs officer paused. Vinnie looked at her blue uniform through his mud-stained visor. Her badge caught the overhead light and flashed back at him. She was writing on a piece of paper.

She handed it to him. "Take this to the inspection area."

Vinnie took the paper. "What for? We told you. We just went to the hockey game."

"Take that paper and drive over to the inspection area." The tone of her voice got firmer.

Vinnie engaged the transmission and slowly pulled away. "Hang on. We didn't break that record on the way down, but I'm gonna need all the speed we can muster right now."

The motorcycle leapt from the inspection area with enough force to nearly pull Dominic off the jump seat. They reached the highway in five seconds. In the time it took for Dominic to get his breath back, Vinnie had sped by one police officer pointing a gun straight at their heads and another yelling through a bullhorn for them to stop and get off the motorcycle.

The Harley's speedometre read one hundred and forty-two kilometres an hour. Vinnie wasn't watching his speed. His eyes darted around looking for the tell-tale signs of flashing police lights. Dominic yelled at Vinnie, who didn't hear him over the noise of the engine and the wind. He wrapped his arms tight around Vinnie's chest and tucked his head behind the driver's helmet. He couldn't see the rolling red, white, and yellow splash of lights drawing closer, nor the rooster tail of road film and water rising ever higher from the rear wheel. Somewhere in the eighteen-hundred-cc engine, Vinnie found the power to pull the Harley to one hundred and fifty-six kilometres per hour. The rain drops grew larger, each one hitting their leather as if fired from a shotgun.

# 29

Dominic felt the pull of the motorcycle toss him to the right and forward as Vinnie geared down and turned. Dominic opened his eyes in time to see a sign reading Fort Erie City Centre with an arrow pointing to the right. They reached the roadway and Vinnie turned the bike left.

It was one o'clock in the morning and the street was quiet. Dominic turned to look behind him. He could see the flashing lights on the highway. The cops hadn't reached the off-ramp yet, but he knew they soon would. There was a low-lying building in the distance in front of them. Cars were parked around it and a crude series of signs was painted on the roof. It was too dark to read them.

Vinnie slowed down as they approached the one-storey building. It was square as a cake pan and just as uninteresting. There were no windows on the building. Vinnie drove around back, stopping the motorcycle near a fenced-off area strewn with dumpsters. He hopped off the bike and ran to the back wall of the building.

"Get off the bike," he said, running back with a water hose. Dominic complied.

Dominic stood silent while Vinnie opened up the hose and turned it on the bike, paying particular attention the license plates.

"Toss the bag behind the fence."

"I'm not getting rid of it."

"We won't leave without it, I promise," Vinnie said.

Dominic set the bag down gently in a shadow. It wouldn't be seen until morning. He hoped that they weren't still here then. "Where to now?"

"Go inside and get a table," Vinnie pointed to the front of the building. "Order some beers. I'll be there in a minute."

Dominic jogged around the building. Splashes of red glowed brighter and brighter on the horizon. Before he could get to the front door, Vinnie zoomed by him. He buried the Harley in a row of motorcycles that had to be fifty deep. He leapt off the bike and jogged to the front door of the building as fast as his squatty legs could carry him.

"I told you to hurry," he said, smiling.

"They're gonna know we're here," Dominic was out of breath. He still had the knapsack over his shoulder.

"They may," Vinnie said. "But knowing is one thing and proving is another."

Dominic and Vinnie tried to sit at a table in the darkest corner of the bar, but the spot was already taken by four bikers and two girls, all of whom Dominic had no desire to be anywhere near. As they moved closer, the biggest of the four men stood up and made it known that Dominic and his short stocky companion weren't welcome.

A haze of blue smoke filled the bar, layered like long, thin clouds. The two men found a pair of stools by the bar. Neon light from beer signs — Miller, Budweiser, and Labatt's — coloured the air. Vinnie bought two drafts from a bartender whose last job must have been pouring out slop at chow time in the penitentiary. The rest of the crowd looked hours away from a parole violation. Dominic had put back half his beer when three police officers came in. The bar's clientele took no notice, as if police visits were as common as a tattoo artist and as regular as a hooker doing shift work.

The police spoke to no one. They walked up and down between

the tables looking at every face. Dominic started to breathe heavily and Vinnie patted him on the back. Vinnie got up from his bar stool and walked towards a group of bikers gathered around one of the two pool tables. He seemed to know one of them, and gave him a fake punch to the gut. The biker put his arm around the little boxer's shoulders. He appeared to be introducing him to the other bikers around the table.

A waitress in a black leather vest with a tattoo of a rose running across her breasts leaned over and tapped Dominic on the shoulder. He almost jumped off his stool.

"You new here?" Her throat had known too many cigarettes and her eyes had seen too much of everything.

"Yeah, came in a while ago. Nice place." Dominic pretended to look around. One of the policemen was walking by the bar. Dominic could see the coldness of his gun, which was unlocked in its holster.

"Well, you can come back anytime," the waitress said. "A girl gets tired of these old things and needs a little fresh blood."

"Thanks. Yeah, maybe later." Dominic took another breath as the policeman looked at him and paused for a moment.

"What are you drinking?" the policeman said.

The question caught Dominic off-guard. He looked down at his glass. "Beer."

"When did you get here?" Any closer and Dominic would have been able to see the sweat forming on his brow reflected in the cop's silver badge.

The waitress came over and pressed her chest into Dominic's shoulder. "He's been here all night," she said. "I got a tab running for him and everything." She gave Dominic a kiss on the cheek. "You should slow down, honey. You're already into me for a hundred bucks."

The cop looked the waitress up and down, apparently more interested in her breasts than in any information she had given him.

"Take it easy, then," the cop said. "We've got a lot a radar traps out there tonight and we're bound to find quite a few drivers who'll blow over the limit."

"I'm only a passenger," Dominic said.

The cop walked away.

"Thanks," Dominic said.

"My pleasure, honey. But you do owe me a hundred bucks."

"Yeah, guess I do."

Vinnie returned holding a set of keys. "I got us a car. Figure they're gonna be looking for two guys on a bike going real fast. A buddy of mine will drive the Harley up to Hamilton. We'll leave as soon as the cops clear out."

Dominic took out his wallet. It was as skinny as he was.

"I'm short at the moment."

"No, you're not," the waitress said. "Him, he's short. But you, honey, I'll take it in trade."

"Rough trade," Vinnie said. "I should let you have him." Vinnie paid the waitress, settling in for a long night.

They waited until three a.m. Dominic and Vinnie spent two hours shooting pool and chatting up bikers who regaled the Hamilton boys with tales of police chases, drug deals gone bad, and long stories about short stays in jail. Dominic saw more women with long, blonde hair and tight jeans than he ever saw in a strip club, and almost as much skin. At three o'clock, Vinnie got behind the wheel of a borrowed Ford Tempo and cruised back to the highway. The trip to Hamilton took an hour, far off Vinnie's record. They passed two speed traps and spotted roadblocks set up on several overpasses, but not a single law enforcement official took any notice of the two men from Hamilton and their overstuffed knapsack.

"What do you think is in there?" Vinnie said

"I really don't want to know."

By the time they passed the Welcome to Hamilton sign, Dominic was fast asleep, clutching the polyester knapsack like a security blanket.

# 30

Tony's first instinct was to meet with Criminisi, let him handle this. On his orders, pieces of that Mustang would end up in every junk yard, pawn shop, and part shop within five hundred miles of the city. But Tony wanted to avoid linking Constantine with the mob, in any way. That was the reason the Mustang had to disappear in the first place. And Tony really wanted to see the car for himself.

He had another strategy. He pointed his Mercedes in the direction of Fortinos market. His goal: make Leo Deluca his bitch.

The butcher had hung around Tony's house around the time Rosemary took Aldo to the emergency ward on the afternoon of the christening. He and Tony had a drink together after most of the other guests had left.

"Dominic's got himself into big trouble," Leo had said.

Tony remembered telling him he didn't want to hear about it. He didn't want to hear anything about Dominic ever again. Not until the phone call from Benedict.

"He's chopping cars for Criminisi," Leo had told him. The two of them were sipping J&B, but Leo didn't have the DiPietro gift for alcohol. Tony could tell that Leo was putting the liquor to his mouth more out of respect than pleasure.

"If you're so worried about it," Tony had said, "you should do something about it. But don't bother me. I don't care if Dominic's in jail, painting cars, or lying drunk on some street corner and living in a cardboard box."

"I can't turn him in. I should, but I can't. I'm just hoping he straightens himself out."

"What you saw today is the real Dominic DiPietro," Tony told him. "I've lived with it long enough. Whatever happens to Dominic will be by his own hand."

But now Dominic had become Tony's problem again. Only this time, without contacting Criminisi Tony had no idea where to find him. Leo, he thought, might be the best guy to let him know. Tony found him where you'd always find a butcher, chopping meat in full public view.

"Leo," Tony said to him from the other side of the display cabinet. Leo looked up and slipped his carving knife into its sleeve. "I need to talk you, in private."

Leo waved him behind the counter. "Let's go in the back."

Leo and Tony stepped into the open refrigerator among the sides of beef, pork, and lamb that hung from steel hooks.

"I need to find Dominic."

Leo looked down. "I don't know if I can help you. I haven't seen him since Aldo's christening."

"I thought you might know where his shop is."

Leo paused and took a deep breath of protein-packed air. "Yeah, he invited me down when he first got started. He actually thought I might want to help him out."

"He's gonna need your help now," Tony said. "He's got himself in deeper with some folks who aren't to be messed with. I need to warn him."

Leo shook his head, "What is it with him?"

"I don't know, and by now you'd think I wouldn't care, but he's my brother. I've been looking out for him for almost twenty-five years. I can't stop now."

"His shop is over on Brampton Street, by the harbour piers in one of those industrial plazas." Tony knew it well. Criminisi had offered him a piece of the building when he first bought it.

"Thanks, Leo. Have you told anyone else about Dominic working with Criminisi?"

"No. I considered calling the police, but it's Dominic's business, I guess."

"That's good, at least for now."

"For now?"

"Yeah. I may ask you to report him, for his own protection. I hope it doesn't come to that. I'll let you know."

Tony stopped his Mercedes a few blocks from the Brampton Street address Leo had given him. It was early. He'd left his home to pay his brother an unannounced visit. It had to be unannounced.

He pulled up to the double garage doors, which had been blacked out. It looked more like a crack house than an automotive business.

The front door was locked, as Tony expected. At least Dominic wasn't stupid enough to allow strangers to walk in from the street. He went around the building looking for the rear door, which he found beside a trailer parked in the back lot. Gino and Sammy were loading auto parts into the trailer. Ignoring them, he walked to the door and let himself in.

The place looked like any other chop shop he's seen in his thirty years in the body shop business. The security was more lax, but Tony knew that was because Dominic hadn't been busted yet. It would only be a matter of time before Dominic had armed guards and a video surveillance system eyeballing the entire building. If he remained in business that long.

What surprised Tony was the Mustang convertible on the other side of the shop. Back from the steel company's sandblasters, it had been sanded clean down to the steel and lay ready for paint like a blank canvas awaiting the artist's arrival. He walked over to the car, pacing an unconscious circle of respect around it. He was inspecting a job his own shop would never see. The car shone even without paint. He ran his hand across the hood and felt super-smooth metal ground so fine that it might have been surgical steel.

"Who the hell are you?" Andy said, emerging from behind the grease-stained vinyl wall. She had been working on the Mustang's engine and power train, and she held a large wrench, gripped like a weapon, in her right hand.

"I should be asking you," Tony said.

She raised the wrench to her shoulder and readied it.

"What are you doing here?" Dominic said. He looked like he just woke up. His hair was pulled in every direction and there were dark circles under his eyes. Tony took his hands off the car.

"Nice work," he said.

"Like I said, what are you doing here? How the hell did you find me?"

"Who's he?" Andy said.

"My brother, Tony."

Tony ran his finger along the trunk. "How are you getting it so smooth?"

"We do all the things here that you wouldn't give me the time for, like proper sanding and acid washes. That, and I've got a sandblaster that'll strip your face down to the skull in twenty seconds. Wanna try it?"

"You'll never make a nickel on a job like this."

"I guess that's my business, isn't it. I'll ask you again: how the hell did you find me?"

Tony swept his hand across the hood of the trunk, unable to hide his admiration. "I told you, Dominic, I know everything you do. All of it. All the time. When are you going to start believing me?"

"How's Aldo doing?"

"He's fine. He spent a week in the hospital, mostly for observation. He'll be okay, we think. But I suspect he'll link the sight of you with pain for a long, long time."

213

Sammy and Gino came in for another load. The sight of the two brothers face-to-face froze them in their tracks.

"Come on in, guys. I assume you've got something to do with this place, too."

Sammy and Gino approached warily. Dominic joined them, hoping that their increased numbers would give him some advantage.

"I'm here to warn you," Tony said.

"About what?" Dominic said.

"Give me a chance and I'll tell you. I figure you've got a couple of days to close this place down before you're all busted."

Sammy said, "I told you this would happen. I warned you, Dominic. We're fucked. We're really fucked."

"Consider the source," Dominic said. "How the hell would you know anything about us being busted?"

"Because I'm the one who's gonna make sure it happens."

"You really can't stand it that I'm on my own, can you?"

"Actually, Dominic, I've come to enjoy the fact that you're not around. The air is a lot cleaner at the shop and my bottom line has improved, too."

"Then what the fuck is your problem? Can't stand the competition?"

"No. I haven't got a problem with you chopping up cars. You gotta do what you gotta do, and I figure auto theft and destruction of stolen property is about the best you can manage. So no, I don't give a shit about you and your business."

"So what is it?"

"It's this car." Tony leaned against the front quarter-panel of the Mustang and crossed his arms against his chest.

"You can't have it," Dominic said.

"Believe me, I don't want it. I just want you to get rid of it."

"What?"

"That's right. Drag this car off to the junkyard and crush it. Hell, I don't even mind if you chop it up and sell the parts. Just don't restore it. Don't paint it, don't drive it, and for chrissakes don't put any plates on it."

Gino said, "I don't understand."

Tony cleared his throat, then spit on the floor. "I don't need you to understand. Any of you. Just do as you're told and get rid of the Mustang. Then you little fucks can carry on with your precious little business. Bury this car or I'll have the cops down here so fast you won't have time to wipe the shit from your pants."

"He won't do that," Andy said. "This shop's protected."

"Yeah, Tony," Dominic said. "You know that, cause you know *everything*."

"I'm not afraid of Criminisi and his thugs, if that's what you're thinking."

"You're not going to do a damn thing. This is just about me. You can't bear to see me succeed. You want me to stay here, chopping cars. Well, it won't work. That Mustang is my future. I won't give it up."

"You gonna have to, or I won't be able to do anything to protect you."

"I've never asked you to protect me."

"But Papa did. He knew you were always going to be a fuck-up. It was his dying wish, you know: *take care of Dominic*."

Dominic pretended not to care what his father had thought about him. He also knew that, coming from Tony, there was a good chance that the words were a pointed lie, barbed and cruel.

"I can protect myself. Your duties on behalf of our father are officially discharged."

Tony backed away from the car. "Dominic, I'll make you a deal. Come back to work for me. You can go back on the paint line. Forget that you ever got involved with the guys."

Dominic lit a cigarette. "You and I are done. Now, I'm asking you nicely, please leave."

"Listen, Dominic. Either you get rid of that Mustang, or I'll have

215

the cops come by and drag it away."

"He can't do that," Andy said to Dominic. "Can he?"

"Watch me, little girl. Just watch me." Tony turned and left.

Sammy said. "What was that all about?"

"Like I said, he just doesn't want me to succeed."

"You really think he'll call the police?" Gino said.

"Not a chance, if only because he wants to keep the DiPietro name out of the papers. If we're busted, his name will appear beside mine, and that would be bad for business. He's not about to do anything that could hurt his image or his pocketbook."

"What do we do now?" Gino said.

"We either move the Mustang, or get rid of it." Dominic walked to the employee lounge. He reached into the old fridge and pulled out a Budweiser.

"You said you'd quit," Andy said, following him.

Dominic flopped himself down on the couch. "I have." He put the unopened Budweiser on the coffee table, the label towards him. "The last thing I need right now is that fuck of a brother of mine showing up and sticking his nose in my business. He's got everyone here all stirred up."

"We're worried, that's all." Andy put some change into the coffee machine. She watched the cup drop and fill with water, coffee, and powdered cream. She put in another set of coins and repeated the process. She sat down on the other side of the couch, putting one of the cups of coffee in front of Dominic. "Your guys are not used to working below the legal radar screen."

"And you are?"

"Are you asking if I've had to do some things that I wouldn't put on a résumé? Yeah. You try raising a kid on your own. You do what you have to do."

"I didn't realize that you had a kid."

"You never asked. You never ask about anything that doesn't have to do with you."

Dominic took a pack of cigarettes from his pocket and offered her one.

"I don't smoke."

"I guess I should have known that, too." Dominic let a cigarette for himself.

"Proves my point."

"Sorry," he said. "I've been a little preoccupied."

Andy smiled, a wry smile, but a smile. "If you buy being preoccupied as an excuse for being self-centered, that's like saying you're sorry for being a drunk when the real problem is that you drink too much."

"If I need my head shrunk I'll call a professional, thank you."

"I'm just saying that you could care a little more about your friends here. We've all taken on a big risk by getting involved in this. You could show a little appreciation."

"I didn't know you'd elevated yourself to the friend category. Don't push it. Gino, Sammy, and I have been friends for years. You need to put some mileage on our relationship before I'd start calling you a friend."

"Friends or not, you're asking a lot of us."

"I'm not forcing anybody to do this."

"You sure as hell are."

"Bullshit. Any of you can walk away from this anytime you want to. Me? I'm not so lucky."

"I'm here on a promise that you're going to make me a partner in your restoration business. Like I said, I've got a kid to take care of. So your dreams are my dreams."

"My headaches are more significant now than my dreams, what with Tony fucking around with me again. God, I really thought I was done with him."

"You're just a spoiled little boy, Dominic. 'Poor me. All my friends are free to do whatever they want and I have to stay inside and work for the ogre.' Christ. My four-year-old is more mature than you."

"Maturity's got nothing to do with it. I'm the one who laid it on the line with Criminisi, not you, not Sammy. Not any one of you."

"You really think we're not on the hook?"

"Not like me, you're not. If we get caught, you guys might get your wrists slapped, pay a fine or something. I'm in charge, which means jail time — and that would be the good part. Criminisi's not the type of guy to let the people who work for him get busted, then squeal on him."

"You think he'd kill you?"

"At the moment, no. I'm just lucky that you can't collect from a dead guy. But if it ever came down to a conflict of interest between him and me, I got no illusions about what side of the grass I'd end up in."

"You gotta get out of this business."

"Get out?" Dominic laughed. "There's no getting out. As soon as I left Tony, I was dead. Criminisi even tried to warn me, like he was trying to protect me, or something. But I wouldn't listen to him, or Tony either."

"There has to be a way."

"If you think of one, let me know. I thought that I could use the Mustang to buy my way out, but I was wrong."

"You still can."

"No way. You heard Tony. He's gonna steal it right out from under me. He's got cops on his payroll. Trust me, if he wants to take me down, he'll find a way, and there's not a thing I can do about it."

Andy stood up. "I think it's time for me to leave."

"When will you be back?"

"I'm not coming back."

"What do you mean you're not coming back? We've got an engine to finish."

"Why would I come back? What's in it for me? At first, it was enough that I was getting to work on this great car. I even got to thinking that I might make a place for myself here. I've got good hands, you know? Real good hands. Know my way around an engine better than anyone."

"You do. You're amazing."

"If I'm so goddamn amazing, why the hell don't you give a shit?"

"I do."

"Just words, like most every other man who's ever been in my life. Words. They make me wanna puke. I thought you were different. I thought you wanted to restore fabulous cars. I thought you wanted to make something of yourself."

"I ..."

"I was going to make something of myself, too. But now big brother shows up and scares you away. Well, I've had enough. I'm not hanging my dreams on yours anymore. I'd rather go back to working with my legs in the air."

"You, you're a ... a prostitute?"

"I prefer not to think of myself that way. But that's right. I was a prostitute, a hooker — whatever you want to call me. With a kid to raise and no one in this town interested in hiring a goddamn woman mechanic. How the hell else was I supposed to make money? But then Gino starts sending me cars to work on. Then that little fucker introduces me to you. You and your little boy dreams."

"Is that where you met the Romanian? On the job?"

"Yeah. He's a john. The place I work for is run by a couple of Criminisi's guys and their girlfriends. They make us put out for their fellow cretins like Nastasi." She spat. "I'd rather flush him back into the sewer he crawled out of."

"I'm sorry."

"I don't want your pity. I want to work on the Mustang. I want to put that car on the road and have everyone know that I got the engine to purr."

"Are you still hooking?"

"Not since I started working on the Mustang. It's been nice being home at night for the kid."

219

"You can't go back."

"I'm going to have to. You don't understand, Dominic. I'm not doing this because I want to. I have to."

"You're quitting on me."

"You're the one who's quitting on me, Dominic."

"I haven't quit," Dominic said. He put the coffee down on the floor. "I just gotta adjust my plans a bit. It's what I always do."

"I can see how well that's worked. I don't know if you're stupid or just plain crazy."

"Neither. I'm practical."

Andy laughed. "Is that what you call it? Practical? Living on a couch in the back of some mobster's warehouse and cutting up cars? You're insane."

"I have no other choice."

"Sure you do."

"What?"

"Stand up for yourself. Stop letting your brother, Criminisi, and especially that Romanian piece of shit push you around."

"That will get me killed."

"That's the risk you have to take. What are you willing to do to make your dreams come true? Are you willing to take a risk?"

"You don't call what I had to do last night a risk?"

"You're just running scared."

"Who the fuck are you to tell me what to do?"

"I'm someone who's taking every sort of risk to raise her kid right. Men. You never get it."

"Your solution is hooking?"

"Being a hooker wasn't the solution. Not being a hooker was the solution, and it's a helluva lot riskier."

Dominic sat straight in the couch, reaching down to the floor to raise the beer to his mouth, then stopped. All the risks he'd taken until now had only dug the hole in his life deeper, as if every step he'd taken was down. Tony's arrival had only sealed the top of the hole. He didn't know the way out, only that somehow, Andy was connected to all this. "I can't just stop working for Criminisi. It's not like I can clean out my locker and walk away from this place. It's not that simple."

"So it's not simple. Are you stupid or something?" Another woman standing in front him, like a mirror, reflecting his every flaw. Yet, he didn't want to lose her.

"No."

"Then figure it out. That's the real reason I'll stick around. I want to get that car on the road, and I know the two of us can do it."

Dominic stared up at her eyes, brown and open, honest and caring. "It's not about mechanics and body work, not anymore."

"No." Andy bowed her head. "When life's going along the way you want it to, doing the right thing is easy. The difference between a good person and a bad person is how they handle the tough times." She brushed back the hair from her face. "Your brother, Nastasi, and guys like them cheat, or quit. Is that what you wanna do?"

# 31

Tony called Constantine from his desk at the office.

"Did you find out who's got the car?"

Tony told him that Dominic had the Mustang and was preparing to put it back on the road, then likely put it up for sale.

"That's good. That's very good. We can keep this quiet."

"I'm working on it. Dominic is not being as co-operative as I hoped."

"You've got to make him co-operate."

"Co-operation and my brother are mutually exclusive. I thought I might get a bailiff to seize the car, as an asset to hold against a debt."

"You'd need a court order," Constantine said. "But that's not the problem. Right now your brother doesn't legally own the car. The estate of Roberto Constantine does. The means me, and I don't want my name attached to this car in any way."

"So the legal route won't work?"

"Not until your brother takes ownership of the car, and by then it'll be too late. The newspapers will be all over him and the car. And I'm fucked."

"You'll be fine," Tony said. "That car will never see the light of day."

"Good. I'm counting on you. You're the only guy I trust to take care of this. Let's hope that by the time we launch the campaign on Thursday, you'll have put this problem far behind us." He hung up.

Tony took a deep breath. He opened up the humidor on this desk and removed a Montecristo. He stared at it for a moment then returned it to the ebony embossed cedar box. He opened a desk drawer and pulled out a local phone book. Flipping though the pages, he found the number for Fortinos.

When he had Leo on the line he said, "Things are going to get bad for Dominic, real bad. We've got to get him into some kind of protective custody or he's going to get hurt, maybe worse … Yeah that's right. Nobody else is going to help him, that's for sure …

"I want you to contact the police. Call the downtown detachment and ask to speak to Sergeant Benedict. He's a friend of the family. Tell him about what Dominic's up to and that you think he's in trouble. Benedict will have him picked up and keep it out of the papers … It's for his own protection, Leo … No, I can't do it. People know that Dominic and I are on the outs right now. Besides, it just doesn't sound right, me calling it in. It'll be better if one of his friends does it. He'll thank you for it, one day, I'm sure."

Tony hung up and walked over to the wall of glass that separated him from the shop floor. He stood there for twenty minutes before he moved, deaf to the whir of business going on below him. Finally he picked up the phone and dialled.

"Alfonso," he said. "We have to talk."


Dominic and Andy left the employee lounge and went into the main garage. Sammy and Gino were wet sanding the Mustang, rubbing the surface with damp emery cloth and sloshing off the remaining rough-edge remnants of paint and steel with the power washer.

"How's it looking?" Dominic asked.

Sammy took his hands off the car. "This baby is smooth, man. I guarantee you there's not a blemish on it." Dominic ran the tips of his fingers around the area on the passenger side where the chrome door handle should be. He smiled like a man enjoying the comfortable feel of a lover's skin.

"Is the chrome back?"

"Tomorrow. Vinnie's taking his Jeep into Toronto to pick it up. He'll need cash — about four grand's worth."

"We'll be ready," Dominic said, feeling a flush in his face that reminded of the times he'd get to drinking and it started to seem as if everything was right with the world. He crouched down by the wheel well on the passenger side and inspected the new steel on the front quarter-panel.

"This is magnificent," he said. "It looks factory-fucking-perfect."

"I told you we had some great guys at the steel company," Sammy said, his arms crossed in triumph. He had taken the damaged fender to work and had a few of his friends refabricate it using rolled steel plate.

"Just take some acid to it," Dominic said. "Etch it down, then smooth it out with more emery cloth. It'll be perfect." He stood up and looked down into the empty engine compartment.

"And the engine?"

Gino said, "Andy was here 'til about eleven last night. She says she got it pretty much back together. You're just working on the electrics, right?"

"Yeah," Andy wiped her wrist across her grease-stained face. "Give me a day, I'll have it turning over. Two days, she'll win Daytona."

"Then we're on schedule." Dominic looked at his watch. "All that's left to do is get this baby out of Tony's reach, and I know just where to put it."

"Where?" Gino asked.

"The last place he'd look. Right under his own nose. Nicky's old shop. I went by there last week. Nostalgia, I guess. The place is empty. Tony hasn't touched it since he bought it. It's way too small for his high-volume operation. But it's got a great paint booth and drying oven." Dominic grinned at Andy. "I'll be able to give this car a better finish than Ford ever gave her."

"Don't you think that's dangerous?" Sammy said. "There's got to be another place."

"Not one that has the paint and body facilities we need to finish the car."

"Still," Sammy said, "you think you can trust that paint wholesaler, what's his name?"

"Janowitz? No way. He's got his nose so far up Tony's ass, he has to ask permission to breathe."

Sammy was pacing, practically spinning in place. "Then what are we doing?" He started breathing heavily.

"Gino," Dominic said. "Get the car on the travellers. Sammy and Vinnie, you're breaking into Nicky's place. We need the car inside and ready to go tonight. I'll meet you there."

"Where are you going?" Andy asked.

"To get the money to finish the Mustang."

The owner of the building had knocked it down a decade before. It was more profitable to use the land as a parking lot and wait for Hamilton's real estate market to come back than to sit on a vacant office tower. Tony liked to meet Criminisi there; a small bribe to the attendant was all that was usually required to hang around undisturbed for as much time as they wanted.

Tony didn't recognize the attendant, who looked like he'd come straight from an aerobics class at the Y.

"Where's Willy," Tony asked.

"Off sick," the attendant said. "You're Tony, right?"

The question put Tony on guard.

"Willy mentioned you. Told me to let you have access to the back stalls along the wall. No charge."

Tony looked at the punch clock in the booth. It was ten thirty in the morning. Criminisi would be there at any moment.

"Thank Willy for me," Tony said. "Let him know I hope he gets better real soon."

"I will." The attendant returned his attention to the *Hamilton Spectator* while Tony drove his Mercedes to the back of the lot.

Moments later, Criminisi's Lincoln Continental appeared. Tony got out of his car and opened the door of the Lincoln, sliding beside Criminisi in the back seat.

"What is our problem today?" Criminisi asked tersely. "I don't like unscheduled meetings."

Teddy Spagnoli sat behind the wheel. "For one, I found your chop shop with one phone call." Criminisi didn't look amused. "If I can do it, so can the cops. I suggest you return to your previous strategy. I figure the cops are a few days away from busting the joint."

"Alright. I should thank you for that information. But why did you feel the need to test our, it would seem, rather lax security?"

"I needed to talk to Dominic. He's got something that doesn't belong to him."

Criminisi puffed out a small laugh. "Everything your brother has belongs to somebody else, or used to."

"Now one of those somebodys wants his property back." Tony told Criminisi about the Mustang, omitting the details of Sal Constantine's involvement and the car's ties to his brother, Roberto.

"We don't chop older cars," Criminisi said. "Late models only. The newer the better."

"This isn't a chop job," Tony told him. "It's a restoration project."

"Why is this a problem for me? This has been Dominic's plan all along. You know that."

Tony frowned. "I want it stopped, Alfonso. This thing is getting way too close to me. And now, with this restoration job, Dominic is about to butt heads with some very important people in this town, people who are very leery about any association with the way you and Dominic conduct your business."

Criminisi fussed with the crease in his pants. "You're no angel yourself."

"No, I'm not. But I got the good sense to operate under the radar."

"As we all try to do," Criminisi said.

"Then listen to me. This car that Dominic's restoring can ruin everything you've ever worked for. Maybe me, too."

Criminisi sat quiet, staring for a moment out the darkened rear window. "I can't lose Dominic, not right now. I need him, unless of course you …"

"You already know the answer to that …"

"Then, I have no choice. The imports are coming in now. Dominic and his team have to begin their real jobs for us. After he's finished, then he could be considered disposable."

"Dominic's your problem now. Just make sure that Mustang of his never sees the light of day."

"I'll need a reason."

"I'll give you one. The Mustang used to belong to Sal Constantine's brother."

"The jeweller?"

"One in the same. This car will destroy Constantine's campaign."

"So it would." Criminisi looked back out the window. "So it would."

Criminisi welcomed Dominic with a hug, kissing him on one cheek before directing him to sit down. Spagnoli sat at one corner of the couch, across from Criminisi's desk. Nastasi sat on a pile of Canada Dry cases high enough to act as a stool. Dominic thought the Romanian looked bored, like he hadn't bloodied anybody's nose in several days.

"I can't tell you how important this is to me," Criminisi said. "I hope you got across the border without any trouble."

"Oh no, no problem," Dominic said.

"I knew you were special as soon as I met you. Have you brought the package?"

"Sure, here," Dominic said. He handed the knapsack to Criminisi.

"Ah, good. I've been anxious to receive this," Criminisi said. He shook the bag as if to inspect its weight to verify that nothing inside was broken. He opened the small padlock with a twist of his hand. It needed no key.

Dominic was as excited to know what he's risked jail time to smuggle across the border as he was to receive payment for the job. Criminisi reached into the knapsack and removed a carton of Marlboro cigarettes, then another, then another.

"That's it?"

"Yes."

"You're paying me five thousand dollars to bring you cigarettes? Five cartons of cigarettes?"

"Yes, you were bringing me cigarettes. Are you surprised?"

"There's got to be something in the cartons, right? Tell me there's something in the cartons, please. Cocaine, or maybe a whole lot of cash. It's cash, right? That would weigh about the same as a carton or two of cigarettes."

"No, my young friend, just Marlboros." Criminisi cracked one of the cartons and took out a fresh pack of US Grade Number 1 cigarettes. He opened the pack, took out a Marlboro, and ran it under his nose, inhaling deeply. He offered the open pack to Dominic.

"You want one? Take one, please. These are so much better than the Canadian tobacco we have to put up with. And the taxes we pay! It's the government who are the criminals, not me." He blew a cloud of American-made smoke into Dominic's face.

"I could have gone to jail for this. I had a policeman pull a gun on me!"

"I am sorry. But you must understand, I had to be sure."

"Sure of what?"

"That you could be trusted."

"Why ...?"

"You offended me young man. You apologized, but still I was not sure." Criminisi stood up from his desk.

"Now I am sure. I can trust you."

Dominic exhaled.

"What would you have me do," Criminisi said. "Ask you to take that *pistola* I gave you and shoot the Romanian here? You think this is the movies where you have to knock somebody off before you are part of the family? No." Criminisi slapped his hand down like he was admonishing a small dog. "I just needed you to take a risk for me, on my behalf. One that you would not ordinarily take."

"I hope I passed."

"You did. With honours. This was an expensive test for me, but you should know it is not without personal reward, as I cannot buy these cigarettes in Canada. And the terms of my agreement with the Government of the United States prevent me from making any unannounced excursions to my homeland at this particular time." Criminisi took an envelope from his jacket pocket and handed it to Dominic. "So while the test was costly, it was not without reward for both of us."

Dominic inspected the envelope, which contained the cash he needed to finish the Mustang.

Criminisi savoured the cigarette the way Tony would a cedar-aged Cuban. "Still, you are not being one hundred percent truthful with me."

"I've done whatever you asked," Dominic answered.

"I understand that you've begun operations out of your restoration shop. A Mustang, I am told."

Dominic glanced over at the Romanian, figuring he had told Criminisi about the car. "Yes, we were working on an old wreck, but it's beyond hope."

"You did not tell me about it. We are partners, are we not?"

"Sure. But I was really just trying to keep my crew busy. The supply of cars had dropped off and I needed something for them to do. Like I said, the car's beyond hope. I scrapped it."

"It's gone then."

Dominic summoned the strength of every lie he'd ever told. "Alfonso, there is one thing other than painting cars that I'm really good at, that's tearing them apart. That Mustang is in a thousand pieces. The man who designed that car wouldn't be able to figure out how to put it back together."

Criminisi appeared to be weighing the veracity of Dominic's assertion. "Alright. But I want you to promise me that should you ever come into possession of such an … opportunity … again, you will discuss it with me. Much could have been made of that Mustang. You are too young to know that the value of many things is beyond what the open market will pay for them."

Dominic was surprised, but kept his composure. "I promise," he said. Criminisi seemed to buy it.

"Starting today, I am shutting down the chop shop." Dominic's eyes grew wide. "Tomorrow, you and your crew start working on the import side of the business."

"We'll be ready," Dominic said. But he did not know for what.

# 32

"We're not alone," Vinnie said. He had scratched an eye-sized patch off the paint on the shop's front window. "There's an unmarked police car sitting half a block down the street. I saw one of them slip out for a cup of coffee."

"You sure?" Sammy said.

"Sure as shit," Vinnie said. "Those guys aren't very subtle. Any idiot could have spotted them."

Dominic came to the window and bent down to peer through Vinnie's eyepiece. "Looks like Tony really went and did it. I wouldn't have believed it." He'd been a pendulum of nerves since he returned from his meeting with Criminisi, alternating between the high of coming back with the cash to finish the Mustang and the anxiety of what Criminisi would expect from him next.

"They might be here because of the border run," Vinnie said.

"I don't know what's going on," Dominic said. "But it's time to get the Mustang out of here." Dominic stepped away from the window.

Gino and Andy came in through the rear loading doors. "I got the U-Haul," he said. "But I'd rather use the flatbed. I don't know if that rusted beast they rented us will take the weight."

Dominic said, "It's gonna have to. There's no way I want those cops to see us hauling that Mustang out of here. I don't anyone to see anything. That U-Haul will hold the car, that's all I care about. Let's get it in."

With Andy behind the wheel, Dominic and company pushed the bare steel Mustang through the shop and into the U-Haul, which was backed into the rear loading doors. The truck was just high enough to reach the loading dock. They pushed the Mustang into the U-Haul's box and rolled down the door. The truck dropped two feet when the car was fully loaded. Its shocks fell to rock bottom.

"Any more weight and we'd be dragging the bumper," Gino said.

"Don't worry about that," Andy said. "It's the engine that's gonna go. My guess? We get about five miles on a flat road before it overheats."

Dominic said, "Then let's hope its all downhill." He tapped the hood of the truck for luck and climbed into the driver's seat. Andy, Gino, and Vinnie squeezed in alongside him. Sammy remained on sentry duty at the chop shop. He bent over and peeked through Vinnie's eyepiece for fifteen minutes before he realized that he could stack several flats of Coca-Cola from Criminisi's overflow delivery and make a stool for himself. He folded a pair of Queenston Vending overalls into a pillow to soften the seat, sat down, and smoked incessantly as he watched the unmarked car watching him watching them.


The U-Haul wheezed and bucked, it's gears ground down through amateur abuse and neglect, but Dominic managed to direct the truck and its precious cargo through the maze of streets from east Hamilton to number 1001 Cannon Street, a drunk's stumbling walk from Ivor Wynne Stadium. Vinnie had broken in earlier and dismantled the security system. Gino and Sammy had cleaned it up, not a speck of dust or cobweb or stray piece of dirt could be detected. Dominic turned on the lights and sought out the power panel. He pulled down a series of high amp breakers. One by one he heard the roar of exhaust fans powering up like vintage World

War I biplanes, and the click-click-click of the paint ovens heating up. Dominic smiled from ear-to-ear. He could barely contain himself. He skipped around the old body shop like a kid left alone in donut shop. He poked at the double dips and licked the maple creams. He drew the smell of fresh roasted coffee into his lungs and exhaled happiness on waves of anticipation. This body shop was his home. He knew it in January. Today, at least, it would be his playground.

Secure in the shop, the Mustang sat like a meditating princess — silent, serene, and ready for its coronation. Its bare steel gleamed — swirls and scratches etched into its surface. It was a naked as a car could be. No seats, no carpet, no roof, no bumpers, no chrome rings around any of the headlamps, no brake lights, no wire, engine, or transmission. The last pieces of its anatomy — the wires that powered it, the wheels and tires, the steering wheel and gaskets — had all been stripped out. It wasn't a car at all. It was a skull. It was up to Dominic to replace its muscle and skin and for Andy to give it back its heart.

Dominic fumbled around in his toolbox. He found filters but no mask. He slipped a sanding mask over his nose and mouth, looking more like a dentist than an automobile painter.

"This is going to have to do," he said. "You guys get out of here. This stuff will kill you if too much of it gets in your lungs."

Vinnie, Gino, and Andy left to hug some cups of coffee and wait for Dominic to finish. Dominic danced his fingers over the Mustang's front fender. He fired the paint gun in the air away from the car and adjusted the mixture of air, primer, and pressure until he was satisfied. He covered the car in a primer coat that was smooth enough for most new car finishes, yet he had three primer coats still to go. Three primer coats, three hand sands, six coats of Ford White, Code M — brand name Wimbledon White — six more light sands, then three coats of clear coat, enough to have the Mustang sparkle under the faintest starlight.

He turned off the sprayer and cleared its nozzle. He slipped off the paper mask and coughed into his hand. Grey primer blended with his phlegm. He wiped it off on the pants of his coveralls.

"Shit," he said. He didn't want to lay down another coat without a proper mask and filter system.

Sammy was sleeping on the Salvation Army couch when he heard the banging on the back door. He scrambled to the door and peered through the peephole. The black holes of Nastasi's eyes stared back at him. Sammy pulled back the deadbolt.

"Where is DiPietro?" Nastasi said. He was alone.

"He's not here. It's just me … and Gino, Vinnie, Leo, and Frankie … Yeah … just me and the guys … all eight of them … just me and the big guys … the ones that haul the parts out, you know … we're waiting for Dominic to come back."

The Romanian looked over Sammy's shoulder. "You tell DiPietro that he and your guys, all them, need to be ready at eight o'clock tonight."

"You mean more cars are coming?"

"Not coming. Going. You will be picked up at eight o'clock, all of you. And don't forget to bring the whore. We got special job for her."

# 33

Sammy paced around the empty shop smoking and wearing a circular rut into the concrete floor. He'd been pacing since Nastasi left. That was five hours ago. It was another two hours before Dominic and his crew returned. The Romanian's order surprised everyone except Dominic. While not having specific knowledge of the purpose of the instructions, he had nevertheless been steeling himself for whatever Criminisi might request.

"Where the hell is he going to take us?" Sammy said. Cigarette butts littered his path with almost as much clarity as dirt gathering beneath his feet. "What's this all about? For Chrissakes Dominic, what have you gotten me into? I'm supposed to just get up and go somewhere and follow this guy, do whatever he tells me to do. I mean, what if he tells us to bury some body or something, or maybe rough somebody up. He's not going to make us part of his gang or anything. I'm not from Romania, you know. His guys, you know, they're gonna start yammerin' on in Romanian or some kind of Slavic European fuck of a language. They could be debating with each other over what's the best way to kill us — knives or guns or bare fists — and we wouldn't know."

"So we'll speak Italian," Dominic said.

"I don't speak Italian. Christ, I barely speak English. You're not going to speak Italian when we get there? Are you? Please. I won't understand anybody."

"Jesus, Sammy, relax. I think he's only gonna have us work on some cars. It's all we know how to do. It can't be anything else."

"Working on cars is all *you* know. I'm a welder. Give me steel and fire I can make anything. What if he wants me to make something — like an iron coffin or something? What do I do?"

Sammy's answer came quickly enough. Nastasi maintained his usual promptness, arriving shortly after nine. The Romanian entered through the rear doors and was greeted by Sammy's Berlin Wall of anxiety.

"Do they teach people to read clocks in Romania?" Sammy said. "Do they have schools, does everyone learn to tell time by looking at the sun?"

"Shut that faggot's face before I do it permanently," Nastasi said to Dominic. "All of you. Follow me. Get into the van and keep your mouths shut." Nastasi looked at Sammy. "Especially you."

They were led to a GMC twelve-passenger van. Nastasi had blacked out the windows with dark tinting film, the kind you would see on street-modified Honda Civics for coolness or on limousines for privacy.

Sammy sat beside Dominic with Andy and Gino on the row of seats behind them. Vinnie took a seat by himself in the last row. Dominic heard the trunk door opening and the pounding metal sound of his toolbox being loaded. There were more shifts of weight as more of the team's equipment got piled into the back.

Spagnoli was behind the wheel. He turned around and tossed an empty pillowcase at each of them. "Put these on your heads," he said. "We're not moving until you do and we stop the first time I catch one of you taking them off. Whoever it is won't be seeing the end of this ride."

Dominic put the pillowcase over his head. It stank of old sweat. So thin was the material that he had no need to peek through the edges. Though darkness had come to Brampton Street, the glow of the streetlights articulated their path like breadcrumbs dropped along the way.

"I'm going to die in this," Sammy said, his voice muffled by the material of the pillowcase. "Either by suffocation or flying through a window, I'm as good as dead. He bobbed his head from side to side. "Did you see what they put us in? It's a GM passenger van. These things roll over and crush whoever's in them. They're death-traps. If this guy takes a corner at over forty miles per hour we're Spam!"

"Shut up back there," Nastasi said. He pulled himself up into the van and sat in the passenger seat. "No talking."

The journey took about a half an hour by Dominic's reckoning. The van rocked over several sets of railway tracks, and lurched to a stop about a dozen times: stop signs and stoplights, Dominic fig-ured. Nastasi obviously thought he was stupid or new to the city. Dominic wouldn't be surprised if the van wasn't taking them a mile or two down the road from the chop shop, somewhere along the waterfront.

"You better be careful," Dominic said. "Cops catch you carrying five guys with bags over their heads and driving around in circles for half an hour, it's going to look a little suspicious."

"I no think you talk so smart when I put knife to your throat," Nastasi said.

"Leave him alone, Bela," Spagnoli said. "You'll get your turn."

Dominic heard the creaky wheels of a large garage door roll open, and the van passed through into a building. Dominic sensed the light growing brighter, much brighter; it was powerful enough to break through the fabric of his hood. He winced in the dark enve-lope in which his head was hidden. The van lurched to a stop and its sliding doors opened. Pairs of rough hands pulled Dominic and his crew from the vehicle.

"Take off your hoods," Spagnoli said. They complied, blinking at the bright overhead lights that illuminated the room. For a moment, all Dominic could see was white light. The room was huge. It was a warehouse — by the harbour, as far as Dominic could tell. In front of him were Spagnoli, the Romanian, and the tiny capo Criminisi. Paulie, Zeno, and a dozen of their friends scattered about the reception area.

There were rows and rows of cars lined up like tin soldiers ready for battle. There were big ones and small ones. Green ones and silver ones, black, blue, and the occasional red one. A smattering of yellow ones gathered in the middle. Some had cracked windshields. Others broken headlights. A few looked good enough to drive out of the building. Dominic thought there were over a hundred cars lined up in front of them, each one a Mercedes.

"Sweet mother Mary and Joseph," Dominic said.

"What the ...?" Vinnie said.

Gino was speechless. Andy dropped her hood on the floor and walked over to Dominic.

"What's going on?" she said.

Criminisi walked towards them. "What is going on, my *doninna allegra*, is that I need all of you to finish some very important business for me. These fine automobiles have come into my possession, and as I mentioned to you some time ago, Dominic, I need you to help me reconfigure them before they go to market."

"What does he mean, reconfigure?" Sammy asked.

"Paint, body work, that sort of thing I'm guessing." Dominic said.

"And more," Spagnoli said. "These cars are from Europe. Germany, France, Italy, like that. They are not set up for sale in North America, not yet. The engines and exhaust systems need adjustments."

Andy had walked over to get a closer look at one of the Mercedes. She stood in front of a blue 1988 260E. "And parts. You're gonna need different parts."

"We know this," Nastasi said. "You should speak when asked, not before."

Criminisi waved his hand. "It's alright, Bela. We don't have time to stand on ceremony. All of these cars need to be road ready in ten days."

"You got a lot of work to do," Dominic said.

"No, my young partner, you and your friends do. I want each of these cars to look exactly like it should if it was a used North American Mercedes-Benz: the right colours, engine components, and, especially, the right mileage."

Andy opened the driver's side door to the blue 260E. "This beaut's got three hundred and fifty thousand kilometres on it. What was it, a taxi?"

"Precisely, my dear."

"So you want us to roll back the odometers," Dominic said.

"If that is what is required," Criminisi said.

"We got a container of used parts to work with," Spagnoli said. "Got Canadian and US parts, odometers, all that kind of shit. You should be able to switch them."

"Good," Dominic said. "The Germans don't take kindly to people screwing around with their odometers. It's gonna be easier to install new ones than roll back the originals."

Sammy had his arms crossed. "Now I know why we chopped up so many Benzes."

"Let us hope you extracted the parts well, my friends," Criminisi said. "For now you have to make use of them."

"You better expect some cannibalization," Dominic said. "Once we're through inspecting them all, I suspect we're going need parts that only some of the cars in this room can donate." He walked toward Criminisi. He spoke to him in a low whisper. "We can do this," he said. "But you mentioned to me that this would eliminate all my obligations to you."

"This is true."

"What about my crew. I can't ask them to do this without payment. Substantial payment."

"I understand," Criminisi said. "I will pay each of you ten thousand dollars for twenty days' work."

"No," Dominic said. He looked down and away from Criminisi.

"You have how many cars here? A hundred?"

"Three hundred and twenty-eight."

"That's more than fifteen cars a day."

"Yes, Dominic. I am aware of the mathematics."

"That's a lot of hours, and every one of my people have other jobs. They'll be spending all of their time here, for you. That means calling in sick and lost wages. They'll need much more money. And more time. Let's say twenty thousand per person, for fifteen days' work."

"Alright. But no more than fifteen days. I need these cars on the street."

"You'll have them. But I also want the cash up front."

Criminisi waved his hand. "You ask too much."

"Then we'll go back to work at the chop shop." Dominic saw cars, cash, and a team ready to work illegally. He believed, for once in his life, he had the power to negotiate. He started to walk back to the van.

"Bela!" Criminisi shouted across the warehouse. Bela nodded at his boss and went over to Criminisi's Lincoln. He opened the trunk. Dominic kept walking towards the van.

"Hey guys, let's go. Back in the van. We're going home."

"Stop right there," Spagnoli said.

"There's only one thing that will convince us to stay."

"We can make you stay. Force you to work." Criminisi said. Nastasi pulled four shotguns out of the Lincoln's trunk. He handed one to Spagnoli. The other two he handed to his biker enforcers.

"I would like to force you," Nastasi said.

"You could," Dominic said. He lit a cigarette. "But then quality control will go for shit. If you want to unload these cars on the public, or dealers, as I am sure you do, they still gotta look like Mercedes when we're done with them, not backyard makeovers."

"You work well, or die." Nastasi drew back the shotgun and pointed it at him.

"Listen, you Romanian fuck! You wouldn't know a good paint job from the one you slap on the outside of your house. And as far as mechanical shit goes, Andy's got more ways to fuck up these engines that you could ever find. You want us, you pay us. Twenty grand each and half of it right now, in our hands, before we so much as lift a hood."

Nastasi cocked his shotgun. Dominic heard the metal slip and click on the three others.

"*Piantala.* Stop it. That is enough," Criminisi said. "We have a deal."

Nastasi shot Criminisi a look of indignant anger.

"I said," Criminisi repeated, "we have a deal. Now put those weapons away and bring me the case. Nastasi complied, partially. He put his own shotgun back in the truck and removed a large black briefcase. The other men remained armed. He handed the briefcase to Criminisi, who opened it on the hood of the Lincoln.

From an envelope he withdrew a handful of hundred-dollar bills. With the practiced hands of a bank teller, he counted out sixty thousand dollars.

"There," he said, handing the cash to Dominic. "Now, you work. I will be back in a few days to check your progress. In the meantime, Bela and his men will supervise. They will also be available for any assistance you need from them. Teddy will take you back to your shop each night and return you here in the morning."

"Agreed." Dominic relished the weight of the cash in his hand. "But you can forget the Ku Klux Klan bit. We can be trusted, and it's not like we don't know you've got us working in a warehouse by the harbour."

"You are correct, young man. I should trust you, and your friends."

"You won't regret this."

"I never have regrets," Criminisi said. "It is the people who let me down who have them."

Dominic gathered his crew and waved Nastasi's men into the circle. "Get yourselves over here. We can't make this happen with you guys just watching. You're gonna have to get your hands dirty."

"I need four men as sentries," Nastasi said.

"Alright. Take whichever four you want. They rest, I get. We don't have too much time left tonight. I only wanna get organized for the morning. Eight a.m. we start working. Sammy, I want you to take charge of organizing the cars. I want each one numbered with a white grease pencil on the driver's side window. I want you to start a file on each car. Type, style, year, and current mileage. Andy will add a mechanical inspection report. I'll add a body report."

"Right," Sammy turned and stared into the indoor parking lot, wondering where to start.

"Andy, I want you to set up your mechanical area first. Gino, you give her a hand. We also gonna need your tow truck to push and pull these cars around. We can save time if Andy's working on some engines while Sammy and I are painting."

"You want me to help you paint?" Sammy pointed a finger at his birdlike chest.

"Yeah. I figure we can use the back end of the building as a paint booth, as far away as possible to avoid over-spraying the other cars. We'll need some kind of production line set-up."

Andy dug her hands in her overalls. "I thought my days on the assembly line were long over."

"Think of it this way: you've stepped up from Crown Victorias to Mercedes. As soon as Sammy's ready, start inspecting the cars. I want to see a list of all our parts and supply needs before the end of the day tomorrow."

"I'll be ready," Andy said. "Though I don't know how."

"Vinnie, you and I are going to set up the paint booth. And you, Romanian boy, you need to assign a couple of guys to go shopping."

"Shopping?" Nastasi looked like he would much prefer to shoot Dominic than to shop for him.

"Yeah, we need shit. A lot of it. We'll have a list for you in the morning."

"Is alright. We do." Nastasi replied, reluctantly.

"And food," Vinnie said. "We're gonna have to eat. It sounds like we can't just take a break and walk over to a sandwich shop."

"Good thinking," Dominic said. "We need catering … breakfast, lunch, dinner, snacks … all of that."

"I will need to talk to the boss," Nastasi said.

"Do that." Dominic felt himself getting sarcastic as a defence. If he was going to make this work, he was going to have to push the Romanian and his thugs around, yet they had all the muscle, and the weapons. His tone of voice was the only tool he had. The veneer of his leadership was thin. All the Romanian would have to do is point that shotgun at him one more time and he'd pee his pants on the spot and do whatever he was told.

"Do something," Dominic said. "But remind *our* boss that a man's hands get shaky without nourishment. Paint tends to splatter. Parts tend to get improperly installed. That sort of thing."

"I'm gonna need lights," Andy said. "It's like a tomb in here. And air power. I can bring in the tools, but I'll need a power source and hoses."

"Add that to your list, Bela. Overhead halogens, the portable kind, and extension cords, lots and lots of extension cords. Plus a compressed air system, hoses …"

"And acetylene tanks, and $O_2$," Sammy said.

"Right … You getting all this, Bela?" Dominic threw his head back and looked down his nose at the Romanian. "Shouldn't you be writing this down? Or do I need to speak Romanian for you to understand?"

"I get. I remember." Nastasi stood there, taking the verbal abuse.

Dominic knew he'd pay for it later. "Make sure you do, because if you don't, we lose time. It's gonna be on your head if that happens."

"You worry about your own head," Nastasi said. "The day will come, soon, when you no longer need it."

"What are we going to be plugging into?" Sammy said. He'd been walking around the warehouse. "There doesn't look like there's enough power here."

"Better add a generator to your memory," Dominic said. "I expect to see all of what we need tomorrow."

"It will be here." Nastasi looked like a wild animal whose instinct told him that this was not the time to fight.

"Good. Then have one of your boys drive us back to Brampton Street. We'll get ourselves back here tomorrow. Then the real work begins."

# 34

The dust of a hundred German automobiles sanded down to the metal filled the air of the harbourside warehouse. As in the chop shop, Dominic had his team separate the work areas into sections, only this time he had a building the size of four football fields to subdivide. On Brampton Street, he split the shop into two equal areas. Here he had double that number, each area twenty times the size of its crosstown cousin.

Section One held all the cars yet to be worked on and led to a line-up of Benzes both big and small waiting with their hoods up for Andy's retro-fit from European to North American standards. Gino handled the part-changing requirements, sped by high-pressure air hoses that spat out power in blaring trumpet blasts. Andy slid from car to car on a dolly that slipped her under each car to check undercarriages, transmissions, shocks, and the exhaust systems.

A biker stood over her, acting as a secretary and pretending to understand the parts and mechanical orders that she barked up from the floor. Clipboard in hand, the biker noted the car's number and ticked off a series of boxes on Andy's handwritten form.

"Shocks … good," she yelled. "Brakes … good enough. Transmission … good for nothing. Exhaust … crap."

The biker checked each code as Andy rattled off her inspection list like a pilot readying herself for takeoff.

After Andy's initial inspection, twenty-four of the three hundred and twenty-eight cars were ready for sand, prime, and paint without any further work. Vinnie led the sanding team, taking each of the ready-to-go cars first. Vinnie organized a group of three bikers and six Romanians into the fastest, if not the best, sanding team Dominic had ever seen. Dominic knew that he would have to fix of a lot of scratches with his paint skills and not with prep work. It took twelve days in a Stuttgart paint line to take a Mercedes from unpainted steel to its final form. Dominic had to lay a convincing colour and shine down in less than thirty minutes per vehicle.

The paint booth was the smallest part of the warehouse. Three car lengths long and just as wide, the floor-to-ceiling drapes kept dust away from the car being painted and prevented any overspray from escaping. Dominic and Sammy pushed each car into the booth after a biker and two Romanians with no language skills between them had taped up the windows and chrome. Dominic would lay a quick-drying primer down on the cars in less than three minutes while Sammy prepped the paint and each of the four spray guns and air hoses that Dominic had set aside. They had about five minutes from the last burst of primer to the first spray of paint. During that short interval, Dominic would check on the status of the next car in line and ensure that the previous car, still wet from the thickest coat of paint Dominic dared to lay on, stayed properly parked under a canopy of two-thousand-watt heat lamps

The work was quick and long. The days started early and finished late. After Dominic and his crew finished eighteen hours of prepping, repairing, and painting a legion of Mercedes, he and at least one other team member — sometimes Sammy, once or twice Vinnie, but most often Andy — retired to the anonymity of the Cannon Street shop. At the pier, Dominic's heart spent most of its time in his throat. He half expected the police to break down the doors and haul them all away. But at Nicky's old shop, at night, his maniacal pace was chastened. His heartbeat slowed. His anxiety faded into the chrome and rubber of the Mustang.

There, a few hours were spent sanding and relaxing, dreaming of the day when the Mustang would take to the road. Each visit culminated in a fresh coat of paint. They left the Mustang alone in the wee hours of the morning and returned to the chop shop for a few hours of sleep before the routine began anew.

Five days into the process, a familiar but out-of-place scene greeted Dominic at the portside warehouse. Rows of multi-coloured pens were aligned on a table by size and shade. File folders were stacked like towers of squatty brown buildings, behind which sat the same woman in the same clean but overworn dress he'd met at Malatesta's insurance agency. She was smoking, the smoke from her cigarette competing with the steam from her coffee.

"You're late," she said.

"I didn't know I was reporting to you," Dominic said.

"You're not," the woman answered. She took a sip of coffee, then placed the cup on the precise spot where she had lifted it from the table. "But I have one hundred and forty-eight insurance files and ownership papers to process in the next two days and I do not want to be wasting my time waiting for some paint sprayer to show up and finish his work."

Dominic smiled and put up his hand defensively. "It won't happen again. We're all as anxious as you are to put this place behind us."

"Well, double-time it there, young man. I got a hair appointment at ten and by the time I get back I want to be able to assign papers and plates to a dozen cars. The same this afternoon."

"Yes ma'am," Dominic gave her a mock salute.

"Treat her well, DiPietro, she's got a present for you." Dominic recognized the booming voice of Louie Malatesta, who was wandering between the rows of Mercedes. He hobbled over to Dominic, wobbly from too many tackles taken too many years before, and shook his hand. "Good to see you, Dominic. Nice operation, eh? When do you figure you'll be out of here?"

"We're on pace for about another eight days, maybe seven, depending on the condition of the cars."

"Sally there has got new VINs, ownership papers, plates, and insurance slips for every car here, all of them as bogus as a Buddha in Saint Bartholomew's. But for you, my friend, she's got a special file. One that is as good as gold."

"You got my ownership papers for the Mustang." Dominic felt a shiver of adrenaline run down his back. "Keep quiet about it, will ya? I told Criminisi that the car was garbage and I dumped it for scrap."

"Why?"

"It was the first thing that came into my head. Seems a lot of people want to make sure this car makes its way back into the harbour where we found it."

"Hand me the file, would ya, Sally?" She handed him a large manila envelope. Malatesta opened it and doled out the contents one piece at a time.

"Here's your ownership papers, all legal and square, and a new driver's license." Malatesta whispered, beaming like a father handing his son the keys to a new car. "What good is one without the other?" He slapped Dominic on the back.

"And here's your insurance forms, same forms ..."

"And the real treat: your plates. Right from the government."

Dominic held the metal license plates in his hands. They were different from the standard issue blue and white ones.

"I don't understand ..."

"They're vintage plates, boy!" Malatesta slapped him on the back. "Sorry," he lowered his voice to a whisper. "You can only get these if your vehicle is over twenty-five years old, and that puppy of yours qualifies in spades. I thought it would be a nice touch. No charge, mind you. My gift to you."

"Thanks," Dominic said, feeling the weight of the metal. He ran his fingers over the numbers.

"You ready to put it on the road?"

"This just about clinches it." Dominic hurried over to his crew and showed them their legal claim to the Mustang.

# 35

"Ladies and gentlemen, the next mayor of Hamilton, Salvatore Constantine!"

Constantine trotted up to the stage, dashing through the assembled throng of well-wishers in an orchestrated attempt to put to rest the question of whether a sixty-year-old man carried too much personal seniority and not enough health to be mayor. Upon reaching the platform, he turned to the assembled crowd, raised both arms, Nixon-style, and flashed a white smile that gleamed hunger. He used the moment to catch his breath. The din of the community hall echoed with music and applause, while masking the exertions of his lungs. Much more slowly, he walked across the stage and shook hands with VIPs and family who had been deemed important enough to require a small piece of real estate on the tiny community hall platform. He shook hands with three of his fellow city councillors, and gave his wife a long hug, a kiss, and a lingering smile. His two adult children, Jack and Marsha, stood in proud awe of their adopted father. They came forward and hugged him together. Tony DiPietro wore a handmade Italian suit of impeccable style and fabric, cut by the same tailor as Constantine in the same Genovese shop they both visited every year.

The mayoral hopeful stepped to the podium. The microphone had been pre-set to match his height and tuned to accentuate the deep timbre of his voice. Once again he held his arms up, lowering his hands slowly to cue the crowd for silence. They eagerly submitted.

The speech lasted several minutes. Constantine recounted his roots in the city, his achievements as a public defender and a city councillor, and the new ground he hoped to break as mayor. The assembled crowd applauded as if on cue, cheering like Constantine was quarterbacking their beloved Tiger-Cats.

Tony spotted Lisa supervising the platters of food and keeping a count on the number of wine bottles left open. She poured him some wine into a plastic glass.

"Thanks," he said. His had to raise his voice to be heard over the rumble that surrounded them. "How are you enjoying the campaign?"

"It's quite a learning experience," Lisa said. She poured herself a glass. "I never realized all the things that go into a campaign. I just thought you put up some posters and people voted. But somebody has to book the halls, co-ordinate the volunteers, order food ..."

"And that somebody is you."

"Yeah. Not like sitting behind a desk at all. Who have you got working insurance claims now that both Dominic and I are gone?"

Tony's face lost any trace of emotion. "I hired a temp. She'll do, at least until you get back. Angelina comes in every couple of days to check her work and handle the more complicated stuff."

"I really do want to come back, you know. This is nice, for a change, but I miss the shop."

"Good. When this is all over, let's take a look at expanding your role. Sal told me he's really impressed. Jackie too, and he's not an easy guy to please."

"I know. He worries about every little detail like the success of the entire campaign rises and falls on the number of pencils we have."

"He's just concerned for his uncle. I remember what it was like to work for my father. It was tough. You can't imagine what it's like if you haven't had to do it."

251

"Still, isn't he supposed to be running the councillor's legal firm?"

"I'm sure he does. But remember, Sal's practice isn't very large. He's wound down a lot of it over the years."

"Well, if you can keep him away from me, I'd appreciate it."

"What? Is he hitting on you?"

"That I could handle. No, it's hard to put my finger on. It's like he's always around, but he's not. Something's on his mind and it's not the campaign. I know that much."

Tony put his arm around her shoulder. "I think it's just that you're in a new environment. You're too used to working with insurance adjustors who are either trying to rip us off or get in your pants. Politics is the art of the subtle. Things are rarely what they seem. Once you get used to it, you'll be telling me what a great guy Jackie is. Besides, you should be nice to him. He's worth a lot of money to us."

Lisa gave Tony a blank stare.

"His uncle's firm handles the local business for a lot of out-of-town insurance companies. Jackie could redirect a lot of business elsewhere if you and he don't get along."

"How come I've never seen his name show up anywhere?"

Tony took sip of his wine. "I've been handling the stuff that Jackie sends us. Sort of as a personal favour, you know. Jackie's very particular about how his clients are handled. That's why I'm happy to see you working with him. When this is all over, I'll feel better about telling Jackie that you'll be handling all of his insurance business."

Tony felt a tug at his arm. He turned to face Leo Deluca. He shook the butcher's hand.

"Tony, can I talk to you?" Leo said.

"Excuse me, Lisa." Tony walked with Leo to a quiet spot at the back of the hall.

"I did what you told me to do," Leo said. "I called that Benedict guy."

"That's good, Leo. Very good. When did you talk to him?"

"Just after your phone call."

"What did you say to him?"

"I told him everything I knew about Dominic's gambling and his work for Criminisi. Benedict made me come down to the station and sign a statement."

"You did the right thing."

"Are you sure? I feel sick about this. Dominic and I have been friends since Mrs. Lucarelli's grade three class. I feel like such a rat. A friend wouldn't do this."

"You're doing exactly what a friend should do." Tony put his hands around Leo's biceps and gave him soft shake, like he was waking up a baby. "He needs your help, Leo. I told you, someday he's gonna thank you."

"I hope you're right."

"I know I'm right. Have you talked to Jackie about helping out with the campaign?"

"Yeah, somebody called me. They want me to organize the workers at Fortinos. Put up posters, that sort of thing. I said sure."

"Great." Tony patted him on the back. "Now go out there and get some wine. I want to come over and talk to you and your wife. Just give me a minute, okay?" Tony wandered downstairs to the basement where there was a lonely pay telephone. He took a notebook from his jacket pocket and scanned it for a telephone number. Cupping the receiver on his shoulder, he dropped a quarter in the phone and dialled.

"Benedict, it's Tony."

"What are you calling me at home for?"

"Because you've had Deluca's statement for two fucking days and I haven't heard word one from you."

"Nothing to tell you."

"What do you mean, nothing? I sent you a guy who gave you a written statement that Dominic is chopping cars for Criminisi. What more do you need?"

"I need a hell of a lot more and you know it." Benedict sounded like Tony had interrupted his dinner or woken him up in the middle of the night.

"What else do you need?"

"I had a couple of unmarkeds out there to watch his place. But my uniforms just sat there drinking coffee. I had to pull them off. They got more important things to do. I'll do whatever I can, but I can't just arrest your brother because he's pissed off some friend of yours."

Tony slammed the phone down into the bakelite cradle, snapping it in two. Half the cradle dropped to the stained linoleum. Tony kicked it along the floor and into a dark corner. He was climbing the stairs to the auditorium when he met Sal Constantine coming down the other way.

"Jesus Christ, Tony," Constantine said. "I've been looking everywhere for you. That *Spectator* reporter showed up and he's asking more questions about the car."

".I was told that the Mustang's been chopped. It should've been melted down into new steel by now," Tony said.

"Maybe so, but the paperwork is still flying around. Batista's telling me that he knows who the car's original owner is. Apparently the government's in the process of issuing new ownership papers and plates."

"Does he know that Dominic made the application?"

"He didn't say."

"Then he's bluffing. He'd be all over you both and me if he had proof that Dominic's got that car."

"He's going to find out soon enough. Shit, Tony, you gotta do something about this."

"Where is the reporter now?"

"He's walking around, having a few drinks. Eating my goddamn food like he was some kind of supporter. The little shit."

"I'll go up and talk to him. You point him out to me. I want to

254

look in his eyes and see if he really knows that Dominic's got that car. There's no way he won't be able to show his cards if he's talking to me."

Tony followed Constantine up the stairs. The reporter was talking to Lisa. Tony came up behind him and put his hand on Batista's bony shoulder.

"Can I, ah … help you with something?" Tony said, turning the reporter around as if he were a long screw Tony was trying to extract from the floor. Constantine stood a discreet distance away, yet still within earshot.

The reporter raised his glass. It was filled to the rim with red wine. "No, thanks. I'm fine."

Tony said, "I mean is there some information you're looking for? Something you need? You are with *Spectator*, right?"

"Yeah."

"I'm Tony DiPietro."

"Oh, Jesus," the reporter said. "I should have recognized your face from your ads."

"Yeah," Tony said.

"My name is Eric Batista. I was hoping to get an interview with Councillor Constantine, but he seems to be avoiding me. Thought I'd just enjoy the hospitality until the crowd thins out."

"I'm gonna have to ask you to leave," Tony said.

"Pardon?"

Jackie Constantine stepped out of Tony's shadow. "What's going on here?"

"This reporter is trying to piece together a smear campaign against your uncle. I was asking him to leave."

"Now hold on a second," Batista said. "I got as much a right to be here as anyone."

Tony placed a large hand on the reporter's insubstantial wrist. "I don't think so. This is a private party. You want to talk to me, that's fine. But the councillor's out of the question." Tony watched Batista's eyes for reaction. All he saw was an inquisitive mind looking for either an opportunity or an exit.

Jackie said, "Tony, hold on. Let me talk to him." Tony ignored him.

"Are you aware of the councillor's past?" Batista said. His left wrist was still encased in Tony right hand.

"You mean, the past that raised two orphaned kids," Tony said, "or the past that opened twenty day care centers across the city, or the past that reopened public swimming pools and kept our water rates flat for the last ten years? Is that the past you mean, Mr. Batista?"

"You know better than that," Batista said. "I am going to break this story, you know. Either the councillor's side of the story leads or I'll run with the one I dig out of the ditch. Both of them are good. It's his choice."

Tony tightened his grip and added his left hand to Batista's shoulder, directing him to the front door. "You run with neither. I put half a million dollars a year into advertising in that rag you call a newspaper. You print one word about Constantine and his brother and I'll pull it all out, along with the advertising of every guy in the automotive business I can convince to come with me."

Jackie watched, incredulous, as Tony dragged the reporter to the door.

Batista shook himself free of Tony's grip. "I'm sure that's a considerable number, Mr. DiPietro. But I'm not interested in your petty little car connections, or the size of your advertising budget. I don't give a shit and neither does my editor. I'd rather see your dirty money out of the paper anyway."

"My money? Dirty? What are you trying to say?"

"I'm saying that the paper doesn't care how your little chain of body shops makes its money. You are not a public figure nor are you running for the highest office in the city. Constantine, on the other hand, is someone we're very interested in. His money is just as dirty as yours."

Tony grabbed the reporter by the collar of his jacket. "*Vaffanculo!* You and your little *bustard* can go fuck yourselves." He started dragging Batista towards the stairs by the front door. The heads of Constantine's guests started to turn. The councillor was standing in front of the stage talking to an older couple. A silence fell across the room, catching the councillor's attention and drawing a glare of politically fuelled anxiety.

"Get your fat dago hands off me!" Batista said.

Tony pushed him to the floor. He looked ready to kick him. Jackie tried to pull Tony back, but Tony shrugged him off, leaned down, and reattached his hand to Batista's jacket collar. He dragged the bucking reporter through the crowd. Tony kicked open one of the double doors at the front of the hall and tossed the reporter through them.

"Tell your editor to expect a call from your publisher!" Tony said. His face was red, his forehead wet with sweat that dampened the edge of his hairline. His eyes bore down on the reporter. "And if I see your face anywhere near this campaign again, you'll be writing your next story from a hospital bed!"

The reporter caught his breath. He rested on one knee while he rubbed his shoulder. "I'll sue your ass off, DiPietro!"

"Sue all the fuck you want. I got lawyers who got more lawyers who spend their entire days dealing with shit like you." Tony straightened out his jacket and ran his hand through his hair.

Jackie said, "Jesus, Tony. What've you done?"

"Nothing he didn't deserve. Calling my money dirty. Well I showed him dirty. One more minute, I'd've shown him real dirt, and he'd be looking through six feet of it."

"What the fuck is going on, Tony?" Jackie demanded.

"This is between me and your uncle," Tony said. "Go work the crowd and raise some money. After tonight, we're gonna need it."

# 36

Dominic handed over the honour of bolting on the plates to Vinnie, as a gesture of respect for the car out of the water. Vinnie's hands shook like a teenage boy trying un-hook his first bra. Andy guided him. With a few twists of a screwdriver, fore and aft, the Mustang was crowned. The coronation party ensued.

"I want him busted!" Tony screamed into the phone. "I don't care what it takes. I want him in jail and I want you to find that Mustang, or whatever's left of it, and bring it to me!"

"I've told you before, Tony, it don't work that way," Benedict said. "We got to have cause. We can't just be breaking into people's places of business and hauling away their stuff — not unless we got a reason. Once we have cause, we can get a warrant."

"I'll give you a goddamn reason," Tony's voice remained piqued. "How about you getting two hundred bucks for every car that every cop brings into one of my shops? How's that for a reason? Or how about the fact that you put that money up your nose with shit you buy from Criminisi's dealers? Is that enough of a reason? Or do I have to tell your bosses about the hookers you're trading favours with?"

"Christ, DiPietro, you're on the goddamn phone."

"I want him busted and I want it to happen tonight. I expect that

Mustang, or whatever's left of it, in my back lot before I get to work tomorrow morning."

It wasn't champagne, but it was clear and bubbly. Gino pulled a full case of Molson Canadian from the back of his tow truck and handed out the tall brown bottles like they were award statues. "To Dominic." Dominic raised his bottle in the air and put it back down again without drinking.

"To all of you," Dominic replied. "And a special thank you to Andy. Without her, this car would only look good."

Andy let out a coy smile. "Yeah. Now, this baby will out-run most low-flying jets."

"So fire it up," Dominic said. He handed her the factory-ordered keys, a bracelet of access and power. "Let's hear the beast behind all that beauty."

Andy grabbed the keys and opened the driver's side door. She slid behind the wheel like she'd been born there. Sammy, Dominic, Vinnie, and Gino surrounded the Mustang's hood and waited. The chrome shone brightly. The tires were new and perfect and centred around spoked wheel coverings. The faces of everyone who worked on the car shone back at them from the perfectly painted surface, six layers deep in clear-coat shine.

Inside Nicky's old body shop, the Mustang started to rumble. The roar of thunder rocked the walls as Andy pushed the accelerator down further. Dominic waved her off.

"Alright already. We're gonna have half the city coming down on us." Andy let the engine purr for a moment longer, then cut if off. Her smile outshone the chrome.

Tony sat alone in his office drinking scotch and smoking a Churchill. The shop was dark save for the spots of light from passing traffic outside. It was three a.m. and Tony was determined not to leave until the police towed Dominic's Mustang into his garage.

259

The phone rang. It was Benedict.

"You're brother is in big trouble."

"You get the car?"

"No. But we did find the Chevy Suburban that was used in the murder of two port police officers a few months back." Benedict coughed into the phone. "Listen, Tony, unless your brother's gone so far over the deep end that I wouldn't even recognize him, I know he's not a cop killer."

"Nothing I hear about Dominic ever surprises me," Tony lied. "Not any more. He's society's problem now, not mine."

"He's probably only chopping the car. But we sure as hell got him as an accessory after the fact."

"Have you arrested him?"

"Not yet. I was hoping you'd talk to him. Get him to come in on his own, or better yet, with you."

"Just bust him. I don't want to be seen anywhere near him. Where's the car?"

"Not there, Tony. There's not so much as a piece of a Mustang at that shop." Benedict coughed again. "Can you at least give me some idea where I could find him? It'll go easier on him if he surrenders to me. I can't promise kid gloves if a uniform gets ahold of him first. A lot of those port officers are ex-cops. Most of the guys here are gonna want to hurt him real bad."

"You now know as much about Dominic as I do. I don't give a shit what you do to him. He's not my brother anymore. All I care about is that Mustang. Find it." Tony hung up.

He picked up again and dialled another number. "This is going bad," he said. "We need to figure out how to put an end to it."

Dominic's crew gathered around the restored Mustang, its hood up, its air-filter rechromed and glimmering like a crown on Andy's rebuilt engine.

"Now we gotta figure out what to do with it," Vinnie said. "It's a shame to sell it. I'd like to keep it, just for the summer … Maybe get rid of it in the fall. I could wait for my dough. But the car, I don't think I can wait for this."

Dominic eased himself behind the wheel, caressing the new seat beside him. "We can't. We have to hide it. Criminisi thinks we've chopped it up and my brother's breathing down my neck. This car stays underground, at least until we can figure out where to move it. Maybe we smuggle it into the States through some native reserve."

"More bullshit!" Sammy said. "I thought we were in the clear with this."

"There's no free-and-clear with Criminisi or my brother. Something's going on and until we find out what it is, this car is a target and so are we."

"We can't leave it here," Vinnie said.

"No," Andy said. "But I do know a place where nobody will ever think to look."

"Good," Dominic said. "I get the feeling we should all lay low for a while. Go back to whatever you were doing before I dragged you into this."

Tony drove his S500 to the portside warehouse and parked outside. An armed biker was stationed by the door. "I'm here to see Criminisi," Tony said.

"Wait here." The biker left Tony alone while he went inside. He emerged a moment later and motioned for Tony to enter.

Criminisi, Nastasi, Spagnoli, Magilla, and Malatesta were seated around a table playing poker. Criminisi waved Tony over. "Come, my friend, take a seat." Tony pulled a chair over to the table.

"Louie you know, of course," Criminisi said. "And Bela and Teddy. As for Magilla …"

"We haven't met," Tony said. "But we are familiar by reputation."

Magilla smiled, creating an extra roll of fat around his neck.

"The cops are after Dominic," Tony said.

"How did this happen?" Criminisi demanded.

"I hadn't heard from you, so I wanted to give Dominic a scare. Make sure he got rid of the Mustang. Instead, the cops raided your Brampton Street shop and found some Suburban that had been used in the murders of a couple of port officers. They're looking for Dominic now."

"Mustang?" Malatesta said. "You mean the car I outfitted Dominic with a set of papers for."

Tony looked at Malatesta. "You started this goddamn thing. You and you fucking phony paperwork."

"You've lived well enough off it," Malatesta said. "Besides, Dominic's stuff is legit. It passed through the standard government channels without a problem."

"No problem? You and my brother are about to bring down the best chance we've ever had to put an Italian in mayor's chair."

Malatesta put down his cards. "I don't know what you're talking about. Dominic's a good kid and I did him favour. Christ, we're making hundreds of thousands of dollars off these cars here. What's a free set of papers and plates?"

Criminisi got up and walked over to Malatesta. He put his hand behind the former football star's head. "You don't remember, do you? Have you forgotten about that car?" He slapped him gently across the back of the head. "American football is very bad for the memory."

"What? It's some old piece of junk that Dominic is trying to put back together," Malatesta protested.

"That piece of junk," Criminisi said, "was the car I buried the harbour twenty-seven years ago!"

Tony said, "You put it there?"

"Yes, I did. Constantine, that son of a bitch, had just gotten me off a break-and-enter charge. His fees were always too high. He gave me a choice: kill his brother or he'd drop enough evidence on the Crown Prosecutor's lap to put me away for life."

"You did Bobby Constantine?" Tony said.

"And his wife. I was young and stupid, like your brother. Salvatore was so upset about the car that he made me promise to get rid of it. The harbour seemed as good a place as any."

"We need to take care of Dominic," Magilla said.

"Yes, we do," Criminisi said. "I want him here tomorrow."

# 37

The massage parlour was a converted three-storey Victorian home on Queen Street. It was unidentified except for the absence of signage on a street dominated by older homes that had been converted to professional offices, hair salons, and discounted fashion retailers. It was after midnight when Dominic and Andy drove the Mustang into the alleyway behind the massage parlour, stopping in front of a newer garage that the current owners had installed several years before.

"Doesn't Criminisi own this place?" Dominic said, as he stopped the car. Andy got out and opened the door to the garage.

"Sure he does, but it's not like he is going look for this car here. I've been using this garage for years to work on my own cars, and no one has ever bothered me." She pulled up the door and motioned for Dominic to follow her in with the Mustang.

"It'll be safe," she promised, closing and locking the door behind her. "I think I'm the only one with key to the place. Besides," she laughed, "if we can paint the car at Tony's shop, then we can hide it a massage parlour run by the mob. Come with me."

Andy led them through the junky remains of the house's back-yard, up a set of three wooden stairs to a small back porch that was as desperate for paint job as it was for a carpenter with a level. "We can stay here for the night. They closed up a few hours ago, and no one will be back until just before noon tomorrow."

"Are you sure about this?"

"Yeah, it won't be a problem. My kid is staying with my mom, and with that going on I'd rather leave some distance between me and them right now, if I can." Andy opened the back door and entered a small mudroom. There was a keypad on the wall. She tapped in a series of numbers and the lights came on.

"There, the alarms are off. All you have to do is choose a room."

The massage parlour was a maze of small rooms and interconnected hallways, the result of the building's transformation from a once-regal Victorian home to its new, seedier and more mundane function. Each room was no larger than a doctor's examination room. They reached a lounge area, which had likely been the house's living room at one time.

Andy opened a small bar fridge and looked inside. She took out two beers and passed one to Dominic. "Here. You deserve it." She spread her arms. "Take your pick. Twelve rooms, no waiting. Unfortunately they don't come with a girl, but, then again, you're not paying fifty dollars an hour." She smiled and took a sip of her beer.

Dominic sat on the long leather couch, putting his feet up on the coffee table, still holding the beer in his hand. "Shit, Andy, I think I could sleep for days." He coughed, leaning forward to take a tissue from the box of Kleenex on the coffee table. He spit into it. "I've sucked in enough paint fumes to recoat this floor." He coughed again.

Andy sat beside him, putting her hand on this shoulder. "You can relax. Sleep here on the couch, if you want. I'll take a room."

Dominic put back the rest of his beer while Andy sought out some sheets and a pillow for the couch.

"I want to thank you," he said as Andy returned, sheets in hand. He gripped the neck of his beer, nervously linking and unlinking his fingers.

"For what?"

"The car, for one. I could never have got it working, let alone purring the way you did. I used to think I knew everything there was to know about cars. You showed me different. Taught me I didn't have to go it alone."

Andy spread a sheet out on the couch. "This place teaches you that being on your own doesn't get you very far. There's only so much you can do when you're left to your own resources."

Dominic smiled. "You're starting to sound like Criminisi. It's all he talks about — the power of partnerships, collaboration, and relationships."

"Well, the old mobster's built himself an impressive little empire by working with other people, you included. If he wasn't a criminal, I might think hooking up with him was a pretty bright idea."

"No choice, darling. You know that." Dominic sat back down on the couch. Andy joined him.

"I'm proud of you." She kissed him on the cheek, then put her hand defensively on his chest. "Don't get any ideas. There's no action here tonight."

A large pounding noise came from the front of the house. Dominic thought it might be a drunk, angry that he was too late for his nightly cat-call.

Andy ran down the hallway. "The cops are here." She puffed the words out. "They never come here. Not on official business, at least."

"We've got to get out of here." The pounding grew louder. They heard the splintering of the wooden front door. "They're using a battering ram," Dominic said. The sound of boots kicking down the broken door echoed through the hallways. Beams of light cutting through the dimness.

Andy took his arm. "There's a stairwell to the basement. It leads to the house next door. The previous owners used to operate two parlours, one beside the other. The passageway allowed guests who didn't want to be seen leaving to exit by back door of a completely

266

different building." She led him to doorway that opened into a closet. In the back was a small door hidden by a vacuum cleaner and other household supplies. She cleared away the obstructions and pushed open the tiny door. "Hurry." Dominic saw her disappear into the darkness.

A strong voice bellowed down the hallway: "DiPietro. Stay where you are." Dominic looked at the door, then back down the hall. The shadowy images of Hamilton police officers filled the entire width of the hallway. Dominic closed the door and stood with his hands up.

An officer approached with his gun drawn and aimed squarely at Dominic's heart. Four others formed a barricade behind him. The officer lowered his gun and approached, levelling a blow to Dominic's diaphragm. "Cop killer. I oughta save the courts the trouble." Dominic dropped to the carpeted floor, the air driven out of his lungs. The officer kicked in the ribs, head, and back until his colleagues pulled him off.

Dominic lost consciousness after the second blow.

# 38

"Is he dead?"

Dominic heard a man's voice, rough and unfamiliar, but as clear as his last shot of silver tequila. So he couldn't be dead. Dead would feel better and couldn't smell this bad.

"No way," another voice, another man. "He's just fucked up, is all. Must've OD'd. They brought him in last night. I saw 'em." Different male voices bombarded Dominic's brain — some harsh, some soft, but each off-the-boat poor and foreign.

The air wrapped around him like a bandage, his head felt ripe for amputation. The scent of flesh pressed too close for too long was putrid and imposing.

His arms covered his head, his body cramped up in knots as he tried, in vain, to shield himself from the smell. He was clammy; sweat enveloped his body in a slick, chilling film. He had to leave. He had to escape the smell, the air, and the pressure that bore down on his body.

Nearby another voice parted the fog. "They threw me in here just after last call. He wasn't here then. I think I passed out after that."

Just before he felt the world slipping away, the contents of Dominic's stomach surged up to meet his throat.

"Jesus, call a guard over here!" somebody cried out. "He's fuckin' puked all over himself."

★ ★ ★

The pinpoint stings of a hundred jets of ice-cold water roused Dominic to attention. He struggled at first, fighting against the flow and the fog of his own head. His lungs started to heave, stretching his ribs past the point of pain. He coughed up a rainbow of colour — running reds, greens, and blues in a watercolour wash of phlegm and spit. Dominic looked down and away to see the colours of his lungs cascading into a Technicolor pool on the floor. He caught a glimpse of a uniform stretched across a well-muscled chest. A large black baton precluded any thoughts of fighting on Dominic's part.

"Feeling better?" the man in the uniform said.

"Where … where am I?" Dominic said.

"Barton Street, the Hole." The guard grabbed him by the scruff of his damp shirt and dragged him from the shower. "Strip those clothes off." Dominic complied, like a dog told to sit.

"What am I doing here?" Dominic was naked, scared and shivering. The only protection he had was his wet, shoulder-length hair. It formed a wall of dirty yellow straw between him and the guard. His teeth broadcast a Morse-code appeal for help that no one could interpret but the demons inside him.

"Like I care." The guard threw him a white paper jumpsuit. "Get dressed."

"Why?" Dominic looked at the thin one-piece garment labelled in black ink: *Detainee — Hamilton Detention Centre.*

"Not a fucking word. It's clean. You're not, and the clothes you were carried in here with should be burned. Some loser's gonna have to wash 'em, though, cause they're your personal property. Your mother should treat you so good."

Dominic pushed the hair from his face and stepped into the paper suit. It was cold; the dampness from the shower made the suit cling to parts of his body he didn't know existed, as if they'd tossed his skeletal frame into a wet plastic bag. Dominic squeezed his ribs so

269

hard they hurt. The guard pushed him into a holding cell and turned him around. Eight other men were crammed into the same space.

"Let me out of here."

"I said, not a word." The bars slid closed and Dominic was left with eight other detainees at the Barton Street Detention Centre. He found himself a spare piece of wall and let his back slide down until he reached the floor. There, his arms wrapped around his knees, Dominic sobbed quietly. He had only tears to wash the taste of vomit from his mouth and they wouldn't come. Sleep did.

The pressure of pent-up bile fired the back of Dominic's throat and jolted him to awareness. Quickly, he crawled over to the exposed toilet and heaved. A strong hand grabbed his shoulder and turned him around. Dominic saw a massive piece of attitude standing over him.

"You got permission to use my toilet?" Attitude said. He was wearing an orange jumper. It was brighter than Dominic's, more permanent, with a yellow stripe running down the outside of both legs. Dominic was eye-level with the behemoth's kneecap.

"Don't start some jailhouse shit on me. I'm in no mood for it." Dominic used the paper sleeve to wipe his mouth.

"I don't ask questions twice," Attitude said. He pulled Dominic to standing position. "Who the fuck are you to throw up in my toilet?" With an arm the size of Dominic's thigh, he threw him against the wall. Dominic's breath shot out from his lungs.

One of Attitude's cousins grabbed Dominic by his paper collar. He was a lily-white Irish kid with hieroglyphic street credentials scratched into his forearms. "He should clean it up. We should make him clean it 'til it shines."

Attitude grinned, highlighting his scraped and chipped yellow teeth. One front tooth had a silver cap on it. It shone as if it lit by a lamp.

"I said, who are you? Tell me or I'll brush out my toilet with your head." Dominic tried to cross his arms in front of his face, but Attitude wrestled his wrist away from him.

"Here it is," the cousin said. He twisted Dominic's hand to reveal a white wristband, which he showed to Attitude as if he'd pried out a secret. Dominic looked too. He didn't remember having it put there.

Attitude pulled Dominic's wrist so hard it almost ripped clean from his elbow. "Dominic-goddamn-Di-fucking-Pietro. Is this you?" He threw Dominic's wrist back at him. "Are you this fuckwit, Di-fucking-Pietro?"

Dominic coughed a bullet of technicolour phlegm into the cousin's sleeve.

"Christ Almighty," the cousin said, looking down at the green, red, and blue bullet wound on his forearm. He pulled away from Dominic, letting him go. "This guy's diseased or something." The cousin ran over to the stainless steel sink and rinsed his sleeve.

A second cousin of Attitude, a smaller man who hadn't yet gained the privilege of prison-issue apparel, approached and whispered in Attitude's ear. Attitude lost his grin. He looked at Dominic, then at his second cousin. His eyes said, *you sure?* The second cousin nodded. *Absolutely.*

Attitude walked over to speak with the phlegm-wounded first cousin who was washing all traces of Dominic's lungs from his sleeve. He glanced at Dominic with the same expression as Attitude, strange and uncertain. The three of them sulked across the cell to the farthest point from Dominic. They whispered amongst themselves and a few of the other men hanging around them, casting occasional glances at Dominic as if they were watching to see if he moved or breathed. He hadn't the strength for much of either.

A high, throaty voice boomed down the corridor: "DiPietro. Detainee DiPietro." Dominic struggled to stand and moved to the front of the holding cell. Attitude and his clan remained as far away as possible, but continued to watch with sideways glances and over-the-shoulder looks.

"Here." Dominic raised his hand like a recalcitrant schoolboy.

The female guard approached. Her eyes looked a hundred years old. Tattoos ran across arms that were as taut as a rope. A canal system of veins ran across the back of her hand. They were scraped and scarred. She looked ready for combat.

"You DiPietro?"

"Yes." Dominic pressed himself against the bars. She grabbed his wrist and looked at the plastic band, then shouted down a distant hallway. "Step back. Crack number four." Her voice rang in Dominic's ears.

"Cracking number four," a disembodied voice answered in a well-practiced rhythm.

The guard pulled open the cell door and motioned with her baton for Dominic to turn around. He complied. She grabbed his wrist and clamped a handcuff on it. Without a thought to his comfort, she took his other wrist and completed the pair.

"Not a word out of you, or your ankles get manacled too." She turned him around by his shoulders and led him out of the cell.

"Locking down number four," she yelled. The faraway voice confirmed the order.

"Where?"

"Not a fucking word." Dominic felt the butt end of a baton poke hard into his spine. "Keep that Italian mouth of yours shut, or I'll gag you."

She led him to a small interrogation room where two police officers waited for him. The room lay a few yards away from the holding cell; its cinderblock was painted grey and it had two doors, one on each side. A small table was placed tight against one wall. On the table were a cassette-tape recorder and some discarded pads of paper. One of the officers was pacing around the interrogation room. He took no notice of Dominic's entrance. He was using a manila file folder to fan the air around his face.

"What stinks in here? It smells like someone took a dump."

"Could be," the other officer said. He sniffed the air. "Or maybe it's this piece of shit."

"I hate being dragged back to this city. Every time I cross that bridge I feel like I have to take a shower." He wriggled his shoulders to feign a shudder.

The other officer stood in front of the interrogation table and smoked a cigarette. He looked over a file folder of his own. "Beats St. Johns in a heartbeat." He looked at Dominic, but had yet to verbally acknowledge his entrance.

"Well, I think you're fucking nuts."

"Like I said, some of us. Until you've felt the chill of January morning coming off an ocean with no fish in it to feed your family, well you got no idea how good this old rotter of a steel town starts to look."

The guard sat Dominic down on a metal chair in front of the table and leaned forward to take off one of the handcuffs. She threaded the connecting chain through an iron loop embedded in the tabletop and reattached the open bracelet to Dominic's right wrist. "You mind your manners in here or I'll be back with these." She waved the leg irons in front of him and left. He heard the solid metallic clunk of the lock behind him.

The Newfoundland cop looked at Dominic. "You like it here in Hamilton, don't you, Mr. DiPietro?"

"It's home." Dominic took a deep sniff of the air.

"Home for a lot of thugs like you. Guys who give it a bad name. We'd be better off if the lot of you packed up and moved out to Toronto where you belong."

The officer standing on the other side of the room was thin, built like a marathon runner. He wore a short-sleeved dress shirt and a tie dotted with images of a police officer on horseback. "Mr. DiPietro, I'm Inspector Ronald Flinders, RCMP, Organized Crime Detachment. This fellow with the Welcome Wagon is Detective Sergeant Frank Shawstak, an associate of mine from the local police department. I guess you'd call him your host."

"What am I doing here?" Dominic said. "Would it be a problem for you to at least take these off?" He raised his hands, feebly. "I can't even scratch my nose."

Flinders pushed away from the wall with his back. He'd been standing in the shadow cast by the harsh overhead light, his arms crossed and impatient.

"Yes, that would be a problem, Mr. DiPietro."

Dominic looked at him. His crimes were petty, at least on the scale his interrogators must be used to. It wasn't like he was dangerous; not to anyone but himself.

Shawstak leaned forward, just out of reach of Dominic's hands. "You did a good job on one of my uniforms," he said.

"I did what?

"You did. Put him right on his back."

"I … I don't remember."

"Sure you do," Flinders said. He was standing, leaning with both arms on the table and looking down at Dominic's white paper suit clinging to his lithe frame. "You got lucky, for sure. The officer is embarrassed by a scrawny runt like you getting the better of him. Can't seem to remember too many of the details himself. But it's true. You knocked him out like you were some kind of middleweight."

Dominic flexed his fingers into a fist. His right hand was sore and tight. It felt the way it did when he spent too many hours squeezing the trigger on a paint gun. The knuckles of his left hand were bruised. He'd kill for a handful of Advil.

"I don't remember."

Flinders pulled over a chair and straddled it. He stared down Dominic. He looked used to getting answers. "How's the jaw, and the ribs? That's what you get, you know, for resisting arrest. Cooperating is what gets you out of here. Resisting gets you more of the same."

"Whatever you say. But I think I should talk to a lawyer."

Shawstak said, "The town's full of them. But they're like towels in a whorehouse. Hard to find one without any stains on it."

"I need a lawyer."

"We'll get you one." Flinders pushed the chair away and stood up. "But you need to start remembering first."

"I don't know what you guys are talking about. Honestly."

Shawstak stood up and took a set of keys from his pocket. "If I take those off, you'll behave yourself?"

"Absolutely. I want to co-operate. But really, I don't know what you're talking about."

Shawstak unthreaded the cuffs from the table, but left Dominic's hands cuffed. At least he had more mobility. He rubbed his eyes with his hands. The bitter taste of bile coated the inside of Dominic's mouth. "I'm thirsty. Can I get a Coke or something?"

Flinders said, "Frank, is there anything around here?"

"Yeah, there's a vending machine in hall, by the john."

Flinders fished around in his pockets. "Got any change?" He pulled out a pair of nickels and few dimes.

Shawstak dove into his pockets. "All I got is a quarter." He handed it to the RCMP officer. "But I think you need seventy-five cents or something to get it work."

Dominic said, "I'd help, but ..."

Flinders said, "Just keep those hands where I can see them." He looked at the coins in his palm. "I'll get you a drink, but when I get back, you are going start talking." The RCMP officer left the room.

Shawstak waited until the door slammed shut, then leaned over the table to within whispering distance from Dominic's ear. "You got yourself in a hell of jam here, boy." The words, if not the speakers, were familiar to Dominic.

"I told you. I don't know what you're talking about."

"Let me give you piece of advice, young man. When that fella from the RCMP gets back in here, you tell him everything you know. It's the only chance you've got."

"So lock me up already. Maybe I'll get a decent night's sleep for once."

"What's going to let you sleep is a clear conscience. Just tell him you hit that cop. Tell him you were scared. You're a young little Italian fuck. He'll believe you."

Flinders returned with a can of Coca-Cola in hand. He pulled back the top and placed it within Dominic's reach.

He took a sip. "It's warm."

"Yeah, some guys were filling the machine when I got there, so all they could give me was this fresh one. Free though. Which is good, 'cause I don't think you're worth the change in my pocket."

Dominic brought the can to his mouth again and chugged the sweet carbonated syrup. The effect was minor, but for a moment Dominic felt human again.

"Now, tell us what you are doing with Bela Nastasi?" Flinders said.

"Who?" Dominic took another drink and held the can in front of his face, the only defence from the unrelenting eyes of the RCMP detective. He needed a place to hide, desperately.

"You know, the Romanian."

Dominic drained the Coke and put the empty can on the table between them. He was going to need a lot more than some useless piece of recycled metal for protection.

# 39

Dominic looked at Flinders. The eyes of the RCMP officer never wavered, staring him down like he would a caged animal. Dominic tried not to show any fear in his voice. "I know a lot of Romanians. Somebody must have off-loaded a whole cargo ship full of them. Which one are you talking about?"

"Now be smart about this," Flinders said. "The only reason we're taking to you at all is that if you give us Nastasi, we might be able to persuade the Crown to look the other way on *some* of the shit you've gotten yourself into."

"Alright. He deals in stolen car parts. He calls me sometimes and asks me to pull apart a car or two for him. That's all."

"This is all you've ever done for him?" Flinders asked. Dominic didn't think the RCMP officer believed him.

"Yeah, that's it."

Shawstak said, "Can you describe him for us?"

The question spooked him. Dominic figured that either they already knew what Nastasi looked like, and this was some kind of test, or the Romanian had slipped through Canadian immigration, the RCMP, the Hamilton Police and a dozen other agencies of the government without so much as a photograph. If so, his description could be lethal, to both of them.

"I've never met him. He just calls me, and I go where he tells me."

"Where do you go?" Shawstak asked.

"It changes. Every time. I've never worked at the same place twice."

"What part of town?" Flinders asked.

"Everywhere. Anywhere. I don't know. East end, mostly. By the harbour. Port lands, most of the time. I've only chopped a couple of cars for him. It's not like I really know anything about the guy."

"You know," Shawstak said, "enough to help us, and yourself."

Flinders paced around the room. He stopped between the light on the wall and Dominic, casting his face into darkness. "If you've never met him, how do you get paid?"

"There's always a couple of other guys showing up. Bikers. One of them pays me. But I don't know who they are, either," he added defensively.

"Seems like you're doing a lot of work for somebody you don't know."

"Like I said, it's only been a couple of times. Surely you can't like lock me away forever on this."

"What we want is information about the Romanian, and his bosses," Shawstak said.

"I got nothing to give you."

"You don't understand, DiPietro. We know better." Flinders had retreated to the wall and was once again using the manila folder to move the air around the room. "We just need you to confirm it."

"I told you everything I know. Every once in a while, the Romanian calls me and I go somewhere and take a car apart. That's it."

"You're lying," Shawstak said. "Or at least you're not telling us everything. Smarten up. The Romanian's into a lot more than illegal car parts, and we know you're his guy."

"I paint cars for my brother. I only did this chop shop stuff for a little extra cash."

Shawstak ran his fingers through his hair like he was trying to straighten out the facts in his head. "Listen, DiPietro. I'm going to tell you what we know, for your own sake. Hopefully it'll pump some reality into the shit you've been trying to sell us. I need you to give that up. I'm not a patient man, so I'm going to lay out the facts for you."

"This is the only chance you're going to get," Flinders said.

"First," Shawstak said, "we know all about your work for Criminisi. He's got the Romanian supervising your chop shop operation. We've had guys watching him for months." He showed Dominic a series of photographs. There was Nastasi going into the old International Truck plant, another of him exiting Queenston Vending, and a third, which appeared to have been taken in a parking lot somewhere, of his brother getting into Criminisi's Lincoln Continental.

"We're not here about chop shops, Dominic," Flinders said. "What we want is your brother."

"My brother is so straight he shits square bricks."

Shawstak picked up the photo of Tony and looked at it. "He's done a real number on you, hasn't he?" He slid the photograph back in front of Dominic, then pulled another half dozen out of his file. In all of them, Tony was talking with Criminisi — in cars, in coffee shops. There were several photographs of Tony at Queenston Vending.

"Let me tell you what your brother's doing with Criminisi," Shawstak said. "He's been running a real sweetheart operation. Tony, you see, makes most of his income — undeclared, of course — as a money launderer for the mob. Criminisi and his cronies, some of whom we know, some of whom we don't, have set up series of offshore insurance companies that specialize in insuring vehicles that don't exist. Criminisi and others, pay exorbitant premiums to insure these phony cars, under equally phony names."

"And then," Flinders added, "these imaginary cars get into imaginary accidents. City-Wide Collision processes a phony claim for a phony car that gets imaginary work done to it, and Tony DiPietro gets paid in very real cash. That money, or at least most of it, gets

279

passed back to Criminisi and his cronies. Dirty money to clean, all facilitated through City-Wide Collision's claims department. Hell, Tony's even got bogus paint and supply orders to back up all the work he's supposedly done."

Dominic was good at putting pieces together; almost as good as he was at pulling them apart. He hoped that Flinders and Shawstak had less skill as policemen than he did at restoring cars. Otherwise, the only cars he might ever see would be in a prison body shop.

"All of this has nothing to do with me," he told them. "You know I've got nothing to do with that."

"Not that you know of," Shawstak said. "Where'd you get the Mustang?"

Dominic felt steel wool binding his throat. "I'm restoring it, as a hobby."

"Just wondering," Shawstak said. He pushed his heavy body away from the table. "Where is it now?"

If they'd been whipping him with a rubber hose Dominic would have felt better than he did at that moment. "You mean it hasn't been impounded?"

"No," Shawstak shook his head. "We haven't got it."

"It's in the garage, behind the massage parlour."

"No, it isn't," Flinders said. "By the time our backup got there, all we found was you unconscious in the hallway of that cat house, and Sergeant Benedict's officers searching the house for evidence."

Somehow Tony had got his hands on the car, Dominic thought. The dream was over, like every other one he'd had before it. "Then I have no idea where it could be."

Flinders crossed his arms across his chest. "Yeah, this *is* Hamilton. Three o'clock in the morning, a good-looking car like that. That's giving some punk an engraved invitation to steal it."

A few blocks away, the triple towers of Lloyd D. Jackson Square stood sentry over the core of the city, at the edge of a decaying downtown, eyes forward towards its post-industrial future. Below them was a mall where street people extended their hands to professionals in business suits. Below that, a three-storey parking lot housed the daily comings and goings of some two thousand cars. Tony had decided that this was the best place to hide a vintage Mustang, for the moment: in the bowels of the city's largest parking lot, in a darkened corner surrounded by people to busy to notice.

It was convenient and discreet. Constantine's law office was spread over one entire floor of one of the towers. Criminisi kept a suite at the hotel for private assignations. Tony had told them to gather at the Jackson Square Mall, Second Level Parking, Area D, Row 3. No one came alone. Tony brought Nunzio. Constantine brought Jackie. Criminisi brought Benedict. Benedict had brought the car.

"We were lucky," Benedict said. "Imagine, figuring he could stash that car at a cat house. Not a bad idea until the security alarm went off. The code belonged to that mechanic you're using. I figured it had to be Dominic and his girl hiding out for the night."

"It cost me my paint and body man," Criminisi said. "I have hundreds of cars to move. Your brother and his crew were supposed to sell them for me. Now what am I supposed to do, open my own lot?"

Tony rubbed the sole of his shoe into the oil and dust of the concrete floor. "Nunzio can take over for Dominic. I can give you Dimitri for a week or two."

"We keep Dimitri, Nunzio, and whoever else we want, for as long as we want," Nastasi said. "And you pay them."

Criminisi pointed an accusatory finger at Tony. "If you'd agreed to this at the outset, we wouldn't have needed your brother." He spat. "Just because you appear legitimate, Tony, don't think you are any better than us."

Tony took a deep breath. The air tasted foul and acidic. He spoke to Constantine. "I hope getting this car off the road was worth it."

The city councillor opened the door to the Mustang and got inside. "How could so little steel cause so much trouble for so many years?" Tony closed the door for him and watched as the mayoral wannabe ran his left hand around the steering wheel, letting his right hand come to rest on the console-mounted transmission shifter. He inspected the clarity of the gauges. "You got the key?" He held out his hand.

Through the open window, Benedict gave it to him. Constantine looked up from behind the wheel. "No one saw you? Right?"

The police sergeant shook his head. Criminisi opened the passenger door and slid inside. "It looks better than the day I dropped it in the harbour."

Constantine pulled down the convertible top, with Nunzio assisting him. He got out of the car. "Tony wants to melt it down to an ingot inside of one Stelco's smelters."

"Which is what I should have done the first time," Criminisi said.

Tony cocked his head. "In a week or two, it'll come back as a new Mustang. Right after they ship the steel to Detroit."

"I hate that I know all this," Jackie said. He had his hands buried in his pants' pockets. A cigarette hung from his lips.

"It had to be done, son," Constantine said. "Your father was too flamboyant, made too much of a show of himself. The authorities were on to him. He was ready to tell them everything, just to save himself. I couldn't let that happen."

"There wasn't any other way?" Jackie sounded as if he was still pleading for his father's life.

"I liked your father," Criminisi said. "Really, I did. He made this ring for me." Criminisi held out his hand, the diamonds of the Scrabble tile ring catching the faintest of light from the garage.

"But he was going to talk to the police," Constantine said. "He had to be silenced."

Jackie sat in the driver's seat. It was a close to sitting in his father's lap as he could remember. He massaged the driver's seat cushion, as if he was trying to feel the ghost of his father behind the wheel. His chin trembled, his eyes watering, but not to the point of tears. "Why?"

"Your father had a good business." Constantine leaned into the car, putting one hand on the wheel and the other, for a moment, on his adopted son's shoulder. "The jewellery business, back then, was a great front for laundering money. Diamonds don't have serial numbers, and we could run tens of thousands of dollars a week through the jewellery shop without anyone suspecting a thing. Even if they did, they couldn't prove anything. Until they caught him and he started singing for his freedom." He stepped back from the door and leaned on the hood, his head and shoulders shining back at him. "And this is the fucking car that did it." Constantine pounded the hood, the noise echoing through the parking garage. "First in Canada. He had to have it. Got his picture in the *Spectator* — front page. And now, Tony, your brother's doing the same thing."

*Brothers are God's curse*, Tony thought. "At least Dominic doesn't realize what he's doing. Bobby was a cheat and a snitch. If Dominic tells them anything, it won't be to save his hide. It'll be because he doesn't know any better."

The elder Constantine said to Tony, "In the end, it doesn't matter. Your brother, like mine, can take us all down."

"Sal, you got the car. You're safe. There's no reason to harm my brother." Tony motioned for Nunzio to come closer. "Let Nunzio take the car away. We'll get rid of it. Nobody will ever be able to connect this Mustang to you. The story about your brother dies in the notebook of that little fuck at the *Spectator*."

"Maybe," Constantine said. "But not if my largest public backer ends up in jail for assault."

"Sorry," Tony said. "That reporter got to me. I lost it."

"This, we can fix," Criminisi said. "One of Bela's men has already visited Mr. Batista at him home. We left a sum of money on his coffee table, just after we broke the legs from underneath it. Batista got the message. His legs, or the money. It was his choice." Criminisi smiled at Tony, the crack in his upper palate showing. "The charges will be dropped, by morning."

Constantine helped Jackie out of the Mustang and let Nunzio take his place. Jackie said, "The charges against Dominic won't be so easy to erase."

"I'll pay whatever it costs," Tony said.

Constantine walked over to Tony and stood beside him. "That won't be necessary."

"I mean it," Tony said. "Whatever it costs. I owe Dominic that much for getting him into this."

"I guess it's too late for Dominic," Criminisi said. He stepped out of the car and stood beside Tony. He held Tony's hand.

"No." Tony looked at Constantine, then back at Criminisi. He even looked over at Jackie, as if Constantine's adopted son might be able to convince his father to change his mind. Jackie was immobile.

"I have people inside," Benedict said. "People die in jails all the time."

Tony exhaled and stepped away. "No. Please. You got everything you need. Dominic … He won't say a word. I promise you … On my own life."

Constantine stared down at the stains on the parking garage floor. "That's a promise you can't keep, Tony." He looked up. "The trial would last right through the election period. My name and your name would be front-page news every day. No, Tony. I want this over with quickly, so the story has a chance to die." He started to walk away. "In a few weeks, the name Dominic DiPietro will be old news, and we can all get back to our business." He motioned for Jackie to follow him.

Criminisi stepped into Nastasi's Cadillac and they drove away. The Constantines followed the light to a set of elevators that would return them to their offices. Nunzio turned over the four hundred and twenty-seven cubic inch V-8 engine, backing the Mustang out of its parking spot, and driving through the maze of stalls and laneways and out of the garage.

As the sweet thunder of its engine faded, Constantine turned back to Tony. "Until this all dies away, you should keep your distance. It'll be best if we're not seen together, at least 'til after the election." He took another step, then stopped. "I liked that smelter idea. Make sure it happens."

Tony opened the door to his Mercedes at got inside. It was an hour before he left the parking garage.

# 40

Flinders knocked on the door, and it opened. The female guard came back into the interrogation room. "Put him in the main detention cells," he told her, then looked at Dominic. "You. We'll talk again, soon."

"What about my lawyer?"

"Your lawyer will be by, I can promise you." Shawstak said.

The guard cuffed Dominic and led him away. She poked her baton into his back, expertly finding the same spot she'd bruised on the way in. She pulled his shoulder back and whispered into his ear. Dominic could smell tobacco smoke in her breath. "Don't worry, DiPietro. You'll find that we can be quite accommodating." She licked the back of his ear. A chill of electric loathing ran down Dominic's spine. "We've had some guys like you in the hole for years," she said. "They've been keeping their mouths shut for somebody, too."

She led Dominic back to the main detention cells through a series of double-locked doors. They passed by prison guards who, Dominic noticed, always kept at least one other guard in their line of sight. The Barton Street Detention Centre was no place to be alone, not for moment.

She stopped at the supply room where a guard who'd gotten too big for his feet to carry was assigned the task of distributing prison gear — blankets, pillows, personal rolls of toilet paper, and soap.

Through a sliding window, he looked Dominic up and down, judging weight and measurements. After a moment searching along a high row of metal shelves, he returned with Dominic's detention kit, complete with a pair of orange overalls and white shower sandals.

He slid them across the counter. "If these don't fit, eat something." Dominic picked up his pile of prison belongings and his escort edged him deeper into the detention area.

"My name's Goose," she told him. "You want something, you talk to me." She stopped walking and took off Dominic's handcuffs.

"No reason for you to walk in there like this." Dominic kept his head down and began to shuffle his feet forward. "You don't ask anybody for anything," she said. "You tell them you need to talk to Goose. Someone'll come get me."

"And when you're not here?"

"I'm always here, darling. I might step out for a smoke or a night's sleep, but for you, someone'll page me." She placed her hand on his backside and gave it a gentle squeeze, then a push forward.

Dominic looked straight ahead as if he could somehow avoid any further contact with her. He was led through a series of doors and stairways that gave him no sense of perspective as to where he was in the building. The journey from the interrogation room to his detention cell took ten minutes.

"Crack 28D," Goose yelled. Another disembodied voice answered, followed by the metal-against-metal sound of a well-worn bolt sliding out of place. The cell door opened and Dominic saw two bunk beds, a cot in the middle of the cell, and a stainless-steel toilet and sink. He also saw Attitude, his two cousins, and a long black male whose skin glowed in ebony perfection. Attitude was sitting on a top bunk, his legs dangling below. His cousins in crime were sitting beneath him, one of them with his back against the wall while pretending to read a magazine. The black male lay on the top of the other bunk. He rolled over to face the door as soon as he heard Goose's command to open.

"Here?" Dominic again felt the dull end of Goose's baton in his bruised back.

"Here. The only choices you get now, darling, are the ones I make for you."

The cell door closed behind him and Dominic looked around for a place to sit. He attempted to avoid eye contact with everyone, a near impossibility in a ten-by-ten foot cell. Attitude broke the tension.

"Take the bottom bunk," he said. "Below the Ethiopian. Unless you want the top. I could always make him get down."

"Don't bother." Dominic placed his prison belongings on the bare mattress.

Goose walked by the locked cell. "Get out of that paper suit. Next time I'm by I expect to see you naked or in detention centre orange, and that biohazard placed on the outside of the cell." She stopped and stared at Dominic for a moment, then carried on with her rounds.

Dominic stood up and began to unzip the temporary clothing. One of Attitude's cousins, the one reading the magazine, tossed his reading material on the cot. "What the hell is that all over your sleeves? It's not gonna make me sick, is it?"

As he slid out of the paper suit, Dominic looked at the palette of colour he'd coughed onto his sleeve. "Paint. Spray paint. I must have painted a hundred cars over the last two weeks." He coughed reflexively. "Kinda fills up your lungs, especially since I've been working with shoddy equipment. So, no, you won't be sick. But I'd appreciate it if you kept your distance, anyway." Dominic put on the orange overalls. Oddly, he found comfort in them, the kind he hadn't felt in a while. They were clean and warm. What he needed now was a bit of food and some privacy, neither of which seemed in his immediate future.

Attitude jumped off his bunk. "Let's set the record straight,

DiPietro. My guys and I were angry when they put us into that holding cell. They cleared us out of our detention cell in the middle of the night and threw us in there with the drunks."

"With you," Cousin two.

"Shut up, Nickelhead." Attitude sat down beside Dominic on his bunk.

"I don't know why they threw us in there, but I was upset about the whole thing. I don't like change, so I took it out on you. I'm sorry. But we're in here together now, and as you can see, they don't give a man too much room to think, so I figure we best make the peace." He extended his hand.

Dominic shook it. "Fine. I just want to lay down and go to sleep."

"Good. My name's Greg Mitchell, you can call me Mitch. Over there on the bunk are Adams and Morreli, but we call him Nickelhead." Nickelhead was the cousin on whom Dominic had spewed forth his paint-fuelled venom.

A long black hand with gently tapered fingers came down from above. A pair of bright white eyes appeared behind it. "I am Tungay. I hope you keep cleaner than these other gentlemen."

Dominic touched his hand in greeting. "I'm DiPietro."

"Ignore the Ethiopian," Mitch said. "They got him in here for overstaying his visa. With any luck, they'll be deporting his black ass back to Africa any day now."

Tungay's voice had a clarity to it that rang through the cell. "Don't be counting on taking this bunk, DiPietro. My immigration lawyer told me to get real comfortable here. The courts are slow, like elephants mating." Dominic could hear his cellmate stretching out above him, the metal squeaking with his every move.

"I'm just gonna lay down and close my eyes."

A detention centre worker came up to the cell. He was pushing a cart with a tray of food on it. "One of you guys DiPietro?"

Dominic got up from his bunk and went to the front of the cell. The worker slid the tray of food through a horizontal gap in the bars. "Goose sent some lunch down for you." He pointed to each item on the tray. "There's some of last night's macaroni and cheese, a salad, some bread — but I gotta tell you it's a little stale — and chocolate pudding. Oh, and there's coffee." He pointed to two identical plastic carafes. "Goose didn't know how you take your coffee, so this one's black." He placed a finger on the left one. "The other ... I guess you'd call it Irish."

Mitch said, "Let's leave the man to his lunch."

Dominic took the tray and returned to his bunk. With the tray on this lap, he lifted the top off the second carafe. The sweet scent of Canadian whiskey filled his nostrils.

# 41

Dominic was staring at the lattice of steel above his head, dreaming into the bottom of Tungay's bunk, when Goose rattled the cell door with the butt of her baton. It was an extension of her body, like an extra arm.

"DiPietro, off your ass." She led him out of the cell and back to the interrogation room. "Sleep well?" she asked him as they walked. She had put him back in handcuffs, and this time added leg irons. They were connected to his cuffs by a long line of braided steel. Goose put her hand on his back. "Did you get my present?" Dominic nodded. "I hope it helped," she whispered.

"What was that all about?" Dominic asked.

"In here, I take care of who I want, how I want, and when I want." She drove her baton into the small of his back. "And it goes both ways." She unlocked the door to the interrogation room. "I'll be back for you later."

Flinders and Shawstak were already in the room. Shawstak was seated at the table, smoking. Dominic shuffled in and sat down. A night's sleep hadn't helped his nerves.

Flinders withdrew a piece of paper from the manila folder on the table. "We'll be quick about this, DiPietro, if you co-operate." He laid the piece of paper in front of Dominic. It was a police statement, signed by Leo Deluca.

Shawstak took over, pointing at the statement. "This says you attempted to recruit one Mr. Deluca to work with you chopping cars, and that you admitted to him that you are in the employ of Alfonso Criminisi."

Dominic looked at the statement, then at Shawstak. "So? Some guy comes in here and lies to you and this is supposed to, what, scare me?" He looked again at the statement. "Deluca. He should be scared. That's not the kind of thing you want on the street. Telling lies about your friends, especially to do with a mob guy."

"We have enough to charge you," Flinders said. "The statement only confirms it. What we're after is your brother and Sal Constantine. Listen to me," he hitched up his pants and sat across from Dominic. "You've got to be smart enough to know that the Crown is not going to let us go after a politico with the power of Sal Constantine based on anything but hard evidence. Very hard. So be the smart guy I know you are. Help us get Constantine and all this goes away."

Dominic closed his eyes. "Never."

"We told the Crown you'd say that," Shawstak said. "So we're gonna have to charge you with the murder of Port Officer Thomas Raymond Murray."

"What are you talking about? I've done nothing like that. Nothing at all."

Shawstak leaned closer, his cigarette an inch from Dominic's face. "The Suburban in your chop shop says different. And, the surviving port officer confirms that it was the same vehicle that attacked them at Pier 24, on the night of March 18."

Dominic scanned the faces of both of his interrogators. He knew they weren't lying.

"So this is it, DiPietro." Flinders picked up the folder. "We know you're not a cop killer. Give us everything we need to nail your brother and Constantine, and this file goes away. If not, what's going away is you."

"I need a lawyer."

"You'll meet him at your arraignment," Shawstak said. He looked at his watch. "You're on the docket for eleven-thirty."

Dominic was led into the courtroom and placed squarely in front of the arraignment judge. The judge was a small woman, no larger than a prepubescent boy, but her face was deeply lined as if she had seen and heard every excuse for ill deeds and cast each aside with the all the concern she might feel for a discarded cigarette butt. Jackie Constantine stood before her too, crisply pressed and comfortable in his polished brogues and hand-tailored double-breasted suit.

The bailiff came forward and read the charge from a blue-bound sheaf of papers. "Dominic Josepi DiPietro, three counts grand theft auto in the first degree, two counts attempt to injure in the first degree, one count auto fraud in the second degree, and one count vehicular assault in the first degree." He handed the papers to the judge.

The judge put on a pair of half-moon reading glasses to review the court documents before her. Despite her size she was high above Dominic's head. Her robed shoulders seemed to rise directly from the oak bench as if she had grown from it. She looked over her lenses at Dominic, then at Jackie standing beside him. Dominic though she was sneering at him.

"I didn't know that Constantine Ross offered a family plan," she said.

"No, Your Honour," Constantine replied. His tone was reverent yet direct.

"It was just the other day that I granted bail to another DiPietro," she said. "Did I not?"

Dominic looked at his lawyer.

"Face the court, please, Mr. DiPietro," the judge said. Dominic complied but displayed none of Jackie's reverence. He was too astonished.

"Yes, Your Honour," Constantine said. "That would be the defendant's brother."

"And how does this brother plead?" she asked.

Dominic leaned over to Jackie and whispered in his ear, "What the hell is going on?"

"Not guilty, Your Honour," Jackie said to the judge.

"Sounds like the family motto," the judge said.

Are they any bail requests?"

The Crown attorney standing across the aisle to Dominic's left wore the same black robe as the judge, with a white, long-collared shirt and matching short tie, squared at the base. "The Crown requests bail at two hundred and fifty thousand dollars, Your Honour," he said.

Jackie cleared his throat. "Your Honour, my client has no prior record. This is the first time he has appeared before this or any other court."

"Your Honour, the defendant has been convicted four times for driving under the influence of alcohol," the Crown attorney said. "I hardly think that qualifies as a blemish-free record. Furthermore, we believe that the defendant was involved in the murders of two police officers."

The judge looked down at the papers before her. "Is the Crown asking the court to amend the charges? Would you like them raised to murder?"

"Not at this time, Your Honour," the Crown attorney grumbled. "But we may."

"You may do a lot of things, but very few of them are allowed in my court. Bail is set at one hundred thousand dollars." The judge looked down at Dominic; her eyes were stern, her face concerned. "Consider yourself fortunate, Mr. DiPietro. Personally, I don't understand why the Crown isn't laying a murder charge."

To Dominic, the courtroom felt as small as a phone booth.

"Your Honour," Jackie said. "My client has neither the means nor the assets to raise that kind of money."

"Then he'd better get used to the Crown's accommodations." The judge took off her reading glasses. "Or perhaps he can talk to his brother. He seemed pretty quick with his chequebook." She slammed the gavel down.

"You're representing Tony?" Dominic said. He and Jackie were in an interview room at the detention center.

"I was. Not anymore. I should have mentioned it to you, but they didn't give me any time." Constantine took off his jacket and hung it on the back of his chair. "You have to trust me. I'm the only guy who can get you out of this."

"I'm fucked."

"You don't have to be. Make a deal with these guys. I'm telling you, Dominic, send those hoods straight to hell."

Dominic took a deep drag of his cigarette. "No. I can't make a deal. I will not flip on Criminisi. I'd rather sit here in jail than find myself toes up on some slab."

Jackie Constantine stood up and put his jacket on. "What makes you think that being in here makes you any safer?"

# 42

The Barton Street Detention Centre is not a prison, it's a jail, and Dominic knew the difference. They send you to prison after you're convicted and sentenced. They take you to a detention centre after you're arrested. There is no exercise yard, no library, no mess hall for meals. A common area for watching television or playing cards is non-existent. Residents like Dominic are called detainees, not prisoners, and spend twenty-three hours of their day locked in their cells. Veterans of the corrections system consider prison a resort compared to detention, which is like solitary confinement, the only difference being the six to eight men sharing a cell designed for four. That's why if a detainee is forced by judicial circumstance to remain incarcerated for six months or more, upon sentencing the detainee gets one and a half to two times credit for time served. This was the singular benefit of extended accommodation on Barton Street. Dominic DiPietro, however, didn't believe he'd make it to six months. He'd be dead long before that. He was sure.

"We want to let you go," Flinders told him. "We want to send you back where you came from, as a mole. Your job will be to gather the evidence we need against your brother, Sal Constantine, and anyone else associated with them. We want them all, DiPietro. You're the guy who's going to deliver them."

Dominic had made a deal with the devil and it had brought him here. He was damned if he was going to make another deal, with a new devil, to get out. At night, when he closed his eyes, he no longer dreamed of the Mustang, only of Aldo. The night screams in the detention centre, the screams that rolled through the concrete floors, and rang inside the iron bars, and echoed like souls dragging their chains in purgatory, could not compete with the screams inside his head. Aldo. Scared and scarred. DiPietro and damned. Dominic stayed quiet, resigned to his fate. Attitude and his cousins, be damned.

Dominic passed the hours teaching Tungay to play cribbage, having convinced Goose to provide them with a board and a deck of cards. He wondered how he was going to pay for it. He had none of the currency necessary to survive detention. No reputation. No cash. No cigarettes. All he had was his ass, and he wasn't ready to give that up. Soon, he worried, he wouldn't even have that.

Mitch and Nickelhead had been out of the cell for most of the morning. There were a lot of comings and goings in the detention centre during the daylight hours. Court appearances, psychological examinations, doctors, and visits by lawyers and designated family members maintained a hum of activity in the hallways. The nights were deadly. His own anxieties battled for attention with the cries of his fellow dispossessed. He listened as they screamed their private torments into musty pillows and tried, without success, to close his ears to the force-fed grunts of male-to-male seduction. It all made sleeping impossible, at best, and, at worst, unadvisable.

Tungay was getting the pegging part of the game alright. Alternating cards running up to thirty-one, though he'd confuse cribbage with blackjack and think he'd score points at twenty-one. Counting his hand was the difficult part. He couldn't understand the repetitive nature of the card count — how a seven could be used with an eight for fifteens, and then again in a run of three to nine. But it passed the time, and for that Dominic was grateful. Plus, it allowed him to avoid Mitch and his cousins. He feared Mitch, and Nickelhead seemed ready to spin into a fit at any moment. He was wound tight but suffered from the withdrawal of any number of illicit narcotics.

Goose rattled the cell door. "Shower time."

Dominic threw down his cards. "You win, Tungay." They left their cell and followed Goose to the showers. The detainees were scheduled in shifts, every three days. Three other guests of the Barton Street Detention Centre were leaving the changing area as Dominic and Tungay entered. Their overalls on hooks, they marched naked into the shower area, the same stalls where a guard had revived Dominic after he'd passed out that first night.

This time, the guards were absent. Dominic was unsure if this was right. It felt out of place. Empty. The authorities were supposed to be near.

Mitch and his cousins greeted Dominic in the shower stall. They were naked, rinsing off after completing their turn in the water. There was a tattoo on Mitch's shoulder; the same one that adorned Zeno. A dragon with a long tail, a spike driven through it.

"Soap?" Mitch tossed a bar at him. Dominic let it drop to his feet. Tungay picked it up, wandering over to a shower nozzle.

Mitch towel-dried his hair, then let the towel rest around his shoulders. "Dangerous places, showers. Accidents happen."

Dominic backed up. Nickelhead was behind him.

"We don't want to hurt you," he said.

"No," Mitch used the end of his towel to wipe his face. "We were told to make it quick."

Tungay stepped out the shower, the water beading on his wiry hair. Mitch looked at him. "You should leave, before you slip on something. Crack that black head of yours wide open."

Dominic guessed that his new Ethiopian friend had been inside long enough to know when a battle could be won, or lost. He read the whites of the man's eyes as Tungay passed by him. Dominic could tell that Tungay's heart was only big enough for himself. "Next time, I'm not letting you win."

Nickelhead came at Dominic from behind, wrapping a towel tightly around his neck and turning it, like a noose. Dominic twisted away, grabbing the towel hard, the strength in his hands and arms like iron from years squeezing a paint gun and pulling at car parts. He got away, but he slipped on the wet floor, sliding into a corner, the back of his head rattling against the wall. Stunned, he stayed down, crouched in the corner where Tungay's shower remained spewing steam. It was the only thing that separated him and Mitch. Nickelhead was shaking, adrenaline replacing the drugs his body was craving.

"You're not making this easy on yourself," Mitch said. He drew his leg back and tried to kick Dominic in the head, but he missed, striking him on the shoulder. The blow threw Dominic back into the tiled wall. Mitch kicked him again, catching him in the jaw. The impact pounded his lip into his teeth, cutting it, a stream of blood washing into the water on the tiled floor. Dead. Cold, naked, and bloodless in the shower of a detention centre. Dominic imagined his pale face blending into the tile as a coroner zipped his remains into a body bag.

The piercing sound of a dozen whistles echoed off the walls of the shower room. Goose and a team of guard rushed in, batons raised, and pounded them into Mitch and Nickelhead. Goose pulled Dominic up by the bicep.

"We're going to have to get you better roommates," she said. "These boys don't play very nice." She handed him a towel, which he wrapped around his waist. Goose looked him up and down. "Nothing I haven't seen before. Now get that cute little ass of yours back in your cell. These guys," she glanced over her shoulder as the other guards shackled his attackers, won't be bothering you for a while."

Dominic started to walk away, but Goose grabbed his arm again.

"What kind of manners did your mother teach you?"

"Thank you," Dominic realized that she was the only reason he was alive, but somehow didn't feel any better than he had a moment before.

Goose pointed her finger at her cheek. "Right here, tight ass."

Dominic kissed her on the cheek.

"Actually," she said, "you should be thanking Alfonso."

"Criminisi?"

"Yeah. He asked me to look out for you. Make sure nothing bad happened. Now, get yourself cleaned up."

Dominic skulked into the change room, grabbing an extra towel to hold against his swelling lip. Another guard escorted him to the clinic where a nurse stitched up his mouth. Blessedly, she handed Dominic a bottle of Tylenol 3s. At least there was a small pay-off for the beating. He swallowed four of them as soon as he got back to his cell.

He wasn't there long before Goose returned with Tungay. "Here's somebody else you should thank," she told him. "If he hadn't found me, my guess is we wouldn't have discovered your body until shift change. I don't want think about what I would have had to tell Alfonso."

"You will still let me win, then?" Tungay grinned through yellow teeth. "I think to myself, Tungay, you and that Canadian boy cannot take on the biker and his friends. So I go find your fairy godmother, and let her do the work."

"If I thought anything of my life, I'd thank you. But somehow, I'm guessing you only put off what is gonna happen sooner or later anyway." Dominic sunk back in his bunk, letting the Tylenols take away his pain and build a wall of fog between him and the reality that surrounded him.

Tungay entered the cell, but Goose left the door open. "Don't go sucking your thumb, DiPietro. It's not becoming. Besides, there's a Mrs. DiPietro here to see you."

300

There were only two Mrs. DiPietros: his mother, and Tony's wife, Rosemary. He prayed his mother wouldn't see him this way. But if it was Rosemary, then she was only there to deliver a message from his brother.

He was wrong on both counts.

"You shouldn't have come here," Dominic said. Andy sat across from him, a wall of chain link separating them. She held a young boy in her arms, a toddler wearing T-shirt two sizes too small. His baby fat belly hung over a pair of scuffed pants.

"We had to. I tried yesterday, but they were only letting your immediate family or your lawyer in to see you. So I told them I was your wife. Frankie's our boy. Don't you like him? Say hi to Dominic, Frankie." The toddler waved with a shy smile. "He likes you. He won't even make eye contact with most people."

"Andy, you gotta get away from all this. Get as far away from me and Hamilton as possible."

Dominic put his hand up to the barrier, his fingers gripping the chain link. "Go back to the shop and look in my blue toolbox. There's a couple of grand in cash. Just take it and get out of town ... you and Frankie."

"I can't just leave you here."

"I'm here until this over, or until I post bail. The only thing we had that was worth anything was the Mustang and now that's disappeared."

Andy closed her eyes. "Your brother's got it."

Tony rules. Tony wins. Always. "It figures. I was dreaming to think we could ever pull this off."

"Stop that. I won't hear it. You're gonna get out of here, Dominic. You've got to. It's not safe. Criminisi's got people inside on his payroll."

Dominic touched his lip. "We've met. But they're not Criminisi's people."

"Then who?"

"I can only figure it's one of Tony's guys. The cops, they want me to wear a wire and entrap him."

"Will you?"

"No. At least not yet."

"You can't stay here. It's not safe."

"A little bird is protecting me, for now. But, I'm not sure how long that's gonna last."

"I'll get you out, I promise."

"Don't worry about me. Take care of yourself. Go back to the shop and take the money." Andy kissed him through the chain link barrier.

"Don't get any ideas," Dominic said. "No action here."


Jackie Constantine looked more wired than usual. Dominic thought the lawyer looked worse than he did. Dressed, but dishevelled, as if he'd worn the same suit for days.

"I can't help you anymore, not as a lawyer." Jackie had been chain smoking since they'd met in the interrogation room. "My career is for crap, anyway. If my uncle hadn't gifted the law school all that money, I never would have graduated. Let me tell you the truth, Dominic. He even paid someone to take the bar exams for me." He stubbed the cigarette out in the ashtray and lit another one. He opened his briefcase, removing a stack of thick files. "I want you to take a look at these."

Dominic took one of the files and scanned it. He didn't know what he was looking at.

"They're incorporation papers," Jackie told him. "Certificates of insurance, partnership agreements, and licenses from the government to operate insurance companies. My uncle owns all or part of twenty-four of them. Every one of them different, and every one of them bogus."

Dominic was confused. Everywhere he turned he was being leaned on or led around by his nose. He couldn't figure out if Jackie was offering him a bridge or burning one.

Jackie took one of the files and opened it, spilling the contents across the table. "They're all phony. I know, because it's my job to keep the paper trail clean."

Dominic stared back at him, quiet and unsure. "He's created a giant pyramid of phony cars with equally phony insurance, all of it operating as a money laundering scheme that buries huge amounts of cash earned from drugs, prostitution, and gambling." Jackie separated three of the documents. "Look. The mob pays these companies premiums to insure non-existent cars. Then they get in non-existent accidents." He pointed at a ledger of transactions. There were several companies listed, but two stood out: Palestra, one of Criminisi's companies, and City-Wide Collision. "The insurance company writes off the cars, then cuts a cheque to the insured owners. One hundred cents in, seventy cents out. My uncle clears thirty, and he's using your brother to do it."

Dominic picked up one of the files and examined it more closely. "That would explain why Tony buys a lot of paint and supplies that never seem to get delivered."

"Yeah. Janowitz is adding another whole layer of so-called legitimacy to the process. Without this paper trail, the cops have nothing. They couldn't bust any of the partners for anything more than creative accounting practices."

The door to the interrogation room opened. It was Goose. She was carrying a small, white plastic bag. She tossed it at him, but, shackled, all Dominic could so was let it fall to the floor. She walked over and unlocked his cuffs. First his ankles, then his wrists.

"I was disappointed to learn you made bail." She gathered up the shackles. "You hurry back, now. I got some things planned for you." Goose threw the shackles over her shoulder and left.

Dominic looked at Jackie. "Who posted —"

"I did. Like I said, I can't help you as a lawyer. But I am in charge of trust accounts that are swimming in dirty cash. So I thought, let's at least do something worthwhile with it."

Jackie was sweating. "Why are you doing all this?" Dominic said.

"Sal Constantine, my loving uncle and most favoured son of the city's Italian community, is just a street hood. The only difference between him and Alfonso Criminisi is that he's got better credentials. Hell, my father was mob too, but he never made any bones about it. Almost thirty years ago, my uncle had my father killed to shut him up. I've known about it for a long time, but the man raised me and my sister. I guess I was emotionally blind to it all. But that changed after I sat behind the wheel of that Mustang you dredged up from the harbour. All I could think about was the time I could have had with my father. Time that my uncle took away."

"You've seen the Mustang?"

"Yeah. It was my dad's. Tony showed it to all us, like it was some kind of trophy. When I sat in it, all I could see was my father. I felt a rage towards my uncle that I've never felt before. Not for anyone." Jackie gathered up the papers. "Listen, Dominic, I'm no hood. I'm a lawyer, and, frankly, not a very good one. But I know enough about what my uncle and your brother have been doing to bury the lot of them.

"I'm dropping off the lot of this to the Crown's office. I'm only hoping that I can make deal. In any event, they won't need you anymore. You gotta disappear. Maybe once all the dust settles, I can find you a real lawyer who can set you up a deal. But you're dead if you stay here."

The bag Goose left contained the clothes Dominic had arrived in. The guard who cleaned him up was right. They'd been washed and folded, cleaner than Dominic had ever managed to get them himself. He took off his detention centre overalls and changed.

"Andy and her kid are outside," Jackie said. "You'll find them waiting for you in a large, black Lincoln."

"That sounds like Magilla's car."

"You do have a memory for automobiles," Jackie smiled briefly. "I hope wherever Magilla takes you, you can make good use of it."

"I'd rather walk."

"You'll do nothing of the sort. Magilla and I are the best friends you have. Andy came to us to get you out. She's the one that convinced me I had to do something. I didn't want another person to die because they got in my uncle's way."

Dominic slid into the back seat of the Lincoln. Andy gave him a hug. Frankie was playing with a toy space shuttle.

"You got a good girl there, DiPietro," Magilla said from the driver's seat. "You take good care of her."

"Her, I'm not worried about," Dominic said. "But why should I trust you?"

"We don't have much choice," Andy said. She held Dominic's hand.

With great difficulty, Magilla turned and puffed out an answer. "You got any better options, I suggest you take them." He removed an envelope from his considerable breast pocket. "Here's twenty grand. It's a going-away gift from the boss. It'll get you and your girl out of the country." He took out his notebook. He flipped through the pages until he found Dominic's account, and ripped out all six pages of it.

"And here's a parting gift from me." Magilla handed the pages to Dominic. "That money's for travelling expenses. I got a guy at the Six Nations' Reserve. He can smuggle you into the States. From there, you got like a whole country to hide in." Magilla wiped his nose with the back of one sausage finger and let go a sniffle that rattled the car. "I'm going to Florida, getting out of this godforsaken city. Clear my goddamn sinuses for once. The boss is even going with me. Says he's connected down there. Go figure."

At the Brampton Street shop Dominic found Vinnie, Sammy, and Gino waiting for him. He expected to see the shop torn apart floor to ceiling by the police, but his crew had already cleaned it up. They'd even rehung the plastic screen that divided the old chop shop from the Mustang's restoration area.

"We wanted to say goodbye," Sammy told him.

Vinnie gave him a muscular hug. "There's just one final job for you to take care of." Gino pulled back the plastic screen, unveiling the 1964 ½ Mustang, white and resplendent under the shop's two thousand watts of halogen lighting. Nunzio was kneeling beside it, buffing off a coat of polish.

"Time for me to choose sides," he said.

"Go away for awhile," Vinnie said. "Get the car out of sight and put some mileage on it. When the time comes to sell it, no one's gonna believe it's got less that forty miles on it."

Dominic teared up, exhaling through ribs sore from the weight of a dozen kicks from a size twelve boot.

"Get out of here," Sammy said. "And, please, be careful. No gambling."

"No problem. My bookie's out of business anyway."

# Epilogue

## A Thursday in Hamilton, Ontario

## May 1991

Highway 6 runs like a straight line between Hamilton and the Six Nations' Indian Reserve. Dominic wanted a more leisurely route, full of curves, soft angles, and open road. He drove east towards Niagara Falls, the Mustang's top down, his arm across the back of the passenger seat, two faces pointed towards the morning sun. Little Frankie slept across the back seat, oblivious to the moment, sleeping peacefully, a child safe from all harm.

The car's radio was tuned to CKCO radio, rock 'n' roll filling the air and competing with the noise of the wind and the road.

*A special newsbreak ... Hamilton City Councillor and mayoral candidate Sal Constantine was found dead this morning, an apparent victim of a shooting at his Hamilton Mountain home. No one has been charged in his death, though his nephew and partner in his law firm, Jackie Constantine, is being held for questioning.*

Andy turned off the radio.

"It's over, Dominic." She put her feet on the dashboard.

"For now. Tony's not going to go down easy. Nor Criminisi. Constantine probably got the easy way out."

Dominic pulled off the road and into a gas station. "We put a lot into this car, Andy. But not enough fuel." He stopped in front of a pump and got out.

Halfway through filling the tank, Dominic heard the rumble of a motorcycle approaching. A biker in Hells Angels colours rode into the gas station, stopping beside Dominic and the Mustang.

He got off his bike, like a cowboy dismounting from his stallion. "Nice ride," he said.

Dominic nodded.

The biker walked towards the convenience store attached to the gas station. He stopped and turned around.

"Damn fine ride," he said. "What do want for it?"

"Not for sale," Dominic said. "Not yet," he added.

The biker took his wallet out and removed a business card. He handed it to Dominic. It read *Marvin Shapiro, Chartered Accountant*.

"When you're ready to part with it, call me."